The Rebel of Lochaber Forest

Highlander: The Legends, Volume 7

Rebecca Ruger

Published by Rebecca Ruger, 2024.

This is a work of fiction. Names, character, places, and incidents are either a product of the author's imagination are used fictitiously, and any resemblance to actual persons, living or dead, events, or locales is entirely coincidental. Some creative license may have been taken with exact dates and locations to better serve the plot and pacing of the novel.

ISBN: 9798325361814
All Rights Reserved.
Copyright © 2024 Rebecca Ruger
Written by Rebecca Ruger

All rights reserved. No part of this publication may be reproduced, distributed or transmitted in any form or by any means, or stored in a database or retrieval system, without the prior written permission of the publisher. Disclaimer: The material in this book is for mature audiences only and may contain graphic content. It is intended only for those aged 18 and older.

Prologue

*Near Strontian Castle
Kilmonivaig in the Highlands
Winter 1306*

"Take 'is head off!"

Cedric MacDuff rolled his eyes and glared at the man who offered that suggestion. "If'n I wanted yer opinion, Daffie," he snapped at the lowly pikoneir, "I'd have gotten it from yer mam ere she left my bed."

Daffie tightened his dirtied hand around the long stem of his pike, briefly lifting it away from where it leant against his shoulder. His jaw tightened as well, and ribald laughter greeted the captain's smear. A lifted brow from MacDuff asked Daffie if he wished to challenge the insult to his mother. He did not, but shot humiliated glances at the smirking men around him.

Momentarily, the captured man whose fate was in question was forgotten and his shoulders slumped a bit with relief, glad to have attention detached from him. Foresight was not something the man, Farley, dealt with often—hence, his predicament now, caught red-handed with the game he'd poached—and thus fear came crashing onto him anew, bolder and more cruel, when the throng of MacKenzie fighting men began to part, making way for a horse and rider.

A chilling dread crept over him, gripping his heart with icy fingers. He swallowed the dryness in his throat, which produced a nervous cough as he watched the man on the glorious black destrier come closer. The man atop the magnificent animal did not stare directly at him but at the body of the red deer not a yard away from Farley's feet, where he'd dropped the poached game when accosted by the MacKenzie men. Augustus McKenzie, Earl of Lochmere, laird of Castle Strontian, sovereign of Lochaber Forest and all the land for a hundred miles around, whose only superior while Scotland was presently kingless and fighting with England, was God in heaven, didn't stop until the nose of his black beast was within a foot of Farley's face.

Holding his breath, Farley gulped down another arid swallow, and met the eyes of the sleek black horse, vaguely believing the animal passed judgment on him with proud eyes. Warily, Farley lifted his gaze to that of the laird. Having lived in and around Lochaber Forest all his thirty-seven misbegotten years, having glimpsed Augustus MacKenzie dozens of times throughout his life, having heard the stories of his swift justice, Farley was not at all put at ease by the lack of obvious fury upon the stark visage of the earl.

Aside from the bright blue irises, the laird's eyes were not so far different from those of his destrier, being hollow and stony and arrogant. The earl did not move his gaze over Farley's face but met his eyes straight on in a diligent manner. He lowered his gaze then and removed his gloves, the leather of which was fine but worn, the palms and fingers chafed from frequently meeting with leather reins and the heavy metal of his sword.

And what a bastard he was, Farley thought, to do so slowly, to draw out the moment and let Farley simmer in his unmanly fright. Leisurely, the earl pulled at each finger of the glove, one at a time until he slowly drew the glove away from first one hand and then another. When he was done, and while he took time to carefully lay the gloves on top of his thigh, being particular about their exact placement, he asked in a deep yet quiet voice, "Caught with the deer in hand?" When the gloves were positioned to his liking, he lifted his gaze to his captain.

Cedric MacDuff, commonly known as Geddy in these parts, nodded solemnly, slanting his wizened gaze at Farley. "An' ye ken it's nae the first time."

The earl straightened in the saddle and moved his cold blue eyes back to Farley, a rumbling fury clearly evident now.

"The least of his sins, by all accounts," he pronounced. He addressed the criminal directly. "Should have stayed scarce, as ye were. But here ye are, on an otherwise ordinary Tuesday, and wee Sìne still brandishing a blackened eye and more wounds, invisible, from yer most recent assault."

Fear, wrought by the quietly murderous glare being leveled at him now, kept Farley's mouth closed.

"Aye, there is nae defense, nae anything ye might say to persuade my thinking," the earl said. He drew a breath and let it settle in his chest before he inclined his head to one of his men, saying "Get the rope."

The young man was quick to scurry away, about his laird's bidding.

To Farley, the earl wondered, "Shall I remove your hand for poaching? Or your wee cock so that ye have nae weapon to attack Sìne again or any another?"

Farley blanched and his jaw fell downward. Frantically, he began to shake his head. It wasn't often he found himself in this situation, shaking with fright, alive with dreadful anticipation. This is how they must have felt, he realized subconsciously, those he'd wronged directly, physically, his own victims.

Sadly, regret was not borne from this consciousness. Instead, he found what remained of his plentiful supply of bluster. "Nae, milord," he spat with contempt. He'd been thieving inside this forest for years, had been—admittedly—bringing a wee bit of terror to the people of Strontian. The auld earl, who was as much a sinner as Farley, hadn't even seen fit to punish him. "Ye canna pass a sentence, nae without cause. And ye canna—"

The blow that came caught him off guard. It followed the smallest movement of the earl's hand, instructing the closest man to quiet Farley. Only the side of an axe was used to deliver the blow so that Farley's life was not snuffed out, but the strike was heavy and swift and dropped him to his knees. Farley's hand connected with the ground, preventing his face from doing so. He blinked several times, his body rigid, expecting another blow. When it didn't come, Farley cautiously turned his head to the side, just in time to see the fine leather boots of the earl land on the ground.

"Get him up," the earl said.

Farley was hauled to his feet just as the earl stepped before him. Thinning his lips, unwilling to allow the earl to see any of the fright that engulfed him, he was forced to lift his chin to meet the cold blue gaze. Panic was hard to conceal, though, since his arms were then lifted to the height of his shoulders, held at the elbows by the loyal and biddable MacKenzie men. Harder yet to hide, the terror, when he caught a glimpse of steel polished to mirror-like perfection, hovering at the earl's side where he held his sword.

Bereft of any control now, Farley whimpered.

"I am nae my father, who allowed such sins upon his own people," said the earl before he took one step back and swung his mighty blade, bringing it down upon Farley's right arm. It banged against his wrist and took his hand with it to the ground. Shock delayed Farley's scream, delayed the presence of pain for one, two, three seconds until it crashed upon him, and he howled.

While Farley cried and screamed, though was kept upright by the hands supporting him even as his knees gave out, the earl coldly wiped the blood from his blade on Farley's tunic.

While Farley watched, his sight blinded by pain and astonishment for how quickly and mercilessly the earl had delivered justice, the earl sheathed his wiped-clean blade and held out his hand, waiting. After a moment, into his large hand was put Farley's severed one, now tied with a length of jute rope round one of his now useless fingers while the other end was wrapped many times, sloppily, around a fist sized rock.

The earl stepped forward, lifting his strong hands to drape the rope around the back of Farley's neck so that the rock hung against his chest on one side and his severed hand laid against his heart.

Clapping his hands roughly against both of Farley's cheeks, the earl met his gaze and said in his steely voice, "If I find ye without this round your neck ere ten years have passed, I'll take off the other hand." He lifted his brows a bit and added, in what sounded a very agreeable tone, "Dinna ever fear I will kill ye, Farley. That would be too easy, too swift. I'll just keep hacking away at all the necessary parts."

When he removed his hands from Farley's face and turned, Farley's knees gave out and he slumped once more to the ground. He was too beset with shock yet, barely comprehending that he'd soiled himself sometime in the last few minutes, to pay any heed to those around him. He stared with mute horror at the hand around his neck, no longer attached to his wrist. His life was ruined now, was all he understood, and would never be the same again.

"What should we do with him?" A MacKenzie asked as the earl mounted his beautiful steed.

"Do with him?" The earl repeated, scowling at his man as if the question were an affront to him. "He is beneath either hatred or scorn, certainly beneath pity. Leave him as he is, as he dropped."

***

She sat upon the ground facing a crude timber frame of shelves, three rows filled with four beehives each. Her eyes and nose were ringed in red from all the tears shed but she hadn't cried in hours now, drained and dead inside.

She had few resources available to her but had found among Finn's belongings a tunic of dark brown. 'Twas not black as was preferred for a mourning cloth, but it would have to do, and she had cut it into squares and draped the fragments over a few of the hives in the home apiary. She wasn't entirely sure of what earthly penalty might befall either herself or Finn's soul, or the apiary itself if she did not tell the bees of their master's demise, but she was well-acquainted with the practice from years spent at Finn's side, tending the bees and soaking up so much knowledge about their upkeep and the customs associated with beekeeping.

"Listen closely and heed my call," she said, her voice a whisper of grief. "Your master's voice no more shall fall. Tell your sisters, tell your brothers: your keeper's gone to join the others."

That was all. It needed no more.

Sorcha Reid was only absently aware of the bees buzzing around her, their wings beating in a steady rhythm that to her seemed to signify the relentless march of time. Life would go on, she understood, even as Finn would not. Oblivious to her sorrow and the depths of her despair, the bees continued their work, gathering nectar and pollen with unwavering dedication.

She sat for a long while, having neither the energy nor the desire to move, or move on.

Surely, if her mother could see her now, she'd blanch with horror. Telling the bees went against all the principles of God and man. Her mother would mourn the spiritual implications of such behavior and would be filled with righteous indignation in the face of such sin—one of many in Sorcha's bucket of sin, as her mother might have said. Sorcha stared blindly at the shrouded hives and supposed that her mother would have demanded that Sorcha spend hours and hours upon her knees, seeking forgiveness for her waywardness, and solace and clarity through prayer.

In all probability, her mother would also suggest that Finn's death was the hand of God at work visiting retribution upon Finn and Sorcha for having sinned. Sorcha shook her head angrily, pushing the idea from her mind. She knew—she'd always believed!—that her mother was wrong about God. He wasn't vengeful or wanting his people to shrivel in fear at the thought of His reprisal. Sorcha looked around and saw only beauty, in everything He created, and believed with all her heart that God was loving and kind.

"How can love exist if not from the Father?" She'd asked her mother years ago. "And why would He surround us with so much beauty if not for love?"

Those simple questions, voiced by a girl mayhap ten and two at the time, had earned her mother's harsh rebuke and more hours spent upon her knees, begging forgiveness from the punitive God her mother served.

It was, in part, what had driven Sorcha into Finn's arms years after that occasion. It still astonished her, how she'd convinced her mother that she prayed more cleverly and felt closer to God when out of doors. Pleased by her daughter's seeming devotion, her mother had magnanimously allowed Sorcha several hours each day to *seek the Lord's counsel* outside the keep.

And there she'd met Finn, not but a few years older than her, following in his father's footsteps, tending the bees at Ballechen. She recalled now with fervent devotion the very first time she'd seen him, the lean lad with shaggy hair the color of honey and soft brown eyes, walking through a cloud of humming bees, his utter lack of fear astounding her, providing to her young mind a testament to his gentle soul and affinity with nature. Though love flowered quickly, it had taken Sorcha a few years to convince Finn to escape with her from Ballechen.

With equal dedication, Sorcha clung to her last memory of Finn.

Shortly after Robert Bruce had been crowned king last year, a laird from the northern reaches of the Highlands, Alasdair MacLaren, had brought his army through Caol. He was a robust old man with a thunderous voice and *a fine good temper*, as Finn had decided. MacLaren visited with Caol's lord, from whom Finn and Sorcha leased land, Lord Aldric de Montfort, and then had proceeded to collect recruits for his army, for which Finn willingly volunteered.

Horrified by what he'd done, Sorcha had begged Finn to reconsider.

With tears and appeals, she pleaded selfishly with him to forget country and obligation.

"Save your life for me, for us," she'd implored.

"I canna, Sorcha," Finn had said. "As did my ancestors, I must fight for independence. I must serve our rightful king and uphold the crown against the English usurpers."

Her astonishment had stayed with her for days, even after Finn had marched away with MacLaren's army after her pleas to make him stay had failed. Never in all the time she'd known him had Finn expressed any devotion to the cause for freedom, nor any wish to be a part of the fight.

From the moment he'd given his oath to MacLaren, the end had come for them. Neither realized it at the time, even as both felt a strange foreboding for the future. But he was now a soldier and no longer a beekeeper, and she a soldier's lover. She hadn't yet learned how to cope, having but a few days preparation for Finn's departure with the army, knowing that every kiss was a countdown to farewell.

"Ye will think of me whilst I'm away?" He'd asked. "Ye will weep tears of joy upon my return?"

She'd nodded frantically. "Go forth safe and well, my love, and may God be kind and watch over you."

One last kiss, one last desperate look, and Finn hoisted his pack onto his shoulder and walked away and was soon lost to the fading twilight.

Barely a month of Sundays had plodded by before news had come of Finn's demise.

The herald of Caol told the tale as it had been related to him, via a message delivered to Lord Aldric. While the townsfolk gathered round him in front of the kirk, Caol's herald's deep, clear voice rang out with the news.

"Naught but a fortnight ago, on a plateau of the Carrick Hills, two armies marshalled in battle array...."

On and on he went, to Sorcha's everlasting disdain and frustration, and a creeping sense of dread.

Possibly five or more minutes had passed before the herald finished his rambling tale.

"Good folk of this noble burgh," the herald said at length, his tone now grave, "'tis with great sorrow that I come before ye to announce the names of our brave sons and brothers who lay still on that hill in Carrick, their guid souls given to God and king."

Finn Drummond was the first name called.

Chapter One

Caol, Scotland
June 1306

The alehouse in Caol, in the parish of Kilmallie, was within walking distance of the narrow water between Loch Linnhe and Loch Eil. Though he seemed to recall someone at one time saying that the only tavern in Caol was known locally as the Bonnie Barrel Inn, no sign hung about the rambling, timber-framed building or sat anywhere on its thatched roof.

Augustus MacKenzie, surrounded by half a dozen MacKenzie officers, dismounted in front of the establishment, glancing around the tiny, sprawling burgh. There were no cobblestone streets but rather lanes made of deeply rutted tracks, the surface worn smooth by countless footsteps, hooves, and cartwheels. Single and two-story buildings, made of timber and stone, were clustered around the alehouse while cottages further away were spaced out at greater distances in either direction. Thatched roofs glistened with evening dew and candlelight flickered in the windows of several homes.

All was quiet and calm, as if the town shut down when the sun did, which struck Augustus as odd. The burgh was small enough—exactly what he'd been hoping for—that even on a busy day, it probably wouldn't be considered bustling, but the absence of any wandering person, or of any noise at all furrowed his brow.

A single door entrance at the front of the establishment led Augustus and his men into the warm and dimly lit interior of the alehouse, where they were immediately subject to the aroma of peat fires and grease smoke, and an ample amount of wary conjecture.

The already subdued atmosphere was reduced to complete silence on their arrival.

Augustus stood near the door for a moment, taking in the rough-hewn wooden tables and benches, and the central stone hearth—one of three that he could see—where crackled a welcoming fire. 'Twas all the welcome they would receive, possibly.

Though it didn't show in his stony countenance, Augustus was suitably surprised to find the inn so full. Nearly every bench and odd stool were occupied, and more men stood around a long wooden counter, behind which an abundance of mismatched tankards hung on pegs pounded into the wall. Several dozen pegs were empty, those tankards already in the hands of the guarded and watchful patrons.

Though the crowdedness of the alehouse was unexpected, their silent and cautious reception was not.

These locals, like any of the small burghs and villages through which they traveled, were accustomed to their own kind, farmers and tradespeople, and were naturally and consistently distrustful of outsiders. They cast glances, some furtive and others not, at the newcomers. 'Twas not unforeseen that the sight of Augustus and the six men standing behind him, stern-faced warriors only hours removed from their most recent skirmish, would inspire a wee guardedness.

Hell, Gryffin's face alone was known to send bairns crying to their mams.

Spying an unoccupied table tucked away in the farthest corner of the taproom, Augustus navigated through the quiet sea of tables, benches, and watchful patrons. Along the way, he glimpsed what looked to be simple but hearty fare, staples like trencher bread, cheese, and stew. To the left of that central stone hearth sat two musicians, their hands and instruments idle while they marked the progress of the interlopers across the room.

While his mood would never have been mistaken for jovial, a particular intensity fueled his steps today, and Augustus moved with a determined purpose. Unfazed by the curious gazes that followed him, he met the eyes of onlookers with stern resolve, his piercing gaze challenging anyone who dared to meet it.

"Change their tune, nae doubt," proposed Geddy, who walked directly behind Augustus, "if they had any inkling about de Blair prowling about, nae more than five miles away."

Augustus slumped down onto the bench at the vacant table, putting his back against the wall and considered his view from here and his captain's words as his men took seats around the table.

Gilbert de Blair was a member of the larger Blair clan that lived and reigned in Banffshire, all of whom had twice now sworn fealty to Edward I of England, first in 1296 and again in 1303. What the de Blair son was doing this far west was only a mystery if Augustus was wrong about what their business might be: having pledged allegiance to the English crown, Edward I likely instructed de Blair to bring round other Scots' noble families to their cause, by way of verbal coercion or simply by leveraging their strength and power to sway the allegiance of northern houses. 'Twas not more than a month ago the Foulis stronghold near Kiltearn had been besieged by the Boyd family from the

Lowlands, Boyd's wife being the sister of Gilbert de Blair. With her castle occupied—savagely by some accounts—the Countess of Foulis was given little choice but to pledge fealty to Edward and England.

Within a moment of the MacKenzies taking seats, the two men with the fiddle and flute began to play, the tune neither lively nor somber but somewhere in between. Many pairs of eyes were yet aimed in the direction of the table in the back corner.

"Aye, mayhap we should have scoured away the bluid," suggested Finlay, a lad easily unnerved by any attention sent his way. "I canna say if they're staring at Gryffin's mug or the proof of a fight."

The innkeep arrived after only a moment, a soiled linen towel hanging over his shoulder.

Rare were the times Augustus met an owner of an alehouse whose temperament was not befouled, in all probability the result of dealing night after night with rowdy patrons, regular sots, and the unruly chaos that often brewed within the walls of such establishments.

This one, short and stout, with naught but a few strands of hair on his head, defied his expectations, offering up a delighted grin.

"What news, mate?" He asked, his round brown eyes sitting anxiously on Augustus. "I might guess ye've come straight from a skirmish, and Caol and I are eager for the tales that cling to your travel-stained breacans."

Augustus gave a nod, his eyes revealing little. He was well accustomed to being sought out to relay news in these small burghs, the residents so rarely venturing far enough away to gather it themselves.

"Trouble on the road," Geddy answered, "and best left there."

"English trouble?" Inquired the squat man, his brow dipping low.

"Nae," answered Geddy, scratching distractedly at his forehead. "Nae this far north. Though we did meet with a party, traitors to the cause of freedom, Scots at that. But they'll nae give ye any grief, nae more anyway."

Colin, the most boisterous and cheery of Augustus's officers—if any of them could be termed as such—squinted up at the innkeeper. "Smells like mam's pottage in here. Got any of that in the kitchen?"

The man nodded but returned his attention to Augustus. "We had an English force march through, but that was a few years back. Cleaned us out of grains and hogs and on their way they went." Narrowing his dark eyes a bit, he asked next, "Ye the rebel they speak of? The Rebel of Lochaber Forest?"

"Rebel of Lochaber Forest?" Augustus repeated, his brows crinkling. He exchanged a befuddled look with Geddy. "That's nae me, mate. But I've heard tales of him. They say he travels with an army one thousand strong."

In fact the army was less than two hundred in number, and at Augustus's command they presently waited well outside the burgh, stationed in posts an eighth of a mile apart, forming a protective barrier around Caol.

"If he did come through, this Rebel," Augustus said, "like as nae he might be willing to accept a few guid men, with long and swift swords and a hatred for any who would betray Scotland."

"And nae loose lips," added Angus, seated to his laird's right. "Nae doubt, the Rebel—this man ye speak of—he'd nae take kindly to any who would bandy about his business, his whereabouts, his activities."

The innkeeper nodded slowly, seeming to consider what to believe, the intuition that said the Rebel sat before him or the lazy denial of this.

"Ale for myself and my friends," Augustus requested mildly. "And whatever pottage is stewing back there, a bowl for each of us."

Another nod answered this. "Aye." And then the chunky, middle-aged man advised, "Extra ha'penny tonight, each man."

"To keep yer lips sealed?" Challenged Geddy, aghast at the very idea, and, some might argue, nearly giving away their identity.

The inn's owner quickly refuted this. "Nae. I dinna care if the Rebel himself warms a chair and sips my ale," he said, settling a glance upon Augustus. "But the beekeeper comes tonight. You'll be paying for the honor of hearing the beekeeper's song."

Geddy scoffed loudly while Angus challenged hotly, "Ye would charge us for a song?"

"Can get that for free," said Colin, shaking his head. "Shite, I've been listening to this one's"—he jabbed his thumb in Finlay's direction—"tuneless whistling all afternoon. I'm nae sure I'm so keen to be captive to more warbling—and to have to pay for it."

"'Tis nae just any song, mind ye," the innkeep was swift to assure them, not at all oblivious to the growing tension. "The beekeeper's song is worth its weight in gold."

Augustus spoke up, his tone measured. "We're nae in the habit of laying out coin for a tune."

The innkeeper met Augustus's gaze, beginning to glow a bit, as if he knew a secret. "Nae offense, sir. It's the way things are done here. The beekeeper's song is a rare gift, and the coin ensures that it reaches every ear in the establishment and that the beekeeper will return, as many nights as the need demands."

A murmur of disgruntlement rippled through the MacKenzie men.

Holding up a pudgy finger, inexplicably grinning now, the man proposed, "Aye, aye, I'll make ye a deal. Dinna pay aforehand but after. Ye be the judge, once ye've heard the song. It's an experience, one I ken ye'll nae soon forget. Ye seek me out when the song is done, ere ye take yer leave, and give what ye ken it's worth."

Though he refrained from rolling his eyes, Augustus met and mirrored Angus's skeptical glance, advancing their mutual displeasure at the idea of parting with coin for a tune that was shrouded in mystery and that—Augustus would wager his last coin—would be delivered in a scratchy, unmelodic voice of an ancient man.

"Will do, mate," chuckled Geddy. "Ye bring us yer ale and yer pottage and for that we'll settle in advance, but dinna mind if we reserve opinion and the coin until we've heard this honey maker's ballad."

"Very well, mates. I'd be Murdo, the proprietor, by the by," said the man, "and that'll be my wife, Myrna, fixing yer meals. Caol welcomes ye."

When Murdo excused himself and retreated to the bar area, Geddy groused, "*Jesu,* a lot of talk in that one. Might've been through half my supper by now if he'd kept his tongue still."

The MacKenzies were briefly quiet, taking stock of their surroundings, as was their habit.

By the time a toothy lass with hair the color of straw delivered a tray of foaming tankards, the men had settled, and after the first few sips, Colin launched into an amused evaluation of today's skirmish. Sure and wasn't there much to appraise and celebrate, sufficient enough to enliven a conversation about how they'd come about their easy victory.

"He dinna account for the dirk gripped in the hand holding my targe," Colin was saying. With his animated face and bright red hair and his easy going nature, he was often underestimated, not expected to be so proficient in hand-to-hand combat. "Eejit. They were nae an army, but bodies pooled together to show larger numbers."

"They dinna move their weapons together," criticized Kael. "Sword then targe, sword then targe, nae ever at the same time, and nae wonder they fell so quickly." He pushed his fingers through is shaggy brown hair, moving it off his forehead. He was a master tactician, always keeping a cool head even in the heat of battle.

"First rule Geddy taught," said Lorne, his large and round eyes scouring the crowded alehouse even as he spoke, "and dinna he drill it still, every day: move yer weapons together. Och, but I'd like to meet their captain, see what he's teaching in place of proper form and rules."

"Do ye ken any who survive learn from us?" Finlay asked, his expression never less than earnest.

Finlay was the youngest officer, still in training in Augustus's eyes, though Geddy assured him that the lad's bouts with excessive enthusiasm were balanced nicely by a genuine sense of duty and a desire to prove his worth.

"What do ye mean?" Angus inquired.

"Well, they see us fighting properly, trained to excess and aye, I'm the first to whinge about the never-ending exercises," replied Finlay, "but I'm always glad to have the proper training, else how would I survive? So those of them who did survive, do ye ken they went back and were like, *Aye, we've got to improve. Did ye take account of those MacKenzie tactics*?"

'Twas mostly shrugs that served as a response to this query.

Gryffin's shrug was accompanied by a grunt. He sat at the end of the table, casting a long shadow over the rest of them for his hulking size. A mysterious and enigmatic figure, skilled in reconnaissance and not at all in polite conversation, he most often lived in silence, observing rather than partaking. Presently, while his broad and thick forehead was crinkled with what seemed unpleasant thoughts, his right hand, calloused and scarred from countless fights, idly traced patterns over his chest, just below his left shoulder, where he was known to keep a concealed dagger, possibly finding comfort in its familiar presence.

"*Jesu*, and dinna I see several blocking their faces with their shield?" Angus added to the condemnation of their enemy's competency. "I 'boot stopped, wanting to instruct the one in front of me—how the bluidy hell can ye fight if ye canna see?"

Kael nodded and added. "Dinna protect their limbs, nae any of them."

"Each limb protects itself," Finlay uttered mechanically, a lesson drilled repeatedly into the lads during their regular training.

They were lads, most of his army. Save for Geddy who'd by now seen four decades and Angus, who was about an age with Augustus's thirty-three years, most of the Mackenzie army were young and malleable, much to Geddy's delight.

Augustus sent a sideways glance to Geddy, watching him nod slowly and steadily, as proud as any parent for the actions learned from him of his 'sons'.

"And that's why we drill, lads, every day, all day," Geddy reminded them, "so ye can sit here and drink yer ale and eat yer victuals."

"And apparently," Colin said, "be subjected to some beekeeper's buzzing."

A round of weary chuckling greeted this remark before the men returned to the topic of their inferior enemy.

Though he could find no fault with his men's assessment of today's enemy and their skill, after a while Augustus listened with only half an ear. He let his gaze wander around the taproom, realizing that despite his advantageous position against a back wall, he could not see all of the tavern. He'd become aware that to the right of the bar itself, there must be another room and more patrons, as several barmaids and sometimes the innkeep himself took full platters and tankards in that direction.

Frankly, he was a wee curious about this, never having known so active a pub as this. Sure, in a larger town and in bigger cities, and certainly on market days or feast days, they might expect to host a crowd of this size. But this, here, was none of those, not a feast day, not a market day—he couldn't imagine that Caol had its own market—not a large town by any stretch of the imagination. So what were all these people doing here?

Possibly an hour or more had passed since they'd entered the alehouse before he had an answer.

Most trenchers at the table were empty, some consumed entirely, and the discussion of today's fight with several units of the

THE REBEL OF LOCHABER FOREST

de Blairs had nearly been exhausted when a hush fell over the crowded taproom.

Instinctively, Augustus laid his hand on the hilt of his sword and motioned for Colin and Angus to stand and investigate.

Before they could, a voice, sweet and haunting, filled the air, and a song, a mournful dirge, crept throughout the alehouse, captivating every ear in the room.

Unmoving in the shadows, Augustus listened to the haunting words and the raw emotions of the melody. The voice was young and beautifully aching. The very first notes were delivered slowly, in a long drawn out tempo.

"*I walk alone*," came the song. "*Or so I thought*." A pause followed, as if the beekeeper was gathering her thoughts. "*Though love is gone, turned to dust.*" Another dramatic pause. "*Comes the starling, 'tis you, I trust.*"

Not a person spoke. No one moved. The crackling fires, too, quieted as if on command, so that her voice was the only sound heard. Augustus blinked, his brow furrowing. Geddy's mouth hung open while Kael's eyes were wide.

The next melody came with greater volume and more urgency. Augustus pictured the singer fisting her hands.

Shadowed is the glen where thistles weep,
In agony I wait, my secrets keep.
Beyond heathered hill and misty sky,
A haunting song, a lover's cry.
Beneath the moon, long shadows dance,
A love lamented, no more a chance.
Your sword laid low, on this your land,

My grief is woven in shifting sand.
Oh, my love, on the battlefield cold,
Through misted eyes, your tale is told.
A candle flickers and memories burn,
In the quiet of night, for you alone do I yearn.

Sensing the owner of the angelic voice was around the corner in that other room, Augustus was a little amazed that the sound conveyed so well and clearly. Her voice, like a mean winter wind, carried an evocative huskiness that wrapped around each note with a melancholic embrace. Each word was delivered as a whispered lament, the ache of enduring grief unmistakable. In the stillness of the inn, her song was not merely heard but felt—a tangible manifestation of the profound sadness that dwelled within her, whoever she was.

On and on it went, many more verses, establishing that she believed—she prayed—that the starling who visited her was her lost love. Entranced by the raw emotion of both the melody and the words, Augustus felt as surely every other mesmerized listener did, a deep sense of empathy and connection, as if the weight of her sorrow touched his soul.

She employed a fiercely whispered plea for the final refrain, the emotion of it staggering.

Let it please be you,
Say that it's you.
Come to me daily, nightly, every hour of the day.
Haunt me, touch me, love me.

Surely every man, woman, and child inside the alehouse held its breath, until the last few words, sung with quiet desperation, broke the suspenseful pause.

Always be near,
My starling dear.

After a long moment of stunned and reeling silence, a slow-coming applause began, hands clapping and tankards tapping, until it grew to some unholy noise, thunderous, as if a thousand steeds charged through the alehouse, the sound pounding in Augustus's ears and raising the hair on his arm.

Without conscious thought, Augustus stood from the table and walked with purpose toward the bar and then to the right, toward that other room, provoked by a consuming urge to see her, to know her. He wasn't the only one with such a mighty desire, he realized as he was trapped inside a moving crowd, with several people calling out, "Sorcha!" and "Another!"

Towering above the throng, Augustus had an advantageous perspective, but little good it did him. He caught a bare glimpse of pale blonde hair, made golden by the inn's warm light, and noted only a petite cloaked figure pulling a blue hood up and over her head, covering the wealth of hair, before he was prevented any further consideration by a body larger than his own suddenly obstructing his view, the man following—escorting more likely—the mysterious figure of the beekeeper through a discreet back door.

The collective sigh of the alehouse patrons mirrored Augustus's own sentiment, a shared exhale resonating through the room in the wake of her departure.

Augustus stood rooted, his sharp and restless gaze fixated on the door through which she'd vanished, an inexplicably profound sense of loss settling over him like a shroud.

Within seconds of her departure the tavern once more buzzed with noise around him, and yet he felt a void, as if something irreplaceable had slipped through his fingers with her leavetaking.

"Ha'penny to hear that?"

Startled out of his reverie, Augustus turned to find Geddy at his side, his gaze on the same door.

"I'd give the whole purse to hear another," the MacKenzie captain proclaimed. "Worth a king's ransom and tell me I lie."

Slowly shaking his head, Augustus stared blindly now. Most certainly, Geddy did not lie. He drew in a deep breath, appreciating that Geddy's presence and his words were a useful antidote to the lingering enchantment cast over him.

He clapped his captain on the shoulder and turned him around, facing the direction of the table they'd shared. "Another ale," he suggested as a cure for the beguilement.

"Mayhap two," countered Geddy sheepishly.

Feeling as if the wind had been sucked clean out of his lungs, Augustus followed Geddy back to their table.

Many years later, long after all the particulars of this day and the evening and this tavern had departed his memory, Augustus would come to understand that it was here, on this night, that he fell in love with the beekeeper, when her song first brushed against his soul.

Chapter Two

Casting long shadows as it descended, the sun created a golden hue over the vast expanse of Caol. A gentle breeze carried the scent of blooming heather, and the distant sound of a murmuring creek added a soothing rhythm to the landscape.

Very close to the creek, not far from a vibrant wildflower meadow, and nestled within a sun-filled clearing inside a protective forest of trees, Sorcha Reid stood within her apiary. The air hummed with the industrious buzz of winged workers, and Sorcha, clad in breeches and a long tunic, moved with practiced ease among the new skeps she and Grimm had made over last winter. Employing careful motions, she paused to lift the veil of her hood, allowing a single drone to escape, the slowness of her release causing no alarm to the bee that had briefly been trapped inside the veil.

She hummed as she worked.

Though she knew Grimm didn't mind her speaking her thoughts aloud, which she regularly did even as she knew he would never respond, she also knew that he far preferred it when she hummed or sang. Dear Grimm wore a perpetual expression of acute pain, his visage flooded with memories too painful to escape. At least that's what Sorcha believed. But when she sang, or when she hummed, she imagined he was given some measure of peace. His rugged and scarred features softened. He was able to rest.

It had been this way since last summer when she'd first met him—or when he'd come to her rescue, as the case had been. She'd been caught up by Hamish McNair one night after she'd sung in the alehouse. He'd harassed her about being a witch, not anything that Sorcha hadn't heard before, an accusation she might have merely shrugged off if not for Hamish having become belligerent and physical, pulling at her hair when she'd attempted to walk on by.

Never in her life had she laid eyes upon Grimm until that moment, when he'd come to her aid, a flash of dark shadow, a flurry of action as he'd disengaged Hamish's hand from her hair and then at least one of Hamish's teeth from his mouth when the quarrelsome man didn't know when to quit.

Grimm hadn't said a word, hadn't replied to either Sorcha's effusive appreciation or her subsequent rising, vocal alarm when Grimm had then proceeded to clasp a meaty paw onto her arm and had walked her all the way home, the stranger eerily knowing the way.

Slow had been the building of their friendship—they *were* friends, she imagined now, despite the fact that he'd not ever spoken a word to her—with Grimm initially proving as wary of her overtures to engage him as Sorcha had been of his constant presence, always lurking. Fairly quickly, she'd understood that his watchful attendance was purely about safeguarding her, and the small distance was maintained so that he didn't trespass into her personal space or privacy.

Sorcha, however, hadn't long suffered his silent, near-but-not-close presence.

She'd stopped one day while walking along the creek, knowing that he was nearby as he had been for weeks. With her hands on her hips, she called out to the trees and the brush and the rocks, "It's much creepier when I can't see you. If you're going to follow me about—and I don't mind it at all—at least do so in my company so that we might get to know one another."

He hadn't, not that day. But Sorcha pretended that he had, knowing he was still close, and had begun to talk to him.

"If you're not going to introduce yourself politely, I will have to imagine your name. I've decided it's Grimm, as you are, ever lurking and wallowing, when you could be here in my company," she'd said to him last summer. "At one time, people found pleasure in being around me. Hard to believe, I know, with how I live now. But once I was the dutiful and respected daughter of an important man and many sought my good opinion in the hopes of currying favor with my father."

Another time, she had tried to cajole him again. "You could be the first, Grimm, or the first in a very long time, to simply enjoy my company, mayhap companionship itself, with no other agenda. I think I might like that with you."

And maybe he was as starved for friendship as she was so that the next morning she found him rather close by so that she left the door to her small cottage open. From inside, she'd called out, "Come in and break your fast with me. I tire of eating alone."

That was the first time he'd entered her home, but he had many times since then, nearly every morning, while they shared a meal together. And every day, he followed her about, around the immediate yard of her cottage as she worked with the bees and her garden there, and often to the second apiary in the forest glade. Several evenings a week, as soon as darkness fell, he walked along with her into Caol proper where she sang her songs. As the weeks had gone on, Grimm had shortened the distance between them until finally he was walking side by side with her.

Unable to resist, she'd teased him when first he'd nearly matched his pace to hers, though he'd been tight-jawed, and staring straight ahead.

"I'm thrilled to have your company, Grimm," she'd said, quite cheery at that moment of supplication, "But you may soon wish you'd remained in my shadow. I am likely to chatter your ears right off." She'd glanced sideways at him, unable to hide her wee pleased smile. "You won't mind, will you, Grimm?" She'd guessed correctly, "Mayhap if I speak in a soft and melodic voice, you won't mind."

Shortly after this, she'd divided the meager coin she earned at the alehouse into two parts and presented one half to him, the coins laid out in the palm she lifted to him.

He'd shaken his head and had given her a stern look, as if offended by the gesture.

"Then leave," she'd boldly said, even as she was half afraid he might. "If you won't share in the bounty, such as it is, then I don't want your help." When he'd only appeared to grow angrier at this, Sorcha cajoled with great and purposeful manipulation, "I want you to have this. I value you and what peace I know with you near." 'Twas true, indeed, since the occasions of her being belittled, harassed, and otherwise pestered had dwindled noticeably since she was so rarely alone but often in the company of the gentle giant. "If you won't take this, we can't be friends."

His lip had curled, evidently displeased to have been given an ultimatum, but he'd reached out his big hand and had plucked one coin from the bunch in her hand. Sorcha had considered it a fantastic victory.

While she'd named him Grimm, the townsfolk called him The Oaf, but Sorcha knew he was anything but a fool. From almost that first night, she'd sensed an intelligence behind his deep set, dark eyes, a haunted quality that she recognized as the weight of memories, none of them good. She had some suspicion that while she had a cache of gorgeous memories of Finn, short and sweet vignettes that sometimes happily interrupted her mourning, Grimm might not have so many fond memories to dull the pain of the bad ones.

"I was thinking that when next we go to market," she said presently while she tended the hives, "that we should buy some hens so that we have our own eggs, whenever we want them."

As she was regularly required to do, Sorcha turned a glance over her shoulder, having to receive his response by expression since he couldn't or wouldn't speak.

He nodded, rather noncommittally, Sorcha thought.

"Or a horse? Should we purchase a horse? Which would benefit us more—a horse, or half a dozen hens?"

At this he scowled so that Sorcha had her answer rather quickly.

"Fine. Hens it is. Fresh eggs in the morning," she exclaimed. "Won't it be lovely?"

She moved now to the opposite side of the next skep, the conical willow hives she'd made and had coated with dung and daub—cloaming, it was called, the weather-proof outer layer she'd applied—so that she faced Grimm now.

Grimm was indeed a giant, larger than any person Sorcha had ever known, with a powerful build that bespoke of immense strength, evident beneath the unkempt layers of clothing that draped his robust frame. His hair, regularly untamed, fell in thick strands around a face weathered by time and trials—more the latter than the former, since Sorcha wasn't quite sure he'd reached three decades yet. Despite the wear on his features, Grimm's eyes held a quiet intensity. Deep-set and most often shadowed by a furrowed brow, his eyes revealed a complexity that Sorcha could sense but didn't fully fathom yet. Aside from the occasional grunts and even rarer chuckles, Grimm was silent, adding an enigmatic quality to his presence.

Delicately, she lifted the outermost straw covering, the hackle, which sat over the skep much as a hat sat on a person's head. This further protected the hive from wind, predators, and most importantly, water. Honey lasted so much longer if, between Sorcha's protection and the hive's industry to keep dry the combs, the water content was reduced as much as possible. Too much water and the honey would ferment and be good for little else than honey mead, which was pointless as so few people could afford honey mead and chose instead to brew or buy the regular grain ale.

The bees, engrossed in their busyness, paid her little mind as she inspected the skep.

"Just as I feared, Grimm," she said absently. "No new eggs." She spotted the queen bee, distinctive because of her longer body—her abdomen stretched beyond the tips of her wings and her back was shiny and bald, unlike the worker bees—and chided lightly, "You have one task, my dear, heart of the hive, mother of all. If you won't give us eggs, well then...."

She pinched the queen from among the hundreds of bees, extracting her with one hand while setting down the skep with the other. Without a word she stepped across the leaf-strewn clearing and transferred the queen to Grimm, wincing as she did so, for what had to be done. His hands, calloused and strong, bore the scars of labor and war. He opened his palm and held his other hand close, his large fingers carefully grasping one wing so that the queen did not escape.

Sorcha turned away before Grimm did what needed to be done. "I'll introduce a new queen tomorrow," she said on a sigh as she replaced the hackle shield over the skep. "I'm done here, but I want to get over to the vale on the other side of the cottage and forage for nuts," she said, lifting the veil from her face. "No singing tonight, Grimm," she decided. "I haven't the energy today."

Often, the prospect of singing felt like an unbearable intrusion into her private grief, a violation of the fragile sanctuary she had carved out for herself after Finn's demise. Away from the prying eyes and whispered judgment of strangers and those regulars inside the alehouse, Sorcha frequently grappled with conflicting emotions. The loss of privacy was a constant source of discomfort, a reminder of the vulnerability she felt whenever she exposed her wounded heart to the world. She'd much rather have kept her grief and her pain, like her sweet memories of Finn, to herself, close to her heart.

Ah, but what choice had she but to exploit her sorrow? Though the sense of exploitation cut the deepest, the knowledge that her sorrow had become a commodity to be traded for a few sparse coins, she knew she must suffer the indignity of it simply to eke out a meager existence with the coin it did afford her. Beekeeping was her love, her last connection to Finn aside from memory, but it barely earned enough yet to sustain her.

Briefly, she closed her eyes and brought Finn's image to mind. His hair was the color of sun-kissed straw with gentle waves that framed his youthful face. His eyes were chestnut in color, warm and inviting, and so often brightened by a smile. She recalled his quiet strength and gentleness, what had drawn her to him years and years ago.

I will never meet another like him, she thought, as she and Grimm walked back home. She had nothing but memory, a bittersweet reminder of the love they'd shared and the dreams they'd once dared to chase.

***

Augustus returned to the Bonnie Barrel Inn the next night and the one after that, and now tonight, growing more desperate after three days for another glimpse of the beekeeper, and more needful, for another performance.

The innkeeper, Murdo, chuckled at his constant presence.

"Dinna I say? I did, dinna I? That ye would be entranced? And so ye are, returned again and again."

"We need to eat," suggested Geddy, who had returned with Augustus, along with Kael and Angus. "But does she nae keep a regular schedule?"

"Sings when she wants," said the innkeep, "mayhap when she has a need. We've come to expect her at least twice a week. A few times, she let me post about it, and kept to a time and date. I paid a lad to run the news all about, saw two, three times as many as she'd normally draw in."

Augustus could not refrain from inquiring, "For whom does she mourn?"

"And there's a tale, tragic in two parts, is it nae?" Replied Murdo. "'Tis said she was born into a guid family, monied ye ken, expected to marry well." He scratched at the side of his head, his eyes crinkling with conjecture. "Milngavie, was it? Mayhap

Bearsden? Dinna matter. But aye, dinna she fall in love with the beekeeper instead and off they run, land here near Caol and are we nae the better for it? Save that her lad was rounded up by the MacLaren, dumped into his army, and lost his life in Ayrshire. That was just 'boot a year ago, if I reckon it right. And now she abides, still keeping bees, living out along the narrow brook in the hovel he'd built for her. Keeps company with the Oaf—dinna ken where he came from, was just here one day— but ye willna see one without the other most days." He grinned cheekily at Augustus. "Ye'll nae get past him to get to her. Och, and haven't they tried? This one, that one, and others. He'll nae let ye within a few yards of her. Safer that way, anyhow, and mayhap that's the way she likes it: untouched, with her grief, her Oaf, and her bees. Mayhap that's all she needs. Nice lad, he was," Murdo continued. "As honest and industrious as she is bonny, I ken that much about him. Says to me when he left, will I keep an eye on her? See that she has peat for her fires and bread for her belly. She dinna ever ask so I guess she dinna need it after all."

Probably not what her man had expected when he'd put in the earnest request. Before Augustus might have commented on this, Murdo shrugged and continued.

"Earns a right guid sum each week anyhow," said the proprietor with no small amount of puffed up munificence. "One-tenth every coin paid for the privilege of hearing her sing."

Augustus scowled at the man over this and could not let this go unchallenged. "One-tenth? She packs your tavern and puts free coin in your pocket—costs ye nothing to provide the venue for her song—and ye sell more ale, take more coin, and her share is but one-tenth?"

"Fair value," defended Murdo, his conceit over his supposed largesse fading quickly in light of Augustus's umbrage. "More'n she earns with honey and wax."

At Augustus's unwavering annoyance, Murdo took himself away.

"Wonder if he'd feel the same were she *his* abandoned lass," Geddy questioned. "Aye, but nae matter. The venison pies are fine and they're warming up to us, the locals. Soon, we'll add to our ranks."

They sat tonight, as they had the last two nights, not at that far corner table furthest away from where the beekeeper had sung her song, but closer to the bar itself, so that both rooms of the alehouse were in sight. Augustus had a clear line of vision to that back door, through which she'd come and gone the other night.

They'd enjoyed two tankards of fairly decent ale and had supped on more venison pies—admittedly coin they didn't need to spend—before the back door swung open. In ran a scruffy lad, breathless and purposeful, scanning the alehouse until he spied Murdo and made straight for him. The lad, not much shorter than the innkeep, tugged at Murdo's sleeve as he talked to patrons at another table. By Augustus's estimation the lad said but two words, to which Murdo nodded before waving him away, off in the direction of one of the barmaids. The lad went to her next, catching her as she wound her way between tables, chairs, and patrons, a tray of tankards in her hands. She nodded as well and soon, all within Augustus's watchful scrutiny, she passed on what news came to another barmaid and soon both of them and Murdo were collecting coin.

She comes, Augustus was almost sure the lad had first said to Murdo.

Anticipation seized Augustus like a sudden gust of wind, sweeping through him with an urgency akin to the approach of an enemy force on the battlefield. Yet, unlike the chaos of combat, here he sat in quiet expectation, his senses attuned to the subtle shift in atmosphere within the alehouse. The patrons, too, seemed to sense the impending arrival of the beekeeper, their voices lowering and the clamor of the bustling tavern softening to a murmur.

Distractedly, he flipped a coin to the barmaid who came to collect, ignoring her startled expression when she caught sight of the dull silver penny, but it was another quarter of an hour before the beekeeper finally arrived. Augustus thought the lad must have been watching her further afield, wherever home was, and had sprinted ahead to alert the Bonnie Barrel Inn.

The Oaf, as Murdo had called him, came first, having to duck his head quite a bit under the low door frame.

Then, from a distance of no more than twenty paces, the beekeeper emerged, a petite and hazy figure cloaked in a once fine but now shabby mantle of midnight blue. Despite the thick haze of grease, smoke, and the pungent scent of unwashed bodies that hung in the air, her presence was unmistakable, a sweet brightness inside the grimy alehouse.

She was at first only a shrouded visage amidst the shadows of that corner, where no tables sat and no patrons gathered, her face obscured by the folds of her deep blue hood, her features veiled in mystery.

Likely she understood that she had a rapt audience and slow was the reveal, her hands lifting gracefully to lower the hood.

There was no gasp at the face revealed, but Augustus thought there should be.

"Saints be praised," breathed Geddy, "but would ye look at her."

Along with every other waiting patron, Augustus did look at her. Time stood still as he drank in the sight before him. Long waving locks of pale gold tresses cascaded in gentle waves around her shoulders, catching the faint flicker of firelight, and shimmering like spun silk. She lifted her eyes to The Oaf, eyes the color of a clear summer sky, while she nodded at him though no conversation was exchanged. Augustus was struck by depths of emotion in her gaze, in those eyes that surely had known both sorrow and joy, but sadly appeared to retain little hope.

Her features were delicate, soft and ethereal, her ivory complexion flawless despite the rosy flush, and yet he sensed a strength in the set of her jaw and the tilt of her chin that spoke of resilience. Though her face bore the marks of hardship and loss, she managed to radiate a quietly stunning beauty that captivated him in its simplicity. Her nose, delicate and refined, held a subtle curve that lent an air of subdued regality to her features, while her cheeks bore the faintest blush, aware of so many hungry eyes upon her. But it was her mouth that truly captivated, full and inviting, her lips curved with a sweetness that hinted at angelic grace, yet their fullness and tempting shape held an enticing allure that spoke of earthly desires.

She was, Augustus decided swiftly, a vision of innocence and temptation entwined.

Before she sang the first note, Augustus understood why her songs held such power over those who listened. Aye, her voice was pure, and the raw pain could not be discounted, but it was the softness of her features and form and the shadows in her blue-eyed gaze, the juxtaposition of her outer beauty with her inner grief that made her song a profound and bittersweet moment. He might suppose that many were or would be captivated not only by her physical allure but also by the vulnerability and strength emanating from her as she shared the echo of her grief.

While The Oaf, to whom Augustus had barely given any attention save to note his immense size, moved a bit away to lean against the wall, Augustus noticed the slight tremor in the beekeeper's slender frame. A silently nervous energy danced about her as she faced forward but kept her gaze downcast.

Slowly, she drew in a deep breath, and lifted her face. She raised her eyes to the low ceiling, her gaze fixed on a point above any person in the crowded room.

She opened her mouth and the first notes of her song spilled forth like liquid gold.

Instantly made a captive to a voice that was at once a force of nature and at the same time seemed to carry with it the weight of centuries of sorrow and longing, Augustus fisted the hand in his lap while his jaw tightened, silently steeling himself against the anticipated emotional impact of her song.

It was no less powerful than the first time he'd heard her sing, her grief no less evident. 'Twas not the same lyrics, but instead a lament about the conflict she faced, not wanting to move forward, leaving his memory behind.

As if she saw her love upon the stained ceiling of the alehouse, her tortured gaze remained there, never once lowering to meet the eyes of any of her engrossed audience.

He attempted once more to approach her when her song was done, but was thwarted again, this time by The Oaf, who steered her quickly toward the door while holding up a large paw meant to keep Augustus at bay.

Augustus carried an imposing figure, but this dull-witted behemoth was larger in both height and breadth, almost grotesquely so, and with hands large enough to squeeze a man's head. Having no interest in tangling with the mountain, who seemed just slow-witted enough that he might not understand the power of a sword or the strength in numbers, with Augustus having been followed by Geddy, Kael, and Angus, Augustus allowed their retreat. He was imminently curious about the beekeeper, but his curiosity would hold and likely be stirred again another night and with another song.

Chapter Three

Sorcha lay in the cool, tall grass, feeling a little drained and melancholic, more so than usual. She watched as the bees swooped and swayed overhead, their hives situated nearby. At the house that Finn had built for her, she still maintained the original colonies of bees that Finn had established when they first arrived in Caol. Finn had constructed a shelter of sorts—a frame consisting of a long wooden bench with a roof made of wood and thatch. This shelter had been placed against an existing garden wall, the only remnant of the former inhabitants of the site. Positioned just west of due south, Finn believed this would protect the hives from the east wind and allow the setting sun to warm them.

The bee bole, Finn had called the protective structure. It held a dozen skeps, and housed thousands of bees, and in the evening, when the sun was golden before it disappeared, and nature's dust motes danced in the air, Sorcha liked to lay there and enjoy the peace wrought, remarkably, by witnessing the never-ending industry of the bees.

In the silence, Sorcha caught the faint sound of Grimm's approach, the quiet swish of his large feet moving through the tall grass. As he drew nearer, she felt his presence, a gentle thud against the ground signifying his arrival. Blocking the sun, he loomed over her, a nightly ritual that always ended with the same unspoken question: Would they venture into town and visit the alehouse?

With a shake of her head, Sorcha declined, offering no explanation. She knew she didn't owe Grimm any justification; he never pressed her for one. Though the tall grass obscured her view, she imagined Grimm settling down nearby. Perhaps, like her, he sought solace in the stillness, a moment for quiet reflection.

After a while, Sorcha couldn't resist breaking the silence. "Don't you ever feel the urge to speak?" she ventured, her curiosity piqued. She knew Grimm was capable of making sounds—chuckles and grunts had punctuated their shared moments—so why not speech?

Not surprisingly, there was no response.

Sorcha sighed, her frustration evident. She often sought answers to her many questions about Grimm, only to be met with his steadfast silence. Some days, more than others, this disturbed her, his refusal to enlighten her. And on a day such as today, when she feared her own melancholy would smother her or choke her, she found herself unable to accept his silence. Slightly miffed, she remarked pertly, "You could at least tell me your real name." When her request was met with yet more silence, she supposed, "Perhaps it's something awful like Mordred or...or Dagda, and Grimm is the preferable alternative." Only a second later, she relented. "Apologies, Grimm. I find myself in a sour mood, but I shouldn't take that out on you." She flopped her arms in the grass above her head.

Moments later, Sorcha was startled by Grimm's sudden reappearance, his looming figure casting a shadow over her once more. His face was etched with anxiety as he swiftly extended his hand towards her. Though taken aback by his urgency and the stern expression on his face, Sorcha refrained from questioning him. Instead, she placed her hand in his, and with a swift motion, he pulled her to her feet.

She glanced around but found no sign of any immediate threat. Grimm, turning his back to her, swiftly maneuvered her behind him by extending his hand and prodding at her hip, urging her to move to the left.

"What—?" she began, but her words trailed off as she then heard the approaching sound of horses. While it wasn't uncommon for people to seek out the beekeeper, the arrival of a horde of mounted riders was highly unusual.

Sorcha instinctively grasped onto Grimm's arm, hoping to see around him, but he shook her off with little regard for gentleness. It was then that she noticed his fingers wrapped around the hilt of the dagger tucked into his belt.

Taking a step further to the left, Sorcha peered around Grimm's broad back and shoulder, careful not to make physical contact with him.

Her eyes widened at the sight before her. A group of a dozen men, mounted on towering destriers, made their way toward her and Grimm. Such grand steeds were a rarity in Caol, and Sorcha couldn't help but feel a sense of unease.

The men were draped in deep blue plaids, their silhouettes contrasting sharply against the fading light of the setting sun. Golden sunlight glinted off the gleaming long swords and metallic components of the harnesses.

Sorcha's gaze was drawn to and lingered on the imposing figure of the man at the forefront of the group, unmistakably their leader. His severity of countenance sent a shiver down her spine. Short chestnut hair, with an intriguing touch of gray at the temples framed a chiseled jawline while striking blue eyes locked onto her, even as she remained tucked safely behind Grimm's protective stance. The man's frank stare unnerved her, the intensity of his gaze causing her heart to quicken its pace.

As he reined in his mount within a few yards of Sorcha and Grimm, the sinewy muscles of his arms flexed beneath the fabric of his tunic, a silent demonstration of his strength. He exuded a commanding presence that left Sorcha feeling both captivated and anxious.

Despite her apprehension, Sorcha found herself unable to tear her gaze away from him, not even to evaluate any other man in his company or to assess any potential threat they might pose. Instead, she remained fixated on the leader, her heart pounding in her chest as his penetrating gaze bore into her. There was a calculated intensity to his scrutiny, a deliberate assessment that sent a chill down her spine. Slowly, methodically, his eyes roamed over her face, as if dissecting her. It was a silent interrogation, a wordless exchange of power and dominance that left Sorcha feeling exposed and vulnerable.

He sat high above her, garbed in his fine breacan and a fierce warrior's mien, a long sword hanging comfortably at his side, its metal sheath dull with age and, she guessed, by constant use.

Refusing to be intimidated, not by the obvious intentions of this stranger to unsettle her, Sorcha took a deliberate step to her left, exposing herself more. She squared her shoulders and lifted her chin defiantly.

"It is customary," she began, her voice ringing with authority, a tone she hadn't employed in years, "for one who arrives uninvited upon another's property to declare their purpose. At the very least, an introduction is expected before subjecting someone to such a prolonged and impolite examination."

As Sorcha spoke, she noticed the subtle reaction of the man. His brows lifted, accentuating the intense blue of his eyes. At the same time, Grimm jerked his face toward her, shooting her a silent warning with his dark and troubled gaze.

The man atop the magnificent black horse grinned. It was merciless, unkind in the extreme, and yet it contained a bit of awareness, Sorcha feared, that her stern attitude—her bravado—was just that. Only that. She was certain he knew that she was quaking in her boots and that her pulse was pounding in her ears.

He did not reply to Sorcha but addressed Grimm, his tone and countenance derisive. "Ye let her speak for ye."

Sorcha startled and swallowed at the sound of his voice, which resonated through her as a deep, reverberating echo. It seemed to penetrate every fiber of her being, sending another shiver down her spine while igniting a flutter in her chest. It was not just the sound of his words, but the laconic and yet commanding presence behind them that seemed to envelop her entirely.

But Sorcha's spine stiffened. "Consider your tone, sir, and rid yourself of whatever contempt colors your words. Though no explanation is owed to you, Grimm hasn't the ability to speak. And I, you may have noticed, do not need someone to speak for me."

"As clear as the ripples on a loch, ma'am."

Sorcha wrenched her gaze from the blue-eyed devil and settled it upon the man sitting closest to him, the one who'd spoken. He sat tall in the saddle, wearing a weathered face, lined with scars. A gray beard framed a stern countenance, and yet Sorcha perceived a lightness in the muted green of his eyes.

"And who are you, sir?"

"I'd be Geddy, ma'am, captain of—"

"I'm not interested in your name, sir," she interrupted imperiously, "so much as I mean to understand why you think I might be concerned about your opinion." When he opened his mouth again, she dismissed him before he spoke. "Pray save your breath, sir. It doesn't matter." She returned her regard to the intimidating leader. "Kindly state your business and pray be quick about it ere you take your leave," she directed crisply.

One corner of the man's most gorgeous mouth quirked upward, and he took his time announcing, "We were only just passing by and thought to make your acquaintance, having recognized ye as the beekeeper who charmed the alehouse with her song."

His tone suggested that *had* been his intention but was not anymore.

It was unsurprising that Sorcha failed to recognize him as part of any recent audience. She had made a habit of avoiding eye contact with the tavern's patrons, unwilling to confront the mixed judgments that often adorned their faces. By keeping her gaze fixed on the ceiling, she maintained a necessary distance, allowing her to deliver her song with greater ease despite the underlying sense of inferiority imposed upon her.

Not quite sure why this man riled her so, save that his initial scrutiny *had* been ill-mannered and his presence—among a dozen mounted, armed men—unsettled her as no other had as far back as she could recall, Sorcha wondered with barely concealed hope, "And has your intention changed now?"

He shrugged lazily and drawled, "I ken I've discovered enough."

He was not interested in knowing her, was her assessment of the cool remark. Perfect.

And now Sorcha smiled. "Very well. Good day, sir."

But the man and his cohorts did not depart.

Instead, he arched a skeptical brow and addressed Grimm. "Tell me, sir," he began, "with a war raging 'round us, with it moving closer day by day, friend and foe often unclear even so far north, why waste your time protecting a mere beekeeper rather than taking up arms against our enemies, near and far?"

Sorcha bristled at his query, laced with so much judgment, aimed at her and Grimm.

As she moved to respond, Grimm swiftly extended his arm, blocking her advance and quelling the verbal assault that threatened to erupt. Glaring at her friend, Sorcha reluctantly retreated, her shock deepening as she observed the uncharacteristically ugly sneer on Grimm's face as he faced the man. Dazed by his unexpected expression, one she had never seen before, she watched as Grimm then gestured with his arm, pointing a finger firmly past the man, indicating where he should go. Away.

"Aye, we'll take our leave," said the man, lifting his hand off the pommel, pulling in the reins. "It was a pleasure to meet ye..." he said and allowed a pause to settle before he finished, "Sorcha, the beekeeper."

Grimm growled his displeasure while Sorcha gasped at his knowledge of her name.

But the man clucked at his massive steed, turning him around, taking his leave.

The man named Geddy pretended to tip a hat from his bare head, grinning like an idiot, by Sorcha's estimation, before he and the others turned and followed their leader, whose name she did not know.

She watched them ride away, her gaze reluctantly fixed with admiration on the broad shoulders of the man with the scorching blue-eyed gaze.

Grimm watched as well, until they were far enough away that only dust risen in their wake remained. He turned on her then, giving her another feral glare.

"What? If you won't speak, then I must," she defended sharply. "We cannot both stand about, mute and terrorized."

Grimm's brows knitted darkly, and he scoffed angrily at this, which effectively let her know that he had not known fear.

Rolling her eyes, made cross by her reaction to the man and his uninvited visit and Grimm's austere manner—sometimes she really wanted to smack him upside the head and demand that he speak!—she belatedly brushed off her skirt, to which a bit of grass still clung, announcing moodily, "We should leave soon. I want to sing tonight."

Grimm was instantly reinvigorated with another forceful opinion, shaking his head angrily. A warning hovered in his gaze. He thought it a foul idea presently, mayhap because that man and his party had specifically sought her out just now.

"I have steam to work off," she argued. "He irritated me, that blue-eyed devil. I need to vent. Song is the best way to do so."

He didn't like it, kept shaking his head.

Sorcha insisted. "I want to sing. Stay behind if you don't want to go," she said, suggesting that she would go, with or without him, knowing very well that he wouldn't allow her to go alone.

Thus, as dusk descended and while Grimm's scowl was even more pronounced than usual, they made their way into Caol and slipped through the back door of the Bonnie Barrel Inn.

Sorcha didn't even bother to pretend she was searching for him in the crowded alehouse, that mysterious man. Though he wasn't positioned front and center, his presence was unmistakable, and much like Grimm's, impossible to ignore. Positioned slightly off-center of where she stood on the 'stage', such as it was, his very presence commanded attention, exuding an air of quiet authority, with the barest hint of menace attached to the ferocity of his countenance, not unlike his regard earlier today.

The man's piercing blue eyes locked onto hers, unyielding and intense, as if daring her to look away. She blinked rapidly and tried to focus, the crowded room quiet now for several seconds in expectation. Once more, and against her greater will, her gaze was drawn to him. Though dozens of eyes watched her, *his* unwavering stare seemed to penetrate the low noise and chatter of the alehouse, cutting through the haze of greasy smoke that hovered high in the room.

With surprising intuition, Sorcha realized that despite the intimidating gaze he projected, she didn't fear the man as much as she feared her own reaction to him. The intensity of his constant scrutiny stirred something within her.

Someone's harsh and hacking cough snapped her out of the hypnotic spell she'd been under.

With a determined lift of her chin, Sorcha directed her gaze upward and began to sing, pouring her heart into each note even as a robust curiosity lingered about the enigmatic figure in the room.

***

Honestly, the fact that she possessed so much fire stirred him even more. That mournful, pathetic creature who'd sung twice before had nothing on this new version, this dynamic, angry young woman with fire in her soul. She'd not only met his probing stare but returned it unblinking for a while. And when she sang, and though it was again a song that mourned, she included in the lyrics a line about the fleeting nature of one's legacy, what seemed like a veiled warning that urged—possibly him—to tread carefully in his dealings lest he be happily forgotten when, as she sang, "the sands of time sweep him away."

He smirked at this, even as she couldn't see it, her regard given to the soot and smoke darkened ceiling while she worked the room with her song.

Augustus was ever watchful and knew what The Oaf was about—Grimm, she'd called him, not very imaginative, since the oaf clearly was quite dour—when he gestured toward a barmaid, bringing her near. Out of the corner of his eye, Augustus watched as Grimm inquired of the harried lass about the strangers inside the taproom, inclining his head in Augustus's direction, his brow furrowed with displeasure.

The barmaid's eyes widened when she saw who Grimm inquired about. After taking her gaze off Augustus, she stood on her toes at the same time Grimm lowered his ear so that she whispered to him whatever knowledge she had about Augustus and his men. Scarcely did it concern him what the barmaid knew, supposed, or shared.

When Sorcha had begun to sing, Augustus had gestured wordlessly to his men, putting them into motion so that presently three of his men were positioned at the back door, thwarting any plan for Grimm and Sorcha to make their usual quick escape.

The seemingly idle wandering of Angus, Gryffin, and Kael and the subsequent strategic positions they assumed did not escape Grimm's notice. The Oaf turned a ferocious scowl onto Augustus, which he purposefully ignored, focusing yet on Sorcha and her song.

In the back of his mind, he did give some thought to the expected confrontation, what would happen when her song was done, and they could not make their hasty retreat.

Frankly, he wouldn't know upon whom to bet, if presented with an opportunity. Augustus feared no man, but couldn't say for sure that in one-on-one combat, he would prevail against the decidedly larger oaf. If anger, guilt, and bitterness alone could see a fight determined, even that would not advise of an obvious choice to win. Augustus might suppose beneath Grimm's seething nature, his steadfast protective instincts toward Sorcha notwithstanding, there lived as much fury and intolerance as what resided within Augustus. Possibly, how many of those inner emotions were self-directed or self-motivated would likely signify a winner; an angry man fought valiantly, but a man fighting inner demons fought recklessly, tirelessly.

As Sorcha's vibrant song came to a close, the last notes ending abruptly as she lowered her head to her chest, a moment of awed silence enveloped the room. This was broken first by a woman's breathy exhale, which seemed to appreciate the intensity and character of Sorcha's song, before the patrons erupted into thunderous applause once again. Their cheers and whistles echoed off the wooden beams of the Bonnie Barrel Inn. Her cheeks flushed with emotion and exhaustion, Sorcha offered a rare, modest smile—an insincere one, Augustus deemed it—before her attention was caught by Grimm, who began to march furiously toward Augustus.

Grimm's expression was dark, his eyes narrowed with determination that Sorcha suddenly seemed intent on disturbing. Amid the din of continued cheers and praise, she rushed after Grimm, taking hold of his big arm.

Whether she understood what Grimm was about, why he meant to confront Augustus, was a mystery presently.

"Leave it," she begged The Oaf when they were but a few yards away. "Grimm, don't."

Her man did not shake her off, but turned his hand around and took hold of Sorcha's wrist, essentially dragging her with him as he bore down on Augustus.

The alehouse went rigidly silent, the applause and appreciation for Sorcha's passionate ballad fading to silent stillness.

Augustus applauded Grimm's decision to keep her close. If he were a man filled with vile intention, the first thing he'd have done was separate her from the Oaf.

When Grimm arrived at the table, with Sorcha still pleading with him to cease, to ignore whatever threat he supposed, Augustus locked his eyes on The Oaf and said mildly, "I only meant to invite the lass to have a drink with me."

"No," she answered at the same time Grimm shook his head forcefully.

The Oaf pointed angrily at Kael and Angus, who blocked the door near the stage they had hoped to use.

Sorcha sent a fleeting gaze in that direction before swinging her blue eyes back around, laying an outraged, quizzical glare onto Augustus.

"I request but a wee bit of your time," he explained to her, just as she opened her mouth to protest, "right here in this public alehouse, at this table. Your man can sit close, can sit beside ye if it pleases ye," he allowed magnanimously. "I dinna ken ye want him using his fists. Me and mine haven't swung yet, and willna, nae first, but swords *will* be unsheathed if he takes the swing he's considering right now."

Sorcha's spine stiffened. She stopped trying to strip Grimm's hold from her wrist.

"Remove your men from blocking the door," she demanded instead.

"Ah," Augustus replied, smirking without humor, "but I dinna want to."

And thus she had no choice. She knew it. Grimm knew it. All the wide-eye and gape jawed patrons knew it. Only moments ago the alehouse had been alive with joy and now a heavy silence hung in the air, every eye fixed on the unfolding confrontation.

Sorcha's spine stiffened, as evidenced by a bit of height added to her small frame, while her blue eyes flashed with stubborn resolve. Purposefully, she yanked her hand from a wary Grimm and slid onto the bench, directly across from Augustus.

He felt a surge of surprise for her boldness, for the quiet determination she carried even as she essentially surrendered. He felt other things as well as he studied her intently, struck by her beauty up close. The soft golden glow of the alehouse lanterns danced across her porcelain skin and turned the strands of her pale blonde hair into spun gold.

Though thoroughly satisfying, Augustus's evaluation was brief, interrupted by Grimm taking a seat next to Sorcha on the bench. The Oaf was furious and didn't mind that Augustus saw this, leveling a steely glare onto him.

Sorcha further surprised Augustus, and perhaps several others, by summoning a hovering Murdo to their table. She smiled beautifully at the innkeeper. "As we are compelled to remain for a bit, Murdo, might Grimm and I have a serving of tonight's pottage? I trow, the aroma has never teased me so much as it has on this evening."

Murdo was taken aback, so much so that one might assume Sorcha and Grimm had never before dined inside the taproom. "But of course," said the garrulous man, "and won't ye be glad ye did?" He cast a sly glance at Augustus before suggesting to Sorcha, "Mayhap you'd a pint of refreshing ale to accommodate your supper?"

"How thoughtful," Sorcha answered, her smile still exquisite. "Yes, I believe we should. Don't you agree, Grimm?" She asked, turning what seemed like an uncomplicated and innocent expression—it was anything but that—onto her friend. "'Twould be rude of us, would it not, if we did not accept this stranger's gratuitous generosity?" She turned her grin back onto Murdo. "Thank you, sir."

The innkeep scurried away while Sorcha gave her regard to Augustus. Her smile vanished at once.

Grimm took it up, smirking at Augustus a bit now, for how he'd just been played.

Augustus revealed nothing of what he was thinking, even as he knew he'd consent to purchasing a week's worth of the Bonnie Barrel Inn's tasty stew, just to have these moments with her.

She didn't know it—how could she?—but this additional little spark, this show of bravado, only made him more curious about her, made him want to unravel the mysteries hidden beneath her façade, to discover the depths of her courage and determination.

He might expect a simple introduction would reveal quite a bit.

"Thank ye for joining me. Apologies, as I have been remiss," he said smoothly. "I have not yet introduced myself. I am the Earl of Lochmere, Augustus MacKenzie."

He was the only one grinning now, his lips curling into a faint smirk, finding a strange satisfaction in their uneasy reaction to his identity. Quite obviously, his reputation had preceded him.

Chapter Four

Augustus MacKenzie.

The Rebel of Lochaber Forest.

The Rebel, *if* the sinister and notorious rumors were to be believed.

There had long been conjecture about the Rebel's actual identity, but the name mentioned more than any other as the most probable culprit—or savior, depending on the source—was the Earl of Lochmere.

A wave of apprehension washed over her, filled with the chilling tales that painted Augustus MacKenzie as not merely a rebel but more akin to the devil. Naturally, she'd heard the stories whispered about him, all of them ugly and vile and nearly unbelievable, whispered in hushed tones, as if speaking too loudly of the heartless Rebel might conjure the man himself.

A shiver coursed through her.

True, she and him might share an allegiance to Scotland—he was reckoned as one of the most formidable warriors throughout all the land, half of his legend borne of his prowess upon the battlefield, his inability to be killed, to hear some speak of him—but that didn't diminish her fear of him. One might expect that a man who rose to the level of his legend must have left behind a wide and long trail of blood. Likely, friend and foe alike had fallen victim to his ruthlessness.

She did not particularly care for the idea beginning to form, based on the smirk he now wore, that he was very pleased to unnerve her. He relished her fright, she believed. And that made him very ugly in her mind, and not quite worthy of her regard. In fact, it made her more determined to show him exactly the opposite of what seemed to please him.

Truth was, she never had been one to tiptoe around fright.

"Do you prefer the Rebel?" Sorcha inquired innocently. "Or is Butcher more accurate? I've heard it both ways."

His response to this, a hardening of his...well, everything—jaw, eyes, lips—gave her pause. What if the tales were true? What if he was as merciless, as gleefully evil as they said?

In for a penny, in for a pound, she guessed. "Is it true that you wear a suit of armor, forged from the bones of your victims—excuse me, I mean your enemies?"

She was aware of Grimm stiffening at her side and felt rather than saw him turn a warning glower onto her.

However, Sorcha kept her attention on the Rebel and his gaze, which had swiftly turned icy and rather helped her understand that while he relished the fear elicited merely by the mention of his name, he also expected, possibly, a wee admiration—and mayhap a bit of fawning—for the fearsome reputation he had cultivated. She refused to be cowed by his formidable demeanor but was determined to match his icy stare with her own unwavering gaze.

"I see that more than merely broad tales have reached even these far corners," Augustus MacKenzie replied finally, his tone chilling, possibly containing a warning. "Be careful what ye heed, beekeeper. 'Tis true what's said that truth is often stranger—and more frightening—than fiction."

With a slight shift in her posture and a tilt to her head, Sorcha subtly conveyed her skepticism, meaning to rile him as he did her. "And what truth might that be, my lord?"

The earl's lips curved into a faint smirk, acknowledging her challenge. "The truth," he said, his gaze piercing, "is that legends are often born from kernels of reality. But whether they grow into towering oaks or wither into mere weeds…well, that is for history to decide."

Laying her hands flat on the scarred wood table, Sorcha goaded him, boldly proposing, "Let us not leave to chance nor to history the fate of your legend, sir. Lay out the facts here and now and write your own story."

Beyond the earl, one of his men snickered aloud, but Sorcha did not remove her gaze from the Rebel, whose smirk grew wide but not necessarily nicer. At the same time, Grimm kneed her leg beneath the table.

But she kept hold of the Rebel's hard blue eyes, unwilling to be intimidated by him.

She didn't understand his interest in her, or his insistence that she keep company with him. She was intent on making sure that this was greatly diminished.

Sure and Augustus MacKenzie wasn't the first to show an interest in her, whether locals or passersby. Thus far, Grimm's presence, and the occasional show of force—such as the altercation with Hamish McNair—had been necessary, but for the most part, Sorcha remained undisturbed by such trouble. She possessed a keen self-awareness regarding both her appearance and her social status. Though conscious that her perceived beauty often attracted unwanted attention, she never doubted the intentions of men—aside from Finn and Grimm, none of it was ever good. While she willingly gave her heart and body to Finn, she had no desire to share either with another. Additionally, she understood that her occupation as a minstrel, coupled with her modest station in life, led others to view her as nothing more than a tavern wench. Men assumed that because she sang for her supper, she was available for other services, and they presumed that for only a few coins tossed her way they might find their ease in her bed.

After a lengthy perusal, meant to intimidate her further no doubt, Augustus MacKenzie said, "I'm much more interested in yer story."

"But you already know it, sir, as it's told right here inside this alehouse several times a week."

"Which reveals only yer current situation," he remarked, "that ye are in mourning and trilling about it."

She *was* bold—she was the daughter of a lord herself, after all, certainly not beneath this man—and was able to easily manufacture a smirk to match his, one meant to show him she couldn't so easily be belittled—trilling, hah!—and that his efforts were paltry and wasted on her.

"Trilling is a curious choice of word, my lord," she said. "It suggests displeasure and then raises the very obvious question: why would you insist on my company?"

They were interrupted by Murdo's arrival, bearing two tankards of ale, followed by the alehouse's server, Maisie, who delivered steaming trenchers of stew, all of which was set down before Grimm and Sorcha.

Maisie cast a glance of concern at Sorcha, then laid a wary one on the earl, before returning her gaze to Sorcha. A thousand questions burned behind her wide brown eyes, readily communicating her unease about this situation unfolding.

"Thank you, Maisie," Sorcha said, smiling pleasantly.

Maisie and Nell, the regular servers, were mostly kind to Sorcha, or rather the least likely to judge her circumstance. They were more likely than any other to exchange greetings with Sorcha and Grimm, even outside the alehouse, as few other people were wont to do.

Neither she nor Grimm wasted any time before digging in.

She broke off a piece of the bread plate, drenched with thick juices and bits of meat, and plopped that into her mouth. The tender meat, possibly simmered for hours if not days, melted in her mouth.

She chewed and swallowed, and licked her thumb, returning her gaze to the mysterious earl. Lifting her chin defiantly, and though he'd not answered her last question, she addressed him. "I might suggest your attention has a certain design. And mayhap you already know but allow me to confirm: I am not interested."

"I have nae said what my *designs* are?"

"You have said very little, sir," she reminded him pertly, "but the manner in which you've conducted yourself thus far gives away enough that I believe my assumptions must be correct and therefore, my interest remains stagnant."

She returned her attention to the savory platter before her, as if any response from him was of little import after all. At her side, Grimm dug in with even more gusto, having made half the trencher and stew disappear already.

Augustus MacKenzie surprised her by replying, "Allow me to rectify such a poor beginning."

Before she could keep it safely tucked inside, Sorcha let out a little laugh of skepticism. "What's done is done, sir." Certainly he didn't seem the type to improve his conduct for another's benefit.

She lifted the tankard of ale and hid her growing consternation behind the width of it as she raised it to her lips.

His eyebrows, which seemed to reside permanently in a downward position, furrowed a bit more, giving him a look of stark intolerance. A fleeting, frightening thought crossed her mind: how may people saw this look last before they were smote with either words or sword? Sorcha swallowed, wondering if she had pushed him too far, if she had provoked him to abandon the facade of civility and reveal his true self, the Rebel who was rumored to possess neither heart nor mercy.

Augustus MacKenzie swiped his hand slowly over his mouth and chin while considering her. "I only meant to discover more about you," he said. "How long have you been living in Caol?"

"Four years."

"Do you perform elsewhere? Or are your songs reserved for the Bonnie Barrel Inn?"

"I sing here and nowhere else."

"And yet your talent is undeniable," he remarked, "and surely opportunities exist outside the area."

"Perhaps."

"Ye are stubborn," he commented now, his expression contrarily softening with this assessment, "and dinna want to give even the smallest morsel." He addressed Grimm. "Is she always like this?"

Grimm harrumphed, the guttural sound filled with displeasure.

Sorcha frowned at her friend, unsure if his response was aimed at the Rebel for what he was doing, or made in reaction to the question, since Grimm knew more than most how stubborn Sorcha could be.

"What do ye ken of the Guardian Stones?" The earl asked then, his probing regard returned to Sorcha.

Bewildered by his swift change of subject, Sorcha's reply was hesitant at first, though she was pleased that she, herself, was removed as the topic. "It is said that the, ah, the Guardian Stones, were erected thousands of years ago by an ancient civilization. According to legend, the stones were placed in that precise circle to harness the energy of the earth and the heavens, imbuing them with protective magic."

Did he ask because he was aware that one of her apiaries was located near the circle of standing stones? Hidden amidst lush meadows and rolling hills of forest, the apiary lay just a stone's throw away from the mystical stones. Would she reveal to him that she'd intentionally chosen that spot, where the towering stones cast their protective shadow over the buzzing hives? Should she acknowledge that apiary was her best-producing?

"You have seen the Guardian Stones?" She asked quietly, wondering at his interest.

"I have nae. I heard mention of them some time ago. 'Twas said that wounded warriors laid inside the circle might be healed."

"I...I have not ever seen this." She'd heard that claim as well and had thought it fanciful. She was only made more curious, though, as he didn't strike her either as someone in need of healing—unless he worried over his surely black heart—or as one who might put stock into supernatural lore.

"Aye, so many wild tales make their way 'round," the earl said mildly.

His words carried a subtle weight, likely a reminder to her to tread carefully in regard to the rumors and stories that swirled around him. A prickling sensation rose at the back of her neck, a silent warning to heed his unspoken caution.

But then, she herself was often the victim of speculation, a fine reminder that people were often quick to invent narratives, but rarely did so with kindness.

Thus, rather with a wee commiseration over this bit of common ground, she nodded in accord. "Tales will be woven, whether you supply the yarn or not."

He smirked once more, this time revealing a bit of humor. "So they will."

Maisie returned once more, removing the earl's empty tankard and replacing it with a fresh one. Sorcha noticed the barmaid's fretful expression, and how smoothly and unobtrusively she made the switch, as if she wished to go completely unnoticed.

Sorcha became aware that the longer she and Grimm sat here with the Earl of Lochmere, the more the patrons' interest in them seemed to wane. Gradually, they returned to their own conversations and companions, no longer fixated on the trio or any of the earl's other men, close at hand.

Unable to prevent herself from doing so, despite the urging of her brain, she looked upon the earl once more. She found his gaze heavy upon her still and was compelled by pride to hold his stare and not cower in the face of such discourteous curiosity. Or was she meant to tremble in the face of his continued piercing gaze? She supposed if the rumors were false—if he were not the Rebel or if the Rebel himself were not portrayed as a ruthless savage—she might look upon him and perceive him differently. If he were naught but a man, a stranger even, if she knew not of his legend, she might imagine him formidable but not monstrous, imposing but not threatening, mayhap even handsome for the mesmerizing blue of his eyes, and for the way his hair fell untamed over his forehead, as if this small thing were only playfully reckless, resisting every effort of his to appear formidable and severe.

Sliding her hands under the table, she made fists in her lap, alarmed by a fleeting and reckless desire to run her fingers over his brow and encourage those wayward locks into compliance. She lowered her gaze, not entirely sure those incisive blue eyes couldn't read minds.

She stared at the earl's long fingers, tapping slowly and rhythmically against the side of his tankard. His hands were large and strong, calloused and scarred, and darkened to a robust gold by the sun. An unexpected, uninvited thought came to her, wondering what it would feel like to have those long fingers caress her bare skin.

Her cheeks pinkened, shamed by her wanton thoughts. She told herself she was not intrigued by him, not at all. Lethal virility did not stir her, she was certain.

How different was the earl's intrusive regard from that soft and loving look she recalled so well from Finn! Sweet Mother of God, but what did he hope to achieve by forcing her company and then subjecting her to this stark and shudder-inducing examination?

"What is your price?" He asked. "For a night with ye."

Her eyes sped back to him. Sorcha's mouth opened in disbelief, but no words emerged. She couldn't help but wonder if, in addition to all the formidable feats he was credited with or accused of—depending on the speaker—the wicked Rebel could also read minds. He just answered the burning question inside her mind.

Grimm, in the act of draining his cup, stiffened, and slammed down his tankard, which wasn't emptied completely after all. A wave of liquid rose out of the top of the tankard and dropped just as swiftly, splashing his hand and the table.

Grimm's low growl was given as the first response before Sorcha was able to find her voice.

"I am not for sale," she uttered imperiously.

"And yet here you are, enjoying victuals and ale, bought with my coin."

While she held his gaze, she pushed the half-eaten trencher toward the middle of the table. "And now we're square," she said tightly. "You've paid for this company now and nothing more."

"It's easy to be brave when you've the mountain at yer side," the earl said, his observation given with lazy indifference.

Indeed, much of what she expressed just now was only bravado. Inside, however, her heart thundered wildly. Unfortunately, it was not uncommon, the tales she'd encountered of women, young lasses even, enduring mistreatment at the hands of greedy, despicable men. Sorcha had witnessed firsthand the harsh reality of women being subjected to abuse, many being taken against their will.

What lore had reached her ears about the Rebel of Lochaber Forest suggested strongly that he might be of that ilk, the kind who didn't bother with polite requests, but was accustomed to seizing. She would go, if that became the case, lest Grimm pay for her refusal, since she knew he would stand in her defense. Her steadfast protector wouldn't have a fighting chance though, not against the imposing figure of the earl and his silent, watchful comrades.

And yet, the earl *had* asked—offensively, of her price—but which gave her hope that he would not only take.

The mountain—Grimm—stood abruptly from the bench. Sorcha followed, wanting to be away from so contrary a man. "It's easy to be brave when offense is given," she countered, unable to deny that there seemed to be some threat in his words, "and when the offending party has earned none of my good opinion."

Truth be told, she was a little surprised neither the earl nor his men had moved, that it seemed they would make no effort to deny her and Grimm's departure. And though she normally didn't like it when Grimm led her around by the hand or arm, she found solace as he took her right wrist and pulled her close while they made their way to the back door. She gripped his thick upper arm with her free hand, unsettled to near witlessness. Heat suffused her entire body.

At the exit, the earl's guard met Grimm's gaze for a few tense moments before slowly stepping aside to allow passage. Sorcha felt Grimm's arm tense under her grip, his clenched fists betraying his urge to force his way through. Possibly, only her firm hold on his arm prevented him from taking action.

They escaped into the night. Never before had their departure come complete with a whoosh of anxious breath released once the door had closed behind them. Sorcha's breath was white in the crisp night air, but she had no time to lift her hood. Grimm did not pause once outside, once the immediate threat was diminished. Instead, he pulled Sorcha along at his side, his pace rushed with anger.

They marched hurriedly along the road with Grimm turning every few seconds, probably to be assured that the alehouse's door did not open and that they were not being pursued.

When they were a quarter mile gone from the Bonnie Barrel Inn and swallowed by the moonless night, Grimm left the road, steering them into a thicket of trees that flanked the twisting lane. Only then did Sorcha know some relief, small though it was. Tension drained from her body, and she exhaled a long breath. And yet she was plagued by her wicked and guilty conscience. She was not ignorant of a man's touch and had understood exactly what the earl had proposed and wanted. Try as she might, she could not refute the truth, that as much as the Rebel's crude offer had frightened and astonished her, it had also tantalized her.

***

Sorcha woke with a start the next morning, having in her mind some recollection of a tale heard not very long ago, whispered inside the walls of the Bonnie Barrel Inn, of a chilling incident involving the Rebel of Lochaber Forest.

Murine, the aged alewife of Caol, had told the tale some months ago. Sorcha heard the words again, as they'd been said then, in Murine's distinctive, craggy voice.

"Small group of travelers was lost in the labyrinthine paths of the forest, they say," Murine had said, "and stumbled upon an ancient ruin, a crumbling castle, its stones seasoned by unkind centuries."

On a good day, Murine was fanciful, always embellishing tales, even mundane ones. A simple transaction, her selling ale to Murdo, could easily become a lengthy and exaggerated story that didn't often or always resemble the exact truth. She loved an audience and had a grand one the day she'd first sang the tune, about one occasion of the Rebel's legend. Several fishwives, laundresses, and other peasants had gathered round and listened raptly. Sorcha was always amazed that no one ever challenged the woman's truth telling.

"Cautiously, they approached," Murine had divulged, "their wary footsteps muffled by the thick undergrowth."

She'd ducked her chin, leaning closer to her listeners, Sorcha recalled.

"A figure emerged from the shadows," Murine had gone on, using an ominous voice. "Tall and commanding, cloaked in darkness, the Rebel stood before them like a shadow of death itself. His eyes gleamed with a sinister light, his presence suffused with an aura of menace."

Sorcha felt now as she had then, the urge to roll her eyes for Murine's theatrical delivery.

"With a voice as cold as the winter wind, the Rebel demanded tribute from the weary travelers, a toll for daring to trespass in his domain, the forest at Lochaber. Ah, but they hesitated, paralyzed by fright, and so he unleashed his fury upon them. In the blink of an eye, his sword flashed like lightning in the darkness, cutting down the hapless travelers with ruthless precision. Their screams echoed through the forest, silent until that moment, and blood painted the leaves crimson."

She'd gone on in her imitable way, to say that when the dawn broke, "and the first light pierced the veil of night", the ruins bore witness to the Rebel's wrath. The forest was now haunted,

Murine had supposed convincingly, before she'd finished, as she often did, with, "And there ye have it and why would I lie?"

In the narrow cot that was her bed, Sorcha stared at the thatch ceiling overhead in the gray light of morning and tried to discern if there was or could be any truth to that shocking account. Did the man who'd inquired with chilling indifference about the price for a night with her slay people without just cause? Did he truly possess a heart as dark as the stories suggested?

Her thoughts wandered back to last evening and that forced encounter with Augustus MacKenzie. Certainly, his piercing gaze had been filled with a brutal intensity, which had made her hair stand on end. But beneath the façade of coldness, was there a flicker of humanity? Or was he truly the merciless villain that folklore portrayed him to be?

Grumbling aloud for the way he'd seeped into her consciousness even as she'd slept and for how he'd managed to torment her first thing in the morning, Sorcha threw back the blankets and climbed out of bed. As she did every day when she'd finished with her morning toilette, she opened the door to her small cottage, expecting Grimm would be near and come soon to share breakfast with her.

She grinned a little to herself as she stoked the small fire under the pot with yesterday's pottage, pleased that the usual pangs of hunger were a little less perceptible today, courtesy of last night's unexpected boon, the supper she'd wrangled out of the earl.

Chapter Five

Augustus leaned against the wooden railing of the farrier's stable, his gaze wandering over the quiet village of Caol, while Cormac, the village farrier, inspected the hoof of Augustus's steed. The man murmured to himself as he worked but hadn't yet seemed to require any input or response from Augustus.

Two women were busy gathering water from the well on the opposite side of the main road. Both were decades older than Augustus, one petite and wiry while the other was taller and sturdier and wearing a handkerchief tied round her head. They'd aimed inquisitive gazes in his direction as they'd approached the well but seemed to have since appeased their curiosity and busied themselves with filling their buckets. Down the lane a wee bit, an even older woman tended to the garden plot at the side of her cottage, bent in half, plucking stalks and roots from the ground. She straightened abruptly, barking out some admonition at a pair of hounds that ran too close.

Four silhouetted men were seen up on the ridge of the fields but otherwise Caol was quiet. Mayhap the dreary skies and constant misting rain prompted folks to tend their indoor chores on this morning that was bitter with cold.

He thought of home, of Strontian's small village, not much larger than this burgh, but was not visited by any nostalgia, not by any wish that he was there instead of here.

Geddy and Angus appeared at the end of the lane, headed toward the farrier's shed, at the same time the farrier straightened up, giving a satisfied nod. "Aye, he's a fine steed, milord. Guid shape he is, for wherever the roads take ye."

"Many thanks," Augustus said, patting the steed's flank before flipping a coin to the farrier.

"Might be wanting to be making yer presence kent to the lord up there," said the farrier, "if ye'll be staying a wee bit in these parts. Seems that ye might be, that ye've found at least one reason to keep ye near for a spell."

Ignoring the man's inference, which certainly referred to the beekeeper and confirmed a long-held belief about gossip in small burghs such as this, Augustus turned toward the northern hills, where the farrier had indicated. "Who is the lord here?"

"De Montfort," Cormac replied and then snickered a bit. "*Lord* Aldric de Montfort, and dinna be forgettin' that part."

The farrier's answer came as no surprise since Augustus had been sent purposefully to Caol to meet de Montfort. *A noble in snake's robes*, de Montfort had been described by Simon Fraser, a most trusted confidante of Robert Bruce, and who had, at the king's behest, charged Augustus with discerning where lay de Montfort's loyalties.

Never one to mince words, he remarked to the farrier, "I've heard he deals poorly with the common man."

Possibly the farrier regretted already how much he'd revealed. As Augustus was essentially a stranger to him, he kept any further opinions to himself. "Might be," was all he said.

Having no further need of the man, Augustus wished him a good day and walked his steed out from under the low roof, mounting just as Geddy and Angus arrived.

"They're all set," announced Geddy, referring to the MacKenzie army, whom Augustus had wanted gathered. "'Bout a mile off, near the bend in the loch."

"Seems the quickest route would take us right past the beekeeper's hut," Angus said, not bothering to hide his smirk.

Augustus gave him a feral glare and wheeled his steed in the opposite direction.

The three men trotted away from Caol, with Geddy advising, "Three of these local lads have joined the ranks, with one's mam scratching and clawing at the lad, trying to keep him from going."

Augustus rolled his eyes at this, a familiar frustration gnawing at him for the widespread expectation that others would fight for freedom while so many were unwilling to make sacrifices themselves. He found it particularly irksome when mothers, fearful for their sons' safety, opposed their involvement in the fight against the English. To Augustus, this attitude was perplexing and hypocritical. How could they expect to win a war without the collective sacrifice and commitment of all? Without individuals willing to fight and endure hardships, victory would remain out of reach.

Once outside the small and narrow lanes of Caol, Augustus gave his destrier his head, allowing him to gallop freely over the rolling hills. The big black's swift pace barred any other conversation, leaving Augustus with his own thoughts, which inevitably circled back to the beekeeper. His encounter with Sorcha last evening lingered like an irritating thorn, scratching and digging at him. He did not curse himself for his lack of finesse in her company, or for any fear that he didn't know how to win favor with a woman. His words and actions had been intentional. He wanted there to be no misunderstanding or doubt about what he wanted. Aye, he would have been mightily surprised if she'd not given the response she had, one of acute offense, but he was pleased to have laid the foundation, so to speak. At any time they met in the future—and he would make sure they did—he wanted there to be no ambiguity about what he was after.

And though he was relatively satisfied with yesterday's engagement with Sorcha and her grim protector, he was indeed vexed at himself for how much time he actually spent thinking about her. He'd passed a rough night, beguiled by recurring visions of her expressive blue eyes, the porcelain quality of her skin, and the sweetness of her voice.

Determined now to put her from his mind, and to instead concentrate instead on the day's ambition, he urged the destrier to greater speed and within minutes met with his army where three tall willows stood sentinel at a sharp bend in Loch Linnhe. He did not stop for any reason but rode beyond the gathered MacKenzie army, along the jagged shoreline of the lake, toward Ironwood, the de Montfort stronghold. His army fell into step behind him.

Naught but a few minutes later, the MacKenzie army crested a tall hillock and the imposing fortress loomed in front of them, its stone walls and battlements gleaming in the late morning sun. A chill wind swept down from the surrounding hills, carrying with it the faint scent of woodsmoke and the distant clang of a smithy's hammer against iron.

He did not approach Ironwood with his full army with any sense of grandeur or intimidation, but rather with a cautious and measured demeanor, as he wasn't quite sure what to expect. 'Twould be a hard sell, despite his reputation, with the numbers he traveled with; the MacKenzie army, fighting since Stirling Bridge a decade ago, was seriously depleted, whereas de Montfort's army, now in residence, was possibly three times the size.

It was often murmured, sometimes with a hint of derision, that de Montfort played only a peripheral role in the war. Rumors circulated about his curious knack for conveniently avoiding major battles, either fortuitously arriving late or finding a reason to skirt around them altogether. Many chuckled, though with little humor, at the notion that whenever forces were consolidated, de Montfort seemed all too eager to offer his company for the rear guard or some flanking position that never quite materialized as needed. It was as if he had mastered the art of preserving his own skin while others risked theirs in the name of victory. With growing frustration, many commanders theorized that hundreds of lives had been lost in battle so that de Montfort could maintain his.

De Montfort was a bit player in the large theater of war, but as Simon Fraser had said to Augustus, "Even the small characters, in only one scene, could wield great influence on the outcome."

Geddy announced their presence at the gate, surprisingly open, where they were advised that twelve might enter and no more. Leaving three officers outside with the bulk of the militia, Augustus, Geddy, and the other officers proceeded through the tall stone archway and dismounted. The door was opened to them and a ghoul of a man in long robes, advising he was Griswald, the castle steward, escorted them into the hall.

Augustus's gaze fell immediately upon Lord Aldric seated at the head table. The middle-aged lord possessed a long face that was notably thin, his frame imagined to be skeletal beneath the folds of his finery. His gaunt appearance lent him an air of austerity, accentuated by the sharp angle of his nose and hollowness of his cheeks, all of which was belied by the bounty of food before him. His expression pinched and haggard, Lord Aldric's eyes darted over Augustus and each of his men in his shadow with a calculating gaze that seemed to miss nothing.

Standing just beyond the earl, behind the chair carved of dark oak stood a woman presumed to be de Montfort's wife. She was twenty years his junior at least, her presence a stark contrast to that of her husband. Thin-lipped and with a fixed gaze that hadn't yet left the back of her husband's head, she exuded an aura of silent obedience, ready to serve her lord.

Around the hall, others loitered lazily, soldiers and servants alike, their movements sluggish and listless. Some leaned against the walls, idly chatting amongst themselves, while others lounged at the table with their lord, their faces obscured by the shadows. There was an air of apathy that hung heavy in the air, a sense that time passed slowly within the confines of Ironwood.

Augustus halted several yards in front of the center of the table and bowed his head briefly.

"Hail, my lord," he said. "I am Augustus MacKenzie, laird of Strontian, come to offer my respects as my retinue crosses through Coal."

Lord Aldric gnawed vigorously on the inside of his left cheek, which twisted his lips in ugly misshapenness to the right.

"Hmph," he snorted. "Cross through or camp in, my lord? Seems ye've been embedded here for several days and this is the first I've seen of ye."

"Pardon, my lord, but I wasn't sure if we were pausing or going," Augustus invented, managing to keep his disdain well concealed behind a tight smile of civility. He was a lord in his own right and effectively on equal footing with the man, and thus was not too keen on de Montfort's superior attitude. "I am under orders from Simon Fraser, loyal disciple of King Robert. I seek either faithless rebels in the area or, at your leave, enlistees for the king's army."

Another harrumphed answered this. Lord Aldric sat with his fingers buried in a platter of haphazardly dissected meat, the grease leaving slick trails across his fingers and staining his garments and chin. "Do ye nae ken yer time might better be spent than chasing small numbers of rebels and instigators?" While leaving his wrists on the table near the oval platter, de Montfort lengthened his thin spine and reclined against the back of the chair, contemplating Augustus through shrewd eyes. "My name is kent in these parts and goes a long way, sir, keeping enemies away from Caol. One can only hope," he said pointedly, raising one thin gray brow, "that the MacKenzies' current presence does nae *invite* the enemy into the territory. I am landlord, leader, judge, father," he barked, "I can call out any man—hundreds of them—to attend me at the chase or to fight under my banner and the mandate is met with ready obedience."

"Ye are fortunate indeed, my lord," said Augustus, wanting to launch himself at the man and quiet his barking with a sword through his ugly mouth. Ah, and he couldn't help himself, putting his mission at risk, but he simply could not leave the boastful statement unchallenged. "Leader, judge, and father?" He repeated, pretending to be impressed. "Ye assume a genial and respectful relationship with your adherents, my lord, but use words like mandate and obedience in the same breath."

De Montfort's eyes hardened at the defiance, but he did not raise his voice when he replied, though a derisive sneer was affixed to his tone. "Ye, instead, are a friend to those who fight in yer name?"

"They dinna fight in my name, my lord," Augustus replied levelly, "but in the name of the king." Often he'd heard of the erroneous impression of the Highland chief as an ignorant and unprincipled tyrant, who rewarded the abject submission of his followers with relentless cruelty and rigorous oppression. Augustus had consistently endeavored to shift such perception. De Montfort, however, proved the exception of the rule Augustus often espoused. "Aye, my lord, many are my friends," Augustus went on, turning and lifting his hand toward the MacKenzies who stood just beyond him. "Many I've kent all my life. Otherwise, duty and an honorable spirit are what join them to my banner."

Whether Lord Aldric was satisfied or annoyed by this response, Augustus did not know. The earl returned his attention to the meat on his platter, clawing with his teeth at the meat on a long bone.

"And what of your castle in Dingwall?" Augustus asked, daring to reveal what he already knew about de Montfort, but also managing to rouse the earl's attention.

Because de Montfort's loyalty had been in question for some time, a year ago he'd been forced to offer some *assurances* to the nobles who stood with Robert Bruce.

De Montfort seethed, "I gave up my strong castles to de Leslie, gave up my son as a hostage to my fidelity." This was uttered with more arrogance than any manner of submissiveness that surely had been attached to him at the time of the surrender. "And how do ye justify making that yer affair?"

He did not say what Augustus had also been made aware of, that Lord Aldric had given also up "fourteen pretty Irishmen" to de Leslie, who had all along been faithful to de Montfort's banner, who were immediately caused to be hanged. It was not well done on de Leslie's part to have taken those lives when de Montfort's treachery had *not* been proven, but it was inexcusably ill-done of de Montfort to have betrayed his own loyal men. More poorly done, if he had indeed risked his own son's life if it should be proven that he *was* working against the Scottish crown.

Augustus shrugged innocently. "Nae my affair at all, my lord. I merely acknowledge what is general knowledge, how much ye've sacrificed in the name of freedom."

De Montfort's gaze narrowed as he measured Augustus derisively, searching no doubt for any hint of deception.

Augustus maintained a carefully neutral façade. It had not escaped his notice, the lack of hospitality extended by de Montfort. There was no offer of a drink or even a gesture to take a seat, or any of the customary courtesies expected of a host. The earl was haughtily contented, it seemed, to leave Augustus and his men standing awkwardly in front of him.

He didn't like him, de Montfort, not one bit.

But then he didn't have to like him. He was gratified, however, to be reminded that fiends resided even in gaunt, seemingly harmless bodies.

There is nae harmless man, came his father's voice in his head, *just as there are nae men without sins*. And who would know better, Augustus wondered internally.

He'd been sent to make conclusions about de Montfort's character and his loyalties. Yet, while all seemed obvious, what he'd surrendered to stay alive and keep his army, 'twas too soon to know for sure and Augustus knew he would be forced to endure many more hours in the man's vile company and domain.

***

Sorcha and Grimm walked along a path barely noticeable, traversed once a month only by the two of them, which turned off the lane and toward the north, where sat Ironwood Castle. Inside the stone walls of the keep built only a generation ago lived Lord Aldric de Montfort and his family, from whom Finn had leased the land and was given leave to build the cottage and with whom Sorcha had subsequently made a deal. Or rather, in the absence of the lord, Sorcha had begged mercy of his wife, Alice de Montfort, who'd conceded gracelessly to Sorcha's pleas to rework the lease after Finn's demise and had allowed Sorcha to pay for her lease with honey and beeswax for two years, almost one of which was nearly gone.

A whole year.

And longer than that since Finn had kissed her goodbye.

As they walked she closed her eyes briefly, her lashed misted by the light rain, trying to bring his image to mind, a pastime which was sadly becoming more and more difficult as time went by. A week ago, she struggled to recall the exact sound of his voice and had wept until she thought she'd recovered it properly. Certainly, she vividly remembered Finn's appearance, but the subtleties of his expressions—his wry grin, his teasing smile, the thoughtful furrow of his brow when he concentrated—were gradually fading from her memory. Like so many people, Finn likely possessed a myriad of expressions and Sorcha lamented the fact that with the passing days, weeks, and months, more and more of them slipped from the grasp of her memory.

Like so many people...save for Augustus MacKenzie, who seemed to have only that one expression: arrogantly fierce.

Her eyes snapped open, and her lips thinned. The last thing she wanted was thoughts of the maddening Rebel supplanting memories of her dear, sweet, perfect Finn. Her breath caught in her throat at the very idea, guilt suffusing her.

Steadfastly, she concentrated on the present, and today's chore, which gave her something else to fret about. She never liked going up to the de Montfort keep. Despite its relative newness, the keep was cold and dreary. Sorcha knew the de Montforts had several children, but she'd never caught even the shadow of a glimpse of them. There was no laughter ringing through the halls, no merry screaming, no bairn clinging to his mother's skirts. For as many times as she visited, she was mostly received by the lady of the keep or her steward and had only rarely met Lord Aldric. For this she was mostly thankful, her initial impression of him unfavorable, but then she wasn't sure his lady wife was a greater substitute. The woman was cold and stiff, the epitome of inhospitality, so much so that Sorcha wasn't sure how she'd been persuaded to accept Sorcha's terms to cover her lease payment with honey and wax or why, in the first place, the woman had allowed Sorcha to maintain the lease. Only a widow could lease land and it was no secret that while they'd lived as such, Sorcha and Finn had been wed only in their minds and hearts.

The small cart that Grimm pulled along behind him groaned as it rode over an exposed rock. The contents of the cart were jostled and shaken but packed so well with straw that nothing was unmoored from its position.

She caught Grimm eyeing her with speculation. Supposing he wondered at her silence for the first half mile, she waved off what appeared to be a question in his gaze.

"My head's in the clouds today," she said dismissively. "Or rather, absorbed here on earth. In spite of her generosity regarding Finn's lease, I can't find it in my heart or head to like Lady de Montfort." She sighed. "I'm an ungrateful wretch, I imagine."

Grimm shrugged, which Sorcha read not as a commentary on her dislike of the woman, but more as if he agreed that there was little to like in the woman.

"They look alike, do they not?" She asked impishly. "The Lord and Lady of Ironwood, both with their long faces and sticklike figures? Do you not find it strange, Grimm, that we've never seen them at the same time—either you and I, or previously Finn and I? Mayhap they are the same person, and—oh, my!" She caught herself, her eyes widening with delight at the idea of a fantastic scenario. "Mayhap Lord Aldric has long been dead, and Lady Alice only portrays him so that she is not compelled to wed another. She is quite young, you know, or she might be, it's hard to tell actually, with the way she squeezes her face so rigidly."

Grimm rolled his eyes at Sorcha while she laughed.

As was often the case, once she began to talk, she sometimes just prattled right along.

And because she spoke freely to Grimm almost always, Sorcha grumbled to him, "And, by the way, I was quiet there for a bit, absorbed in thoughts of Finn until that wretched Earl of Lochmere intruded upon my happy thoughts." Mayhap they were not so much happy as they were sacred thoughts, she clarified to herself. Though she found joy in the memory of Finn, the loss of him was both inescapable and heartbreaking still.

Grimm sent her a look of scathing rebuke, at which Sorcha shrugged.

"Oh, you don't have to tell me, Grimm. Trust me, it appalls me as much as you."

The next look he sent her way clearly said, *And make sure it stays that way.*

They trudged on, Grimm pulling along the three-wheeled cart along a level field of tall grass before they were forced to climb upward the last couple hundred feet, as Ironwood sat upon a small beinn, "as lofty as the lord," Sorcha had commented to Finn at one time.

They strolled in through the gates unchecked and Sorcha thought that there must ever be a person watching for people approaching as it had been many months since she'd been compelled to bang upon the thick wooden door and announce herself. Today it was pulled open by Griswald, de Montfort's steward, who wore a face much as his mistress, devoid of any good humor.

"Lord Aldric is expecting you," Griswald intoned, his lips barely moving inside a face that was pasty white.

A bit taken aback, both at being expected—there were still three days until the end of the quarter—and by the news that she would be received by de Montfort himself, Sorcha exchanged a raised brow with Grimm and followed the steward as he slunk through the dark halls of Ironwood. Grimm left the cart outside the door.

They were led directly to the keep's main hall, which would never be considered fine as it was without windows and thus light and was furnished with but one long table. Sorcha had often and peculiarly likened it to a dungeon, the table being where prisoners might be strapped down and tortured.

Many surprises greeted her as she glanced toward the far end of the hall.

First and most unnerving, standing in front of the lord's table was a small group of MacKenzie men, all of whom turned at their entrance, which Griswald announced scratchily. Sorcha's eyes passed right over all the faces, landing immediately upon Augustus MacKenzie, who stood at the helm of his men, so to speak.

His hypnotic blue eyes fixated on her, and she might have supposed that he was just as surprised to see her as she was him. Her breath caught in her throat, and she abhorred what had caused this, not fear but a prickling sense of womanly awareness. Damn him!

Grimm's timely and purposeful hand on her arm steered her forward, and there she met the next shock: Lady Alice standing behind her husband while he supped at the table. Any harsh opinion of the woman evaporated instantly as Sorcha considered her stiff and fearful mien. Good Lord! But was Alice instructed, under the threat of violence, to keep her eyes only on Lord Aldric, even as the hall became quite crowded with guests?

She felt as if she'd entered the wrong keep or another dimension.

But then she settled her gaze on Lord Aldric and a bit of normalcy returned. Lord Aldric de Montfort sat behind the long table, spooning pudding or some such delight from a silver cup while he watched her approach. She'd forgotten that about him, that she rarely if ever saw him when he wasn't eating something.

She smiled mechanically but insincerely at Lord Aldric, often required to resist a shiver in his presence. His face was gaunt and pallid, with sunken eyes that bore into any subject with a disturbing intensity. His thin lips were drawn into a perpetual sneer, often revealing crowded and crooked teeth that were nowhere near white. His hair hung limply around his haggard face, adding to his disturbing aura.

Lord Aldric passed a displeased glance over Grimm as they approached the table. His bony fingers continued to spoon pudding into his mouth. Previously, Sorcha had wondered if he would simply shrivel and die if he ever stopped eating. Was he hollow, and his skeletal frame needed constant filling?

Possibly, Lord Aldric had only met Grimm on one occasion, having been absent so often in the last year. She recalled now what she'd noted on that other occasion, that the lord was not pleased at all that Sorcha had found herself a protector. On two occasions since Finn had gone, Lord Aldric had ambiguously let it be known that he would be pleased to waive her rents due if she would accommodate some of his needs. She'd been quick with her refusal, using her grief in a self-serving manner—the first and only time—while somehow managing to refrain from gagging in front of him.

"Ah, the beekeeper," Lord Aldric intoned indistinctly, his mouth full. He swallowed and sent a clearly discontented glance at Grimm. "And the Oaf."

"Good day, my lord," she said, her voice shaky. She blamed the Rebel for this and not the earl. Having come abreast of him, and while her gaze was trained on de Montfort, she could *feel* the radiant heat of a pair of striking blue eyes. "I've brought my rents due for this quarter, my lord," she said, her voice stronger, "and I wonder if I might—"

"Ye dinna march straight in and go straightway to nattering. I've guests or have ye nae eyes in yer head?"

Bristling internally, Sorcha said tightly, "I meant not to waste any of your time. And I have met Lord Augustus." She turned and looked only at his broad shoulder. "Good day, my lord. I did not intend a rudeness."

"Good day, lass," the Rebel responded in a fair tone. "Rest assured, I would nae ever assume any impoliteness from ye."

Her eyes flew swiftly to his. Did she detect a scant hint of mockery directed at her? Aye, she supposed she had, and which she silently acknowledged was not out of line, for how discourteous she had been to him last evening.

"I dinna want these cakes," Lord Aldric barked to a serving wench, pushing the platter back into her stomach as the girl had just brought it to the table at his side. "Bring me the ones with the currants." He banged the flat of his hand on the table when the girl took time to steady the plate and bow to his favor. "Move, girl! Now."

With a bit of lingering annoyance, Lord Aldric turned his dark gaze onto Sorcha, whose eyes were wide now, not for the treatment of the kitchen girl, but that he'd not concealed it from the small crowd in the hall.

"What now?" He asked of Sorcha. "What are ye meaning to blather about?"

Wanting only to be away from all that was awkward and uncomfortable presently—more so than on any other occasion—Sorcha rushed out, "I seek leave, my lord, to construct a third apiary, as had been Finn's wish, in the—"

"Nae! Nae!" Lord Aldric blustered. "What need have ye of another? 'Tis nae my business to satisfy yer personal greed."

"My lord, consider the amount of honey I would be able to deliver to you," Sorcha implored tautly. "I would have to lease more space and thus you would benefit from—"

"I said nae. Enough with yer bees and yer hives." A look of annoyed confusion claimed his haggard features. "And what is your purpose inside Caol, Oaf? What occupation do you claim?"

"He doesn't speak, my lord," Sorcha gritted out, "as you might recall." Should recall, since he brought it up at each of their other meetings.

"Dinna speak, aye. Tongue might be broken but his hands are nae. He canna exist with nae—"

"Grimm is not without an occupation, my lord. He is my assistant, same as I was to Finn. The apiaries require continued attention, my lord, and when comes the time to claim the honey and—"

"Aye, aye, aye. I recall now. He serves you, Sorcha the beekeeper. But in what other capacity does he service you?"

Of course, he'd not misspoken by accident, the slimy old man.

Her cheeks flamed red at what he insinuated, knowing who stood among the audience.

"Grimm is my assistant, my lord, and aside from being my dearest friend, he serves as a loyal protector." She'd reached her limit and realized she couldn't hold back any more her opinion of him or his behavior much longer. However, in spite of her want to verbally berate him, she maintained her composure and only hinted at his dishonor and vulgar attempts at manipulation. "The nights here in Caol are fraught with dangers."

The beginnings of a nasty smirk curled one side of his mouth as he glared at her.

"Might be dangers of your own doing," he suggested in a tone meant to be interpreted as a father counseling his daughter, but which essentially reminded her that his protection was available.

Aye, if she didn't mind parting with her dignity, her sanity, any shred of pride, or for that matter, her very soul.

Sorcha met and held his gaze, smiling artlessly, all the while recalling what he'd said to her at the end of last year when they'd last met. He'd been much more open in his lewdness.

"I've said, have I nae, that I could make it so your life was far more comfortable?" He'd asked her last autumn, leering at her malevolently from that same chair.

"You have, my lord," Sorcha had returned stiffly on that other day.

"Or utterly more miserable," Lord Aldric had threatened then, too pompous to have veiled it, all because she'd failed to produce the appropriate amount of gratitude, or to accept his coarse offer.

Presently, without any expectation of gaining his approval to construct another hive, Sorcha bowed her head at the earl. "I won't take up anymore of your time. Good day."

With her anger ignited by the earl's mistreatment, Sorcha turned and faced Augustus MacKenzie, intrigued by a brazen plan to swipe at Lord Aldric's arrogance—a move for which she knew she would likely face consequences. She grasped her threadbare cloak firmly and swept it out to her sides, lowering herself into a deep and reverent curtsy, a gesture of humble homage that she would forever withhold from de Montfort. One that, if not for her dander being raised and her wanting the last word, she would never have bestowed upon the Rebel.

"A great pleasure to see you again, my lord," she murmured to the ground.

When she rose and lifted her face, the mesmerizing blue eyes of the Rebel of Lochaber Forest brimmed with amusement.

He knew exactly what she had done and why.

Sorcha could have cared less.

With the aplomb worthy of a queen, she pivoted gracefully and took her leave, calling for Grimm to follow.

Damn both those earls!

Chapter Six

Flashes of lightning illuminated the cottage every few seconds, the piercing light flickering between gaps where the lone window met the wall, casting eerie shadows about the cottage. The light also appeared as a multitude of streaks in the window's shutters and glinted through spaces around the door frame. The door and shutter shook and rattled with the force of the wind that drove the storm. Rain pounded against the thatch overhead with a relentless intensity, the likes of which Sorcha could not recall. The drumming of the rain, coupled with thunder that came as harsh blasts of noise and sometimes as low grumblings of a seething tempest, drowned out all other sounds.

    Sorcha's heart raced with anxiety as she huddled in her narrow cot, listening to the persistent onslaught. Rain dripping onto the bottom of her bed, from where she'd moved her feet and the bottom of her blankets, worried her much less than what the fierce winds and driving rains might be doing to her apiaries. With every gust of wind that whistled ominously through her tiny cottage, she imagined her beehives toppling over or worse, yet being blown away entirely, those precious, industrious bees scattered, lost to the storm. She'd braved the lashing rain only briefly, an hour ago, to step outside and assure herself that her home apiary, inside the protective frame Finn had built, was undisturbed, having been greatly relieved to discover that the care Finn had taken to situate the hives away from the most common easterly wind had been prudent, and in this instance, lifesaving. There, on the southwestern side of the cottage, the skeps tucked under the sturdy frame were barely bothered by the wind or rain.

She had not dared to venture further, off to the forest apiary, not in the pure blackness of the night that was barely relieved by silvery rain. She would have to wait until morn to know its fate.

Before she'd returned to the relative warmth and calm inside her cottage, she'd called out for Grimm, wanting him to find shelter inside with her. He'd not responded and hadn't shown himself, which hadn't worried Sorcha so much as it had annoyed her, that he wouldn't seek refuge with her but somewhere on his own. His concern for propriety sometimes irked her; what did she care what the sometimes narrow-minded and often judgmental citizens of Caol thought or her? Their opinion of her was never going to improve, was only ever going to get worse, whether she behaved in a manner that suited their conveniently strict morals or acted the whore they imagined her.

She slept only intermittently and when morning came the hard earth inside her small house was littered with half a dozen puddles, as quite a bit of the thatch of her roof had been torn away by the fierce wind. Sorcha gave that mess little heed for now but stepped outside and tossed an exasperated glare at the clear blue sky—*where were you last night?*—checking first on the home apiary. Not even the smallest breeze lifted the hair off her shoulders or bent a single blade of grass now.

"If ye dinna like the weather, wait five minutes," she'd heard Murdo say more than once.

With an annoyance directed at a very fickle Mother Nature and her savage outburst of last night, Sorcha now squinted against the sun, checking the skeps under the lean-to once again before scouring the area for Grimm, who was still nowhere to be found. But she could not and would not wait for him and began to march away from the house, heading out on the rain-soaked path that led into Caol, but which she would abandon well before the burgh, making a left off into the woods and the apiary in the clearing.

Twenty minutes later, she'd just made that turn off the lane and was stomping through an area of wind and rain matted grass when it dawned on her that concern had overridden good sense, and that she'd not brought any tools with her to address any damage she might find among her hives. Disgruntled anew with her own lack of foresight, Sorcha continued on anyway, deciding she might best first discover what, if any, damage there was. She was still clinging to a nebulous hope that the thick forest all around the clearing might have provided some protection to her bees and hives.

The remainder of the trek, through a woodland thick with mud, downed limbs, and scattered forest debris, took twice as long as it normally might. Her sturdy but worn boots were caked with mud, and what had seemed only a trace of water but had turned out to be a puddle a half foot deep, alerted her that there was at least one hole in the toe of her boot and her left foot was wet inside and out, and thus, Sorcha's mood was not only anxious but sour by the time she reached her distant apiary.

Her mood was not improved when she arrived, but rather devastation sank heavily upon her at the sight of the once neatly aligned row of skeps, which were as she'd feared, toppled, broken, and vacant, the bees having flown elsewhere.

A small cry escaped her as she rushed toward the upset hives, picking up one overturned hackle and skep, frowning at the damage done to it. The protective straw hackle was shredded, and the hardened cloaming skep looked as if it had been beaten repeatedly against the ground or a nearby tree. Sorcha bent and picked up a remnant of another skep, turning it over, examining the woven willow, and then tossing it aside when she failed to find any part worth saving.

After a while, after she'd examined a dozen different pieces, she stood outside the circle of destruction, hands at her sides even as they held yet several broken sections of arc-ed willow, her mouth open as she stared with growing puzzlement at the mess made of her apiary. She had to imagine that any number of forest critters—raccoons, birds, ants— could have taken advantage of the initial destruction and helped themselves to a succulent treat of honey.

Straightening her back, Sorcha took a deep breath and considered the damage once more. 'Twas more than only her means of support destroyed, but her connection to Finn as well. He'd chosen this location, he'd built the first skep, and had said he'd construct others when he returned.

Disheartened and discouraged by the whims of Fate, Sorcha lifted her arm and twirled, flinging one of the willow sections with some force, the action committed to and performed before she realized that she was not alone. As soon as she released the brown wood piece she clapped her hands over her mouth, horrified as she watched the Earl of Lochmere duck out of the way of the flying missile.

She held her breath and waited, a frisson of fear teasing its way about her heart, tightening the organ in her chest.

Truth be told, she was as fascinated by the swift and smooth motion he used to avoid the airborne skep section as she was by how vibrant and virile he appeared against the backdrop of the earthy green forest. He bent backward at the waist, his torso and head moved out of the way with a fluid grace that belied his size, while at the same time he planted a foot behind himself to maintain his balance. 'Twas all done rather poetically, she didn't mind thinking, a wee bit mesmerized by the elegance of that motion. At the same time, he was awash in gorgeous color, which shimmered in the russet strands of his hair, in the brilliant blue of his eyes, in the rich fabric of his plaid. This, coupled with the athleticism of his action, evoked a sense of striking masculinity and vigor, and briefly overshadowed her initial fright at having essentially if unwittingly lobbed an assault at him.

When he straightened and though he scowled, he whistled low and turned around to where the willow landed innocently several feet beyond him.

"Was that meant for any who intruded upon you in your apiary?" Augustus Mackenzie drawled when he faced Sorcha again. "Or was that aimed at me directly?"

Dropping her hands from her face, she was quick to acknowledge, "I am...I'm sorry. I didn't know—I thought I was alone."

"Venting frustration then," he guessed, his piercing gaze scanning the scene before it settled upon her with that almost-familiar-by-now powerful scrutiny. "'Twas a rough night indeed," he said absently, his gaze raking over her with nearly offensive diligence.

She imagined she appeared unkempt, that she showed signs that she'd rushed from her bed and from her cottage with little care for her appearance, while he appeared quite fresh, as if he'd not been disturbed by the storm overnight, as if he had no care about the destruction left in its wake. Perhaps she should be thankful for the blush his prolonged inspection caused to rise, since it likely added color to her supposed weary paleness. And then she wondered why on earth she should care what this man saw or thought about her.

"This is not..." she began, though she did not have any full thought in mind, was only wanting to put words into the silence that accompanied his piercing stare. When her voice trailed off, she returned his regard, suddenly struck by many questions, not least of which were about his presence here and now, in this remote spot. "This is not as bad as it seems," she said, fabricating an end to her sentence.

"Where is your man?"

"Grimm? He's about," she said, aware now of her circumstance, alone with the Rebel, deep in the forest. "Of course his name is not Grimm, as you might have guessed," she said next, aiming for an indifference she most certainly did not feel. With no intention of keeping company with the Rebel at this time or in this place, Sorcha fisted her hand into her skirts and lifted the hem a bit, stepping over some of the hive debris, murmuring, "Good day," as she walked away from the disturbing scene. There wasn't anything she could do here now, and she neither wished nor had reason to remain.

To her surprise, the earl fell into step beside her, holding the reins of his large destrier.

"What...what are you doing?" She asked nervously but kept moving.

"I canna have ye walk alone," he said idly. "If yer man willna safeguard ye, I suppose I must."

Unable to help herself, she barked out a laugh, "Is there not some adage about the fox guarding the hen's quarters? Or is it the wolf keeping safe the sheep?"

"If I intended to take, I'd nae have offered to pay for it," he said starkly, displeased by her inference, if anything should be gleaned from his chilly tone of voice.

"And why did you, by the way?"

"Ye want me to catalogue your charms? Your beauty? Do ye nae hear it—"

"No, no. I don't mean that—I wasn't trawling for compliments. I meant, well, why me? Why someone who isn't interested? Do not swooning and coy females throw themselves at you? Is that not incorporated into so lauded and terrifying a legend? That women throw themselves at you?"

He frowned severely at her. "Ye dinna seem sheltered—canna be, nae for the way ye left home with the beekeeper and made yer life here, but damn, if ye dinna sound like a child, with queries such as that."

Neither did she gasp at his knowledge of her nor wonder from where it had come. If not Murdo, any of the townsfolk would have been happy to share gossip about her. She'd bet her last halfpenny he'd had quite an earful from people always ready to mock her.

Only partially chastised by his statement—more embarrassed than scolded—she lowered her head and joined her hands in front of her. "Pardon me, for having so little exposure to...to extravagant legends or...loose women, or whatever type might be the sort to throw themselves at you."

"Why are ye so sure there are any women throwing themselves at me?"

"Well, I mean," she began, lifting her hand, waving it at him, her gaze returning to his striking visage. She caught herself, though, before she might have revealed that she found him ruggedly handsome in a frightening and fascinating way. Dropping her hand, she shrugged and faced forward again, knowing her cheeks were as pink as rosy apples in early fall. "I guess I imagined the lore and legend of your reputation might draw...curiosity seekers."

"It's nae something I bandy about, that other moniker."

"And yet it is with you—you didn't deny it to me the other night," she reminded him. She sent a spare glance out of the corner of her eye at him. "One might almost believe you revel in the chaos it causes a person, when they discover who they are actually speaking to."

"Ye are speaking to Augustus MacKenzie."

"Ah, but you cannot disclaim the other now, not at this late date. You might have refuted the rumor straight away. Methinks you enjoy the intimidation."

They walked on for a bit in silence until the earl guessed, "Ye come to a lot of conclusions inside your own head, do ye nae?"

Ignoring the inference that she shouldn't trust her own judgment, she maintained, "You didn't refute it when you had the chance and, therefore, I will keep to my opinion. Mayhap you believed my head would be turned by the strength of your reputation?"

"'Tis nae your head I aim to turn."

"Aye, my body," she provided boldly, even as she understood the content of this conversation was enormously improper. Simultaneously, she veered a little to the left of the earl so that more space separated them. "You wish to spend the night with me, ravish me," she said, a bit flustered—her own doing, for delving into this topic—and waved a hand impatiently, "or what have you. All pointless, I must say. My heart is not mine to give." She glanced forward, wondering, hoping that they were close to the edge of the forest, that she might soon be relieved of his company.

"I made no mention of your heart."

"Mm, yes. I am aware," she replied, slightly breathless now for the speed of her march and the racing of her pulse. "But as it is attached to my body, neither is available for purchase."

"Belongs to another?" He asked casually.

Sorcha was frustrated that he didn't sound out of breath and that it appeared he didn't need to either lengthen or quicken his stride but was able to keep pace effortlessly with her. "Yes, for some time now," she answered when she recalled he'd posed his last words as a question.

"And how long still? I hear yer man's been gone for almost a year."

"Love has a time limit?"

"Nae, but life does."

She harrumphed a laugh. "I'm not so long in the tooth that I need worry about that yet."

"Ye are nae a maid, though, are nae a lass with fewer than a score of years behind ye."

"Sweet Jesus, but are you always so offensively forthwith?"

"Am I expected to squander time with politeness, when the next minute is nae guaranteed to us."

A bit peeved at his lousy response, which seemed to want to justify his rudeness but failed miserably in her estimation, Sorcha glanced around the quiet woodland. "I believe we might both assume we have at the very least, several more moments, and that no terrible end awaits us near or on the horizon. I do not require an escort, my lord. Last night's storm was more dangerous than anything here and now."

It was, wasn't it? Or *was* she in danger at this moment, in the company of the Rebel of Lochaber Forest?

Augustus MacKenzie retorted promptly and with little emotion. "Did your man subscribe to that opinion? Did he—or ye—believe he would return? That many tomorrows awaited ye?"

Knowing she would not discuss Finn, a good man, with this one, who most certainly was not, Sorcha clamped her lips and marched on.

"Ye are afraid of me," he drawled, his guess not far from the mark.

"Was that not your intent?"

"It was nae."

Flippantly, and despite a niggling of anxiety that coursed through her now, she said offhandedly, "Isn't that wonderful, when we are able to achieve greater results than we set out to accomplish?"

"Ye're a spiky lass," was the earl's response to this.

Against all the wise counsel inside her head, she was, admittedly, not unmoved by the sound of his rich voice, all his words delivered with the laziness of a disinterested drawl. Recalling the direction of their improper conversation and ignoring his accusation, Sorcha declared, "I don't understand you, or your curiosity. You've said, outright, that you…well, you've made your aim clear. You professed especially that you are not interested in my head or heart. So why the—" she stopped walking and talking and turned to stare at the earl, her brow knit. "Oh, dear Lord...is this your attempt to woo me? By showering me with what is expected to be either unthreatening or pleasant conversation, but which has mostly given offense?"

Before he answered, he responded with a feral scowl. At length he stared at her, as if she'd spoken a language he did not understand.

"And now ye smile?" He said after a moment.

"Yes." She hadn't realized she'd done so, though. "The apprehension of safety will do that. Unless you intend to force yourself on me—I am beginning to believe you will not—you will not succeed either in winning my affections or having what you want. You haven't the means to lure me away from Finn's memory." Her smile improved and she proclaimed triumphantly, "I am safe."

Though his countenance remained fierce, his next question surprised her for where his mind had gone, for what he'd heard in her statement.

"That's your fear? That's what keeps ye happily mourning? That you'll dishonor his memory?"

Lifting her chin, irritated with herself for giving anything away regarding Finn and her grief and annoyed with him, this stranger, for how callously he dismissed her grief, she said through thin lips. "I have no fear that Finn's memory will ever be overshadowed. He was...an exceptional man, a saint among sinners."

The earl of Lochmere crooked his head at her, his brow lifted quizzically. "Was he all that while he lived, too?"

Sorcha gasped at his insinuation that Finn had been anything but, or that she might only cherish sweet memories, having disregarded any other.

To her growing annoyance, the earl shrugged and moved on, as if any response she might give to his query—asked only to rile her, she was sure—was of little import to him, or perhaps not to be believed.

"Mayhap I begin to see why ladies of good character or other might *not* be throwing themselves at you," she crowed, making sure her voice was loud enough for him to hear as he walked several yards away from and in front of her.

But he only vexed her further, sending back a chuckle, which sounded amused and not infuriated. His laughter was deep and surprisingly warm, grating doubly on her nerves for how delectable the sound was.

Soon enough, they reached the edge of the woods, where the earl paused and faced her as she caught up with him.

"Here comes your man," he said, "nae doubt ready and willing to take off my head."

Sorcha glanced across the storm-swept tall grass that led to a meandering path that would take her home. Indeed, Grimm was spotted, stalking along toward her, the grass little hindrance to his long legs. He wore a fresh or renewed scowl, though she couldn't be sure since she hadn't seen him this morning.

Sorcha glanced back at the earl, somewhat belatedly surprised that she had emerged from their encounter wholly unscathed. Yet, her surprise swiftly turned to fascination as she beheld the sight of his eyes. The sunlight bathed them in a pure light, causing them to gleam as brightly blue as the sea itself. Her lips parted in wonder. 'Twas a sin, really, that such an infuriating man should be so very compelling.

Before Grimm came within hearing of them, the earl bowed his head slightly at her.

"There are nae saints, lass," he said, in reference to her earlier remark about Finn. "Nae in this world."

He did not at that moment take his leave of her but embarked upon a lengthy perusal of her person, from head to toe, his gaze potent enough to send a shiver down her spine.

He turned and walked off with his horse then, inclining his head to Grimm as he approached.

Sorcha watched as the earl mounted, trying to make sense of the man. Purported to be a vicious rebel, he'd been anything but with her. Vexing, to be sure, but neither merciless nor overtly cruel.

Before Grimm reached her, she stared after the earl, worrying her lips now, wondering if she'd woken a sleeping dragon. Had her flippant, occasionally hostile remarks been taken as a gauntlet? The intensity of his gaze when she'd announced he posed no threat to Finn's memory said as much, did it not? She'd sensed that he'd found great disfavor being relegated to so small a threat.

She acknowledged Grimm's quizzical frown but said nothing. Shaking her head, troubled by the way these interactions with the earl left her...unfulfilled—Sweet Mother of God, as if she wanted more—she began to stomp through the grass herself, forcing Grimm to retrace his steps. By the time she reached the path where the grass struck the lane, Sorcha was more sure than she'd been after any previous meeting with the earl that she'd not seen the last of Augustus MacKenzie. The stomping then, was conceived in an attempt to hammer out her frustration with herself, for being nearly giddy at the prospect. She must put the Rebel from her mind! How selfish and indecent she was to entertain a fluttering belly and tingling nerves when Finn lay cold and dead in some unmarked grave.

Chapter Seven

As was his practice in any new environment, Augustus rode his destrier far and wide over all of Caol. He didn't know that presently what he gleaned of the area would be useful but as with a dozen other locales he'd investigated, he appreciated having knowledge of the terrain and its features. It was a habit born from his years leading an army, where familiarity with different counties and parishes could often mean the difference between victory and defeat on the battlefield. So, he rode, taking in the rolling hills and meandering streams, committing the landscape to memory in case the need for such information should arise in the future.

He knew it wasn't precisely by chance that he entered the forest where days ago he'd met Sorcha in another of her apiaries, which had sadly been destroyed by the storm. As he allowed the destrier to pick his way through the forest, shafts of golden light filtered through the thick canopy overhead, dappling the needle-strewn earth with patches of light and shadow. Grinning, Augustus wondered if his horse knew the way as well, as without much guidance he seemed to be headed in the direction of the glade where had once been a dozen skeps.

Just as he considered that there wasn't much chance of running into Sorcha now—nothing remained to bring her to the glade—Augustus was jolted from all thought by a soft wave of music that drifted toward him, the unmistakable melody of Sorcha's song. As he'd just decided she had no cause to be in the forest, he was surprised by this, and he paused, his senses coming instantly alive.

Instinctively, he moved closer but not close enough to reveal his presence. One brow raised at the content of her song today. No mournful hymn this, and though it was not quite a rousing tavern tune, 'twas the first song he'd heard from her that was rich in cadence, and not a lament. After a moment, as his ears tuned to her voice, his lips parted and a slow grin formed, realizing that she sang what was commonly known as *òrain obrach*, or work songs, normally sung by laborers, weavers, and sometimes marching armies to coordinate their movements.

Less than half of the words reached his ears, but the pulse and the timbre of her voice was easily discernable. There was something familiar and soothing about the sound and Augustus was loath to disturb either it or her. Unhurriedly, he dismounted, securing the reins around the pommel. His destrier might wander, but it would not be far, and a curt whistle always brought him back.

Content to simply listen to Sorcha's mesmerizing voice, he leaned against the smooth bark of a silver birch and slid down until he was sitting. He closed his eyes and allowed himself to be further enchanted, welcoming the respite, a moment of peace that was rarely afforded him. In no time at all, tension and worries of the world slipped away, replaced by an unfamiliar calm, a tranquility he hadn't experienced in years.

'Twas a fine reminder that his fascination with Sorcha was not based solely on how exquisite she was, or by how she amused and enchanted him with her constant displays of spirit—a mighty soul, his *màthair* might have claimed she possessed—but that he was equally attracted to her song, which he'd begun to believe had the power to heal.

So soothing was the sound of her voice and song that Augustus felt himself losing the battle against wakefulness.

When next he opened his eyes, he understood immediately that he'd actually dozed off, and he realized that there was no more song. *Jesu, but how long had he—*

Climbing to his feet, he was caught unawares by a huge black shape on his right periphery, amid what should have been a forest of green. Reaching for his sword, he turned to confront...Sorcha, holding the reins of his destrier, standing thirty paces away, motionless and staring at him with a softened expression, biting her lip as she contemplated him.

As he breathed out a sigh of relief, that he'd not encountered a more dangerous animal or man, Sorcha came forward, leading his horse.

"I won't tell," she said, humor brightening her eyes, "that the Rebel sneaks off from the retinue that surrounds him day and night, only to take a nap in the forest."

She said *take a nap* in such a way as to suggest he was a bairn, still in nappies. While he didn't find it amusing, he found he wasn't provoked by the insinuation.

Augustus shrugged sheepishly. "I'm nae saying yer song was dull, lass, but it does have a certain calming effect."

When she wasn't bristling with indignation, when she wasn't trying to evade him for some imagined fear that he would pounce on her—when she wasn't standing up to de Montfort and goading him, to her great peril, by curtsying to Augustus!—he learned that she was or could be fairly forthright.

"Grimm sometimes falls asleep as well," she said. Her eyes remained lively, and a smile teased her lips. "I keep hope in my heart that it's the soothing song that lulls him and not only him pretending to sleep so that he's given a respite from my regular chatter—which would *deaden an ear*, as Finn used to...say."

Her smile faded and once more, she bit her lip, an inclination of hers that he found quite charming. He had a notion, whether accurate or not, that it wasn't merely the mention of the deceased man's name that caused her hesitation, but rather the revelation that her lover had deemed her overly talkative. With little deliberation, Augustus concluded that the dead man's judgment cast Finn in a negative light, and much less so Sorcha.

She cleared her throat and announced, "I found this brute wandering near the glade."

Augustus lifted his hands and collected the reins from her, his fingers brushing hers.

"He's not quite as fearsome as he looks," she commented.

He rather expected that she would follow this with some remark that the same could not be said of the destrier's master, and quite frankly, Augustus knew a wee disappointment when she did not.

He frowned suddenly, realizing what had escaped his notice until now. "That's twice now I've found ye deep in the forest and the oaf naewhere around."

"His name is Grimm," she insisted.

"I'm sure it is nae," he countered.

Shrugging, Sorcha admitted, "No, it's probably not. And he probably hates it, but it's his own fault for not providing me with his actual name."

Though he was reluctant to offer any defense for the man, Augustus was compelled to remind her, "He dinna speak."

"Well, I know that, but there are other ways to convey his name—I'd once offered him honey and a sheaf of bark that he might write it down, but he refused."

"Mayhap he canna write."

Sorcha harrumphed with little grace, her nose wrinkling.

Once again, he found himself smitten, this time marveling at how effortlessly she engaged him in conversation. It seemed as though she had become relaxed enough to share her frustrations about her silent guardian.

Augustus returned to the issue he'd taken with her, which she'd adroitly sidestepped.

"But lass, I've seen enough of Caol and its citizens to understand the need for the—for Grimm's presence, and so why do ye tempt fate by taking yerself deep in the forest, where no one would hear ye scream?"

"Oh, he's busy with the roof," she said petulantly, "and I grew tired of waiting on him." As if reminded of something, she glanced down absently at her hand, turning it over to investigate her palm before she quickly closed her hand and buried it in the folds of her skirt.

Scowling, having caught a glimpse of redness and rawness, Augustus clasped her wrist and lifted her hand up for his own inspection, his face darkening at the damage done to her small hands.

"What is this?"

"It's nothing, but that stupid thatch," she said, trying to yank her hand away. "It's just that I'm not familiar with the method of thatch-making and…well, this is the result."

Augustus found her other hand and examined that one as well. Her palms bore the tell-tale signs of the labor-intensive craft. The once smooth skin now displayed a patchwork of welts and cuts.

Holding both her wrists, he brought his gaze to hers, his forehead creased in concern.

"Ye should have worn gloves," he scolded mildly.

"I am obviously ill-suited to such detailed labor," she answered, withdrawing her hands from his grasp, "but I do generally possess good sense, my lord; if I owned gloves, certainly I would have made use of—why are you making that face? You look as if you just swallowed some unidentifiable morsel of meat."

"Ye say guid sense, lass," he challenged lightly, "and I have to wonder where that was the other day when ye provoked de Montfort as ye did."

"I did no such thing!" She boldly lied.

"I'm nae saying that I was nae entertained, but de Montfort was much less so, I promise ye," Augustus said, ignoring her misplaced indignation. "He seems the type who dinna forget an affront. Ye dinna want to tickle that wolf's tail, lass."

Adopting a portion of that noble mien she'd deftly employed the other day—and which he was since certain she had in fact been born to—Sorcha dismissed his concern. "Fine, it may have been a bit of tickling the wolf's tail, as you say, but it's the least he deserves. A nastier, more vile, sorrier human being I'm sure I've never met." She lurched a bit and lifted her startling blue eyes to him, and quickly refined, "Unless you are well-disposed to him, and I shouldn't give vent to my frustration in front of you—in that case," she said, smiling benignly, "Lord Aldric is quite lovely."

Augustus chuckled at this, wonderfully amused by her at this point, and put her mind at ease.

"Nae, ye had the right of it—nasty, vile, and many other ignoble things, I agree."

Sorcha smiled at him. "I knew it."

His eyes devoured her rawly, feasting upon every gorgeous line and angle of her face, her high color, her pale countenance, eyes she swept downward at his lengthy scrutiny.

As if the shuttered gaze had boarded up her responsive personality as well, she withdrew—from him and from what ease and casualness they'd achieved today.

"I-I should get back," she said nervously.

She licked her lips and a coil of heat thrummed in his groin.

"Aye, unless ye prefer to ride," he said, a bit thickly, mayhap tellingly so, "I'll walk ye back."

Sorcha had turned in the direction in which they would go and now glanced over her shoulder. "I shall walk, thank you, but you needn't—"

"But I will."

He was annoyingly aware that he'd missed his chance—was well aware and sorry for it—that he'd missed an opportunity to kiss her.

***

An hour later, Sorcha stood beside Grimm as they stared up at the roof. Grimm had, sadly but necessarily, made the holes bigger in an attempt to remove all the damaged parts of the thatch.

"It wears the look of calamity, does it not?" she asked. And because he'd been grim-faced since he'd discovered her with Augustus MacKenzie—again, as the Rebel had returned her to her front door—Sorcha tried to bring out a grin. "Pray never say that it wears calamity better than I do."

He was displeased about something more than only the damage from the onslaught of the storm or having found her with the Rebel, but she didn't pursue his anger issues. If he wouldn't speak, there was little she could learn.

As twilight fell, they made their way into the village.

"I'm just sick about the damage to the forest apiary, Grimm. All that work destroyed, and most the bees gone," Sorcha said as they walked. She sighed. "For the present, I'll need to sing almost every night simply to collect enough coin to make up for what will be lost with all those hives destroyed." She put into words an idea she'd been toying with all throughout the day. "Maybe, Grimm, it's time to move on from Caol."

She met his gaze when he jerked his face toward her and studied him for a moment, attempting to gauge his reaction by his expression, judging him more surprised than alarmed. She did not read in his dark eyes any great reluctance or disagreement.

Grimm lifted both hands, asking a question with some annoyance.

"Where would we go?" She imagined he might be wondering. "I have no idea. And of course, you are not beholden or expected to simply follow blindly—or at all if you…if you would rather part company."

He rolled his eyes at this, to which Sorcha knew some relief. She hadn't known true fear in some time, hadn't felt alone—an awful feeling—and would rather not return to that status.

"I've thought a bit lately about returning to my family and Ballechen. It would be a trial, I'm sure. As I've mentioned previously, I wasn't always happy there, didn't so much enjoy being treated as an object, whose sole purpose was as an ardent disciple and fanatical believer—I wasn't very good at it, you might imagine. That's very selfish, I know. I am selfish and self-serving. And yet...while I truly enjoy my autonomy, I am weary of wondering when I'll eat next or if I'll survive the harsh winter or...ah, this is just me whining, feeling sorry for myself now in the wake of the ruin of the apiary." She paused and thought for a moment about going home and then wondered, "What does it say about me, Grimm, that I give hardly any thought to my father or mother, and even less to my sister and brother, than I do to Finn? I should miss them, shouldn't I? Long for their company and the sweet embrace of home?"

Grimm harrumphed quietly.

"Aye, maybe it says more about them and home, neither of whose embrace was actually sweet." She sighed as another thought struck her. "But then, please don't ever believe that I *only* left with Finn simply to escape. That was not the case. Finn was...Finn gave me life. He let me breathe when I only ever felt stifled by convention and expectations. He wasn't perfect, by no means, Grimm, but I knew love and felt love and it was...it was lovely."

The Bonnie Barrel Inn came into view as they rounded a copse of downy birch at a bend in the lane.

"We don't need to make any decisions straight away," Sorcha said, flipping up her hood over her loose blonde hair. "But you understand, do you not, that my *trilling*—as the earl calls it—will grow old here in Caol? I mean, how long can I really expect the fill the tavern ere they grow tired of the same doleful songs, night after night, week after week?"

At the back of the inn, Grimm opened the door, bringing to them the scent of garlic and onions and wood smoke.

As she followed Grimm inside, Sorcha said quietly at his back, for his ears alone, "I wish you would talk to me. It would be so much easier to debate ideas with another's input."

What seemed a rowdier than usual din took a moment longer to quiet. The sensation of this was always unnerving, knowing she now became the focus. Her heart thudded inside her chest and ears.

She lowered her head as she followed behind Grimm's broad figure. He ducked to enter while Sorcha walked straight forward, the door frame a full foot or more above her. Keeping her gaze on the timber floor of the inn, she counted seven steps inside, as she always did, and then stopped. Slowly, she lifted her face, her eyes closed briefly while she removed her hood. She did not open her eyes again until she'd lifted her face to the low ceiling.

Staunchly, she pushed away thoughts of the MacKenzie man, and that he might be watching her at this very moment. She tried to, anyway, but then wondered if she would feel his presence, his persona and aura being so large and bright and intimidating. A heated frisson coursed through her. Immediately, she dubbed the sensation displeasure and not delighted expectation. Named it such, even as she knew she lied.

Because her emotions had been high and low in the last few days, which had brought with it more tumult than she'd known recently, she'd not given thought to a new song but employed one she'd used before, since it required little awareness or preparedness and was most appropriate after the recent inclement weather.

"*In the quiet of the morning, when the storm clouds clear,*" she began to sing, "*a weight still sits upon my shoulders, hope consumed by fear.*"

She continued to sing, knowing it wasn't either her best song or her best effort. Though she failed to hit one note as well as she'd have liked, she was rather pleased with the performance overall. She'd always thought the final words—"*Let the rain fall down upon me, let the thunder roll; Come the sun and your birdsong, there is peace within my soul*"—was a fair representation of her truth.

When she was done, she closed her eyes again and lowered her face, no longer startled by the raucous applause as she had been when she'd first started singing here. After a moment, she opened her eyes, expecting that Grimm would be near, ready to escort her out through the same back door. Instead, she blinked, her gaze meeting with Augustus MacKenzie, who sat stoically—he was not cheering as was almost everyone else, including his man, Geddy, at his side—his gaze shuttered and unfathomable, so very different from what he'd shown her in the glade.

Grimm was engaged in a silent contest, chest to chest with one of the MacKenzie men, a rare person who could stand eye to eye with him, not half a dozen feet away from where Sorcha stood.

Sorcha bristled at the earl's presence even as she half expected it this evening. Still, she didn't appreciate the way he stared at her with such familiarity, as if he knew her, as if her curves were familiar, as if the texture of her skin and hair were already known to him. While she did not welcome the intimate stare, she recognized her own response to it, which was akin to how she'd felt this morning in his presence, not unmoved by it despite all hope and conscious effort. She wondered if her pulse didn't race so, if she might internally label his staring as leering.

It was then she noticed the heavy presence of so many men clad in the de Montfort colors and she realized the inn was crowded more with soldiers than village folk. And that's when she also realized that sitting at the same table with Augustus MacKenzie was Lord de Montfort himself.

A wretched feeling engulfed her, knowing she could not ignore the lord's presence. He had, unfortunately, the power to make her life miserable, as he liked to remind her. Likewise, she could not pretend that she wasn't aware of Lord Aldric curling his fingers toward himself, beckoning her to their table in a regal manner.

Pasting a slim smile on her face, Sorcha stepped off the dais and approached the table, where sat a total of four men, the two earls and two MacKenzie officers, including the one named Geddy.

Possibly more than one person might have noticed how she dragged her feet as she stepped off the small dais and made her way to the table where sat the two earls.

Certainly, the Lochaber Rebel observed her unwillingness. He stood and smirked knowingly at her as she neared, possibly recalling the opinion she'd shared with him, what she thought of Lord Aldric.

This smirk, unlike others she'd seen, was actually painted with a bit of humor. It gave gorgeous life to his stunning blue eyes, and Sorcha couldn't take her gaze from him. A dangerous man, indeed, for owning so brilliant a pair of laughing eyes.

"My lords, good evening," she said, standing before the round table where unfortunately one more chair sat empty.

The MacKenize earl indicated the free chair and did not sit again until Sorcha had reluctantly taken a seat. Lord Aldric did not stand. Out of the corner of her eye, she saw that Grimm was close again, alert and watchful.

"Ah, but it's been too long since I've heard your song," snapped Lord Aldric as if the fault were hers. Aye, the bark of his speech was normal, but it disagreed presently with the alleged praise of his words. "My own fault, of course, for how long gone I was, but here, now that's corrected." He turned a shrewd eye to Augustus and to Sorcha's shock, made bold statements that were clearly false. "It fairly distresses me," he said, the clip of his tone suggesting *infuriates* should have replaced *distresses*, "when I think of her condition, her present circumstance being so far removed from her past."

Sorcha scowled at him. He had no right to use her as the subject of any conversation—certainly not in her presence while acting as if he were not. Yet, short of leaving his company, Sorcha didn't know a way to stop it.

"But ye saw her yesterday at Ironwood," Lord Aldric continued. "Sharp of tongue and filled with ideas, things beyond her comprehension."

As if ignorant to the slight, or even as ignorant as he suggested, Sorcha focused her gaze on the shoulder of the MacKenzie captain directly across from her, who sometimes glanced at her though he did not let his gaze linger long.

Ye dinna want to tickle that wolf's tail, lass, Augustus had cautioned her.

Oh, but a large part of her really did.

But she did not, only sat stoically, barely attentive, wondering what the odds were that another raging storm might pass through Caol, twice in two days. Storms of that strength had the power to clear the taproom, she was sure.

Naught but wishful thinking.

She scarcely paid attention to the conversation, her mind drifting back to her first few months in Caol with Finn. Those rare occasions in the earl's company had taught her that little was expected of her, and she reflected on the earl's narrow-minded perspective, which deemed women as having only one purpose in life.

Instead, she eavesdropped on a mundane conversation taking place at a table nearby. Much more pleasant, much less provoking, those three men and their discussion about the local agriculture. Caol, she'd heard many times, was considered a region of poor soil. The wheat crop was specifically discussed, and apparently needed only two bushels per acre of seed, but would yield from the same space almost three hundred liters of grain.

Sorcha considered this, trying to recall if the same numbers would have or still did apply to Ballechen.

Lord Aldric's voice cut into her purposeful reverie.

"That wretched fool Harrington," he growled, his tone dripping with contempt. "Caught with his hands in the wrong bluidy pocket again, the spineless cur."

"And lost his head because of it," Augustus replied. "As it should be."

Though she did not show it, Sorcha was taken aback by the Rebel's nonchalant attitude toward an apparent execution, finding his indifference disturbing.

Maybe she should not have been surprised, but should have been guided by the rumors that preceded the advent of the Rebel into her life.

As difficult as it was to prevent any thoughts of Augustus MacKenzie from creeping into her consciousness, so too she found it nearly impossible not to compare the two earls.

Both men were gruff in their own way, and she supposed the MacKenzie might be more primitive than refined—courtly manners he did not possess—but clearly then Lord Aldric should be deemed a heathen by comparison, as coarse as he was. Though she wasn't quite sure who would rise to the top in her estimation, to her surprise, she discovered that she definitely preferred the MacKenzie's piercing and unsettling regard over de Montfort's lewd ogling.

She did not respect Lord Aldric, no more than she liked the man, but she feigned—mostly—the appropriate submissiveness, knowing she would suffer otherwise. She had some suspicion that Augustus MacKenzie would not only *not* find such submissiveness an attractive quality, but that it would possibly negate a person's worth if he was subjected to it.

If, under duress, she was forced to say one good thing about Lord Aldric, Sorcha might have guessed that she appreciated that he didn't conceal his evil nature or intentions. What you saw was exactly what he was.

She could not say, not with even the smallest degree of certainty that the same could be said of the MacKenzie earl. She simply did not know and absolutely did not trust that her intuition about him wasn't governed by his effect on her.

***

It was a struggle, to be sure, to endure the company of the earl so calmly, certainly while his disdain and mistrust festered like a wound that refused to heal. Every moment spent in de Montfort's presence was an eternity, each word exchanged a test of patience and endurance. Truly, his capability in subterfuge and reconnaissance were being tested. Despite the loathing crawling up his skin, Augustus knew he had little choice but to maintain civility. His mission demanded it.

He offered no defense for Sorcha, nor would he. De Montfort was not one to tolerate criticism, let alone alter his behavior to avoid it and thus any words spoken by Augustus in this regard would fall on deaf ears. Moreover, Augustus harbored a deep conviction that defending Sorcha would only put her at risk. If De Montfort proved to be a traitor, any hint of any possible affection for Sorcha on Augustus's part could make her a target or a pawn in de Montfort's machinations of war.

Occasionally as he sipped from his tankard of warm ale, he stole glances at Sorcha. When first she'd come to join them at the table, she'd glanced up through her lashes at him several times but had since become nearly immobile, almost trancelike as she stared at Geddy.

He thought it laughable how often he'd brought to mind the wee smile she'd shown him yesterday and the casualness she'd exhibited in his company today. *He* was laughable, he supposed, for being smitten with only a smile. Ah, but the brightness in her eyes at that moment, surely enough to turn the devil himself toward goodness.

Bluidy hell, and now I wax poetic.

Still, he allowed his gaze to seek her out often. Presently, while de Montfort yapped out some horseshite about his role and that of his army in a pitched battle against the MacFie of Colonsay, in which Augustus knew with certainty the earl had not been a factor, Augustus traced with his gaze the length of one long blonde tress as it hung aside her cheek and tumbled over her shoulder. Its texture was unknown, but surely it would feel as velvet when finally he caressed it between his fingers, would it not? His thoughts were captured by this idea, though to be fair, the thought was neither unbidden nor unexpected. He'd wanted just that, had he not? The chance to touch her, to run his hands over every inch of her flesh, to stroke her silky hair and take her sweet lips in a scorching kiss?

He did not let his gaze ever sit too long on her, unwilling to draw de Montfort's attention. He was not in the dark about de Montfort's desire for Sorcha—it was palpable, the sidelong sinister intention. Lord Aldric's first bit of conversation, after Sorcha had joined them, all about Sorcha—as if he knew her well and for years—bore the suggestion of an intimacy that Sorcha's stark, disgruntled gaze clearly said was false, as if her words to Augustus this afternoon had not already advised him of her feelings for the earl. However, Augustus saw de Montfort's behavior for what it was, staking a claim on Sorcha, not so subtly letting Augustus know Sorcha was not available to him, as if Lord Aldric had such power.

Considering her precarious circumstance and in light of de Montfort's intent to display his dominance tonight, Augustus spared a glance at Grimm, her protector, gratified to find de Montfort the subject of that silent man's intense regard. Even as he wondered if his own intentions regarding Sorcha might sooner or later be thwarted by Grimm, Augustus was at the same time grateful for the man's diligent protection of Sorcha.

Chapter Eight

Two mornings later Sorcha woke, not entirely well-rested, with the sun and got about her day in the usual manner, stoking the fire beneath the kettle and completing her toilette before throwing open the door to admit Grimm so that they might break their fast. It had been days since she'd added anything new to the kettle so that the pottage, though steeped well in flavor, was mostly broth. It had been weeks since they'd had barley to make porridge, and sadly, years since she'd enjoyed a fine oat porridge as she grown up with. She might have liked to forage for berries today but knew instead she would need to continue to work on gathering and binding straw for thatch, which she'd begun yesterday. 'Twas a task at which she did not excel, having only learned the basics of it in the last year. While she'd labored painstakingly over such yesterday, Grimm had begun replacing some of the exposed and worn hazel rods to the roof, the wooden stays, so that the new thatch might be attached to them.

And just as she opened the door and told herself the sooner she completed the necessary but unpleasant task of making the thatch sections, the sooner she could get to work on replacing the ruined skeps and hackles, she nearly tripped over several full yokes of long straw, a veritable gift of ready thatch there at her door.

Sorcha stared, stunned, and then lifted her gaze to find Grimm walking toward her. His face and much of his hair was wet, as it normally was each morning. She imagined he began his day at the small brook closest to her plot, performing his own morning ablutions there.

When Grimm realized her presence in the doorway, Sorcha pointed to the bundles, her brow knit with confusion.

"Did you make these?" She asked, even as she didn't suspect he could have. Grimm was a man of many talents, but these yoked bundles, at a quick glance, seemed to have been made by a craftsman.

Grimm's response, immediate and animated, suggested the idea was absurd. He reached her stoop and touched the bundles before Sorcha might have, investigating the foremost one, inspecting the fine quality.

"I don't know who might have...." Sorcha began only to trail off. She glanced down at her hands, at her palms which Augustus had looked upon, seemingly with genuine concern. For being separated from the task of working with the straw over the last two days, since it needed to dry first, her hands had improved quite a bit. The redness was reduced and most of the slivered cuts were closed over.

Bent at the waist while inspecting the boon, Grimm lifted only his eyes to her, this new expression informing her that she'd have to be daft to not be able to guess who might have given her this gift.

He then swung his arm up at her, shoving something light and floppy into her hands.

Sorcha recoiled slightly and just for a moment until she realized that though it was animal skin, it was not alive as she'd fleetingly feared.

"What...?" She collected the soft leather, startled to discover a pair of women's gloves, crafted of fine deerskin, which might serve her well in summer for unpleasant chores or during the winter to keep her hands warm.

Her gaze filled with wonder, she asked of Grimm, "Were these in there? They came with the thatch?"

Grimm nodded and planted his hands on his hips as he stood, marking her with a level stare. His brows were lifted, conveying a sense of anticipation and expectation. The corners of his lips were turned down in displeasure and his eyes, always so demonstrative, silently urged Sorcha to connect the dots to imagine the source of the unexpected favor. He lifted his brows further, the motion rife with impatience.

But Sorcha only pretended ignorance, knowing exactly who was behind the generosity.

"Don't look at me like that," she said pertly to Grimm, befuddled by what the Rebel—supposedly—had done for her. "I didn't ask—I hadn't anything to do with this. You know that." At his prolonged look, she thinned her lips and considered the high-quality of the thatch compared to the lone bundle she'd managed to make a day ago, which was messy and made with straw that wasn't as dry as it should have been. She lifted her chin, squeezing the precious gloves in her fist. "As it is, and no matter the source, it would be criminal not to put it to good use, either the gloves or the yokes." At Grimm's next look, Sorcha declared, "Just because I accept the gift—charity, really—doesn't make me beholden. I didn't ask for it." She shrugged. "I'm simply not an idiot, to refuse what is necessary. Certainly, my pride is not greater than my annoyance with that stupid opossum and her clicking and hissing right above that largest hole in the roof, and certainly pride would be further diminished when the nights turn cold, or rain comes again. And no, I won't feel indebted to him and there will be no payment, mark my words."

Though Grimm's countenance remained severe, he gave her no more silent grief but walked into the cottage.

Sending one last glance at the beautiful sheaves of straw and now clutching the gloves to her chest, Sorcha followed Grimm inside, briefly wearing a secretive smile. Until she *realized* that she was smiling and smoothed her expression into implacability. She had no interest in the Rebel's not-so-subtle attempt to force an appreciation of him, she reminded herself. Everything, each small act of supposed kindness, had a price, one that she wasn't willing to pay, as she'd just vowed to her friend.

And yet she could not escape the truth, that the MacKenzie earl had managed, as no other had been able to do, to infiltrate her thoughts, encroaching upon the cherished moments she had reserved solely for Finn. Unlike the gentle and comforting memories of her late husband, the earl's presence was invasive, disrupting her tranquility of mind.

Betray the memory of Finn for the MacKenzie? For the Rebel? Absolutely not.

Several hours later, Sorcha worked beside an old ladder nestled against the front of her cottage collecting all the debris fallen down from Grimm's work up on the roof. He'd begun at the eaves, and little did Sorcha know of the application, but had to wonder if Grimm knew any better. Rather than attach all the gifted yokes of thatch to all the open spots and then complete the repairs with the cutting and raking, Grimm worked in small sections, affixing, raking, and cutting each part.

On the ground, required only to pass on tools that he'd laid them on the roof but which had fallen, Sorcha busied herself filling a barrel with the raked and cut straw which Grimm had dusted from the roof, and which at some times, had stood in piles as high as her shins.

Sorcha waved her hand in front of her, dispersing the straw dust that glistened gold in the morning sun and floated in front of her. She was quite sure she would blow her nose at some point today and find her kerchief straw colored.

Her focus was interrupted by the distant but unmistakable sound of riders approaching. The rhythmic thud of hooves against the earth pierced the tranquil air and turned her around toward the horizon and the direction of Caol proper. Upon spying a party possibly as large as twenty men, and thereby assuming that the MacKenzie earl came, possibly to receive what he might expect was hearty thanks, Sorcha bristled, even as she couldn't deny the sudden racing of her pulse.

As she recognized that the small scraping sound of Grimm's work had ceased, she realized as the riders closed in on the cottage that these were not MacKenzie men, but rather outfitted in the de Montfort colors, green and gold, and that they came at a great speed.

Grimm climbed down the ladder, hopping off without employing the last few rungs to land at Sorcha's side, and exchanged a wary glance with her. He stepped forward, holding out one hand to indicate that Sorcha should remain under the eaves, while in his other hand he held the knife he'd been using to trim the thatch.

Though curious about the coming of the men from Ironwood, she knew no alarm until they reined in, and several soldiers dismounted straightway and drew their swords. Knowing Grimm could not or would not speak and that she must, she rushed forward as they came.

"What is the meaning of—?"

"Mind yerself, beekeeper!" Called out a still-mounted man, his tone sharp and laced with superiority. 'Twas Malcolm Blackwood, de Montfort's bailiff, known for the pleasure he derived from menacing the folks of Caol. "'Tis nae ye we're after but the Oaf."

"Grimm? For what? And why do you draw your weapons?" She reached Grimm's side and curled her fingers into the rough fabric of his sleeve while the rest of the horsemen surrounded her and Grimm in a half-circle.

"And dinna I say to ye, to keep clear?" Asked the same man, urging his steed near.

The three sword-wielding men kept coming.

Grimm flipped the long dagger until he held it by the blade, offering the handle to the first man to reach him, who flicked it out of his hand with a swipe of his sword.

While Sorcha clung to him, Grimm lifted his arms in supplication.

"What is happening?" she asked, truly puzzled, at both the arrival of de Montfort's henchmen and Grimm's easy surrender. She fought against the man closest to her, when he latched onto Grimm's huge arm and tried to pry Sorcha's finger from his person. "Stop! Why are you—?"

The backhand across her face was unexpected, taking the words and the breath from her, knocking her onto the side, where she stumbled and, unable to right herself, fell to the ground, landing hard on her hip. Stunned by the unprovoked attack, and tasting blood inside her mouth, tears pooled in her eyes.

A scrum followed, Grimm's roar of fury being the loudest element, none of which Sorcha could see, with her hair covering her face and because momentarily, bright dots of white danced in front of her eyes. When she righted herself, she saw Grimm now being attacked by more armed men. He butted his head against one, sending him staggering backwards, and struck out his fist to meet with the side of another's helmed head. It took eight men and plenty of kicks, shoves, and punches to finally wrestle him into submission, forcing him to the ground. Three men took up various positions directly over him, with knees, swords, and hands pressed into his back while his hands were bound with rope behind him.

All the while Malcolm Blackwood called out loudly the reason for the fracas.

"Effie, the weaver, says ye raped her, Oaf," claimed the bailiff. "Used and bruised her against her daft will."

Aghast, Sorcha glared at Malcolm Blackwood. "That is absurd. You lie," she spat, coming to her feet. Wobbly she was for the first half second, until she shook off the dizziness and tried to reach Grimm. "Stop this at once. De Montfort will know of this debacle!"

"Sent at the lord's behest, beekeeper," called out the nearest man, shoving her away again.

"No! It's all a mistake," Sorcha persisted. "A lie, either yours or Effie's. I won't stand for it."

A dark shadow was cast over Sorcha as Malcolm Blackwood walked his horse between her and where she wanted to be, with Grimm.

She pushed the hair out of her face and looked up at him. He was a hulking man, with a belly as wide as his shoulders, as ugly in countenance as he was in spirit. His face, weathered and scarred, and his eyes, cold and calculating, mirrored the cruelty for which he was known.

"Cease, wench," he commanded, giving a kick with his foot, stirrup and all, which connected with Sorcha's shoulder. "He'll nae be strung up swiftly. There'll be a court session for 'im."

"This is—"

"*Jesu*, will ye stop with yer bluidy havering!" Blackwood spat. "The oaf's done got 'imself caught, and innit what he gets for terrorizing the peasants hereabouts?"

Her lips curled but she ignored the menace atop the horse, attempting to go around him and his mare. Blackwood taunted her a bit, moving the horse backward and forward as needed so that Sorcha could not pass. He chuckled while he did so, the sound as ugly as all the rest of him, until finally with a heckling chuckle he allowed her to move around him.

Grimm was on his feet once more, his red face a mask of stony rage, his hands secured behind his back. A rope was placed around his neck. While his fury was directed at her, it was not for her but for the situation and likely for Sorcha's mistreatment, which was renewed when next she went to him. She thought to slap her way past two soldiers barring her progress toward Grimm but received a jab to her stomach from the butt end of a sword, dropping her again to the ground.

Once more she flipped the hair away from her eyes, just in time to see Grimm's bared teeth before he was yanked forward by the rope in Blackwood's hand.

"Off we go, rapist," chirped the bailiff, forcing Grimm to jog along so that he did not stumble and fall, and risk being dragged, possibly to his death, by the rope around his neck.

"You're a vile wretch, Blackwood!" Sorcha called after them, struggling to her feet. "You'll answer for this injustice!" She swung her fist in the air, but there were no witnesses to her wrath and promise of retribution.

Her chest heaving, she stood still for a moment, until indignation spurred her to move. She raced inside and unearthed the buried coins, what few she had, and shoved them into her pocket. Without care for her disheveled appearance, she left the cottage. She did not hesitate, did not wait until Grimm and his captors were small specks in the distance but followed immediately after the party. She didn't need to arm herself, as she had no weapons but her small dagger and a tongue she wasn't afraid to use, even if it meant begging for his release. She would first appeal to de Montfort or his lady wife and offer all the coin she had to compel Grimm's release.

While she marched after them, she was plagued with equal amounts of puzzlement and worry, wondering why Effie might have lied—or who might have induced her to. Not for a minute did Sorcha believe there was any truth to the charge.

***

Augustus watched Lord Aldric and a small company of his army ride away, parting from them about a quarter mile from the main street in Caol, where a rarely used path ended at a short stone wall, which enclosed all the meadowland belonging to Ironwood. They'd been out all morning at Lord Aldric's invitation to participate in a bit of scouting as Lord Aldric professed to have evidence that the MacNabs, loyal to the English, had been recently noted in the area. According to de Montfort, though the MacNab stronghold was only a few miles yonder, there was no reason for them to be "sniffing round these parts".

While it struck Augustus as a vague justification—the possibility of this sighting being manufactured occurred to him as well—he was tasked with discerning where lay de Montfort's true fealty and thus he wasn't about to squander any occasion to be in his company.

Little did he learn, save that de Montfort liked to talk about himself, liked to extoll his virtues, and plenty time he'd had to do so as they'd covered as much as a dozen miles in their travels by Augustus's estimation. Curiously, not only did they fail to discover any MacNab in the area, but they found no evidence of any riders being someplace they should not. With the most recent savage storm, which likely would have eliminated any trace of a person or group loitering inside the de Montfort demesne—the supposed sighting came *after* the storm—it should have been easy to find evidence of this.

Turning his horse around, he led his small unit of twenty men in the opposite direction, along the stone wall in grass as tall as his destrier's hocks.

"Sore's on his arse and mark my words," suggested Geddy a moment later, from Augustus's right. "Man's nae more used to the saddle than me auld mum, may the guid Lord keep her...there instead of here."

"Posing is what it is," suggested Angus, on Augustus's left, after a brief chuckle at the captain's quip. "I wonder if he ken what we're about, spying on him, and only putting on a guid show."

"A farce, ye mean to say," was Augustus's opinion, still half believing they'd been chasing invented ghosts today. "Aye, and mayhap he does suspect what we're about, and that was his attempt to keep us occupied and oblivious to other goings-on."

Their debate about the unfathomable earl was disturbed by Augustus's sudden stop, drawing his horse to a halt while he squinted out across the sea of grass on the north side of the low wall, given pause by the sight of a woman traipsing across the grass, headed toward the wall.

With so much distance between them, only a small figure was revealed and yet the unfiltered sunshine assisted in identification, reflecting brightly off a head of pale gold hair.

"Other goings-on, ye say," Geddy remarked. "There's a strange one, the lass oot and aboot and nae oaf at her side."

"On a mission, is she nae?" supposed Angus, referring to her determined gait.

Behind them Gryffin snorted something mysterious.

More than a hundred yards away, possibly oblivious to their presence, Sorcha scrambled over the low wall with a clumsiness not previously noticed and continued on. Frowning a bit at her purposeful stride and as Geddy mentioned, without her man in sight—though he himself had encountered her twice with Grimm nowhere around—Augustus clucked his tongue, urging his destrier forward. He made an arc in his pursuit to be able to come straight at the wall, his large horse easily able to vault over it.

Sorcha's steps faltered as she climbed the hill of green pasture inside the enclosure, as if a sense of unease settled over her when she realized she was being followed. She turned sharply, her brows furrowing in annoyance as she caught sight of Augustus and his men trailing behind her. Their unexpected presence seemed to irk her, evident in the slight downturn of her lips and the tensing of her shoulders. With a frustrated huff, she pivoted back around and resumed her ascent, trudging up the hill with steps more determined than just a moment ago.

"I have no time for this today," she called out loudly, well before they'd come upon her.

Augustus did not respond until he came abreast of her. "Nae time for what?" He asked, scowling over her unkempt appearance, in that her hair was as disheveled as he'd ever seen it, mussed all around her face. Her left shoulder was caked with a bit of dried dirt and several sections of her skirt were dusted with dirt and debris as well, as if she'd rolled on the ground.

She didn't look at him. A hand sneaked out from within the folds of her cloak and spun around several times with impatience. "This, whatever you are about. And neither do I have a wish of company."

"Getting somewhere in a hurry," Geddy commented.

Having recognized an unusual wobble to her voice, Augustus moved several paces in front of her, angling his face downward to have a look at her. "Sorcha," he said sternly when she did not lift her face to him.

"Please just leave me be," she begged, tucking her chin nearly to her chest, lifting her hood to cover her head.

He didn't yet know her well enough to distinguish emotions in her voice but was perfectly able to identify the sound of fear. When he moved his steed closer to her, she overreacted, cowering and jerking a full foot away from him.

Nonplussed, Augustus hopped off his destrier and grabbed her by the arm to make her stop.

Shrinking away, as far as his hold would allow, she turned a startled expression upon him.

He'd opened his mouth to question her unaccountable rudeness, but no words came. Instead a surge of rage swept over him at the sight of the bruise marring the perfect porcelain of her face.

The injury was fresh, the skin around her mouth softly red and slightly swollen. Her lip was cracked in the corner and stained with a wee bit of blood.

Unconsciously, his fingers tightened on her arm.

"Who did this?" He ground out. "The oaf?"

Sorcha's frown came as quickly as had his fury. "What? Grimm? No—he would never. He was...it doesn't matter. Please leave me be. I must get to Lord Aldric."

Augustus refused to release her, even as she tugged forcibly at her arm. "Who did this?" He persisted.

Her eyes closed briefly, and mayhap she decided it would benefit her to simply spill her truth so that he might leave her to her task. "Blackwood did this—Ironwood's bailiff," she said curtly. "He and his goons did when I opposed his arrest of Grimm on a grotesque charge. Grimm wouldn't hurt a soul—I know it's all a lie."

"For what crime was he apprehended?" Augustus asked, his brain jolted in another direction with this startling news.

Again, she closed her eyes and lifted her chin, shaking her head. "He didn't do anything! It's all a lie—"

"What *dinna* he do, but which they claim he did?"

"Assault Effie, the weaver," she snapped.

"Assault?"

"Rape," she cried, opening her eyes, staring at him as if her were a simpleton, as if he couldn't imagine what kind of assault a man might perpetrate against a woman. "But it's all a lie," she maintained tersely before her shoulders shrunk, fear briefly overpowering her resolve. She asked plaintively, "How could he have done something like that when he's always with me? When he saved me from the very same thing?"

Augustus ground his jaw tightly, staring at her, trying to make sense of what had transpired and why.

"They attacked him," she cried, possibly further distressed by the ferocity of his dark gaze, "as if he'd already been found guilty, and then struck me when I tried to stop them. Please release me," she begged anew. "I must speak to the earl."

Finally, he lightened his hold on her arm, though he did not let go completely.

"Aye," he said, turning to collect the reins of his destrier. "The MacKenzies will escort ye."

Sorcha's brown knitted anew. "What? No. I don't need an escort."

"Aye, ye do," proclaimed Augustus, closing the distance between them, horse in hand.

"If they're nae true, lass, the charges," Geddy said, "ye should nae be alone. If false, it begs the question: why would someone want him arrested and out of the way? What's he ever done but provide protection to you?"

Possibly sensing they meant neither to harm her nor detain her, Sorcha lost a bit of her rigidity as she directed her responding query to Geddy. "But why would someone—I don't understand. What do people care about either Grimm or me?"

Another of Gryffin's incomprehensible snorts earned a glare from Geddy.

Why did the townsfolk care about her? Like as not, they did not. But Augustus would wage his last coin that any man, given the opportunity, would happily spend any amount of time in her company, minutes or hours, engaged in either their carnal dreams or simply attempting to draw a smile. Regarding the same matter, the exquisite beekeeper, Augustus would also wager a guess that there were few women who didn't envy her beauty, perpetrate broad and false rumors about her character to denigrate her and thus elevate their own comprehension of themselves, or outright loath her for how their men desired her. Possibly if the oaf was capable of speech, he'd have enlightened her in this regard.

"Aye, and let's go and discover what lies beneath these claims," Augustus suggested. "C'mon up."

In all likelihood, the utter trauma of her assault and Grimm's arrest had befuddled her so that without a quarrel she allowed Augustus to lift her into the saddle. She did not groan aloud but with his gaze trained with such steadfastness upon her, he did not miss the wince she gave when he did so, his hands large and strong at her waist.

"Did I harm ye?" He asked as she grimaced once more, situating herself more comfortably while Augustus stood at her side, one hand on the pommel and the other on the cantle, about to hoist himself upward.

Sorcha shook her head. "'Tis nothing."

It was *not* nothing, Augustus knew. He shoved aside her skirt to step into the stirrup and mounted directly behind her, exchanging a look with Angus, who was closest to the pair. Angus's darkly quizzical look suggested that he might be imagining what Augustus was, that she'd been struck more than once.

His nostrils flared with renewed rage, and he ground his teeth tightly, but he was gentle as he wrapped a hand around her middle, advising, "Hold on to my arm," so that he wasn't compelled to embrace her too tightly as they rode.

And while he might have preferred to catch Lord Aldric unawares and still upon his horse, having not yet reached Ironwood, he was not of a mind to exacerbate whatever other injuries Sorcha might have and thus set the pace at a slow canter, upward, over the hill.

Geddy rode beside Augustus and Sorcha.

"Ye sure ye ken the oaf well, lass?" He wondered. "Nae much to tell of his nature, as he dinna say anything by which to judge."

"Enough should be gleaned," Sorcha retorted pointedly, "simply from his protective nature toward me. Do you suppose he safeguards one person so diligently and then abuses another?"

"De Montfort up to something?" Geddy surmised next.

"That'd be my guess," chimed in Angus. "He's unlikely to get at the lass while the big man stands in his way."

Sorcha swung her face quickly in Angus's direction, her profile showing a heavy scowl and lips parted in furious wonder. While Augustus subscribed to Angus's theory, he'd rather that it hadn't been mentioned to Sorcha so frankly—or at all for that matter.

Her fingers curled into his forearm, bringing a different awareness to him, of their proximity, of her soft bottom nestled into his groin, the feel of her long hair brushing against his cheek as the wind moved it, the scent of her—did he imagine it, or was she enveloped in the sweet musk of honey and heather?—the curve of her lip, even tilted downward disagreeably, her lips were delectable, a temptation almost beyond reason or, apparently, fair timing.

"I don't care very much for that inference, sir," she stated pertly. "I am not something to be *gotten*."

"Yes, ma'am," Angus replied mechanically, catching his beard point with his broad fingers. "But Lord Aldric might see it differently."

Sorcha made no response but drew in her bottom lip with some conjecture so that Augustus supposed she'd not been completely oblivious to de Montfort's yearning for her.

The remainder of the journey, naught but another quarter mile, was made in silence. Along the arm wrapped around her, Augustus felt Sorcha's large inhale when they crested the last knoll and Ironwood loomed before them.

They rode through the gates shortly after the de Montfort had, this timing discerned by the stable lad just now walking his lord's horse into the stables. Other men of de Montfort's cavalry milled around inside the bailey, some still mounted.

Augustus wondered if some of these soldiers might have been assigned to Blackwood this morning.

He ducked his head a bit, putting his cheek against Sorcha's silky hair. "Do you see any of the ones who struck ye?" Blackwood himself was nowhere in sight.

Shaking her head softly against his cheek, she answered quietly, "No."

Their entrance through the gates was neither questioned nor challenged, an oddity over which Augustus mulled, considering that de Montfort had expressed that concern about MacNabs in the area.

He dismounted in the middle of the yard and reached for Sorcha, being careful with her person. He thought she might have schooled her expression to show no pain now. Seeing again the thick and reddening bruise at the side of her mouth reinvigorated his wrath.

When her feet touched the ground, she gripped his shirtsleeves and lifted plaintive eyes to him.

"Grimm is innocent, I swear to you," she said.

Though he leaned toward that belief, Augustus nodded but said nothing.

As he led her toward the arched doorway of the hall, he heard Angus say in a low voice, "Kael and I will hang about here, see if we canna discover who it was raised a hand to the lass."

"Aye, ye do that," Geddy said as he and others followed Augustus and Sorcha. "And quietly see that they are unable to do so again."

Chapter Nine

De Montfort was found in much the same circumstance as when last Augustus visited Ironwood, sitting at the boards at one end of the hall, a feast laid before him, including a bright silver carafe of wine near his silver goblet. A dozen soldiers idled about the hall but snapped to attention when Augustus and his party entered. Likely it was one of the few times Sorcha's presence, her very appearance, did not command all attention.

The lord's wife, Lady de Montfort, stood as she had previously beside her husband, hovering at his elbow as if she only awaited commands to see to his every need. Her pinched face showed a great dismay at the sight of the intruders, her eyes wide with a silent alarm. 'Twas the first time that Augustus noticed her gaze removed from the back of her husband's head.

To Augustus's chagrin, Sorcha rushed forward with great urgency before he could stop her, pleading for the Oaf's release before she'd reached the dais.

"My lord," she began, her voice quivering, dropping to her knees a few yards before the table, "I beg of you to have mercy on Grimm. He is innocent of the charges brought against him. I swear it," she vowed, clasping her hands together. "Please, release him from your possession and allow him to defend himself against these false accusations."

To one not acquainted with the beekeeper, and possibly to some who were, Sorcha appeared a beggar, a pleading supplicant at the feet of the lord. Her cloak, once elegant, now bore stains, her skirts were soiled, and her hair fell untamed around her face. One side of her mouth was swollen, a sight not uncommon among peasant women. Yet, despite her battered appearance, she spoke with unwavering strength, in an authoritative tone honed over many years rather than conjured for this occasion alone.

Lord Aldric's reply came with a veneer of politeness, his eyes betraying a bit of amusement to have Sorcha begging before him. "My dear lady," he began, his tone smooth and measured, almost unrecognizable, "I appreciate your concern for your...companion, but the matter at hand is not easily dismissed. Grievous harm was caused—these are serious accusations—"

"They are lies!" Sorcha interjected fiercely, sitting back on her heels. "Where is Effie? I want to speak to her, to hear from her own lips what—"

"Rest assured," Lord Aldric continued, raising his voice though he did not increase the tempo to out pace Sorcha's urgently given demands, "the Oaf will be given a fair trial, and all will come out. If indeed he is innocent, he shall be released unscathed." His thin lips curved into a faint smile.

Unmoved by this promise, Sorcha rose to her feet and pointed a slim arm and trembling finger at de Montfort's bailiff, Blackwood. "And what right has he to cause injury to my person? Is it your practice, my lord, to keep in your company men who abuse women? Will you arrest this man for his assault on me same as you have Grimm for his supposed attack of Effie?"

With a gaze as sharp as honed steel, Augustus fixed his eyes upon Blackwood, who seemed oblivious to Augustus's rage, mayhap unaware that Augustus would have cause to seek retribution for raising a hand to Sorcha. Silently, he vowed to seek vengeance against him.

After an intemperate look at the smirking Blackwood, Lord Aldric snapped his ire at Sorcha, "Interfering with the lord's business is a crime as well, lass. But I shall overlook it in this instance as you—"

"Interfering with the *king's* business is a crime," Sorcha corrected smartly. "There is no law against questioning the actions of those in power or against outrageous, patently false accusations, especially when those actions result in harm to innocent people. If you wish to be seen as a just lord," Sorcha ranted, "you would do well to hold all your men accountable for their deeds, regardless of their station. Or does justice only apply to those who serve your interests?"

Lord Aldric's facade slowly changed, his previously glib chuckle fading into a menacing silence. His expression, once filled with casual disdain, burned with a newfound fury. The air in the hall thickened, heavy with the weight of his growing rage. Surrounded by an armed retinue, every movement he made, from the curl of his pasty lip to the clenching of his pale fists, exuded a palpable threat.

"In these parts, lass, I *am* king." He said these words in a hard voice and then looked pointedly at Augustus, as if to remind him of this as well.

"My lady," Sorcha implored, "have pity. Please."

Lady Alice's eyes narrowed as she lifted her chin piously, but she made no response.

Having followed Sorcha forward, Augustus now set a calming hand on the small of her back, the action containing a bit of a warning to her as well. She turned to him at his touch but before she might have voiced an objection or questioned his familiarity, Augustus addressed de Montfort.

"If I might intercede on behalf of the beekeeper and her man," Augustus began, only to be cut off by lord Aldric.

"Bah," he scoffed, waving his eating knife as he spoke while a tender morsel of meat flopped back and forth with is action. "What is it to you, MacKenzie? Leave the law-keeping in these parts to those who dwell in these parts."

Maintaining the tenuous hold upon his own temper, Augustus replied, "We have become friendly over the last few weeks, the Oaf and I," Augustus lied evenly. "I suppose it might be possible that I—"

De Montfort snickered crudely at this. "Friendly? With a man who does not speak? I can hardly fathom it, MacKenzie."

Augustus stared him down for an extended moment. In the same manner as he would establish dominance over a horse or hound, Augustus stared unblinking and let de Montfort be the first to break eye contact.

"As an agent of the king, my lord," Augustus clipped in a sharp tone after de Montfort had looked away, "I should like to convey to him that all is governed satisfactorily *in these parts*, in a manner befitting his expectations."

True, he'd tipped his hand a bit. De Montfort might now believe he was being spied upon or, just as possible, he might simply equate Augustus's tactic with a juvenile attempt to gain the upper hand, equivalent to a bairn threatening to tell his mam what his sibling had done. Augustus did not care what the man presumed of the barely concealed threat.

"Is the prisoner to be allowed visitors?" He asked blankly. "Or will I be denied access?"

'Twas evident that de Montfort neither expected to be nor relished being challenged. His florid face showed a bit of agitation, literally spasming a wee bit, until he settled his countenance and affected a disinterested mien, as if he only wished to be done with the matter for now and move on with his day. "Go on then," he said, flapping his hand impatiently. "Take him down—the Mackenzie only," he insisted to the closest hovering de Montfort soldier. "He's nae going anywhere, the Oaf, nae until the court session at the end of the month," he reminded Augustus.

Augustus inclined his head, acknowledging this, and sent a meaningful glance at Geddy, which his captain should understand to mean keep an eye on the goings-on here in the hall and particularly, on Sorcha while he went below.

"Why do you deny me the same access you allow the MacKenzie laird?" Sorcha railed.

Twirling around, Augustus caught her arm, and was subsequently favored with a murderous glare from a pair of enraged blue eyes.

"Take yerself off, with Lady de Montfort, if ye please," called Lord Aldric indifferently.

"I do not please," Sorcha snapped, fisting her hand, making her arm rigid in Augustus's grasp. "I will not be denied. I don't want to be—"

Augustus stepped in front of her, blocking de Montfort's view of her.

"Cease," he said quietly. "Right or wrong," he continued, his voice only loud enough for Sorcha to hear, "he has the power just now. Let me confer with your man while de Montfort allows that and later—"

Tears fell, along with her shoulders. "But it's not right. He didn't do anything."

Fleetingly, his thumb stroked up and down against her trembling bicep. "One thing at a time, Sorcha. I ken ye have nae reason, but ye have nae choice but to trust me now."

"I don't *know* you. I trust Grimm and no one else and look what they've done—"

"Shh," he cautioned when her volume increased. "Let me speak to Grimm—"

Sorcha bristled impatiently, reminding him through clenched teeth, "He doesn't speak. *I* can understand him, but you cannot. How does this help?"

Geddy and Colin had come to stand near Augustus and Sorcha, so that the four of them appeared huddled in a small group.

"Lass, nae matter what I learn or dinna," Augustus advised her, "or what ye might have gleaned had ye been allowed access, Grimm is nae leaving here. Nae today and nae for a while."

"Patience, lass," Geddy advised. "The process has to play itself out."

Before Sorcha might have argued further, Augustus said to Geddy, "Send one of the lads out for the remainder of the army. Bring 'em all in. Take Sorcha back to her cottage—hush," he commanded when she opened her mouth to gainsay this directive. "I'll meet ye there when I'm done here. Leave only Angus and a handful with me."

"Aye, he dinna like the pressure here, with a full unit of ours and he nae done with his meal," Geddy concluded, his hand resting comfortably upon his sword. "Ye get on to see the oaf and aye, nae sense in being coy. We'll camp out all around that wee cottage, hem her in against de Montfort's designs."

"I am not leaving without Grimm," Sorcha persisted, ignoring Geddy's insinuation while appearing incredibly small between Augustus, Geddy, and Colin.

Geddy spoke the words Augustus would have. "Ye'll do as I say at this moment, lass. Until we ken the *who* and *why* behind this—presuming the oaf's innocence at yer say so, by the by," he said, lifting a weighted brow at her, "we'll keep everything tight."

Though her bottom lip trembled, and her neck and jaw were rigid with tension—and a want to argue further, no doubt—Sorcha nodded.

Geddy and Augustus pivoted to face the head table, where Lord Aldric sat motionless, his glare fixed upon them, clearly displeased by their whispered conversation.

Geddy chuckled, the noise loud in the quiet hall. "Aye and we've got her all squared away, my lord," he announced, seemingly in good humor. "Needs but a certain way, these lasses, to make them understand who's who and what's what."

"You are abhorrent," Sorcha ground out in a whisper.

Augustus turned a fierce stare onto her but then was stunned himself to hear Geddy's next words.

"Ah, but ye ken all about that, do ye nae, milord?" Geddy pointed to Lady Aldric. "Another spitfire there, am I right? Firm hand, ye ken all about that, I'm sure. I'll take the lass out of doors, in my firm hand, and ye'll nae be troubled nae more." With that, he bowed his head slightly and latched his thick paw onto Sorcha's arm.

'Twas a good ploy, Augustus decided, so that de Montfort didn't suppose they'd been conspiring and conniving with Sorcha, but now might believe they'd been quietly scolding her for her disrespect.

Sorcha did not see the benefit of it, but fought against Geddy's heavy hand, scratching at his flesh, crying, "Unhand me this instant! Let me go, you fiend! You're as bad as they are!"

"Come along, spitfire," Geddy said calmly over her protests, pulling her toward the door while her feet slid against the cool stone floor, her feeble strength no match to his.

When they were gone, with Colin following, leaving Augustus as the only MacKenzie inside Ironwood, two armed de Montfort lads beckoned Augustus to follow. With a bow of false courtesy at Lord Aldric, Augustus pursued one and was trailed by another through a passageway that twisted and turned, and down a musty set of stone steps that opened up into an expansive cellar. They proceeded, Augustus was sure, from one end of the keep to the other, underground, before reaching a locked portal, which the foremost soldier accessed by turning the key that had been left in the door.

The lad then collected the torch that burned in a sconce on the damp wall and handed that to Augustus, his gaze earnest upon him. "That way, milord," said the lad as he stood aside, allowing Augustus to pass.

Briefly he wondered if he were now to be locked beyond the door, along with Grimm, but dismissed any concern over this; Geddy would know where to find him. Ducking under the low doorframe, Augustus was pleased that once past the door, he was able to stand straight again. Torchlight illuminated the space inside, an open area flanked by four cells segmented by iron bars and gates. The air was heavy with the scent of damp stone and mildew, and the sound of dripping water echoed in the distance. The walls were rough-hewn and coated with moisture while the floor was uneven and littered with debris.

The lads who'd escorted him must have gone—he didn't believe they'd only politely allowed him and Grimm some privacy—as their voices were heard further away, as naught but muffled sounds. The door that separated the dungeon from the rest of the cellar remained open.

"Grimm," he called, having no need to raise his voice.

The sound of shackles being moved pulled Augustus's attention to the cage on his right. He moved closer and upon spying a hulking form beyond the bars, he set the torch into an iron holder on the wall.

Grimm stepped closer, coming as near to the bars as the shackle upon one wrist would allow. His face was illuminated by the flickering light of the torch, but immediately Augustus could not read his expression—not until Grimm smirked meanly, which Augustus read quite easily.

"Nae, I dinna have anything to do with your circumstance," he enlightened the man, whose face was battered and bloody. "I and my men ran into Sor—the beekeeper—upon returning from an outing with de Montfort. She was, ye may nae be surprised to hear, stomping across the fields, intent upon coming to your rescue." He was unperturbed by Grimm's initial judgment, which supposed Augustus had been behind his incarceration. He'd have suspected the same if he were in his shoes.

Grimm received this slowly, seeming to consider it, before he froze and grimaced mightily, and appeared to grapple with an unseen force for an excruciating ten seconds, much to Augustus's growing frustration and bewilderment.

What he wrestled with was revealed in the next moment.

"Where is Sorcha?" The once-silent oaf inquired, his words slackening Augustus's jaw with disbelief.

Augustus's mind raced, trying to process the sudden turn of events. Not only had Grimm broken his silence, but his thick and decidedly *English* accent added another layer of bafflement to the already perplexing situation. It was a confounding moment, leaving Augustus at a loss for words, as he'd not been as far back as he could recall.

"So there," Grimm said in his flawless English, though he kept his voice low, "there is the reason I do not speak."

Finally regaining his composure, Augustus stared hard at the man and said, at length, in a low rumble of residual shock, "I guess that there is reason enough." He shook his head, as if to clear cobwebs. "*Jesu*, an Englishman posing as a mute Scot. What the bluidy hell—?"

"It was necessary," Grimm said.

"Explain yourself," Augustus growled.

Grimm sighed. "I was part of a caravan heading to Stirling Castle when we were overtaken by a force under the direction of Magnus Matheson, and left for dead by my fleeing comrades," he said. His voice was gravelly, rusty with disuse, and the words came slowly, as if speaking, words rolling off his tongue, were indeed new to him. "A...a woman took me in, hid me from her neighbors, and made me well again. She was...it doesn't matter, but it became dangerous for obvious reasons for me to remain with her. Even before I was well enough, I left her but then I was behind enemy lines and not quite well enough to make a straight run for it." He paused, looking at the bars between them and not directly at Augustus. "I found myself near Caol and meant only to skirt around, out of sight, going south. But then I heard her song." He raised his gaze now, and some bit of torture was briefly glimpsed before he shuttered his expression. Another sigh preceded his next words, "It was the first bit of relief I'd known since I'd left the...the woman who healed me. All the battle noise and screams inside my head were quieted." Again he raised his dark eyes, gauging Augustus's reaction. "I remained close, initially simply to hear her song. But then, as you might guess, it became evident how vulnerable she is. I made my presence known one night when she was being accosted by one of the locals and then...how could I leave her, knowing how susceptible she was to danger?"

"And ye needed her song," Augustus reckoned.

Grimm nodded.

Augustus studied him intently. "She dinna ken, does she?"

Grimm shook his head.

"And by name in truth, you are...?"

"Wycliffe" he said begrudgingly. "Richard Wycliffe." Reluctantly, he added, "Of Winteringham."

"Bluidy hell." Some vague recollection, a mention of a Baron Wycliffe, with lands in Lincolnshire, teased at the periphery of his mind.

For a long moment, Augustus and Grimm—nae, Richard Wycliffe—stared at each other. Internally, Augustus struggled to piece everything together. At length, he said, "Let's start anew, with what we have. Did ye assault the weaver?"

The baron's response brimmed with instant indignation.

"No," he confirmed. "and how could I have? *When* could I have when I am every hour and every day in Sorcha's company?"

Augustus countered, "I met her twice in the last few days, including the morning after the storm, at the apiary in the forest. On both occasions, you were nowhere in sight."

Wycliffe growled. "I was gone but a moment from her shack and upon my return, she had left already. I met her upon her return, after she'd tangled with *you*. For all your blatant and obsessive study of her, it should come as no surprised that quite of bit of my time is spent chasing her down. She does as she pleases, with little regard to her safety, and with an inflated opinion of her own capabilities."

No, that certainly did not surprise Augustus. "But then what is at play here?"

"I have no idea, other than the obvious, but that which is *so* obvious, it's almost inconceivable that he could be so foolish as to attempt it?"

"De Montfort?"

"Yes," Richard stated hotly. "You were there. You saw how he salivates over Sorcha. She'll never willingly lay down for him, but he's a man used to taking." He shrugged. "I stand in his way."

"What about this weaver? Why would she commit to this falsehood?"

"Effie is weak, easily cowed, and has no man to stand for her. She has neither the pluck nor the resolve of Sorcha. De Montfort likely threatened her. I haven't laid eyes on her in a week perhaps, but I wager she'll be bruised and battered, to have compelled her testimony and to align with the narrative of my alleged assault."

Pushing his tongue over the front of his teeth, Augustus considered this and the man telling it. He was eager to believe him, if only for Sorcha's sake, but he simply lacked the ability to trust without tangible proof.

Needing to know more about this man, to understand him better, he said, "But ye...ye dinna hang about, silent and creeping, only to hear her song."

"I did."

"Ye are in love with her," Augustus accused.

"No," Richard insisted. "She's exasperating and too headstrong and impossibly outspoken—her voice drips with noble birth at times—but otherwise perfect. I would not stain her with my sins." He quirked a brow at Augustus. "Will you?"

Wycliffe's sins, Augustus had to imagine, were related to all those battle noises and that incessant screaming inside his head, something Augustus was not entirely unfamiliar with. "What you consider sins, I call necessity," he said, in regard to his conduct during war, how many lives he'd taken, and all the cries he'd quieted with his blade. "I sleep verra well at night."

"You are to be envied then." Grimm paused. "Or deemed a liar."

"Your opinion is negligent."

Wycliffe nodded and pursued that topic no more. "There is no truth behind the charges," he said, returning to his claim of innocence. "And now Sorcha is...she's vulnerable again. And you are absolutely the last person I would ask to safeguard her, but I sense, beneath all the rumors behind the legend, that there is some honor in you, that you wouldn't have a lass only by foul or underhanded deeds, and thus...."

"Ye have nae choice but to trust me and my character," Augustus finished.

The baron's lips curled derisively. "It does not sit well with me."

"But ye are desperate, because de Montfort is powerful."

"But *you* are the Rebel and so I put more stock in what you can accomplish, meaning if anyone can keep her out of his hands, I wager you can."

"So much gambling."

Wycliffe scoffed humorlessly. "In this position, hope is all I have."

"But dinna tell me ye aren't in love with her."

"I am not. At any rate, she knows only him, her lost lover. I wouldn't jeopardize what I have. It would ruin everything, take her song away and I...I, Lord help me, I need her song more than I need her."

"Ye are in love with the woman who healed ye then?" Augustus ventured. Sorcha's healing song notwithstanding, a man simply did not dedicate so much time and effort to protect a person who was not kin to him, who was a stranger until she needed help, without reason. Ah, but perhaps it stemmed from a place of love, a desire for another to experience safety, born from that other woman.

Wycliffe returned his steady regard but gave nothing away and offered no response.

Though few conclusions had been reached, Augustus felt he'd asked all that was pertinent and had what answers he desired. For now.

Augustus raised a brow, glancing beyond the huge man into the darkness of his dank prison.

Wycliffe shrugged. "I knew eventually I'd have to figure it out, how to silence the noise in my head. This seems a safe place to start."

Augustus considered him with a jaundiced eye. "Dinna do anything foolish."

"Neither you," Wycliffe advised. "Was that you? Laid the thatch and gloves outside her door?"

"Aye," he replied, and waited but the topic was not pursued. "Sorcha gave de Montfort plenty of grief up there," he said. "I'm guessing he was about three seconds or one more slur fired at him away from tossing her down here. So now—"

"You would not have allowed that," Wycliffe contended.

"I would nae have," Augustus acknowledged briefly, but did not elaborate. "Geddy and the lads took her back home. She's nae in any danger now."

"Not even from you? I swear if you harm one hair on her head, I will make it my life's mission to hunt you down and visit upon you the—"

"Calm yourself, English," Augustus suggested, holding up his hand. "I've nae more plans to injure Sorcha than ye do."

"She doesn't want what you're hoping to give her, or be to her," Wycliffe said.

Augustus nodded, but only in consideration of that man's claim, not because he believed it.

"I'm nae the one deceiving her," he said.

Wycliffe growled at him. "I am helping her."

A harrumph erupted from Augustus.

"She needs to help me, or to *believe* that she is," Wycliffe explained, "otherwise, she wouldn't allow herself to accept my protection."

"She is pursued, often I imagine," Augustus supposed.

Wycliffe shook his head. "No. She is an outcast. There is no polite pursuit, only the illicit variety, for which she has me to thwart. The locals have caught on; they know I wouldn't hesitate to kill any who tried."

August nodded, digesting this. He set his hand on the cross bar of iron and tapped it twice with his palm. "Be smart, English," he said as farewell.

"It was Blackwood, Ironwood's bailiff," Richard said next, "and a man called Milton that struck her. I assume you will address that." At Augustus's nod, Wycliffe reiterated firmly, "Don't let her out of your sight."

After one last nod, and after pretending to forget the torch, Augustus took his leave.

Out in the courtyard, he noticed a ruckus inside the stables, one that apparently had drawn de Montfort from his feast. Only mildly curious, Augustus hung around only long enough to discern heavy cries from what surely was an injured man, and someone hollering that "Milton's been impaled."

Smirking, imbued with greater knowledge than he should have possessed of Milton's injury—his men had apparently worked swiftly and effectively outside while Augustus had been inside the keep—Augustus collected his steed and vacated Ironwood's bailey.

Chapter Ten

"Still nae speaking to me?"

Sorcha whirled around, a bit unruffled by the presence of the man at the open door of her cottage. Actually, that was an understatement; she was, in fact, completely rattled and utterly discomposed by the totality of today's events, so much so that she'd yet to wrap her brain around all that had transpired.

But to Geddy, the MacKenzie captain who stood in her doorway now, she shook her head wearily.

"Pray pardon my rudeness, sir," she said. "I truly do understand why you behaved as you did."

She hadn't at first, had been too immersed in her rage at his manhandling of her to have reasoned it out.

"Needs must and all that," Geddy said sheepishly, "but lass, I do beg yer pardon."

She tried on a smile, and though she believed it was as drained as she was, she said, "I've greater concerns at the moment, as you mentioned. Consider yourself wholly exonerated."

They'd returned to her house only a quarter hour ago. Sorcha had gone directly inside, hoping to find some solace in the comfort of home, which sadly, she had not. Before that, while they'd ridden, Geddy had tried to explain himself upon their jaunt back to her cottage, telling her he didn't want Lord Aldric to believe they were 'in collusion' and thus had to take the upper hand as he did. It only reminded Sorcha that sometimes she really hated being female.

"How long do you think your laird will be?" She asked. "I am fretfully anxious about Grimm."

Geddy chuckled, the sound craggy and slightly charming. "Yer man dinna speak, and my laird is nae kent as being chatty, lass. I dinna ken he'll be too long gone."

"Geddy, be honest with me," she appealed. "Is there any danger that Grimm might be...executed for what they say he's done?"

The lightness of his expression evaporated. He straightened away from where he'd leaned against the doorjamb and hooked his thumbs into his belt. "Now, ye dinna need to go there, lass, wringing yer mind with worry like that. We like to take things one moment, one calamity at a time."

Possibly he saw that these words did not offer her any relief. In fact, Sorcha's eyes widened at the use of calamity.

"We willna let it come to that," he was quick to aver, tipping forward a bit with his statement. "We're nae in the habit of standing passively while justice is perverted."

Which begged the query from Sorcha, which she asked with drawn brows, "But why do you care? Any of you." She waved her hand toward the front of her cottage, looking out the lone window beside the door. "Camped round my house, dozens of MacKenzies, as if sent by king to guard his kin, while I'm naught but a stranger, and Grimm more so." Clasping her hands, worrying her fingers at her waist, she lowered her eyes to the ground beneath her feet. "And when I've been...so horrid to all of you."

The MacKenzie captain pulled his hand away from his belt to scratch at his short white beard. "Dinna make excuses for what behaviors ye need to adapt, living as ye do, desiring safety and security. We're nae here because of who ye are or how ye've treated us, lass," Geddy said, his voice carrying the weight of sincerity. "It's about justice, plain and simple. We canna turn a blind eye to wrongdoing, nae matter who's involved. Last week it was the victims of de Blair we fought for, this week it's ye and the mute. Tomorrow, it could be anyone—could be de Montfort himself in need against a true enemy, and we'd be there just the same, ready to defend what's right."

Sorcha nodded and said sheepishly, "That only makes me feel smaller, for how noble are your principles compared to how caustic I've been."

A knowing grin spread across Geddy's face as he met Sorcha's gaze. "At the same time, let's nae ignore the obvious, lass. The laird has a personal stake here, and he's made that clear to ye. He was nae about to let ye—"

"I did not ask for his help," Sorcha bristled. "I will not be beholden to—I won't consider myself in his debt," she avowed, her voice strained again.

"And he willna either," Geddy said lightly, unaffected by her vehemence, "and ye'll get to ken that about him." Geddy waved his hand. "That's enough of that. Remember," he advised, "more pressing matters to consider."

Sorcha nodded agreeably, calming a bit, and then showed a small wince. "Speaking of more pressing matters, Geddy, I'm sorry to say, I haven't either the means or the knowhow to feed an army. I suppose I might be able to—"

"Och, lass," he butt in, "we've been in the field for nigh on a year. We dinna require a supper laid out, are well-used to providing our own meals. Might be, we're hosting ye, preparing a nice stag on which to dine."

With some politeness settled between them, Geddy having graciously excused her prior behavior toward he and his fellow MacKenzies, Sorcha smiled at the very idea, unable to recall the last time she'd dined upon venison, or any meat of larger game.

Her diet, and Grimm's as well, consisted mainly of nuts and grains, with the occasional rabbit or squirrel considered a treat, and the even rarer advent of fish a true feast in their eyes.

"Thank you, Geddy," she said.

The MacKenzie captain nodded and promptly tipped his ear toward the exterior of the house.

"Aye and here he comes now, the laird," he said.

In a flash, Sorcha rushed the door, which Geddy had vacated as he stepped outside.

Unable to disguise her disappointment, her shoulders dropped significantly when she saw only Augustus MacKenzie approaching. Grimm was not with him.

At the same time, she could not help but admire the way Augustus effortlessly commanded his horse or how he looked doing so. Mounted atop his towering destrier, he exuded an air of innate athleticism and masculinity, appearing entirely at ease, at home, in the saddle. Tall and proud, he sat the horse with confident ease, his broad shoulders squared and his back as straight as a lance. Muscles rippled beneath the fabric of his tunic, evidence of years of training and physical exertion. His grip on the reins was firm, comfortable, and yet his gaze was focused, scanning the horizon and all the flat acreage around Sorcha's cottage as he neared. As he drew closer, he passed his gaze over Geddy and other MacKenzies idling just outside before fixing his blue eyes directly on Sorcha.

Dismounting, he handed off the reins to a waiting lad, one who was possibly too old to be a page or squire but certainly was too young to be a knight and was not outfitted with a long sword.

"Ye got back all right," he said, merely as an opening to conversation as he passed Geddy, who promptly fell into step behind him on the approach to Sorcha in the doorway.

Stepping backward to allow them entry, Sorcha nodded and checked herself, for where her thoughts went.

His unexceptional comment brought to mind the differences between riding atop a horse with Geddy and sharing the saddle with Augustus MacKenzie. Each occasion seemed to exist in its own separate universe, with the emotions attached to it as disparate as night and day. Riding with Augustus had been a revelation—and this despite the fact that there was plenty at that time to have held her nervous awareness!—a reluctantly acknowledged rush of exhilaration and awareness that had nearly left her breathless. Though he was fierce and formidable, his imposing yet protective presence had ignited a fire within her, stirring desires she hadn't known she'd harbored.

In stark contrast, riding with Geddy had been a mundane affair, devoid of any spark of excitement, welcome or not. She had scarcely noticed his size or strength, her mind preoccupied with Grimm's predicament. There had been no heightened awareness of his person, nor his arm around her middle, no racing heartbeat or flushed cheeks, all of which were present during her short time in the saddle with Augustus.

Presently, inside her small home, she covered her cheeks with her hands, hoping her current blush went unnoticed. *How can I behave so?* She wondered, chastising herself internally for giving even a moment's thought to so inappropriate a desire as what she'd known in his close company.

"Grimm?" She asked when Augustus did not immediately launch into any explanation about what had happened and why

Grimm was not with him but was busy taking stock of her home, the aesthetics being something to which she rarely gave consideration prior to this moment.

She looked around as well and saw what he saw.

His gaze swept over the single room, taking in the humbleness, the complete lack of extravagance. Sparsely furnished, the cottage provided only the essentials for daily living. A rough-hewn wooden table occupied the center, surrounded by two mismatched stools, one with three legs while the other had four. A small hearth nestled against one wall, its stone façade blackened by the residue of countless fires. Above it, a simple iron kettle hung from a hook. Shelves lined the entirety of one wall, displaying a small array of clay pots and wooden utensils, and a wee stack of linens, that which she'd smuggled away from home three years ago. A narrow cot, barely raised off the ground, its bedding plain but clean, occupied one corner. Sorcha knew firsthand that it offered meager respite from the toils of a long day.

Certainly, it was a far cry from what she had known in life prior to leaving her family with Finn. Curious, that she'd never known cause to be embarrassed about it until this moment.

"Grimm?" She prompted again, when Augustus turned his piercing regard upon her, his look fathomable enough that she supposed he was trying to reconcile her, with this being her home.

"Aye, as ye ken—as de Montfort stated—he'll nae be released any time soon, nae until the court session—if he should prevail—or...nae at all."

"But you saw him," she pursued. "You would have seen it. In his eyes, in his countenance, in what I am sure what a righteous fury marring his face in response to such a false allegation, so you know, aye, that he did not commit this crime."

"He assured me he did nae. Said it was a lie."

"Naturally, but what can be done—?" she stopped abruptly. "What did you say?"

He wore a peculiar expression on his face, the usual intensity of his blue eyes softening almost dramatically as he stared at her, looking decidedly uncomfortable.

"He assured you?" Sorcha repeated while the MacKenzie laird seemed to struggle with no small amount of indecision. "He *said*?" She asked and then held her breath.

Augustus nodded. "Aye, he spoke."

Sorcha's mouth fell open. In the confusion of feelings that ripped through her, her eyes watered. "Grimm spoke," she restated, testing out the sound of that, the very idea of it.

Into the awkward silence that followed, Augustus said, "He is nae Grimm, as ye ken. His name is Richard Wycliffe."

"Richard Wycliffe," she echoed breathlessly. "Oh."

Recognizing instantly that her foremost reaction, the most oppressive sentiment known in receipt of this knowledge was a pain in her heart, Sorcha spun around, putting her back to Augustus and Geddy, the MacKenzie captain a silent observer. She busied herself at the hearth, adding a block of bog peat to the barely smoldering fire. Crossing her arms over her chest, she let her gaze be transfixed by the morning's red coals, which came back to life.

"An Englishman," Augustus said next.

Though her eyes widened with shock, Sorcha barely moved otherwise.

Behind her, Geddy blew out a startled breath that vibrated his lips.

"An Englishman," she murmured. "I see." Of course it was too much, too overwhelming to dissect and accept all at once. Nodding jerkily, she whirled around. "Very good," she said without making eye contact with either man. "Thank you, my lord, for letting me know." She walked across the room and picked up a basket from behind the door, which contained a variety of small tools and a few small bundles of coiled hazel wood fibers, and walked outside.

Though she'd been advised the MacKenzie army would convene upon her cottage, and though she'd glimpsed some evidence of this over the last half hour through the open door, she was unprepared for the sight before her. Spread out before her like a crowd at market day, dozens and dozens of men of varying shapes, sizes, and age dotted the landscape in every direction, lads, men, and horses, their presence large. Some were engaged in tasks, building a fire pit, tending mounts, sharpening swords, while others milled about in small groups, subdued banter and the occasional chuckling filling the air. They all bore the unmistakable mark of warriors, their hardened expressions and steely gazes betraying a readiness for battle. Saturated with a surge of apprehension that was tinged with awe at the sight, Sorcha lowered her gaze from those that noticed her and proceeded around the side of the cottage.

Sweet Mother of God, she groused internally, terribly unnerved by this current circumstance, a lone female surrounded by the formidable army of the Rebel of Lochaber Forest. Worry and hurt over Grimm's predicament briefly faded, wondering at her own safety. Not long were emotions regarding Grimm and all things considered lost to her.

Richard Wycliffe, she reminded herself.

Ignoring the forgotten mess of trimmed and shaved straw that was littered all around the front stoop, Sorcha rounded the west side of the cottage, annoyed to find three MacKenzie soldiers—lads several years younger than herself, she presumed, by way of the downy fuzz about their cheeks and chins. Before they realized her presence, she saw that they were inspecting the stacked rows of skeps. While one of the lads swatted at the bees buzzing about, another was striking a long stick against the hives.

"Stop that," she cried, rushing forward. "Get away."

They jumped at her cry and stood erect, and guilt-ridden for their prying.

"I don't want you here," Sorcha said, moving to stand between the lads and the hives. "You've no right to trespass like this."

Their three gazes lifted over her head and one lad's face lost all color so that she was completely surprised to discover that Augustus Mackenzie must have followed her.

"Go on now," he said, his voice low but firm. "And dinna encroach again," he instructed his men.

Sorcha whirled at him as the lads quickly scurried away. "I don't want you here either. Not any of you. Go away. And take your army with you."

"That is nae a wise course of action at the moment," he remarked. He was not looking at her, but at the hives themselves, seemingly more curious about the set-up and the industry than he was perturbed by the bees buzzing all around them.

Attempting to simply ignore his presence and desperate to occupy her mind, Sorcha lifted the hackle from one of the hives and set it aside. Beneath, the skep was intact, with bees crawling in and out of the aperture located on the side. She wanted only to investigate whether or not the new queen she'd introduced days ago had been accepted by the hive. Familiar with the healthy sound of a hive, Sorcha sensed no agitation or loud buzzing, all good signs. Slowly tipping over the bell-shaped skep, she peered inside. Though she did not immediately locate the queen, she saw that she had eaten her way free of the brood comb, another positive milestone. Next, she recognized new eggs laid and a moment later, spotted the queen herself, crawling undisturbed over other bees.

Satisfied that the hive had accepted the queen she'd moved in three days ago, Sorcha replaced the skep in its position on the frame shelf Finn had lovingly made and covered it once more with the protective hackle.

When she turned around, she found Augustus MacKenzie perched lazily against the stump of a tree, his arms folded over his chest while his feet were crossed at the ankles. She frowned, though she could not say why it bothered her that he'd made himself so comfortable.

Long dead the tree had been when Finn had cut it down. There was really no reason to have done so, but the stump had since served as a handy counter of sorts, where she sometimes set down the basket she'd brought with her today. She couldn't quite put her finger on why the sight of the MacKenzie lounging against Finn's old stump unsettled her, but just as she was about to ask him to move, another of his soldiers popped up around the corner of the house, stifling her intent.

"Och, laird, there ye are," said the young man, who was as long of face as he was of limbs. "Are we expected to put up the tents?" He asked, his gaze darting back and forth between his laird and Sorcha.

"Aye, as ye see fit," Augustus answered indifferently.

"Aye, but we came soon as Peiter fetched us, laird, and left our camp as it was," the lad qualified.

He responded with a level of patience she hadn't expected from him, leading her to wonder if it was solely for her benefit. "The camp should be moved here."

"Aye, laird, and that we'll do." With one last inquisitive glance at Sorcha, the lad bobbed his head a few times and took his leave.

Maintaining her silence, and with the basket hung over her arm, Sorcha returned to the front of the cottage, having to sidestep several men who'd gathered round Geddy near the door. Once inside, she closed the door, feeling oppressed by the presence of the MacKenzie army. She felt heavily the lack of peace, of privacy, and closing the door shut out sunshine and much daylight so that little solace was found inside. She busied herself tidying up, getting about needless tasks simply to evade the thoughts in her head but did not stay long indoors, quickly irritated by the feeling that she had little choice to seclude herself against the army that was making camp, dwarfing her tiny abode. Feeling suffocated by the four close walls and the unnatural dimness at this time of day, Sorcha threw open the door and exited the house once more.

The party just outside her door had wandered off. She saw Geddy nearby, examining the hoof of a huge destrier with a man just about his age, but recognized only a few other faces in the sea of them right in front of her. And though she could have chosen to stay nearby, focusing on the tangled thatch just outside her door, she longed to be unseen as she grappled with the events of the day and their consequences.

Sorcha retreated from the busyness around her cottage, her steps purposeful as she walked around the left corner of the cottage. She made her way through a dense copse of pine trees, their fragrant boughs brushing against her as she passed. The earth beneath her feet softened as she reached the narrow brook hidden beyond, its gentle babbling unfortunately failing to provide a soothing backdrop to her troubled thoughts.

Though she did not find peace, there was quiet, and yet this was soon enough intruded upon when she realized the presence of another, coming in her wake through the pines.

She was not surprised, somehow, to find Augustus MacKenzie stalking her.

"Am I to be allowed neither freedom nor privacy?" She asked tartly, her voice tinged with frustration.

She faced the narrow waterway and crossed her arms over her chest, unable to shake the unease that settled in her chest. She understood that what he was doing was noble, taking up the role of protector in light of Grimm's arrest, but she couldn't find it in her heart to be grateful, and neither could she shake the notion that this circumstance served Augustus far better than it benefitted her. His presence at the moment felt more like an intrusion, a furtherance of his own agenda, an unwelcome imposition at a most inopportune time.

Another consideration unsettled her further. Was it possible that she was more affected by Augustus than she cared to admit? Was she attracted to him, beguiled by his imposing presence even though she knew she shouldn't be? The very idea both intrigued and troubled her.

"'Tis nae a guid idea for ye to be alone at the moment," he said, closer to her than she'd thought but several feet behind her still. To his credit, he did sound very sorry to have to tell her this. "As ye put up with Grimm's presence, and what peace it offered, so now ye will have to bear the presence of the MacKenzies."

"But it's not the same," she countered, turning to face him. "You—and more so your men—are strangers. I *know* Grimm. He is my...he was my friend. I thought he was, at any rate. I thought I knew him." She clamped her lips until she thought to remind him, "I did not ask for your protection."

Augustus chose to address her remarks about Grimm—*Richard*, she needed to keep reminding herself.

"He dinna have a choice but to speak to me."

"But why...why did he never speak to *me*?" She finally wondered aloud the thought that had burned in her brain for the last half hour.

"I canna answer for him."

Sorcha narrowed her eyes at him. "But you suspect a reason or two?"

"I might, but that dinna make it truth. Ye take that up with him."

"Will I be able to? Will I be allowed such an opportunity? Or will he be tried and executed first?"

Rather than answer that, Augustus shrugged his broad shoulders and asked, "Ye had no idea? None at all?"

Sighing, Sorcha admitted, "I did sometimes suspect. They called him Oaf and made him out to be dull-witted, naught but a mindless hound keeping his mistress safe. Of course he wasn't that. From the start, when first we met, I saw the intelligence in his gaze. I guess he didn't speak because he didn't want to give away his origins, the dangerous truth of who he was." He hadn't trusted her, she thought sadly. "He's tortured and restless and frustrated with some untold reality, but when I sang he was never restless. I always believed—and mayhap I was only fooling myself—that he knew some measure of peace. Sometimes he would close his eyes and let down walls." However, they always returned, sometimes stronger and more obvious than before.

Made morose by all the day's events, Sorcha spied a raven flying overhead. She tilted her face up toward the sky and charted its course as it twisted and rolled and then dove with aplomb, disappearing into the trees on the opposite side of the brook, quite a distance away. Oh, to be so free, so removed from earth and man and all his human foibles!

Augustus's next words brought her back down to earth.

"Perchance Grimm's silence was his way of protecting you from the burden of his past," he suggested. "Some wounds are too deep for words, and silence becomes a sanctuary."

Sorcha stared at him incredulously, as if he'd spoken in another tongue. His words hung in the air, pregnant with sincerity but lost inside her untimely and inappropriate want to giggle. She could barely contain the laughter bubbling up in her chest, unable to prevent a short chuckle from erupting behind an unexpected smile.

In response, while Sorcha's lightheartedness grew, so too did Augustus MacKenzie's scowl.

"I'm not laughing at you," she was quick to say. "Well, I am, actually, but...ah, pray forgive me, but that was much more philosophical than expected, and..." she grinned anew, "delivered so...earnestly, like a knight in shining armor, wielding a sword of wisdom."

Realizing the MacKenzie found nothing amiss with his statement, certainly no cause for laughter—he contemplated her gravely, as if he'd never heard laughter before—Sorcha sobered swiftly. "He's allowed to have his secrets," she said in reference to Grimm. "We all are. He owes me nothing. I guess I thought we were friends. Maybe he isn't capable of trusting. Not everyone is."

"Are ye?" Augustus asked without hesitation.

She nodded. "I trust too easily, I fear."

He raised a brow at this.

"I was broken by loss, not by betrayal," she informed him. "I have no dark past and—the loss of Finn notwithstanding—no traumatic event that would made me skeptical of people's intentions."

"Do you ever think about returning home? To your family?"

She looked askance at him, wondering what he knew about her family, about her in general. He offered nothing by way of explanation. Shrugging, Sorcha replied, "Maybe that's my dark secret, that I have disappointed my family, that I would not be welcomed back with open arms. My father—well, perhaps my mother to a larger degree—they are...they are not merciful people."

"And this is preferable? Barely eking out a living, living in danger, rather than returning to the bosom of your family and what I might assume would be a greater society of security."

"I don't think...I'm not the same girl who ran away from them—from home. I'm not that person, and as it was, she barely fit in with their ideals."

"This life suits ye better?"

"It does. Certainly it did while Finn was alive."

"Did he wed ye?"

The question startled Sorcha. No one had ever asked her that.

She shook her head. Though she believed she owed no explanation to this man, in her own mind she defended the lack of formal vows, a defense honed over several years of self-justification. To her, the bond with Finn had transcended the need for a formal union sanctioned by society or church. Their love was pure, untainted by the constraints of marriage vows or legalities. They'd shared their lives, their hopes, and their dreams, and in each other's arms, they had found the truest form of love. She'd needed no more than that.

It was a long moment before she met the blue eyes of Augustus MacKenzie again, but she did not examine at length why his reaction to or opinion of this should concern her, save that she might assume what many would call her sinfulness, how she'd lived with Finn, might embolden this man's belief that she was available for purchase.

His eyes betrayed him. Sorcha recognized the burning within his gaze and knew he would kiss her.

And what more today? she wondered, shocked to discover that she had no wish to stop him.

Chapter Eleven

While his rugged face appeared chiseled from stone, his riveting stare caused Sorcha to hold her breath. Was he thinking as she suspected, that because she hadn't wed Finn properly, that she possessed a weaker moral code? That she might be amenable now or soon or one day to his original proposition to spend a night with him?

Sorcha licked her dry lips and saw that his gaze followed the motion of her tongue. Against all better judgment, she did not move, not one muscle, when Augustus MacKenzie slowly closed the small distance between them, his blue eyes locked with hers. She stiffened when he touched her, when he lifted his warm hand and cupped her chin, but she did not pull away. Even as her pulse raced and her stomach knotted, she kept her eyes fixed on his as he applied slight pressure to raise her face to his and brought his mouth down on hers.

His kiss was powerful but not overpowering. And still the entire world faded from awareness until nothing remained but mesmerizing warmth, a surprising gentleness, and a beguiling friction that tempted her lips to part. He brushed his lips softly against hers before he opened his mouth and slid his tongue past her teeth. His tongue was as velvet, offering sleek enticement, circling inside her mouth, sensuous and searing.

Sorcha's breath fluttered outward.

But oh, the taste of him, the silky sway of tongues, the butterflies that roused to flight in her belly, the slow roll of tension that trembled within her. Everything in her cried out to plunge hard into the kiss, to drive forward at him and grasp tightly.

She'd wondered, had she not, about a kiss from another? From someone who was not Finn, the only man she'd ever kissed before this moment. At one point she worried that she might have forgotten how, that she would be drowned in guilt at a moment such as this, but...she was not. She knew and felt only Augustus. His strong hands framed her face, his long fingers threading in her hair. Tilting his head, he nipped at her lips, and she answered, more than willing, allowing her tongue to dance with his. Funny, that she didn't recall the overwhelming surge of sensation, how every nerve and fiber and bit of flesh lit on fire.

So well-remembered, the act of kissing, and yet so brand new. She didn't remember being awash in wanton need, not as she was now. Her hands relaxed, her fists unfurling. She moved them toward him, awkwardly gripping at the first thing they touched, the fabric of his tunic near his waist. Augustus was tall and broad, and Sorcha felt small and safe in his arms. That sensation startled her nearly as much as his breathtaking expertise, how easily he'd made her not only complicit, but become the aggressor, lifting herself onto her toes, sliding her hand up around his neck, drawing him down to her.

Any warning her brain might have offered was repressed by the blood pounding in her ears, by the shocking delight of being held in the arms of the man whom she'd vowed should not be allowed to unsettle her composure. His embrace grew firmer, drawing her closer, while a strong hand circled her nape, and skillful fingers soothed the tension in her neck.

When finally he released her mouth, he lightly traced his forefinger along her bottom lip and stared down at her with a smoldering gaze for what seemed an eternity before he said, "I rejoice in your passion, lass, but sadly, 'tis nae the time nae the place to get carried away."

His voice was deliciously husky, generating a warmth between her legs to which she was no stranger. Dream-like images and titillating scenarios flashed inside her head, of bare flesh and entwined limbs. Sorcha bit her lip, nearly undone with yearning at the idea of him naked. Finn had been a tender and simplistic lover; she'd bet her own precious freedom that the Rebel was anything but, that he was ardent and vigorous. He teemed now with a physical desire, his jaw tight and chest heaving, his gaze wild.

Trapped yet in a haze of peace and an incomprehensible joy, Sorcha answered intuitively, "It's been so long."

"Aye, but nae more."

The beautiful bedevilment was quickly overtaken by a late-blooming guilt, for her actions, and for her betrayal of both Finn and Grimm, the latter's circumstance being more dire presently. The knot in her stomach turned distinctly uncomfortable. Her cheeks flushed with color that hadn't anything to do with desire and yearning. Awkwardly, she pushed against him to be free.

Guilt was a curious thing, choosing to manifest and then vanish as it pleased.

"Release me," she said, which was intended to be a command but sound like pleading.

He did, his large hands slowly falling away from her neck and face, sliding provocatively down her shoulders and arms until Sorcha stepped out of his reach.

While she stared at him, imagining words she might hurl at him to falsely accuse him of an attack, solely to exonerate herself, Augustus cocked a brow at her.

"Ye canna kiss me like that and expect that I'd be satisfied with naught else—or have me believe that ye would be. And dinna deny what ye feel—what I just caused ye to feel. I will nae believe it, that yer response was manufactured."

"It was not," she murmured before she thought better of it, and then frowned. "It's too...too soon, too difficult...."

"Aye but it dinna have to be."

Angered at his lazy attitude, at his laconic tone, Sorcha bristled and took another step backward, wanting to get away from his unnerving scrutiny and from the nearness of him and his kiss.

"Oh, but I wish you hadn't—" she began with annoyance. Though she'd been secretly thrilled and hugely titillated, she knew she would never admit this to him. "What are you about anyway? Taking advantage of...of today's catastrophe. With all that's happened, *this* is what you're thinking about? You're a...a hound—a bounder," she accused, struck by inspiration. Staunchly, she refused to make any reference to her own part in their kiss, to her response, which in no way could be construed as reluctant. "You imagine me weak, loose mayhap, and now without Grimm to stand in my defense—"

"I kissed ye because ye smiled," he said, quite calmly, as if his heart did not pound like thunder inside his chest, as did hers. Without smiling, still using a husky bedroom voice, he clarified, "Or rather, I kissed ye in response to the effect of the smile. *Jesu*, Sorcha, but ye should do that more often."

Preoccupied and bewildered, she shot back the first thing that entered her mind, in a pert tone, "Says the man who does not own a smile." Realizing what she was arguing about, she waved her hands and strode past him, aware for the first time in many minutes the sounds of the existence of others, all around her house, any of whom might have witnessed their kiss. "Stop. Leave it be. Leave me alone now. That is unfair advantage to take, when you know so well how anxious I am today."

"Distracted by a kiss is nae a bad thing, lass," he called after her though he did not follow.

"And stop that," she commanded, throwing the words over her shoulder. "Making light of it, as if...as if—just stop."

Her brain and the thoughts within were tangled, the excitement of his kiss tousling with guilt and thoughts of dear Grimm and his decidedly less stellar circumstance. And then another thought surfaced, one she was aghast to have nearly overlooked. She spun around and retraced her steps, striding with fervor toward Augustus, who remained where she'd left him and crooked a never-before-seen grin at her return.

When she stood directly in front of him, she planted her hands on her hips and chastised, "You are a knave! A hypocrite! You accuse de Montfort of treachery, yet you commit the same offense. You propose he had Grimm arrested so that I was left unprotected, and you insist the MacKenzies will now safeguard me and yet you do this! You are no better than de Montfort, if what you say about his intent is even true!"

Augustus captured her arm in a tight grip, hauling her up against him once more. "Enough!" he clipped, his body stiffening and heightening with fury, his short-lived grin gone, replaced by a steely glower. "Dinna question my integrity," he growled, "nae when ye stand on the shaky moral ground over which lives your response to my kiss."

Sorcha gasped. "How dare—"

"Aye, I dare," he snarled, all evidence of desire washed from his furious façade, "and will continue to do so if ye keep on with rubbish such as this."

Though her knees quaked, she forged on. "You live up to your legend, don't you? The Rebel of Lochaber Forest, who takes what he wants," she accused, her voice trembling with a mix of anger and uncertainty. "Perhaps I shouldn't be surprised by your actions. 'Tis said you manipulate situations to your advantage—is that what you've done with Grimm? Was it your plan then? To bend me to your will?"

Augustus's grip on her arm tightened, his eyes flashing with anger. "Dinna ever again accuse me of such low treachery," he warned, his voice low and dangerous.

Augustus released her arm with a forceful shove, his blue eyes darkened, blazing with anger as he took a step back. Without another word, he turned on his heel and strode away, his wide shoulders tense with fury.

Stunned by the intensity of his rage, Sorcha watched him walk away.

***

Unable to shake off the sting of her accusations, the way she'd likened him to de Montfort and what Augustus truly believed were that man's evil designs, Augustus stormed away from Sorcha. He was further annoyed to have the memory of that burning kiss tarnished by the aftermath.

Still, as he walked, the weight of his own actions bore down on him. He had warned her of the possible danger she faced, and why she needed protection, and yet he'd kissed her, realizing now the full implications of his actions. It was a reckless move, not entirely out of character save that this was not in the heat of battle, where impulsiveness might save lives. Still, in that moment, when the effect of her smile was fresh and intoxicating, he could no more resist the pull of her presence or the beckoning softness of her lips than any other red-blooded man.

Thus, he was briefly torn between indignation and desire, anger and longing. While part of him resented being chastised for crossing boundaries, for having dared what he did, another part of him refused to regret it. The thrill of Sorcha's kiss had branded him, and a rush of adrenaline still coursed through his veins so that, despite the consequences, he was glad that he'd acted on the impulse. He refused to let doubt creep in. He would face whatever repercussions she hurled his way—save for comparing him to the despicable de Montfort—but he would not apologize for following that path of desire.

And yet, there was one fleeting regret. His legendary status had gained him respect and admiration and allowed him to command loyalty and obedience more easily. More importantly, his legend had served him well, dissuading thieves and brigands, and sometimes effortlessly intimidating enemies. He had never wished to be anyone else—until today, when Sorcha had thrown his reputation in his face. For one brief moment and for the first time in his life, he wished he wasn't that man.

Augustus strode purposefully across the camp taking shape, while clusters of soldiers rode in and out, either to or from their previous campsite. At present, only a few tents had been erected, barely taller than the long grass which stretched forever across the lane from Sorcha's wee cottage.

Still wearing a dark scowl, he scanned the faces until he found Geddy, who was conferring with Angus, Kael, Colin, and Griffyn. As he approached, Colin noticed his coming and though he straightened to attention, the lad did not lose the smirk he wore but seemed to direct it at his laird.

Assuming the sly grin meant he'd witnessed Augustus kissing Sorcha—and suffering neither shame nor guilt over this—Augustus grimly stared down the lad, causing the smirk to dissolve by the time he'd reached the group.

Shifting his attention to Geddy, Augustus asked without preamble, "How will ye break 'em up? I want at least two units surveying Ironwood."

"Aye and we'll keep a close eye on Lord Aldric and what goes on there," Geddy answered promptly. "I'm just telling Angus he'll take that watch."

"And send John of Skye and Angus the Black over to the Bonnie Barrell," Augustus instructed. "Chat up the barmaids. I want to ken what's being said and be advised if there's any mention of a court session or trial or any news regarding the prisoner."

John, formerly of Skye, and Angus the Black, distinguished from several other soldiers named Angus by his mane of long black hair, had been employed in this regard more than once. Both were fine looking lads with easy charm, the kind that didn't come naturally to Augustus. This wouldn't be the first time they were dispatched with similar instructions: extract information from forthcoming wenches or tavern patrons using their charismatic demeanor.

The next instruction he might have given was disrupted by the advent of a swiftly moving rider. He came from the south and even while he was still at the furthest end of the quietly bustling camp, the speed of his approach and his distinctive red and gold tabard caught the eye. Hands that had instinctively reached for hilts of their swords relaxed, recognizing the colors of their king, Robert Bruce. As he drew near, the royal insignia emblazoned upon his chest could be made out, further identifying him as a messenger of the king.

Augustus's tent had yet to be erected and thus no banner was displayed to guide the messenger to him. Geddy raised his arm and gave out a short, low whistle, which drew the man's attention to them.

Though he'd never met a messenger who was not serious and purposeful, reflecting the gravity of his position, this one wore a mien of particular sternness. Augustus exchanged a quick glance with Geddy and Angus, a silent communication passing between them as they braced themselves for whatever news the king's messenger might bring. They remained still as the rider was allowed to approach without interference.

The messenger searched the faces of Augustus's group and, having decided his target, focused on Augustus alone as he reined in. His expression did not lose its grimness as he announced, "I bring urgent news from Robert Bruce."

He did not dismount but withdrew a scroll from inside his tabard and stretched out his hand.

Kael, closest to the man and horse, received the scroll and brought it to Augustus.

Augustus first inspected the unbroken seal carefully before snapping the wafer and perusing the few words plied to parchment.

"To our dear friend and loyal confidante, earl of Lochmere, please hear these words," read the instruction, the notice of which was signed in the king's own hand, the script familiar to Augustus. 'Twas not uncommon, to put no words to paper, certainly not when the message must be carried across a great many miles.

Augustus raised his gaze to the messenger, lifting his brow. "What news?" He asked, his voice steady despite the underlying sense of anticipation.

The messenger nodded and drew in a breath, and then proceeded to deliver his lengthy message in an informal manner.

"Though Sir Douglas has rejoined the king, swelling his numbers, new and unexpected perils awaited them," he began. "Recently, the Lord of Lorn, a notorious sinner, aligned with the English under Pembroke, bringing eight-hundred treacherous Highlanders with him. To their shame, they also brought a large bloodhound—an old dog—committing a grave betrayal by turning man against his loyal beast. This was especially poignant as the king himself had raised the bloodhound from a pup. Dutiful he was, the hound, and nearly effected a capture, having pursued his first master with the utmost eagerness and certainty." The messenger barely moved as he spoke, using not his hands or more frivolous expressions, but only his mouth to convey the message. "Aye, but the king has refined the practice of dividing his force upon any retreat, and as such, they dispersed into the mountains when Pembroke believed he had them pinned. And then into play comes the hound, milord, let loose and seeking his master, fixing on one of the three tracks as the one the king had taken, leading the enemy in pursuit." He crossed his forefinger over his heart, the first motion he'd made since the beginning of the tale. "Saved by the grace of God—and how could it nae be?—when an arrow shot from one in pursuit killed the hound and nae any of the men fleeing. Lo, he lost his banner, the king did, and to his own nephew, Randolph, who since his capture at Methven, is now fighting with the English ranks. 'Twas nae a firm rout, milord; the king put to the sword the detachment of two hundred of Pembroke's finest, those who'd followed the hound and his trail. And Pembroke, at that time, weary of his service to Longshanks, withdrew to Carlisle."

Imagining there was more—the king did not send a messenger merely to update Augustus about his near escape—he put his hands on his hips and waited.

"Aye, but come again, the Pembroke Earl," continued the middle-aged messenger, "advancing into Ayrshire with a force of three thousand cavalry."

"At this moment?" Augustus asked. At the messenger's nod, he queried, "How many are attached to the king now?"

"Six hundred spearmen has he, and knowing of the ability of men of this ilk in battle, especially against cavalry, the king is resolved to oppose Pembroke's advance. He desires you to join him, as Pembroke informed him of his intention to march by Loudon Hill. He challenged our king to battle there on the 10th day of May, milord, and bring adherents as you can pull to your banner."

Geddy cursed, "That's more'n a hundred miles," he said, and consulting his fingers, added, "and less than five days."

At Augustus's right, Griffyn shrugged. "Thirty miles a day is nae hardship."

Geddy swiftly turned a scowl onto Griffyn, his face clearly suggesting otherwise.

Augustus addressed the messenger. "Ye've stopped elsewhere ere ye reached me?"

"Not I, milord," was replied promptly. "But aye, other missives were delivered by other messengers."

Robert Bruce was calling in everyone, which sadly, considering the state of the dissention within the nobles, might not be enough to defeat Pembroke once and for all. Pembroke's army was mighty and had been in serious, devastating pursuit of the king since Robert Bruce had pulled the crown down on his head last spring. The battle that had taken place near Methven last year had nearly seen the newly crowned king captured, his stunning opposition to England and Edward I a breath away from dying a premature death.

Becoming aware of the chatter around him, Geddy and the lads discussing the chances of reaching the king's side in time, Augustus formulated his response to the messenger in his head. It didn't matter what task he'd been given here in Caol or that it was not yet completed. A summons from the king himself was not to be avoided, certainly not with a battle looming, and neither did Augustus have a desire to ignore it. Rather, the very idea of returning to action quickened his pulse.

The messenger's demeanor softened, his gaze drifting away. Augustus followed his line of sight, noticing Sorcha nearby as she worked on tidying the thatch chaos outside her door. Until that moment, the messenger had been reserved and professional, his expression somber. Presently, his entire façade appeared to melt, affected by wonder at the sight of her. No surprise there, for she was an exquisite pale rose among the thorn of her cottage, a brilliant beacon amidst the mundane army camp.

Her presence brought to mind her predicament and Augustus's own self-appointed role of protector. Lifting his hand, he rubbed his cheeks and jaw, considering her and this new turn.

"Och, but the lass...." Geddy said, having noticed her presence as well.

Augustus nodded, his mind racing with ideas and strategies, and said to the messenger, "Ye may relay to our king that we will attend him anon," he pronounced, drawing the messenger's fascinated attention back to him—and a barely concealed snort from Kael, who might be wondering how they would make so many miles in so short a time.

The man cleared his throat and bowed his head in acknowledgement of this, and with little aim to conceal the action, he cast one more glance at Sorcha, lingering for a moment before he spun his horse about and departed.

"We leave today," Angus said when the man was well gone, "and still we'll struggle to arrive in time to be of any use to the king."

"Coming in fatigued will be nae help against Pembroke," Colin predicted.

"There'll be nae time to construct any siege engines," Geddy contributed, "nae time to outfit the archers proper-like."

"Are you suggesting we ignore the king's summons?" Augustus asked the group in general.

An immediate chorus of "Naes" responded, putting an end to the discussion that it couldn't be done, or couldn't be accomplished suitably.

"Then let us prepare," Augustus instructed. He glanced upward at the sun's position. "Plan to move out in two hours' time. We'll travel by night as well as day."

"And the lass?" Geddy wondered.

Augustus chewed the inside of his cheek, his attention drawn to her while she unknowingly swept loose pieces of thatch away from her stoop.

"Canna leave her here," Colin decided. "We dinna ken that de Montfort is behind the oaf's arrest, but then we dinna ken he isnae."

Griffyn, who rarely spoke, offered what Augustus and possibly others were thinking. "Some men would commit all sorts of offenses to have her."

"But that assumes," Kael proposed, "that the weaver—what's her name? Effie?—lied and this lass here is a guid judge of the oaf, and how do we ken that, when she dinna even ken the oaf was English?"

Narrowing his eyes at Sorcha's petite figure, his mind and body yet filled with the memory of her kiss, he couldn't help but ponder the extent to which de Montfort would go to claim her for himself, even at the risk of invoking Augustus's wrath. He didn't doubt for a moment that de Montfort was the type who would exploit her vulnerability. Sorcha, in his eyes, was immeasurably superior to any other woman he had encountered, both in appearance and in the strength of her convictions and courage. Even her sharp temper, her fighting spirit, held a certain allure.

"We canna take her with us," Geddy supposed, scratching his head, "unless we deposit in Glasgow or secret her way near Galston while the fight is on."

"Irvine is near to Loudon Hill," Angus reminded them, "and is sympathetic to the Bruce, possibly a safe haven temporarily. I've kin there," he said and scrunched up his face in consideration of this, "or I did at one time. Unless they got themselves kilt, might still be around those parts."

"What about the oaf?" Colin wondered. "Do we trust that Lord Aldric will nae hurry along the trial and punishment while we're gone, in light of yer support?" When several sets of eyes turned toward him in question, Colin lifted his hands defensively. "What? Ye ken Lord Aldric dinna ken why we were there, and with the laird speaking on behalf of the lass?"

Knowing he could not in good conscience leave Sorcha behind, certainly not while Grimm was still imprisoned, and strongly suspecting Sorcha would not leave willingly while Grimm was yet in chains, Augustus turned his narrow gaze onto Geddy. "Ah, but will we nae invite de Montfort to ride to Loudon Hill with us? Should he not? Being so loyal an adherent to Robert Bruce?"

Geddy nodded and Griffyn smirked as they understood. The messenger had called for recruitment, and an entire army, larger than the MacKenzie force and claiming to be on the side of right, was housed nearby. Should they not be expected to also race to the king's side?

Augustus had one more idea.

"Any chance we can spring her man from the dungeon while we're convincing de Montfort to join us?"

Angus let out a low whistle, aptly conveying his surprise.

Augustus sensed the same all around him, in the other faces.

"Och, shite," was Geddy's response. But at the same time as he shook his head disagreeably, a slow grin evolved. "Only one way to find out."

Chapter Twelve

Still in possession of the scroll with the king's introduction of the messenger, August returned to Ironwood, with only Griffyn and Finlay at his side. Once more he was not prevented from riding directly through the gate nor from entering the keep itself. He shook his head at this, what he considered de Montfort's arrogance.

Finding Lord Aldric yet at the boards, Augustus was caused to wonder if the man sat anywhere else or engaged in any other activity. While platters surrounded him and his hand rested possessively on a pewter goblet at this hour, he was engaged in a lively conversation with two men while a robed man carrying leather-bound ledgers awaited his attention. None had been invited to sit at the table or enjoy wine with their lord.

With only a fleeting glance at the others, Augustus focused his gaze on Lord Aldric as he approached. The displeasure de Montfort tried to hide did not go unnoticed.

"Ah, MacKenzie, back so soon," the earl drawled, lifting the goblet to his mouth and taking a long sip, his narrow eyes shrewd as he watched Augustus over the rim of the cup. "Mayhap you came to give your sympathies to young Milton," he said when he set the cup down, "who most curiously fell upon a four-tined rake in the stables. Though not dead, in bad shape he is. Another moon will have to come ere the lad doesn't breathe through the holes in his chest."

"Tough break," Augustus said, feigning ignorance but not having to pretend that he didn't care. "Let us hope infection dinna claim him in the meantime." With little time to spare, he laid the scroll on the tabletop and pushed it toward de Montfort. "God is guid," Augustus said, "having me so near to ye when came the call to arms. A battle looms at Loudon Hill and King Robert requests our presence."

Having briefly perused the parchment, de Montfort raised a brow to Augustus. "It says nothing of the sort, my lord."

"Nae, but the messenger who brought it had plenty to say. We can manage twenty-five miles a day and arrive in time to ride under the king's banner in his time of need."

"Arrive where? And for what?"

"I've just said, at the king's side near Loudon Hill, to fight for right." He gave up no more than that, unwilling to mention Pembroke while he maintained a suspicion that de Montfort was not loyal to the Scottish crown.

Lord Aldric did not stutter with any swift resistance but stared steadily at Augustus, his mind quite obviously scratching and clawing for any justification to refuse.

Augustus staved off any possible excuse by saying, "Praise God ye keep yer army in guid stead, as ye said only this morning—*ready to march at a moment's notice*, ye said—and how provident that just now we are called to move. The king desires that I be accompanied by all the loyal supporters I can muster."

De Montfort knew damn well he was being challenged, that his loyalty was being questioned at this very moment. Little recourse Augustus had at the moment if de Montfort refused to follow, but by doing so Lord Aldric would effectively give away his true allegiance and repercussions would come, tomorrow or another day.

"We must make haste," Augustus urged when de Montfort hadn't yet decided upon his response.

"Yes, yes, of course," he finally said. He flicked his fingers at one of men in his audience. "Bring Blackwood to me."

Augustus frowned. "Blackwood is yer bailiff. Do ye nae mean to consult with the captain of yer army, to prepare for departure?"

De Montfort went still, and his expression turned icy. "Naturally," he contended, "and so I will. But first I must set to rights the affairs of my house if I'm to be absent for any length of time."

"I see. Do so quickly, my lord," Augustus suggested. "And let us convene at the bend in the loch in two hours' time."

De Montfort's jaw tightened, clearly displeased to be given instructions. Though they were equal in rank, Augustus rarely played at politics and was far below him in wealth and noble influence, and thus de Montfort would imagine himself superior. Likely, because of that wealth and the power it afforded him within their society, and in no small part due to his natural arrogance, de Montfort imagined himself superior to many.

Tight-lipped, Lord Aldric nodded. "Of course. Two hours. I look forward to the opportunity to be of assistance to the king."

With an astute grin, Augustus sketched a brief bow and turned, walking away, believing it had been no mistake that de Montfort hadn't mentioned the king by name.

Again out of doors and returned to their steeds, Augustus, Griffyn, and Finlay made short work of the distance between Ironwood and Sorcha's cottage. There, he found little evidence of the camp that had barely begun to take shape, all belongings and supplies removed from the tall grass. Men moved hurriedly, packing two wayns with what remained of their grain, bread, and ale stores while horses stood at the ready, laden with a warrior's gear.

He found Geddy just finishing his discussion with the MacKenzie surgeon, waving him off, telling him, "I'm nae much caring for what yer saying, Hamish. We're moving and yer going with us, and those what's nae healed should be loaded again into the hospital wagons. We're nae leaving anyone behind."

The captain turned at his laird's approach, squinting up at Augustus as the sun shone directly on him.

"What'd the auld hog say?"

Shrugging with indifference, Augustus advised, "Claims he'll meet us at the loch." His tone suggested he wasn't quite ready to believe it until he saw it. He paused and gave a short whistle, drawing the attention of many, but waving Angus forward from where he attended the shoe of his steed thirty yards away.

"And ye still mean to free the Oaf?" Geddy inquired. "Still believe that's necessary?"

"Aye, I do. At the very least, it will go far in convincing the lass that she must accompany us as well. She'll nae leave him, nae any more than he would her. De Montfort called first for Blackwood—nae his captain—so I imagine he might give orders regarding either one or both, Sorcha or Wycliffe."

"Might be," Geddy conceded.

Angus arrived, standing beside Geddy.

"Angus, I want ye and your unit, plus Griffyn and Finlay, to hold back, separate yourselves now from the army and head over to Ironwood unseen. As soon as de Montfort and his men leave, get in there and retrieve Wycliffe. I assume ye can take on Blackwood and the house guard without difficulty." At Angus's harrumph, which suggested he was offended that Augustus might have thought otherwise, Augustus continued, "If they dinna assemble and depart as de Montfort just assured me he would, we'll have nae choice but to abandon that plan until our return."

"Which might be too late," Geddy supposed, scratching at the bald spot in his crown.

"Aye, it might be, but the king's command takes precedence naturally, and we've little time to waste. If ye do recover him, ye'll have to ride like the wind to catch up, but keep Wycliffe out of sight of de Montfort's men. Disguise him if ye have to."

"Ye want us going in covertly," Angus inquired, "or dinna ye care if the earl kent it's us and what we're about?"

"I want Wycliffe out of the dungeon," Augustus stated, "and I dinna care how ye accomplish that. I'll lose nae sleep if Blackwood gets roughed up in a scuffle, I ken that much."

Griffyn grinned, rather sadistically, which bade Augustus caution him, "Dinna kill him."

"Mayhap only make him wish he were dead," Geddy suggested.

"But keep in mind the time, of which we've little to spare. I need ye rejoined before we reach the king." He turned to Geddy once more. "Ye have the ledger?"

"Aye, Mouse has it. All set. One hundred forty-six presently accounted for."

The ledger, as it was simply known, was a record kept in a worn and weathered leather-bound journal, where were written the names of all the men in his company, battles they'd participated in, acts of valor achieved, and details of injuries, large or small. Sadly, it also chronicled the deaths among his men, each loss marked with a heavy heart by the squire, a young lad called Mouse for his skittish demeanor and small stature.

Sadly, one hundred and forty-six meant that they'd lost more than sixty able-bodied fighters, all MacKenzie kin, in the last year since Robert Bruce had been crowned king.

Nodding, Augustus finally dismounted. "Have someone check his shoes," he said, handing off the reins to Finlay, "and make sure he's fed and watered." He headed toward Sorcha's house, calling over his shoulder, "Let's see how much trouble the lass will give me."

Geddy's chuckle followed him while Angus called out, "Give a yelp, laird, if she's too much for ye."

***

Inside the dimly lit cottage, Sorcha paced back and forth, wearing a light pattern on the packed-earth floor. The only source of light filtered in through the lone window, casting faint beams that barely illuminated the space. The door, closed tight against the outside world—the entire MacKenzie army camped outside her door—offered little relief from the oppressive atmosphere within.

Her mind whirled with a myriad of conflicting emotions. Anxiety gnawed at her gut as she fretted over Grimm's unjust arrest and his fate. She couldn't shake the feeling of helplessness, knowing he was locked away in a cold, dank dungeon. She felt trapped herself to some degree, but in no way could it compare to Grimm's circumstance. Still, disdain for the entire situation simmered beneath the surface of her grim-faced façade, fueling her frustration. Frankly, the MacKenzie's encampment felt like an invasion of privacy—being hemmed in by the very people who claimed they wanted only to protect her—suffocating her with their sheer proximity. Oh, how she longed to erase all of today, all the last few weeks for that matter, to that time before the Rebel had come to Caol.

Contrary to this heartfelt wish and grappling for notice in the chaos of her thoughts, one memory persisted with stubborn insistence: the memory of Augustus MacKenzie's kiss. Naught but an hour old, it haunted her already, refusing to be banished to the far recesses of her mind, and this despite everything else that should engage her concern. Riled to anger with herself for allowing it to occupy so much space in her thoughts, Sorcha reminded herself that she was entertaining ideas of a man who represented everything she should detest. With each turn across the floor, Sorcha purposefully brought to mind his high-handedness, his pride, his overbearing manner, any or all of which should have negated the effects of that searing kiss.

A firm rap at her door startled her. She froze for a moment, supposing such a decisive knock could only belong to the Rebel. Further annoyed by the way her unfaithful pulse sped up at the idea, Sorcha yanked open the door and glared at him, for indeed Augustus MacKenzie had come calling.

He stepped inside, not waiting for her to invite him or back up out of his way, but rather forcing her to do so.

"Mother Mary and Joseph and their sweet babe, will you learn some manners," she cried.

He offered no apology for his actions, his tone curt as he delivered the news. "A summons has arrived from the king, and I am obliged to heed it," he informed her. "I will take my army away, quite a distance, and I fear there is nae choice but that ye should accompany us."

Driven by instinct and a deep-seated aversion to being commanded, Sorcha's response was swift. "I refuse to comply. I will not."

"'Tis nae safe—"

"You cannot simply decide my fate—I am not a pawn in whatever game you play. I have a life here, responsibilities. Grimm is here!" she reminded him, her voice nearly shrill to match her upset. Her hands covered her cheeks, in awe of his audacity. "Here you are, once again, imposing your will without considering my perspective."

Tightly, Augustus admonished, "Put aside, just for a moment, your distrust of me. I vow to ye I have nae agenda but yer safety."

"But why? Why do you care?" A staggering kiss and his intent to have one night with her aside—that was all the consideration she merited in his mind, she was sure—*why* did he care? She was, essentially, a stranger to him.

He could not or would not answer, his mouth thinning with displeasure at her query.

"All very suspect," she decided.

"Nevertheless, Sorcha, ye canna stay here, and ye might like to ken—and ye would have, if ye listened rather than hastily reacted—that my men mean to release Grimm—Wycliffe—from Ironwood."

This caught her attention. Hope rose briskly and Sorcha stepped closer to him. She raised her hands and squeezed her fists with anxiety. "Will they? How will they make it happen? Do you plan to—oh, but it comes with a price, does it not? And now I owe you and what will you want? I daresay a kiss will not suffice, will it? The cost will be much steeper. Again, it leads me to believe that it was you who arranged to have Effie raise that hue and cry, to have Grimm arrested and removed from—"

Growling an unintelligible curse, Augustus clamped his hands on her arms and hauled her up against him, crashing his mouth down on hers. He kissed her fervently, thoroughly. And though it was different than his first kiss, this one wild and tainted with either anger or impatience, and somehow more spontaneous, her senses reeled all the same. Sorcha lost focus as Augustus held her close and moved his lips firmly over hers, again and again, each time kissing her more deeply than the last, and that before he entered her mouth with his tongue, teasing her with needful strokes until she was feverish and weak. Breathless and dizzy, she made no move to break away and gasp for air. Instead, she instinctively wrapped her arms around his broad shoulders, clinging to him as if her very life came from him. The world spun around her, and she braced herself for the possibility of losing consciousness at any moment.

Augustus withdrew, abruptly, cruelly. The kiss broken, he stared down at her, angrily, as if he'd been forced to kiss her.

Sorcha recovered herself, to some small degree. She stammered a newly realized belief, "Y-you...you kissed me to silence me."

"Aye," he acknowledged tersely, "and when ye speak of things at which ye only guess—incredibly, ye have so many things wrong—I will let that be my response, as that seems to stifle your ridiculousness. I dinna have time, Sorcha. The king summons me and my army. We will depart Caol at once, and ye will accompany us, as ye canna stay in Caol. I canna promise that my men can make Wycliffe free, but I vow that by my orders they are set to try."

A question burned inside her. "But tell me why you concern yourself at all with me? I won't go anywhere with you until you answer," she proclaimed childishly.

"The king will wait on ye?" He challenged irritably.

"You are free to leave, to keep to your schedule."

"I have concern for naught but that a vulnerable lass should nae be terrorized. And ye ken the other truth, that I want ye, paid or nae I dinna care, but willing and eager, with as much zest as ye bring to our kiss ere it strikes ye wrongly that ye should nae be liking my kiss. I'm nae likely to have that if I return and find ye beaten, broken, or brutalized, am I right?"

Taken aback by his candid response, Sorcha could only nod.

"And the fact is ye do," he said.

"I do what?"

"Like my kiss," he replied, "and want more of them."

Her spine straightened with indignation. "You are...you're—"

"Aye, I ken what I am and what ye believe. Ye've made that clear. Now pack a bag—only bring the bare necessities—

"You're going to bring me to war? Where I might suffer a worse fate? Where I might very well be killed?"

His expression hardened dangerously. "Unless I am slain, Sorcha," he said tightly, "I vow that ye will live."

She had some suspicion that she'd offended him by suggesting otherwise.

Unabashedly, she let her eyes roam over his broad shoulders and thick arms, at his fierce expression and his strong hands. "You look like someone who might be hard to kill."

He surprised her by grinning—oh, the beauty of it!—and then by pecking her lips with a kiss. "Make yourself ready. We will depart within the hour." His suddenly lighter tone spoke volumes about his certainty that she would argue no more.

He would see that Grimm was freed! How could she say no?

She stared at him, her eyes drawn once more to the smattering of gray hair at his temples, deciding it suited him, complementing his authoritative nature, something that certainly did not come with youth. Still, it was a shame that she found him so bloody attractive. A man with his reputation should not be allowed to own eyes so magnificent, so mesmerizing.

Augustus didn't depart immediately, but she didn't sense he was only waiting on a formal acquiescence from her. For a man who'd mentioned the matter of time often in the last few minutes, he seemed suddenly as someone who had plenty of it, returning her gaze.

Blinking broke the spell, but only barely.

"Is there any chance," she began, a fresh concern harassing her, "I mean, Grimm won't be killed while they attempt to free him, will he? That won't happen, will it?"

"Angus and his unit will nae make an attempt if it seems unlikely to work in their favor, or too risky," he informed her, "but aye, even plans that seem tight can go awry. But then, Wycliffe dinna strike me as one to go down easy. I wager we'll see him soon."

Though she suspected he would be angry with the question, she had to ask, "And you swear to me, this is not some plot of your own making...?"

Augustus shook his head slowly, seemingly unoffended by her nervous question.

"If what you say is true, then I am being a shrew—an ungrateful one." A hint of pleading entered her gaze. "But please don't allow that to…" she paused and then started anew, attempting a conciliatory tone. "I apologize for my behavior. I am grateful for whatever aid you and your army can lend to Grimm and me." Nodding jerkily, having said that, she winced a bit and thought to warn him, "I cannot ride one of your monstrous war horses. If there is a mare available or mayhap a wagon," she said, "I would be more comfortable."

"Ye'll ride with me," he declared. "'Tis my vow to keep ye safe and that is best achieved with ye kept close."

A flutter of unease mixed with tingling anticipation. The idea of riding with him again, feeling the warmth of his body and the strength of his arms around her was as unsettling as it was enticing. Despite her concerns about the impending dangers of war and the attempt to free Grimm, she couldn't deny the allure of being so close to Augustus.

"I'll…make myself ready," she said after a moment, her voice oddly husky, which caused her to duck her gaze from Augustus.

She lifted her eyes again when she sensed movement and found that he'd pivoted and had left. For a fleeting moment, before he turned left outside the door, he was a perfect shadowy silhouette against the sunlight opening, his shoulders meeting both sides of the door frame at once.

Bemusedly, she tipped her head back and ran her fingers down the column of her neck, still heated after their exchange. Her gaze landed on one of the remaining holes in her roof.

She recalled that upon waking this morning, her only plans for the day, over which she'd been quite put out, had been to assist Grimm with repairing the thatch.

She prayed there were no more surprises waiting to be sprung on her today.

Putting off readying herself, Sorcha went first to tell the bees.

Chapter Thirteen

Had they been preparing to depart from Strontian, had they been fresh to or long gone from war, there would be more instructions to give and greater amounts of supplies to load ere they departed Caol. As it was, gone now more than a year from home, and with both men and supplies reduced, their preparations were limited and quickly achieved. This was not a raw troop heading off into their first foray. These men had been at the rout that was Methven, had seen the king nearly trampled and slain, had fought at Dalrigh, had engaged with both English and Scottish foes. Little encouragement did they need from their laird and commander, for they knew what lay ahead. They fought bravely for the cause and for their comrades, kinship being on of the great factors of war, Augustus believed.

Geddy was a fine captain, effortlessly commanding respect, fear, and admiration. His meticulous attention to detail ensured that no MacKenzie movement went unnoticed; he knew the composition of each unit, from the vanguard to the rear guard, and monitored the number of soldiers in the sick wagons. This dedication to understanding every facet of their operations allowed Augustus the freedom to focus on strategic planning for battle. However, knowing that King Robert would have mapped out his own strategy for the battle against Pembroke, Augustus understood that his schemes would not come into play until the battle was well under way, and adjustments, if any were needed, might need direction in the midst of the fight.

Presently, as the army maneuvered into their marching formation, Sorcha exited her cottage, draped in her long cloak and clutching a worn satchel. She looked decidedly ill-at-ease, evident in the searching gaze as her blue eyes scanned the line of mounted men. She bit her lower lip, an endearing habit of hers that revealed her bouts with indecision or anxiety. Her gaze paused when it landed on Augustus and eased a bit as she strode toward him.

Having positioned his steed just behind the vanguard, Augustus dismounted and awaited her approach, peripherally aware of all the eyes upon her—her pink cheeks betrayed that she was aware of this as well. Tension pinched her features, and she gave only a flat smile as Augustus took the bag, which was surprisingly light. Having expected it would have been bulkier, or that there would be several satchels and thus need to be stored in the provisions' wayn, he determined it might well remain with them and affixed it to the horse's flanks, opposite his own saddle bags.

"Have ye a horn for water or ale?" He asked as he knotted the straps to the saddle.

Sorcha shook her head, her blush darkening.

"We can share mine," he said. "Ye have a knife on ye?"

She nodded, patting her hip. "Yes."

When the bag was secure, he faced her. "Ye'll have to ride astride," he said. "It will be more comfortable as we'll be moving swiftly."

Another nod, another nibble on her lip as she removed her gaze, eyeing the broad back of his destrier.

Sensing her heightened agitation, Augustus took hold of her hand, drawing her gaze back to him. "Sorcha, all will be well. Ye will be reunited with Wycliffe shortly and the two of ye set aside somewhere safe ere we engage in battle. I dinna take this on lightly, the idea that ye should accompany us."

"Thank you," she said, her voice small. "But pray bear with me, as my nerves are on fire."

He grinned at her phrasing and let his gaze linger on her, his jaw tightening briefly as he was reminded of her injury, her swollen upper lip, the area showing the beginning of a purple and yellow bruise.

She was well named, 'Sorcha' meaning bright or radiant. She was both, exuding light and beauty that stirred within him a deep desire to protect her.

Meaning to put her at ease, he assured her, "Ye'll settle in. Willna take long at all."

When he moved to assist her in mounting, she held up a hand to stall him. "I can do it," she insisted.

A soft chuckle erupted. "Nae, lass, ye canna." Unceremoniously, he lifted her by her waist and set her up on the saddle. As she swung her leg over the horse's back and settled in, adjusting herself until she was comfortable, he told her, "Ye're too small, lass, and would nae be able to reach the saddle or lift your foot as high as the stirrup."

"But shouldn't I learn how to do so?" She asked as Augustus hoisted himself up behind her.

He reached his arms around both sides of her, collecting the reins from the pommel and adjusted his own seat until her bum was nestled in his groin, likely to be hell on earth, but necessary for an easier ride.

"'Tis nae anything to learn, lass, as I imagine you've climbed atop plenty of mares." He thought this might be true, being that she was raised in a noble family. "'Tis only a matter of size and ye are simply too petite."

He glanced around, noting that all appeared ready and lifted his hand, twirling his finger around until Geddy's voice could be heard, his deep tone ringing out. "Forward march! Keep those ranks tight!"

At the head of the vanguard, Kael called out his customary, "Aaa-oooh! Off we go!"

In flawless formation, they marched with purpose, their shields, swords, and helms gleaming in the late day sun. The rhythmic sound of shoed hooves striking the earth echoed across the glen while a gentle breeze and their growing speed waved the MacKenzie banners at the front of the line.

Sorcha sat stiffly before him, her spine straight and her chin raised.

"Nae, lass," Augustus said after only half a mile, "dinna tense your body. Ye'll ache for hours afterward."

"I'm nervous," she said and did not relax her form.

"Ye still wonder if my designs are nefarious?" He asked, a bit of an edge to his voice. Aye, he was often impatient, sometimes fierce, and was renowned for his quick temper, but he was certain he'd given her no reason to have so low an opinion of him, or such high expectations that he would dishonor or harm her.

Without answering him directly, she said, "I'm worried about Grimm and his circumstance and I'm sorry that I didn't take more time to secure the home apiary by inspecting the skeps more thoroughly or reinforcing the hackles."

Relieved a wee bit by this confession, Augustus said, "I ken the bees have been around for thousands of years, lass. I surmise they might manage to hang on for a few days while you're gone."

"Will it truly only be a few days?"

"Actually, nae," he was sorry to tell her, to have misspoken. "A few days it will be simply to reach the location where we will meet the king."

Her shoulders sank a bit, and Augustus said no more, supposing that her drooped figure at least meant that her body was less rigid.

He said no more, how the battle and aftermath might last more days, or that their might be a continuation of battle if the initial fight were reckoned a draw, and he didn't remind her that they would then need several more for the return trip to Caol. And certainly he didn't mention that once reunited with Wycliffe, and under his protection, she and the baron might make their own decisions and their own path.

Eventually they climbed out of the valley, riding over the smallest beinn of an extensive range of tall hills. On the other side was the loch, shimmering under the sun dropping lower in a cloudless sky. From the vantage point of the top of the hill there was no sign of de Montfort's army and Augustus gnashed his teeth in exasperation. He neither desired to wait overlong for the earl to arrive at his leisure nor was he willing presently to consider what it would mean, and what retaliation would be required, if Lord Aldric failed to show entirely, thereby proving his lack of allegiance to Robert Bruce.

They slowed their pace on the descent, with several lads putting hands on the sides of wagons to prevent them from rolling carelessly downhill. The degree of the slope meant that Sorcha was forced to lean backward, likely imbued with a sense that she would pitch forward over the destrier's head otherwise. Augustus fitted the reins into one hand and wrapped the other around her midsection, mindful that there might live a bruise there.

Five minutes later, the last of the MacKenzie army had just reached level ground when came a thundering of horses along the trail on the east side of the loch.

Frankly, Augustus was riddled with a wee shock, hardly having believed de Montfort would show.

Breaking formation, Augustus urged his steed forward, ahead of the vanguard. Geddy and several other unit commanders followed suit, riding beside or just behind Augustus and Sorcha.

While the sight of the earl's complete numbers was impressive—Augustus frequently longed to have so many men under his command, an army of three hundred or more—De Montfort looked no more comfortable in the saddle this afternoon than he had this morning. He was a paunchy ghoul in a soldier's costume, no more fit for battle than his lady wife. Sitting upon a fine charger, wearing an elaborately decorated helm, outfitted in a bright green tabard and armor off which the sun glinted sharply, Lord Aldric looked entirely out of place, even as his retainers were similarly adorned in garish colors and armor that was likewise too shiny. One might guess the de Montfort soldiers spent the majority of their time polishing armor rather than training; clearly none of this metal had ever seen the harsh action of a battle.

With some attempt to convey his superiority, de Montfort reined in first so that Augustus and his army were compelled to ride further and arrive at him, rather than two men and their armies meeting mutually. This scarcely rankled Augustus, who was too entertained by the shock of Lord Aldric's gaze as they drew near, when the earl realized the presence of Sorcha upon the same horse as Augustus.

There could be no question now, who sponsored Sorcha's protection.

"What is this?" De Montfort challenged in a huff even before Augustus had halted his steed. "What is the beekeeper doing here? With ye?"

"I was knighted by Willam Wallace, my lord," Augustus said matter-of-factly. "He bid me pledge that I would honor my vows to protect all the loyal citizens of Scotland, most especially women and children." He waited for that to sink in before elaborating, "With her guardian imprisoned and his fate unknown at this time, it was decided to be in Sorcha's best interests to nae abide alone. Where better safe than with a knight of Willam Wallace?"

Augustus hadn't reached the advanced age of three and thirty without being able to read people. Lord Aldric's face had frozen with his shock, but there was evidence of a larger irritation, which advised Augustus that possibly the MacKenzies had now foiled some nefarious plot of the earl. The man was clearly peeved to realize that she would not be alone and vulnerable, left behind in her tiny cottage in Caol.

Regaining a bit of composure, the earl snarled disdainfully at Augustus, "Ye bring her to war?"

"I take her away from Caol," Augustus refined. "And she will be a ward of the MacKenzies and dinna fear that ye would be expected to concern yourself with her welfare as we march."

Having encountered the stone wall of Augustus's resolve, Lord Aldric turned his attention to Sorcha, leveling her with an exasperated glower, one that lengthened his long face and scorned this very unorthodox arrangement.

"And ye—what are ye thinking, lass? Ye imagine yourself safe with him, a man of war, and whom ye only just met, and nae securely ensconced in yer own home?"

"With Grimm's unjust imprisonment, I trust this man's word, that I am safer with him."

Augustus knew a certain level of pride at her strong voice and tart opinion. Geddy had the right of it—spitfire indeed.

"We've many miles to cover and little time to reach our destination," Augustus observed. "I suggest we leave off with any remaining pleasantries and make our start."

Twenty or more feet separated Augustus from de Montfort and yet he still was aware of the earl's low growl.

Lifting his face until only one saggy and crepey chin was visible, de Montfort proclaimed imperiously, "My own vanguard will take the lead, sir. Nae doubt few would argue my superior rank or that my army is more disciplined, nae to mention far greater in number." He speech as usual could be likened to the growl of an angry dog, each word snapping out with a sharp, biting edge. "My captain—nae yers—will march at the head."

"By all means, my lord," Augustus readily agreed.

Another few minutes passed, in which time the de Montfort militia moved with some disarray and shoving of horse rumps until they were finally positioned in front of the MacKenzie force.

"Why do you not challenge him when he speaks like that?" Sorcha quietly asked Augustus.

"There are greater battles to fight, lass. Nae need to expend energy where it is nae deserved. We're all going to the same place. Dinna matter if I arrive at the head of the line or nae."

When finally it was time for them to move, Augustus's army kept their formation as they fell in behind de Montfort's walking and riding troops.

"Is that true, that ye trust me?" Augustus queried after a while.

"Given that I scarcely have another choice," Sorcha answered promptly, turning her face toward the side. "I suppose I must."

"I will interpret that as an 'aye.'"

"Naturally, I supposed you might."

They rode for several miles in silence then, conversation difficult to have while they maintained a bruising pace. Augustus was easily able to keep track of Lord Aldric, his attention drawn to the distinctive helm with its comically tall crown and protruding swan's feather. Plenty of noble commanders he'd met that he did not like, some that he outright distrusted, such as de Montfort, but he'd fought alongside them, personal grievances set aside while the fight was on. He wasn't sure he would be willing to fight alongside de Montfort, still suspecting him of duplicity at the most and spinelessness in the least. And still, he was pleased to bring to the king and to the battle with Pembroke and army more than twice what Robert Bruce was expecting. 'Twas unlikely King Robert would long endure de Montfort's faults, whatever they were in whole or in part. Less likely, the probability that the king would allow any man to act the coward in his presence.

They rode for many miles for nearly two hours when they came upon Ashgill's Pass, a narrow trail nestled between towering crags. The path was so constricted that they could only proceed three or four abreast, creating a tense atmosphere typical of such confined spaces. Augustus's gaze darted about, ensuring the movements of de Montfort's vanguard, scanning the looming cliffs overhead, and keeping a watchful eye on the treacherous terrain underfoot, made all of jagged rock. The shadows cast by the surrounding mountains seemed to deepen the crevice, adding to the sense of foreboding that permeated the air.

Though he was distrustful of Lord Aldric, scarcely did he entertain any notion that the man would brazenly attack the MacKenzies *while* they marched. In a thousand years, Augustus would have imagined the earl too cowardly to even attempt a fight of any sort. True, their numbers were vastly superior to that of the MacKenzie force, but still and always, even the slightest of skirmishes could result in many casualties.

And yet from high above, small pebbles began to fall, followed almost immediately by larger rocks and small boulders. Transferring the reins to one hand, Augustus freed his targe and lifted it above his head, shielding both him and Sorcha from the onslaught of descending stones.

"Bluidy hell!" Geddy groused nearby.

A guttural scream was heard from somewhere ahead, possibly in the MacKenzie vanguard, and Augustus realized a brawl was underway. Sorcha shrunk in front of him, keeping herself low, her back pressed into his middle.

"About! About!" Augustus shouted, recognizing the trap that had been laid for them.

The men all around him began to turn at Augustus's command, and a bit of chaos ensued for the trouble wrought by the narrow confines. Horses whinnied and shields bumped. Randolph, the tanner's son, fell from his steed when clubbed by a falling boulder. He was pulled onto the horse of another. After a slight scramble, the MacKenzies faced north and began to evacuate the crevice.

Sorcha cried out when a falling rock glanced off the inside wall of the crag, shattering, sending out a spray of shale, some of which sprayed against her cheek.

Somehow, furiously, Augustus was not surprised to see that rearguard was already engaged, with de Montfort's men, in all probability men held back, to come up behind as part of the ambush.

"Hold the targe!" Augustus commanded Sorcha, needing his hands free to battle those closest and maneuver his destrier out of the melee. "Cover yourself!"

He used his newly freed hand to draw his sword, knowing he would be better served avoiding any combat, since Sorcha was in such a vulnerable position. Better it would have been to have her behind him, but no time would be allowed to make this change.

"Clear a path!" Geddy commanded his men. "Clear a path for yer laird!"

And so they did, allowing Augustus and Sorcha to pass nearly to the end of the constricted pass before he was forced to use his sword, taking off the arm of a man in a green tabard.

Dozens of men fought in front of him, backing up the enemy with the ferocity of their fight and pursuit. Sadly, while the formidable prowess and efficiency of the MacKenzies played to their advantage, the simple matter of numbers worked against them. There were simply too many de Montfort men. The fight was lost before it had begun.

"Pull back!" He roared above the sounds of clashing steel and anguished cries. "Disperse! Disperse!"

They needed to clear the passage so that those trapped previously ahead—but now behind since they'd turned about—would have an escape.

"Get her out of here!" Griffyn roared nearby. "We'll hold them off ere we run!"

It was the only choice he had. He simply could not fight efficiently with Sorcha in front of him.

He kicked the sides of his destrier, needing him to go from that a standstill to blazing speed if they stood any chance of survival.

Very soon it became clear, with so many de Montfort soldiers in pursuit that he and possibly Sorcha were particular targets. Imagining it was pre-arranged and because de Montfort hadn't known until they'd met that Sorcha would be with him, Augustus didn't imagine the assault was made solely to kidnap the lass.

Geddy's voice sounded very far away but strong and hot-blooded when he ordered, "To yer laird! To yer laird!"

At the same time, Augustus realized that they would not be allowed to ride straight and free, but instead he would be forced to fight his way clear.

His destrier was a weapon in its own right, often as deadly as his sword, crushing one de Montfort man beneath his hooves as they escaped.

A soldier discharged his spear in the direction of Augustus and Sorcha, but his hasty aim and the speed at which they were moving sent the shot wide of the mark, the lobbed spear impaled upon the earth, its end wobbling as it went no further.

THE REBEL OF LOCHABER FOREST

While Sorcha now gripped the shield at her chest, Augustus managed the reins in one hand and his sword with the other. When another assailant was almost abreast of them, Augustus stabbed his sword with mighty force and the de Montfort man threw up his hands toward the hole in his neck and toppled over, falling from his charger.

The sword thrust of the next man did no fatal harm, Augustus causing his destrier to rear so that the man's intended aim was put off. Augustus's sword arm came down with his destrier's front hooves, the blade striking the man's shoulder with such force that it nearly cleaved his arm completely from his body.

Soon, however, they were surrounded by four or more sleek chargers, seated by crazed men wanting to be the one who felled the Rebel. Augustus used his larger destrier as a battering ram, ploughing through the throng. A blade swiped at his back but only grazed his quilted gambeson, the blade rejected by the metal plates that reinforced the vest. Another glanced off his arm and sliced his skin, but not deeply. Augustus wielded his sword deftly, unleashing a fierce counterattack, keeping his war horse constantly moving so that no blow found its mark. With swift and decisive blows, he dispatched one and then another. He kept swinging, blood pounding in his ears, and at the same time channeled the raw power of his destrier, charging forward, driving a path through the encircling but dwindling enemy horsemen with relentless force.

Yet, while he fought his way out of that tight melee, more de Montforts surged in front of them to await their coming. Augustus eyed with purpose the forest just beyond them.

His gallant destrier, long beloved and adept in battle, was no match for the overwhelming numbers coming up against him.

It was only a matter of time before one of the adversaries decided to strike at the steed instead of the man. When came the blow, it was ably tossed from that group that blocked any advance into the forest, so that the lance struck the destrier directly in his broad chest. Another pierced his flanks beyond Augustus's right thigh. With the spear swaying jerkily left and right, struck into the thick flesh of the horse's chest, 'twas inevitable that he would collapse. Augustus urged him forward, wanting to at least gain the trees. "Go, boy! Get on!" He did but only for another moment, carrying his load for a few fitful leaps before he fell sharply to the earth, hurling his riders over his head, some half dozen feet short of the pine-strewn forest.

Augustus did not land fully atop Sorcha. Her smaller figure was tossed further so that when he met the earth, his shoulder collided with only her leg. The soft earth beneath him did no worse injury than to soil his face and garments. Half a second later, Augustus was on his feet, sword yet in hand, and tugging at Sorcha's wrist, hauling her upward.

Help was on the way, the blue plaids of the MacKenzies visible beyond the wall of de Montforts giving chase, but they were not close enough, and Augustus could not take on eight riders coming at him *and* protect Sorcha.

"Run!" He ordered, pulling her along as he did so.

'Twas all that was available to him now as a strategy. To stay and fight would only see them soon surrounded and heavily outnumbered and both of them killed—if they would be so merciful to Sorcha, though he suspected not. The river was close, possibly the falls at Glenwood as well, if his reckoning of their location was correct.

Truth be told, though Sorcha was quick, her smaller stature meant that there was no way she could possibly keep up with the strides of his long flanks, and indeed she slowed them down since he wasn't about to release her hand. He kept on though, keeping to his quickest pace so that he thought she might be flying behind him, her feet barely touching the ground as he yanked her along. Nary a cry or complaint was heard, and her fingers gripped his hand as tightly as he did hers.

His arm burned where the skin had been pierced, the outside of his thigh as well but he recognized that he was fortunate to have no graver injury. He prayed Sorcha had not suffered any other wound but a glancing blow to her arm he'd caught sight of. He forced her to run at his pace, leaping over crevices in the ground and sidestepping trees and heavier brush, ducking under low hanging boughs. His sword swayed up and down with each long step he took. They ran where horses could not, through dense brush and tightly clustered trees, but he thought his pursuers hadn't yet abandoned their chargers nor imagined a tactic that would see them outrace Augustus and Sorcha and be waiting ahead of them.

Soon he became aware, over the pounding of his heart in his ears, of the sound of the river itself and the raucous noise of water gushing over the short falls as they came upon it, running parallel to the river. Switching directions, Augustus jerked Sorcha to the left, little delayed by her stumble for his grip remained strong and his swift speed did not allow her to fall. She regained her feet just as they erupted from the trees, into the light of day, and straight in the path of a racing horse. Augustus crashed into the steed with the underside of his arm, his sword raised and cutting into the man's side. The man howled and bent over, and it wasn't until hours later that Augustus realized he should have pushed the wounded enemy from his charger and taken the horse for himself. Instead, he kept moving, dragging Sorcha under the horse's head and past that quickly-stifled opponent.

Their potential salvation lay in the fact that none of their pursuers were armed with bow and arrow.

Beyond the man and horse, Augustus came to a crashing halt as the earth ended abruptly, and he found himself standing on a precipice a dozen feet over the river. The clomping of others in pursuit spurred him along, to run along the shelf above the river, trying to gauge the depth of the water, wanting to know if a jump from this height would break limbs or worse. He looked for darkened pools where the water was not clear at all, and no bottom could be seen, imagining spots such as those would give them a four-to-six foot cushion of water to break their fall. No such place or opportunity presented itself, and the sounds of pursuit were drawing near so that Augustus paused again, sheathing his sword before dropping to his arse so that his feet hung over the ledge.

"Oh, sweet Jesus," Sorcha whimpered, even as she mechanically scampered down beside him.

"Let go for just a moment when your feet hit the side," he said, and without further ado, he tugged at her hand until her bottom left the ledge. As carefully as he could manage, and using two hands, he lowered her against the side of the crag. She touched nothing but air for one brief moment until her hip bounced against the rock.

"Augustus!" She cried when she felt his hands loosening. "Noooo!"

"Drop and roll!" He shouted as instruction, hoping she managed not to roll off the three foot flat bank of the river at the bottom of the crag and directly into the swiftly moving water.

A body hurtling itself at him forced him to drop her sooner than he'd have liked. Sorcha screamed and a scraping noise and thump followed while Augustus wrestled with the man who'd idiotically leapt from his horse at Augustus rather than striking him with his blade. If it weren't for the folly of a vast number of his enemies over the years, possibly Augustus would long ago have been slain. With half his upper body hanging over the cliff, Augustus managed a tight hold on the smaller man's breastplate, able to hold him close while he pummeled his face repeatedly. When the body above him went limp, Augustus threw him off.

With little thought but that no matter how he got down there he was likely going to bruise himself, he angled his feet out and down and allowed himself to slide limply down the sharp slope of the crag side. He muttered a curse for all the places along his head, back, and thighs that met with the pointed shale. At the bottom, he couldn't stop his forward momentum and tipped over, landing hard on his knees, though he was able to plant his hands to prevent himself from eating a mouthful of dirt.

While on all fours, he paused just a moment to draw a deep and needed breath.

"Augustus," Sorcha said, and he felt her small hand on his back, "they're still coming."

He lifted his hands from the earth just as Sorcha slid her hand under his arm. He arrived on his feet just in time to duck from a lance sent through the air toward his head. Blindly assuring himself that his sword was still attached to his person and keeping half an eye on the goings-on over their head while one of de Montfort's goons raced back and forth on his charger, having no means to subdue or injure the pair below since he'd launched his lance, Augustus perused Sorcha's face and body.

"Ye guid, lass?" He asked, his chest heaving.

She nodded and glanced upward. "But now what?"

"Into the water," he said, "It'll carry us faster than our feet."

Her chest rose and fell drastically as well, her hair shooting out in all directions, her cheek and left hand decorated generously with blood, she somehow managed a shaky smile and breathy laugh. "You are trying to kill me after all," she decided.

Her quip was not misplaced, despite the disaster of the hour. Augustus knew that often, in moments of intense terror or fear, it was not uncommon for people to experience a peculiar reaction, where they might find themselves laughing or making lighthearted remarks. He'd always imagined it was how frightened people coped with fear.

Gravely, he assured her, "Twould be my greatest sin if I did."

Inhaling deeply and exhaling slowly, he lifted his hand, presenting his palm to her.

Without hesitation, Sorcha put her hand in his.

"Dinna let go, nae matter what."

And with that, Augustus led her into the raging river.

Chapter Fourteen

They emerged well downstream, miles and miles it had felt like, broken and battered by the rocks, the falls, and the surging water. Sorcha coughed for a full minute, trying to express all the water she'd taken in. Truth be told, it had been almost comical, floating and spinning past the men of the de Montfort army, whom they'd sailed right by as the original fight had happened so far downstream. There was no man willing or instructed to give chase in the river and so none did.

Sadly, the river widened and deepened after the falls and though they were spared the abuse of the rocks beneath the surface, the depth was more treacherous and several times Sorcha lost contact with Augustus. The last time was the worst, being parted from the security of his strong hand for more than a minute, having to navigate herself. She could not control her progress and found herself a prisoner of the whims of the river. He'd appeared out of nowhere then, near the shoreline with the lowering sun behind him, his head barely visible above the churning water, clinging to the protruding limb of some leafy brush, slapping his hand against hers as the water tried to push her past him, his fingers clamping around her wrist.

Bereft of all strength at that moment, Sorcha had no idea from where he culled his, but he managed to draw her near, at the same time hiking his hand further up the branch until his feet touched the bottom and he was able to stand. Sorcha was dragged the last few feet, her tangled skirts preventing her from finding the bottom itself.

He'd tripped over some root or rock upon the shore and toppled backwards, and Sorcha, having only just gotten to her feet, collapsed with him, falling hard on his chest.

For a long moment, she didn't move, or couldn't move. She went limp on top of him, laying her head against his chest while her legs were entwined with his. She thought she cried but couldn't be sure, her body wrecked, and her mind wracked by a thousand heightened emotions. Augustus dropped his hand heavily on her back and she felt, unreasonably, irrationally safe, and extremely fortunate to be alive.

Too soon, the fullness of her position, draped so intimately over him, prompted her to crawl off him, plopping face down in the sand next to him. Her feet were still lapped by water. On her stomach, she pressed her cheek into the sand, facing away from him, her gaze finding a small cluster of vibrant purple crocus. The deep purple tube flowers held her gaze and somewhere in the back of her mind she recalled her beloved grandmother saying the crocus represented hope, and "better things to come".

"The river became a loch," she said hoarsely after another moment, supposing that would explain why the speed at which the water moved had lessened, and why the shoreline was sandy.

"Aye," he said, as breathless as she. "Becomes Loch Eilde Mor, if I recall."

Hardly could she make a frown come, but she felt it inside, having not understood how close they were to home—her old home, where her family still resided, as far as she knew. She did not divulge this news to Augustus.

"They were after you specifically, were they not?" She asked instead.

"Seems so." After another moment, he said, "We canna stay here, have to keep moving."

Sorcha turned her head around, laying her other cheek in the sand so that she faced him. "Will they come for us, your army?"

"They might, if they survived, or those that did, but there's no way of telling if they even ken where we'd gone. We first ran east but the river took us fairly south."

"When I'm able to move—I'm not suggesting I am at this moment—what do we do?"

"Find cover. 'Tis nae safe to be out in the open. De Montfort canna allow me to live, imagining rightly that I'll take word of his treachery straight to King Robert."

"He is a traitor? That wasn't personal."

"It might well have been personal, but aye, he is a traitor, as we suspected."

"You suspected?" Had she the strength, she might have raised her voice with incredulity. "And you still made those plans with him, essentially invited him to march with you."

"I suspected but was nae sure. I would have been much happier to have been proved wrong."

"And now the king has neither the MacKenzies nor the De Montforts to rise to the challenge of Pembroke?"

He frowned at her, possibly wondering how she knew of their objective.

"I have ears," she told him, her voice still weak. "And Geddy's voice carries."

He closed his eyes and grinned. "Aye, it does."

"Are you more angry over de Montfort's deceit, his attempt to kill you, or that he prevented you from reaching the king?"

"That I will, in all likelihood, nae be able to be at my king's side."

"In all likelihood? Are you even now contemplating how you might still make it in time?"

"Aye, and if we could meet with any others, I would make haste to get to Loudon Hill."

"Do you wonder if...if Angus and those men with him had been with us, would it have made a difference?"

"Sadly, we'd still have been outnumbered two to one."

Another few minutes passed before Augustus sat up, blowing out yet another slow breath.

"I'm not ready to move," she warned him.

"But we must, lass."

With that, all energy and vigor were restored to him. He went easily to his feet while Sorcha barely managed, her body protesting all the way, to roll over onto her back. She contemplated the innocent looking sky, deep blue in the twilight, and wondered why she felt as if the sky should be crowded with storm clouds instead.

Augustus reached down his hand to her.

"Where are we going?" She asked when she was brought to her feet.

Standing before him, she noticed immediately the subtle shift in his demeanor. Normally formidable and proud, it seemed now a weariness weighed heavily upon his shoulders. His usual air of invincibility was tempered by the toll of the last hour, reflected in the fatigue etched upon his features. His usually piercing blue gaze, which gleamed so often with purpose, was dimmed now with a shadowy effect. He remained impossibly handsome; even drenched from their plunge in the river, with his dark hair soaked and tousled and his lashes spiked with water, he retained a rugged attractiveness that was difficult to ignore. And yet the weariness was stark and Sorcha realized that even Augustus Mackenzie, the infamous Rebel of Lochaber Forest, with all his strength, his enviable pride, and his towering presence, was not immune to the vulnerabilities of human frailty.

Lost in this reflection, she blinked when he spoke, trying to focus.

"Ye just reminded me of Angus's unit, and Griff and Finlay with him as well," he said. "We ken the path they'll take. We're naught but ten miles from Caol. If we canna find others, there might still be time to intercept them as they try to catch up."

"So you want me to move yet more?" She asked, quirking a grin, imbued with a sense that she should make him smile.

"Aye, and quickly."

"I don't ever want to travel again with you."

Wearing a scowl that lacked all the menace of his usual frowns, he lifted his hand and gentle as a breeze, brushed the sand from one cheek and then the other. He said nothing.

Sorcha withered in front of him.

"I'm sorry. I should not be flippant, not at all." She laid her hands over his at her cheeks. "Some of your men are dead, I imagine." She wrinkled her nose as tears gathered in her eyes. "Mayhap dozens…I am so sorry, Augustus."

He only nodded an acceptance of this but said nothing, and though his expressions were oft inscrutable, his tightened jaw and the flaring of his nostrils advised that he was not unmoved by the losses.

Pulling his hands away from her face, he laid his hand on the hilt of his sword, his fingers curling around it, as if he drew comfort from its presence. "Let's go."

"But we can't go back the way we came," Sorcha protested. "We're bound to run into de Montfort's men if we do."

"We're on the opposite side of the water now," he reminded her. "And we'll keep to the shadows if they come." He frowned anew and looked her over. "Take off your cloak."

"What?"

"Your cloak. 'Tis too heavy to dry and will prevent your léine and kirtle from drying as well if ye dinna remove it. Either carry it or discard it."

Discard it? "But I haven't another," she lamented. She laid her fingers protectively over the frog closure at her neck.

"And ye'll have nae need of another if this one kills ye," he admonished, "either by slowing us down or by freezing ye, trapping all the cold against yer skin."

"But my gown and kirtle are wet as well," she protested, even as she understood his concern. The cloak *had* nearly drowned her and now, the sodden wool was oppressive for the weight of it.

"And they will dry sooner if nae encumbered by the cloak." He held out his hand. "I'll carry it."

Begrudgingly, Sorcha undid the clasp and removed her cloaked, surprised to realize the full weight of it in her hands and for how much lighter she instantly felt. She handed the cloak to Augustus, who tossed it casually over his shoulder.

"Let's move."

Off they went, walking along the banks of the loch until Augustus stepped off into a path littered with heather and thistle. Walking a few steps behind Augustus, Sorcha turned toward the west, where only a quarter of the sun was visible, beyond the mountains in the distance, it's fading light filtered through a closer woodland of tall pines.

Inside of an hour, they were walking in near complete blackness. Sorcha had no idea how Augustus knew where he was going. If there was a moon, and she didn't regularly pay attention to that orb in the nighttime sky, it was obscured by inky black clouds.

Several times she wanted to say, *Enough*. She could walk no more. Her legs had been as pudding since they'd come from the water. But just as Augustus hoped to find some part of his army, even one man, so too did Sorcha, understanding how defenseless they were, Augustus's prowess in battle notwithstanding.

She revisited the fight, the carnage and chaos, the likes of which she'd not have been able to imagine if given ten lifetimes. In truth, she thought her memory played tricks on her, for the ravages she'd witnessed, for the utter brutality of that ambush. To some degree, because of the life she lived, and the risks she'd taken, she considered herself worldly. Oh, how foolish she had been to think so, to believe that she lived a brave and fearless life. The horror of that fight, Augustus's brutality in particular, advised that she was decidedly more *un*worldly and sheltered than she could have ever imagined. In hindsight, as she thought upon it now, she reckoned that the Rebel, as a caption to his legend, was grossly understated, wholly inadequate to capture the ferocity and ruthlessness he had displayed in that fight.

And try as she might, she could not help but insert Finn into that monstrous melee, wondering for the first time exactly how he'd perished. Her lip quivered as she considered that he might have had his head cleaved from his body, as Augustus had made sure one de Montfort soldier had. Or had he suffered a sword strike to the body and been left for dead, cold and alone upon the bloody ground?

Had he died slowly, thinking of her? The very idea filled her with sorrow and despair. She couldn't bear to imagine him suffering alone, his life slipping away as the sounds of war raged all around him.

A whimper escaped her, she being too weak to hold it back.

Ahead of her, Augustus's shadowy figure turned at the sound.

"I'm sorry," she murmured. "I can't go on." She did, in fact, fear she was about to collapse, and was so far gone into exhaustion and fright that she didn't even care what Augustus thought of this, or that he might now be wishing he'd not insisted she accompany the MacKenzies today. He might consider her a great nuisance or hindrance, but she was simply too drained to care. "I'm done," she said as Augustus turned and approached her.

Though his gaze was unfathomable in the darkness, the blue of his eyes glittered like black stones. When he stood in front of her, he reached out and touched his fingers to the sleeve of her gown before he moved his hand downward, tracing a section of her skirt, plucking it away from her body.

Sorcha watched him silently, her weary heart beating a little faster at his nearness and his touch, though she felt no urge to pull away. In but a moment she realized that he was merely gauging the dampness of her garments.

"I am wet and cold and cannot take another step," she declared dully. True, her léine and kirtle were not so sodden as they had been, but they were by no means fully dry.

"Aye, we can pause here—"

"Pause? No. I want to sleep," she insisted, "for the next twenty-four hours, if you please."

His teeth flashed white in the darkness, which had in the last half hour been lightened a wee bit as the clouds had cleared and a half moon shone overhead.

"I'll give ye several hours, lass, but nae so much as a day," he said, his voice returned to normal, devoid of the weariness that yet plagued her and grew steadily.

He glanced around with a practiced eye, his gaze sweeping over the shadowed landscape.

"This way," he said, taking her hand, leading her in a different direction than where they'd been heading.

The terrain stretched out before them, a patchwork of rugged hills and dense woodland, veiled in the cloak of night. Tall trees loomed overhead as they moved away from the open fields. The faint rustle of leaves and the sound of their soft footsteps were the only sounds heard.

Deep inside a forest of trees, Augustus led her to a clearing that offered both concealment and a measure of protection, having decided upon a spot where an outcropping of tall rock provided a useful wall against the cool breeze that chilled her to her bones. Assuming that walking had at least kept her blood moving, she wondered if she would only be colder for being still.

The rock sat adjacent to an old and massive fir, and a depression in the earth directly below the tree and on one side of the rock was filled with forest debris and protruding roots. Augustus hopped down into the shallow cavity and reached for Sorcha's hand.

"Merciful Lord, there are probably spiders everywhere," she bemoaned as she took his hand and climbed down to stand beside him in the small space.

Politely, Augustus cleared a bit of the debris with his boot, and then with his hands, scooping up handfuls of leaves and tossing them aside.

Sometimes when she was overtired, she did become a little giddy and said tartly now, "Great. Now you've woken them up."

Whether he knew she only jested, he ignored this and suggested, "Ye need to consider removing at least one layer," he said as he plucked her cloak from his shoulder and tossed it aside. "And before ye grouse about that, ken that two layers of damp will nae keep ye warm but likely make ye sick." He didn't stare at her, awaiting a verbal response or even consider her frozen, distressed expression but removed his padded leather breastplate, undoing the buckles blindly and dropping that to the ground as well, out of the way. Next, he pulled his severely disheveled plaid out from his belt and discarded that as well until he wore only his tunic, which hugged his body, hinting at a strongly muscled torso.

As Sorcha watched, and with little shame, he proceeded to lift his tunic over his head, unveiling the chiseled flesh beneath. A line of dark hair rose from his breeches, where they hung low on lean hips, and spread across his broad chest. His taut stomach rippled as he moved. He was a beast of a man, beautiful and virile, and Sorcha swallowed hard at the sight before her. Embarrassment finally burns her cheeks, for her unabashed ogling. But then she squinted into the darkness, her gaze focusing on dark impressions cut across his otherwise perfect form.

She gasped at the sight of what appeared to be a most serious wound. Thus bestirred from merely eyeing his body, Sorcha closed the small space between them and inspected him for other wounds. Augustus lifted his right shoulder and arm to peer down at the deep in his side. There were other cuts as well, but none as severe as the largest, which had sliced open a swath several inches long, but which thankfully was no longer actively bleeding.

Collecting herself, she stammered, "We have to—Augustus, the blood. We have to bind your wounds," she urged, her voice clearer and stronger now.

"Flesh wounds," he advised, brushing aside her concern. "Nae more than that."

"Um, I disagree—I strongly disagree."

"I've nae passed out yet, despite the miles we covered. It can wait until morn."

"No. It can't wait. I won't rest, I won't be able to now, with you bleeding all over the place. My God, Augustus, if you—"

"Hush," he said, weariness finally overriding all else.

More gently, Sorcha proposed, "At least let me bind the most grievous one—that I can see—the one on your side." Unwilling to be deterred, she reached for her cloak and tried to tear strips from it. When she could not, she handed it to Augustus.

"Nae, dinna destroy yer cloak," he argued. "'Tis all ye have, ye said."

"Then my kirtle," she said, lifting the hem of her gown. Beneath, her linen kirtle was yet damp but thinner by some degree than the fabric of her cloak and already threadbare so that she was able to wrench the garment at the hem and tear strips. No one long piece came apart all at once and so she tied several strips together while Augustus stood motionless beside her.

"I don't suppose we could make a fire?" She wondered. "Or no, I guess we haven't the means."

"Nae unless ye can snap yer fingers and produce flames."

"I cannot, more the pity."

When the torn strips had been fashioned into one long length of linen, Sorcha moved closer to Augustus.

"Lift your arms," she beckoned and when he did so, she applied the first end of the linen directly over the ghastly wound and coiled it about him, wrapping her arms around his midsection to find the linen at his back and bring it around. He was very broad, which often brought her chest and cheek into fleeting contact with the fabric of his breeches and the expanse of his abdomen as she endeavored to transfer the linen from one hand to another at his back. His skin was warm and while impressively solid, it was surprisingly soft. Though he smelled of sweat and blood, she did not find the scent offensive, but rather comforted by his sheer masculinity.

"You are quite proficient in this arena," he commented, his voice hoarse now whereas it was not a moment ago.

"Finn was nearly perfect save for an odd habit of not knowing where his body was in relation to the rest of the world," she answered lightly, feeling so much better to have Augustus's injury attended. "He was forever getting scraped and scratched and was once cut deeply by the blade of a plough. I've done this before."

He winced as she secured the linen, making it snug and tying two ends together at his middle, but at his left side and not directly over the wound.

"Nearly perfect, was he?"

"In my eyes, yes," she answered succinctly.

When the task was done, Sorcha straightened and inspected her handiwork, all that she could see in the darkness. Little could she improve upon it until both daylight and better supplies availed themselves to her. Reaching for the tunic he'd set aside, she offered that to him.

"Nae, tis still too wet. I'll be warmer without it. And the same applies to ye. Lose at least one of those layers."

She knew he was right, that without the weight and icy coolness of her long-sleeved léine, she might indeed be warmer. Possibly, the night air, though cool, was warmer than the fabric of her léine. Still, it took her a minute to come to terms with the idea.

Rejecting propriety in favor of her wellness, she stepped back, still inside the depression in the earth and lifted her clinging léine up and over her head. She felt an immediate brush with severe cold and rubbed her now bare arms with her hands.

The Rebel of Lochaber Forest was either immersed in politeness or disinterest, as he paid no attention to her but sat gingerly, not without a wince, with his back against the bottom of the rock, carefully stretching his long legs out before him.

With few other options and none that appealed to her, she sat beside him, leaning back as well, only to jerk forward for the shock of her back touching the cold stone. Drawing her knees up to her chest, she wrapped her arms around her legs and waited to become warm. She was shivering within a minute, but suspected this was due in part to her preoccupation with her body temperature.

A hand, gloriously warm, landed on her bare shoulder. "Sit near me, lass. Ye'll be warmer."

Her lips rolled inward, and she went rigid with shock, contemplating such a thing, nestled against his naked chest. Truth was, if he'd asked without touching her, she would have objected outright, but the heat of his touch, and that found only in one hand, suggested there was a large body of heat nearby, willing to warm her. Without a word though her cheeks were painted with a bright red blush, she scooted closer to him. Apparently it wasn't close enough to suit him; Augustus wrapped his arm around her and drew her closer and she hadn't the will to resist. Not only hadn't she the resolve, but as soon as she realized the heat wafting off him, Sorcha craved his warmth and made the last bit of space between them disappear, scooching as close as she could get. As his arm was up and around her shoulder, she snuggled closely against his chest and closed her eyes.

"This is glorious," she murmured into the hands near her chin.

"Mm," agreed Augustus.

Sorcha pictured him with his eyes closed, the events of the day finally catching up with him.

The distant hoot of an owl echoed in the stillness, punctuating the quiet of the night. The same small wind that chilled her carried with it the earthy scent of damp soil and pine.

The exhaustion that had threatened to make her drop as she walked was suddenly nowhere to be found. Indeed, she was invigorated by Augustus' presence, his warmth, and her own lack of fear. Plenty had she to worry about, but she was most curiously not afraid at this moment.

"I'm sorry about the loss of your horse, Augustus," she said quietly.

He didn't respond immediately and she wondered if he was asleep.

But then his low voice pierced the silence, his words vibrating in his chest against her side.

"I trained him from a foal. He'd been with me for almost seven years—the bravest destrier I'd ever known."

"You will train another?"

"Eventually."

"Do you not fear dying yourself?"

"*Rugadh mi a 'sabaid agus gheibh mi bàs a' sabaid*," he said softly.

The lush quality of the foreign words, delivered in Augustus's rich voice, captivated her.

"My Scots is poor," she admitted.

"Born fighting and I will die fighting," he translated.

She wondered if another had ever been this close, warm in his embrace, and shared nighttime conversation with him. Augustus's voice in the night was a deep, velvety rumble, soothing and lulling Sorcha into a greater sense of calm.

"Were you ever—or are you—wed?" She ventured boldly.

"Long ago, I was," he answered after only a moment's hesitation. "Right bonny lass she was, guid wife."

"Did you love her?"

"I dinna ken. I admired her, being that she was forthright and hard-working and dinna shrink from any duty. Mostly we got on well, but...I never ken a great desire for her when we were parted."

"Where is she now?"

"Buried, deep below Strontian, in the crypts with my sire and màthair."

"Did ye have children with her?"

"Nae, we could nae conceive."

"How did she die?"

"Same as a dozen others, my sire included, when a fever went round the village and keep."

"Did you...do you mourn her?"

"I mourn her for her faithfulness. I dinna ever believe she liked me so well, but she never misspoke about me to another and was a dutiful chatelaine to Strontian."

Sorcha considered how sorrowful it was, that a woman lived and married and managed a stronghold and when she died, it was done. No one carried on her name, manners, or memory.

"I want to have children," she said into the silence. *I want someone to love, and someone to love me; I yearn for the affection of true love,* were her innermost thoughts on the matter.

"Ye are nae beyond a time that ye might," Augustus commented, in what she thought was a careful tone, or carefully chosen words.

She tipped her face up to him, wanting to see his expression, which the darkness would not allow.

Without warning, Augustus dipped his head and captured her lips.

Sorcha sucked in her breath, but a jolting thrill overcame her surprise.

The kiss was slow and tender, possibly all that could be managed after the day they'd had. His mouth moved over hers and Sorcha lifted her hand to stroke it along the stubble on his cheek and jaw. She responded, seeking his lips and tongue with a hunger she'd ignored for too long. Long and languid was his kiss, as if he tried to transfer to her a thousand deep emotions that swirled inside him. Or was that what she was doing? Undeniably, she wanted more, to be completely naked beneath him, to feel him thrusting into the part of her that ached to be filled.

Once again, twas Augustus who broke the kiss.

"Nae," he said, slightly breathless. "I must keep my wits."

Her body, roused so swiftly with hope, deflated against him. She buried her head once more against his chest but couldn't find it within to chastise herself.

And yet, she didn't mind chastising him a bit. "Saying that I wanted children was not meant as an invitation to make them."

His responding chuckle was nearly silent, but it rumbled against her body where she touched him.

"Why have ye nae bairns?" He asked. "Ye and yer man were together for some time, were ye nae?"

"His name was Finn," she told him. Shrugging, she said, "Mayhap I cannot conceive."

Which would make her unsuitable as a mate to almost every man, but certainly to an earl, the chieftain of a large clan. Not that, for one instant, she supposed he was considering her as a wife.

Silence prevailed then, a long stretch of it until Sorcha finally drifted off to sleep.

Before she did, she realized she was both thrilled and horrified by her craving for Augustus's kiss—and so much more. As quickly as had come and gone his kiss, so too did Sorcha's fleeting want of atonement, for how she'd responded—several times now—to this man. She'd been lonely too long, and Augustus stirred something inside her as no one else had since Finn.

Possibly more than Finn ever had, she began to consider.

Immediately she was consumed by guilt, for how her thoughts betrayed her love of Finn.

Some hours later, Sorcha was gently shaken from a sound slumber. Slow was her wakefulness. Initially she was aware only that a warm hand caressed her cheek. Groggily, she laid her hand over the one at her cheek, smiling softly as she opened her eyes.

Her smile dissolved upon finding that it was not Finn stroking her face as she'd sleepily imagined, but Augustus, and that sometime overnight, she'd fallen into his lap and was staring up at him and he down at her.

Augustus saved her any grand mortification, announcing briskly, "Time to go."

She stiffened and sat up, only able to absolve herself of any further betrayal of Finn by knowing that she'd smiled because his touch had been warm and soothing and because she'd believed it had been Finn.

Even as her brain was shrouded with the fog of sleep, and before she managed to rise to her feet, she knew that she lied to herself.

Chapter Fifteen

He was annoyed with himself for all the hours wasted sleeping, hours in which Angus and those MacKenzies with him might have covered many more miles and might now be well south of Augustus and Sorcha. More irritated still, for the weakness proven in him by how many minutes he let slip by while he sat awake but loath to rouse Sorcha, who'd been sleeping so serenely in his lap.

He'd done that, repositioned her so that she was more comfortable. When he'd woken after a few hours of fitful sleep, he'd noticed that her head kept drooping jerkily against him. It would fall and then she would startle and lift it again, every other minute, until Augustus put a wee bit of space between them so that she could, essentially, fall into his lap.

"Five more minutes," she'd murmured then and had promptly fallen back asleep.

Powerless to resist the temptation, he'd stroked his fingers over her silky hair, pushing it away from her face. When all was brushed back, he did not stop running his fingers over her hair and temple.

So aye, their predicament now was the negligible chance of finding any of his army for how much time he'd wasted in that sublime circumstance with Sorcha. Thus, he wore a grim expression while he waited, hands on his hips with a return of his impatience while Sorcha saw to her needs not too far from where they'd slept and where he waited now, still near that large boulder in the forest.

He had little awareness of the hour—another irritation, not having any true idea how long he'd slept—and could only guess by the quality of darkness that it was still several hours before the dawn.

Though she wasn't terribly noisy, he heard her before he saw her, her footfalls disturbing crunchy leaves and cracking at least one twig.

"I feel like I slept but a quarter hour," she said as she approached, garbed again in her léine.

His eyes were well adjusted to the inkiness so that her smile, tired but winning, did not go unnoticed.

"Where to, my lord?"

And just like that, nearly half his fury evaporated.

Mentally shaking himself, he turned and began walking, expecting that she would follow. Once again, her still-damp cloak was tossed over his shoulder.

"I canna be entirely sure of our location," he admitted, "but we kept along the river for quite a distance, and if I surmise correctly our general location, I expect we might be near to a guid spot to run into some or parts of my army."

"Augustus, shouldn't we—I mean, will we go back to...to where they ambushed us? Should we check for survivors?"

Several things about her very careful query intrigued him. First, in all probability, he would never grow accustomed to his name being said by her tongue—and he was fine with that. There was a certain intimacy in the way she said his name—in the very fact that she used his Christian name—that transcended the more formal titles of *sir* or *my lord*. In his mind, it signified a level of trust and comfort that went beyond their roles and position and their circumstance.

Next, he was a wee bemused by her use of *us*, referring to de Montfort's ambush. The use of the collective further indicated a connection between them that felt genuine and personal. He was hard pressed to take issue with either of these points.

"We will, lass," he stated, "but we could nae have returned yesterday, so soon after the rout, would've been too dangerous. And we canna go alone, just ye and I—again, it simply is nae safe."

"Where are we that you believe we might happen upon other MacKenzies?"

"There are plenty of the old roman roads, snaking up from the Lallans," he explained, "but we dinna keep with them even though this is nae so far south. So the lads will ken to search out the nearest trails and roadways used more frequently by friendly locals. Because we move often across the region, we've grown familiar with where these roads might be. If I'm right, we're in or near to Balquhidder and Loch Voil, and there's a well-maintained path that abuts against a barren field. Stone wall, covered in moss, small church and cemetery, the spire is painted—"

"Saffron yellow," Sorcha finished.

Augustus came to a halt and turned on her, awaiting an explanation for how she might know this. "Aye, saffron yellow. And why is that?"

Sorcha stopped as well when she came abreast of him. Swallowing what might be dread, though he couldn't be sure, she answered, "They wanted God to see them, amid all the green and brown on earth and the black hearts of sinners."

His jaw didn't drop but only because he caught himself.

"If you're right about that," Sorcha said, "where we are, I, um...I believe we're fairly close to my father's house."

He had questions, plenty of them, most pressing about the *black hearts of sinners.*

"My father's house sits on the Balvag River," she said. "A thousand acres has he."

"Yer father's house? Nae yours?"

She shook her head but gave no explanation for the curious distinction.

He was cautious with his response, saying mildly as to give no offense, "Ye dinna go far from home."

"No. I'm not so brave after all."

"Ye are though," he claimed, "remarkably so."

"It's easy to show little fear with...well, with someone of your stature and experience."

"I was nae with ye when ye left home," he reminded her, as he'd not only been speaking of her bravery yesterday, where likely she'd witnessed a scene such as she never had before. "I was nae with ye when yer man left nor when ye learned of his demise, nor when ye made yer own way, choosing to remain in Caol by yourself. Ye are brave, with nae help from another, lass."

Sorcha stared at him, her mouth open, a wee bit of wonder creeping into her gaze.

"I am, aren't I?" She asked with a smile.

"Aye," he said, noting how easily grins came in her company. "C'mon, let's find the lads and then ye can decide if ye want or need to pay a visit to yer kin."

"Ooh," she said and made a face that wrinkled her nose. "Unless someone is in dire need of healing—Ballechen has a superb healer—I don't see any reason to go by there."

Which then made it impossible to resist asking, "Would ye happen to be one of those sinners? With the black heart?"

She lifted her chin and nodded, trying very hard, he guessed, to show no shame.

"Ye're nae sinner, lass," he pronounced with no small amount of disgust for whomever told her otherwise, "nae more than I am a saint." He frowned, wanting to attach all the puzzle pieces that made up the image of Sorcha Reid. "Is that why ye ran off with the beekeeper, because they called ye sinner?"

"They called me sinner and I left with Finn for the same reason: because I loved him."

"And ye'll nae go back?"

When Sorcha shook her head, Augustus nodded, signifying an end to his queries for now, satisfied to have been given a few more insights into her character.

They marched again, mostly in silence, over stretches of fallow fields, through dense patches of woodland, and as the sun rose in the east in a red sky, over rolling hills until Augustus unceremoniously clutched at Sorcha's hand and drew her down to the ground, having discerned, he thought, the unmistakable jangle of a harness. They crouched in place before the crest of a knoll while Augustus listened intently, before he carefully lifted himself just enough to see over the ridge.

A hundred yards beyond the bottom of the hill rose a wall of trees and he recognized movement between the boughs. Hope soared as he believed the pathway he sought was just beyond that shallow but lengthy stretch of trees, and who but someone wanting to keep a low profile would avoid the open tracts of land for the safety of the trees?

He didn't realize Sorcha had risen carefully as well until she whispered, "Their plaids are blue. Augustus, those are ours. They're MacKenzies," she declared with some excitement.

She did it again, established a relationship to him and his men, saying *ours* in reference to his army. Later, he thought, he would investigate further why this pleased him so. A fleeting idea spun round his head, wondering if *ours* as opposed to *theirs* or *them* was employed simply as her way of distinguishing between good and bad company.

"Wait," he cautioned, ducking low once more.

Tipping his head upward, he emitted a prolonged whistle, imitating the *tee-cher, tee-cher* chatter of a great tit.

On her haunches at his side, Sorcha watched but did not question his objective.

A half minute passed before they heard a returned call, the short trilling song of the blue tit.

Augustus nodded quickly, with great relief, to Sorcha's animated query of, "Is that them?"

"Aye, let's go."

Still, he rose carefully and held Sorcha yet by the hand, keeping her low as he examined the line of trees. His relief expanded when he saw that indeed, some of the men there were draped in the MacKenzie colors.

He stood fully, bringing Sorcha with him, and together they crested the hillock and descended the other side while the men inside the trees came forward, showing their faces. He hadn't been hoping to see any one person or unit more so than another but knew a slight start to see that it was Angus and his unit, those that had remained behind to free Wycliffe. Narrowing his eyes, he searched the faces but did not see Grimm.

But just as he questioned the disappointment that visited him, Sorcha tugged at her hand and shouted, "Grimm!"

Augustus released her and watched as she sped down the hill, her arms held out to maintain balance as she floated over the thistle, grass, and rock.

He saw him then, the last man to emerge from the fir trees, walking tall and seemingly unhindered by any injury.

As the object of his desire ran toward another man with such unfettered joy, Augustus contemplated Wycliffe through a new lens. He was far enough away yet that his expression could not be observed, and though he stepped forward ahead of the rest of the party, he did not rush out to meet her. And whether or not he would have opened his arms would remain a mystery since, to Augustus's eyes, Sorcha throwing herself at him appeared rather a last minute decision, preceded by a bit of a stumble. Wycliffe did, however, wrap his arms around her and embrace her for several long seconds, in which time her feet were lifted off the ground an entire foot.

Having jogged after Sorcha, Augustus met first with Angus, exchanging a grateful embrace.

"*Jesu*, ye're a sight—believed ye dead, we did," Angus said in his ear.

He exchanged greetings with Griffyn, Finlay, and more than a dozen others, never more pleased to see the men of his army, whole and hearty.

"Aye, ye sprung 'im," Augustus said, referring to Wycliffe. "But how did it go? Suffer much resistance?"

Angus snorted and sneered. "Blackwood, much to my displeasure, was nae where to be found."

"And aye," Griffyn added broodily, "we looked hard for that one."

Before he might have questioned this further, Augustus's attention was drawn to the conversation between Wycliffe and Sorcha, the latter whose feet had since been returned to the ground. Though he'd already spoken to the English baron, apparently it was going to take some time to get used to the foreign sound of his voice.

"I knew she lied—Effie, that is," Sorcha was saying, "and just wait until I see her. I've a mind to—"

"Calm yourself, Sorcha," Wycliffe urged gently. "We cannot but imagine that duress was the source of her accusation."

"Sweet Mother of God, but look at your face, what they've done to you," she went on, her distress clearly not about to be diminished by a simple directive. "But is that it? Are you free? Or will they hunt you all your life?"

"Remains to be seen," Wycliffe acknowledged. "I am under the impression that at this time, De Montfort has more to concern himself with—"

Sorcha gasped, right in the middle of Wycliffe's statement. She smacked at his chest, catching the oaf unprepared so that he did not have time to deflect her slap.

"Oh, but I'm not speaking to you!" She said testily. "Almost a year—a year, sir!—you've been in my company and never not once said a single word to me."

"I could not," Wycliffe defended. "Surely you understand the many reasons that justify my silence."

Crossing her arms over her chest, Sorcha admitted in a small voice, "I would have trusted you, if my role had been yours."

Nonplussed, Wycliffe shrugged helplessly, wincing a bit.

Augustus found it curious that when mute, he'd had so few expressions, showing little emotions but anger and annoyance. Now, with speech, so much more was gleaned in his features.

"Greater matters at hand than the mute now talking," Angus proposed.

"Fine," Sorcha conceded with little grace, and after turning an infuriated glare onto Angus, "but will someone please remind me at some later date to take him to task for his behavior."

"Aye, ma'am," Angus agreed.

Sorcha pointedly turned her back on Wycliffe, by which his amused grin said he was quite entertained. He stepped around her and approached Augustus, extending his hand.

"I have you to thank, sir," Wycliffe said, "and I do, heartily and sincerely. I know you did not need to do what you did."

Augustus took his hand and pumped it several times. "I'm glad it all worked out," he said, leaving out the obvious truth behind the reasons for such an action: *I did it for her*.

Griffyn moved into Augustus's line of sight. "What the bluidy hell happened at the pass?"

Augustus sighed, expecting the entire awful tale would have to be relived in order to be conveyed. "An ambush. And I'll tell ye all about it as we ride, but I want to return to the pass and search for—"

"There are nae survivors," Angus said heatedly, his brow etched with fury. "Naught but bodies and blood. We finished off what de Montforts were still breathing, but—God forgive us—we dinna stay around to bury our own, went right out searching." He shook his head, wrinkling his face in such a way that it was clear they'd stumbled upon no other MacKenzies, or none that were alive.

"That is our first priority," Augustus announced, "recovering as many as we can, alive or nae. Let us go first along the local lanes and pathways. Just as we happened upon each other, so might we meet more of our own. Have ye a steed for me?"

"Four steeds we have, laird," Finlay proudly informed him. "Found them racing back toward Ironwood. That's when we figured something was amiss."

"Verra guid. Angus, take the lead, south first for five miles and then we'll retrace our path, and finish north. Were the wayns left at Ashgill's pass?"

"Gone," Angus said bluntly. "All of them. Or nae trace of them."

"Then we'll need to resupply a bit, assuming several days marching and then for the siege we will lay against Ironwood."

More than one pair of eyes widened at this revelation.

"Lay siege to a bluidy fortress?" Angus challenged. "With naught but twenty of us?"

"We'll find them, Geddy and many more I'm sure," he said confidently, even as he hadn't the heart yet to ask how many MacKenzie bodies they discovered in and around the pass. "And I willna rest until de Montfort pays for this crime."

Angus was unconvinced, of either the prudence of entertaining such a plot to attack Ironwood or that they would, actually, find more of their scattered comrades. He puffed out a breath of disbelief.

"Actually, you might be able to accomplish an effective siege with only these numbers," Richard Wycliffe contributed.

Angus rolled his eyes at this.

But Augustus favored him with a quizzical glance.

He'd hovered outside the group until now, but stepped forward, his size and startling statement drawing all eyes.

"There are tunnels beneath de Montfort's keep," Wycliffe disclosed. "Two of my guards, young lads, were talking outside the door to the dungeon," he explained to everyone's silence and skepticism. "One was bragging to the other, for his knowledge of the tunnels. The second one did not believe him and the lad who insisted they were there, said that he'd stolen into them at times, then proceeded to give way their location. A warren of tunnels, he indicated, winding all around below the keep. One arm even opened up directly under the armory, he said. Outside the wall, he said they exit at some place near a cluster of ancient oak trees. And there I sat, not ten feet away, with the door closed between us but the lad's voice rising in indignation for not being believed. He detailed the entire path of the tunnels and crypts."

"He dinna," breathed Angus in disbelief, at the lad's grievous misstep of giving up such valuable information, even inadvertently.

Griffyn chuckled darkly with satisfaction, amused by the chatty lad's carelessness.

"He did," Wycliffe assured them, grinning a bit himself.

"*Jesu*," Augustus drawled, "but that increases the possibility of success tenfold. All we have to do is get in and open the gate."

Angus pulled his hands off his hips and ticked off on his fingers the order of operations as he understood them. "Riding now, looking for our captain and any others. Resupply, and now to include what's needed to attack Ironwood—what we can accomplish by way of coin available—and then perpetrate an attack. Willna happen in one day, I guarantee ye that."

"And yet it should happen soon," Augustus decided. "We are nae use to King Robert now, too late and too depleted for his battle in a few days' time, but we can slay two birds with one stone by taking out de Montfort: vengeance for his crimes against the MacKenzies and to disrupt any plot he might be hatching against the king. He did nae ambush us merely for personal reasons. He wanted to prevent us from reaching the king and giving aid against Pembroke."

Hands returned to his hips, Angus shook his head. "Christ, de Montfort doubtless soiled his silk breeches—pardon, lass—knowing ye live yet."

"Bring me a steed," Augustus said at length. "Let's get to it."

While young Edwin moved swiftly to obey his laird, Augustus went to Sorcha, reaching down his hand. Though she looked resistant—to him or their plans, he could not say—she laid her hand in his and allowed him to pull her to her feet.

"Ye can rest while we ride," he assured her, but at the briefly disgruntled look she gave him, which suggested that was highly unlikely, he amended, "Ye can relax, at any rate. Safer now, we are."

She was no less exquisite for how weary she appeared, for the dark circles under her eyes and the still-growing colorful bruise aside her sweet mouth, nor for her rumpled hair and garb, but doubly attractive for her resolve, for how she'd coped with tragedy and horror thus far—and then she was twice more appealing for her response.

"Shock and a dreadful fright governed my last twenty-four hours, sir," she quietly told him, "but in hindsight, I cannot say that there was any one moment when I thought my end was near. I expect that will remain true so long as I am with you."

High praise indeed, respecting the fierceness of yesterday's ambush and what at times seemed like their imminent demise, that which was denied by their hard-fought and blessedly earned escape.

Rather than give her any choice or allow another to interfere, Augustus walked Sorcha over to the horse Edwin approached, intending that she ride with him and ready to gainsay any who might have other ideas. 'Twas not a large destrier as he was accustomed to, but a sleek charger built for speed, about which he was not upset.

Though she might well have mounted this steed by herself, as she'd been unable to do when he'd possessed his beloved destrier, Augustus lifted her into the saddle without giving her the option. He mounted behind her and set his arm around her middle, drawing himself closer to her until he was fully seated on the saddle.

Around them, all his men and Wycliffe too climbed atop their steeds and as they began to move, following Angus's lead, Sorcha laid her palm over the back of his hand at her middle and slunk down against him, laying her head against his chest.

A feeling, warm and soothing, enveloped him, for how trusting and at ease she was in his company, in his arms. While it didn't provide a complete respite from the weight of his current burdens, it offered a rare internal peace that had eluded him for many years.

Chapter Sixteen

The wind proved a nuisance, whipping through her hair and disheveling the strands around her face. She tried to gather it all to one side and hold it there, but her efforts were futile against the persistence of the brisk wind. Finally, she drew up the hood of her cloak and pulled it close around her face and knew some relief. She was thankful for the plaid that Augustus had requested for her. Before he'd laid it around her shoulders, she'd had a difficult time imagining that she might ever be warm again.

As did every man in their party, Sorcha tirelessly scanned the horizon, her eyes darting from one direction to another in search of their missing comrades. Over the head of the gray charger, lush green hills rolled on endlessly, presenting a daunting challenge.

Despite her focus on the task at hand, Sorcha couldn't shake the unease that gnawed at her whenever she stole glances at Grimm—dammit, Richard Wycliffe, she needed to keep reminding herself—sometimes riding fairly close to the gray horse. He'd been a constant presence in her life for more than a year, yet now, knowing the truth of his identity and hearing his voice often while they rode, she felt as though she hardly knew him at all. The realization left her feeling unsettled and adrift, questioning the nature of their friendship, and unable to help herself, wondering what other secrets he might be hiding.

Admittedly, he appeared quite natural in the saddle, as well attuned to the steed beneath him as Augustus was. For a while, Grimm rode directly in front of Sorcha and Augustus, and she found herself staring at his wide back and dark hair with fresh eyes, and once more she suffered some distaste for the fact that he'd not trusted her with the astonishing facts of his name and heritage and ability to speak.

Augustus bent his head and his voice whispered close to her ear. "Dinna hold onto anger, lass. He did what was necessary to survive, as ye or any other might have."

She tensed a bit, wondering how Augustus had been able to read her mind, and certainly not enjoying the fact that he could so accurately.

Soon, a stretch of uneven terrain, thick with vegetation, required them to slow, to navigate carefully to avoid accidents. Augustus caught up with Grimm and allowed the horse to proceed at the same speed as Grimm's.

"The lass is worried, Wycliffe, that ye might have suffered irreparably down in that dungeon," Augustus stunned her by saying.

Grimm laid his dark eyes on her, one corner of his mouth quirked. "And why does *the lass* not express this herself?"

"Aye, to that, ye ken she's still nae speaking to ye," Augustus responded.

"I did not say that—and I did not—" she stopped abruptly, deciding she might not be speaking to Augustus either right now! How dare he!

Encouraging Augustus's foolishness, Grimm said, "You may tell the lass that I suffered no lasting effects. I daresay if Lord Aldric hadn't been occupied by other concerns, those which you brought to him, my lord, he might have found time to harass his prisoner."

"I will let her know," Augustus stated.

Sorcha knew for certain now he was making fun of her. If she did not need to hang onto Augustus and the pommel to steady her seat, she'd have crossed her arms over her chest in crossness. As it was, she murmured petulantly, "It pleases me so much that the two of you find such humor in the whole affair."

In truth, she was undeniably unnerved by how different Grimm was behaving. He was not the same man she knew, she decided, but seemed instead so much less drowned by torture. Or had she only imagined that, his bouts with melancholy and the greater anguish?

She rationalized that in all likelihood, being able to finally speak and because of recent events that nearly saw him in dire straits, he might have been stirred to life, to this...normal person. Sadly, she did not know this man. Sorcha was certain that the minute he spoke, she'd lost her friend. Her sadness over this was nearly shattering.

Biting her lip, she wrestled with a question burning inside her, which was pitted against her serious desire to not speak to him, her childish attempt to punish him for hurting her.

Curiosity won out over annoyance.

"Was there...was there ever a time when you really struggled *not* to speak?" She guessed she might have gone batty if she ever found herself bereft of her voice.

He did not answer, which drew her gaze to him as he rode beside her and Augustus. He might have been waiting for her attention, because he did finally answer when she met his eyes, the intensity of his dark eyes as telling as his words.

"Every day, Sorcha. The fight to remain silent was a constant battle."

Though he faced the path ahead of them once the words had been spoken, Sorcha stared at him a moment longer.

He wasn't so very different from Augustus in one regard—possibly many, but only one that she could detect thus far: he used his face and mouth to great effect, able to utter volumes without speaking a word.

While they were still proceeding slowly, Grimm turned and looked at Augustus, saying cryptically, "The unholy carnage of Lord Aldric's ambush, while horrific, might have roused a purpose within me. The screaming voices now shout for justice."

Sorcha could only guess at what he meant, but Augustus's prompt reply suggested he knew for sure.

"And yet ye're still English," Augustus reminded him.

Grimm shook his head. "I'm a man who abhors all things unnatural and ruinous, deceit and treachery, the greed behind war, frivolous deaths."

"Will you fight for right? With the MacKenzies?"

"I will abide for a while," Grimm declared, "until de Montfort gets his due."

"Verra well," said Augustus, "and dinna mind if we put ye to guid use."

"Little choice you have," Grimm commented. "At this point, I wouldn't bet against ye taking up beggars, lepers, and old women."

"If they can fight—if they possess fury enough about those who practice such villainy: deceit, treachery, mayhem wrought by greed—I'd put a sword in their hands, too."

Sorcha lent only half an ear as their conversation continued, having instead latched onto Grimm's intention to remain only so long as it took to lay siege to Ironwood.

Grimm would leave. Not once since she'd known him had she entertained any thought or idea that he might. While she didn't give much thought to the future, save for things related to her bees and her own needs—weather, her plans to grow her hives, when she might next eat—she'd not ever considered that one day Grimm would walk out of her life.

He couldn't stay in Caol, no matter the outcome of Augustus's plot for revenge against Lord Aldric. He was an accused rapist, and whether or not the accusation was disproven, he would not find welcome in Caol. Or rather, would find demonstrably less welcome than he'd known so far.

She wasn't brave enough presently to ask him if he'd been planning for some time his departure.

Her entire life had changed in an instant, gone up in smoke, she realized; nothing would or could ever be the same. *And what will I do?* She wondered.

"I sense a disturbance in ye," Augustus said at length, when Grimm had moved forward and paced himself with Angus.

"I haven't said a word in five minutes," she defended, still agitated by so many things out of her control.

"I can feel it in ye. Ye tense or slouch depending on yer thoughts. And what has ye so dispirited now?"

She debated only a moment before revealing, "My life...everything is different now, in ruins."

"Was it nae ruined when ye left home? Was it nae devastated when ye got word yer man had fallen in battle?"

"My life improved dramatically when I left home," she countered easily. "But yes, when I learned about Finn, when the notice came to Caol with all the names of the men lost to war, I felt as if all the life had been sucked out of me. So, aye, I'm rather peeved about having another upset. It isn't fair. Haven't I endured enough? What more tragedy awaits?"

"Ye believe these things are measurable," he asked mildly, "and everyone must suffer their fair share of grief and pain and tragedy, but no more than that?"

"I have no idea how it works. I'm simply saying I've had enough."

"And yet ye will endure, as ye have. And aye, more heartache might arrive at yer doorstep and ye'll endure that as well."

"Over and over until I die, is what yer saying?" She asked tartly, unmoved by his stoicism.

"Ye sing yer mournful song and I ken that's ye, living in the past, lamenting the loss of that life and that man, but lass, it dinna really open the door for anything but more grief to come yer way."

"A very philosophical rebel you are," she sneered, unwilling to be admonished by this man, the Rebel.

"Ye ken I speak true, that living in the past is nae really living."

"It's a little difficult to embrace what's come to my door now, sir."

"'Tis nae the end, mayhap nae anything changes, but if ye dinna see opportunity in what has—"

"You say all that to remind me—annoyingly so—that I must think positively."

"Aye, ye can boil it down to that. At the verra least, lass, embrace what comes lest ye perish—in body or spirit—for trying to avoid it."

"Embrace...what?" she asked.

"Ye might be pleased that Wycliffe *can* speak, and that he finally did," Augustus suggested. "Ye might ken you've got youth and beauty yet on yer side—"

She snorted at this. What good had that done her?

"—ye might be grateful ye were nae on the receiving end of any blade."

She conceded that point internally, knowing she had only Augustus to thank for that. She was grateful for him, for more than only that, for what he'd done for Grimm as well.

"You might consider that what occurred in Caol—losing your hives to the storm, enduring the townsfolk's mistreatment, and learning for certain of de Montfort's treachery—could be a sign to make a fresh start in a new location."

Of course, it was possible that he was right. But she didn't much feel like admitting it. And frankly, did he—a powerful man with resources, who likely had never not once in his life ever been the victim—have any idea how difficult that was for a lone woman to accomplish?

She wanted the conversation done. She didn't want to discuss this with Augustus, who seemed to have an answer for everything. She much preferred him brooding and terse.

"Can you not simply let me wallow for a while?" She asked. "Without chirping in my ear that every problem has a solution? Can't I just be morose for a wee bit?"

He chuckled, which subdued a bit of her irritation, the rich sound having such an effect on her.

"Aye, I can do that, lass."

Sorcha folded into herself. Despite the flippancy she projected, she was in fact reluctant to exhibit any more of that deplorable melancholy and woe. She truly abhorred when she allowed herself to be brought so low. And yet, *Embrace what comes lest ye perish?* Hmph.

She gave a start and clutched instinctively at Augustus's hand around her waist when he drew hard on the reins. Someone's mount close behind them snorted his displeasure, likely having been stopped abruptly as well.

"Look," Augustus said, directing gazes to the berm beyond a narrow and meandering stream, more than thirty yards away. "Riders."

The raised bank was shrouded in tall brush and the occasional birch tree, but scores of shoulders and heads were visible above the tallest vegetation.

The entire party halted, waiting. Upon these endless, undulating knolls, their party could not go unnoticed.

Though it was not yet possible to identify faces, one horse and rider turned toward them, breaking through the brush to stand just beyond the stream.

A loud and familiar voice echoed across the glen. "Bluidy lost sheep! Where the hell ye been?"

"*Jesu*! The auld bastard!" Angus said, chortling either at Geddy's shout or the very fact that the captain of the MacKenzies had survived. "'Ow many times 'ave I said: the auld man canna be kilt!"

Several whoops and hollers sounded out, coming from both groups, all of them filled with cheer. Sorcha gasped with delight at the sheer number of men that emerged from what appeared to be a hedgerow of brush, so many more than she would have ever guessed able to have survived Lord Aldric's ambush.

Little did she know these MacKenzie men in truth, save for Augustus who was still an enigma to her, but she found herself roused from her melancholy and smiling as both parties began to race toward one another.

"Yah," Augustus urged his steed, a lightness detected in his tone.

As they came together, none dismounted, but allowed horses to converge, fusing deeply into the other group as men on both sides celebrated their rediscovered comrades. Augustus and Geddy rode straight at each other, the first to meet, and clasped forearms and held on for many seconds.

"*Jesu*, and ye've got the lass and the oaf, too!" Geddy exclaimed, even as he kept his gaze on Augustus, the much younger laird. "I kent ye were dead, believed I'd come across yer quarters, strewn about Caol when I went back to slay de Montfort."

Sorcha blanched at the image imagined from Geddy's words. The *auld man*, as Angus had called him, appeared much as his laird did, unkempt and covered in stains of blood and cuts to his breastplate and breeches, and still he managed to convey a robust figure, broad and strong, wholly indestructible.

"I kent ye dead as well," Augustus remarked. "Could nae imagine an outlet for ye, either going forward or back out of the pass."

"Was on yer tail, fighting right behind ye," Geddy informed him, "but as ye rode straight away from the pass, I went right, taking on a guid following. Our destriers were nae ever goin' to outrun their coursers, but aye, pulling them all apart, separating them as we did, at the front and the back, was the key. We were naught but fish in a pool waiting to be speared inside the crevice. Outside of that, I ken we could handle them, two or three at a time, each of us." He turned his attention to Sorcha, winking at her. "Death's been knocking for years at my door, lass. I just tell 'im I'm nae at home."

Her smile returned at this proud witticism and Sorcha said, with great sincerity, "A wise decision, sir, for which we are all thankful."

He accepted this, a broad grin creasing his craggy features. The smile faded, however, as quickly as it came.

"Och, but those gone, Aug," he lamented, and began to list the names of those who hadn't survived. "Colin, Daffy, the lad Eagan, Brodie, Niamh the fisher, Finnigan the weaver's son, Colle the wheelwright—*Jesu*, too many and how will we make de Montfort pay?"

To have names put to the dead nearly broke her heart. She hadn't been introduced to but a few of Augustus's men of course, save for Colin, who had once responded to Augustus's call and had come running, his bright red hair flopping about his head, his expression eager.

Augustus's hands tightened on the reins and around her middle at the mention of specific names, and her heart ached for the sorrow that surely dwelt in him, having led his men into that ambush.

"We aim to supply ourselves hereabouts," Augustus answered, "and march straight away for Ironwood. Wycliffe has tossed us a boon, as he'd heard mention of tunnels beneath the keep that open up outside the curtain wall. In we'll go and we'll nae depart until I've severed de Montfort's head from his body."

Geddy nodded enthusiastically. "And aye, will we nae rest easier when his head's rolling on the floor." He glanced around a bit, beyond the combined reunited army, which by now had settled down—many were close and silent, attending this conversation—and squinted along the western horizon. "Seems I recall this area and nearby sits a burgh or market town."

"Aye, we kent the same," agreed Augustus. "Angus believes it's just there," he said, pointing toward a wall of trees, "beyond the forest."

Indecision gnawed at Sorcha, for what she knew that they were only guessing at. She swallowed thickly and announced, "Tis Gylmyne, and it's actually there," she said, pointing a bit east of where Augustus had indicated.

Several curious gazes were aimed her way.

"And if it's Tuesday—I believe it is—then the market is taking place," she added, and then held her breath, praying that no one questioned her knowledge of this.

Though one of Geddy's brows was raised in conjecture, he did not put forth the obvious query.

"To Gylmyne it is," Augustus called out, his words felt along her back.

As Augustus wheeled the horse forward, Sorcha heard Angus caution Grimm somewhere behind them, "And best keep yer Englishness to yerself inside the burgh."

The forest was naught more than half a mile wide, and not more than a quarter hour was needed to pass through the trees. Beyond that, the pathing leading into Gylmyne twisted and turned through verdant fields and a sparse wooded vale. Sorcha's gaze swept over the outline of Gylmyne as it gradually came into view, stone and timber buildings rising against a backdrop of white-capped beinns. The bustle of market day was evident even from afar, with colorful stalls and bustling crowds dotting the landscape.

As they neared, Sorcha considered the scene with a mix of familiarity and dread, but not with any nostalgia for the place she had eagerly left behind.

Stalls lined the cobbled street, displaying an array of goods and wares, including fresh cut meats, handmade leather bits, and plenty of baked goods. Vibrant colors and lively chatter saturated High Street. The air was filled with the aroma of savory meats, baked bread, and fragrant spices. Market vendors called out to passersby, enticing them to visit their stalls. Memories of her childhood were stirred, but they were memories she had long since buried.

Fairly quickly, as the long line of MacKenzie soldiers made their way, two by two, down High Street, there was a noticeable shift in the atmosphere. The lively chatter and laughter of market day faltered as they passed, replaced by hushed whispers and wary glances. Townsfolk and vendors alike paused in their activities, their expressions guarded, as they watched the unfamiliar sight of armed soldiers marching along their street. The tension could not be ignored, and Sorcha felt it down to her bones. Unconsciously, she buried herself a bit more in the MacKenzie cloak.

Neither Augustus nor any of his army seemed unnerved by either the attention or the wariness aimed at them.

"Let's find the livery," Augustus said mildly, "and sell these extra steeds."

At the center of the town square stood the mercat cross, a stone pillar adorned with intricate carvings, where merchants paid their toll. The mercat cross was also the site where the herald called out news, where public rejoicings and lesser punishments were announced and performed. Executions as punishment, though rare in Gylmyne, took place outside of town, upon the hillock known as Scourge Hill.

The initial hush that fell upon Gylmyne with the arrival of the MacKenzies was short-lived. It wasn't long before the vibrant clamor of the market resumed, reassured by the absence of any ominous intent from the passing soldiers.

The livery was at the far end of the market and knew its own commotion for all the horses ridden to town and kept here. Augustus reined in amid a sea of horses, his eyes scanning the scene. The soldiers were given leave by Geddy to do as they pleased within the market, with the warning, "And dinna make me regret letting ye loose!"

Augustus dismounted leisurely, keeping one hand on the reins, his fist on the part of the saddle he'd vacated.

"Ye might wish to stretch yer legs, "he guessed, "but I dinna suggest ye gambol about while I see to some business, unless Wycliffe would escort ye."

Sorcha shook her head, silently bemoaning the loss of his warmth at her back and having no desire to get about the market. "I'll wait here."

He narrowed his eyes broodingly at her but said nothing before handing the reins to her. "I'll nae be long."

She idled away the minutes taking in the active scene all around her, so different from the persistent dullness of Caol. Despite the activity around her, Sorcha felt a distinct sense of detachment from the town and its people. Gylmyne may have looked familiar, but it held no warmth or comfort for her.

As Sorcha's gaze swept over the crowd, her heart skipped a beat, aghast to discover among the throngs of people, her own mother and sister. Stricken by this discovery, she stared unabashedly at the pair, who were arm in arm as they considered the wares offered in a booth directly across the cobbled street from the livery.

Unconsciously, her hands tightened on the reins.

While her mother appeared to have changed not at all, was still that austere figure with a perennially severe expression and adorned in her customary pious wimple, her younger sister, Gelis, who would be almost seventeen now, had grown significantly. How beautiful she was, with her white-blonde hair and delicate features. A softness melted Sorcha's heart, recalling Gelis's sweet voice and her generous spirit. She knew a bit of shame, for having abandoned Gelis and brother to her parents' overbearing and oft harsh household. Though it was possible that what was true then remained so now: it had always and only been Sorcha who'd borne the brunt of their disapproval, displeasure, and recrimination.

Her father, Gospatric Reid, was a tyrant inside his home, pompous and domineering, deeply devoted to the Church, and all too eager to administer punishment to any who broke the laws of God. Her mother, Bessetta, despite the stern façade, was as meek and timid as her husband was loud and brutal. Long ago Sorcha had known a great sympathy for her mother, being married to such a militant tormentor, but as she grew into adulthood, she began to understand that her mother was relieved, almost pleased, when Sorcha had begun to bear the brunt of Gospatric Reid's rage and aggression. She had been forced to be present at all of Sorcha's punishments, many of which involved a willow rod, and hadn't on any of those occasions, as far as Sorcha knew, shed a tear, offered a defense, nor begged mercy for her child. She'd stood and watched, her hands folded calmly before her, her lips thin with displeasure, while the rod was administered to her daughter's back.

She was startled out of her unhappy reverie by the return of Augustus and Geddy, but she did not turn in their direction as they approached, speaking quietly to each other.

And yet the content of their conversation pulled at her awareness as they arrived at their horses. She kept her gaze on her mother and sister, though, as she listened to Geddy speaking with some urgency to Augustus.

"That was de Montfort's doing and nae yer own."

"God as my witness, Geddy," Augustus said, his voice nearly agonized, "I kent at most—if he tried *anything*—he would wait until we reached the king. He'd want to ken the Bruce's location. And aye, he might have attempted something there, once we met with the king, but he'd be outnumbered at that time, and be trounced easily."

"Aye, and we talked about it, and I agreed," Geddy responded. "We canna be faulted for failing to understand how desperate he was to keep his true allegiance from the king. And likely, we'll nae ever ken why he acted *when* he did—ye or I, we'd want to get to the king, at least ascertain his whereabouts—shite, I was certain he'd have waited until the battle with Pembroke was under way and ambush us then, all the king's army, hemming us in between himself and Pembroke. Lad, ye canna harass yerself with guilt. Ye ken it has nae place, nae in this war, and nae with regard to men such as de Montfort."

Still observing Bessetta and Gelis, who were in the midst of a purchase of some textiles, Sorcha's heart constricted with compassion for Augustus, recognizing the depth of his suffering, struggling to come to terms with what he considered the consequences of *his* orders.

Briefly, she removed her gaze from the pair across the street as Augustus approached but could find no obvious trauma etched on his rugged features; he appeared as brooding and fierce as always.

He paused a moment at her side, collecting the reins from her. She returned her gaze to her mother and sister, filled with as much anticipation and fear that they might see her.

Bessetta and Gelis Reid completed their purchase and turned away from the merchants stall at the exact same moment that Augustus lifted his hands, gripping both the pommel and the back of the saddle in order to gain his seat. Though aware of his proximity, the fact that he didn't immediately climb onto the horse's back did not register with Sorcha.

Instead, she froze as Gelis spotted Sorcha almost immediately, her gaze likely drawn to the number of horses gathered near the livery, and possibly to Sorcha because she was the only person seated atop any of the horses.

The eyes of her younger sister widened in recognition, surprise and a quickly-birthed longing evident on her face as she stared at Sorcha with her jaw slightly agape. Wordlessly, Gelis tugged at her mother's sleeve and pointed discreetly at Sorcha, who held her breath, awaiting her mother's reaction.

Bessetta Reid followed her daughter's direction and Sorcha's gaze clashed with blue eyes not so different than her own. Again she held her breath, searching for any hint of warmth or joy in her mother's expression.

She didn't quite understand that her search was painted with a brush of hope, didn't realize this until any possibility of a reunion was squashed when Bessetta looked her over, her gaze scathing. With a thin-lipped glance, Bessetta Reid raised her chin and averted her gaze, pretending not to recognize Sorcha amidst the ragtag army of the MacKenzies.

Sorcha considered what her mother saw: her wayward daughter atop a war horse, with Augustus's hands familiarly set around her, Sorcha sitting vulgarly astride with her calves bare to any onlooker, and her entire person undoubtedly disheveled beyond civility.

Sorcha experienced a sharp stab of pain as she watched her mother and sister hurry along the cobbles, away from the textile vendor. Although years had passed, the rift between them seemed as wide as ever. There had not been the tiniest hint of joy on her mother's face at seeing her daughter, for even knowing that she lived.

Though Bessetta pulled Gelis along with her, her sister sent back a gaze filled with shock and yearning, which tugged at Sorcha's heart. Though for a moment only twenty or so feet had separated them, the emotional distance between them felt insurmountable.

Her vision blurred and her lips trembled.

"Sorcha," Augustus said at her side, bringing her awareness of him into focus again.

She blinked and met his gaze, belatedly aware of the concern of his tone, the tone softer than any she'd ever heard from him.

"Ye look as if ye've seen a ghost," he said, his brow furrowed, "and have become one yerself, white as snow ye are."

Sorcha loosened her clamped lips and gave her regard to the horse's mane, absently stroking the coarse hair there, reflecting upon the sighting and the pain in her heart.

Shouldn't a mother love her daughter?

"If the ghost wears a blue léine and linen wimple, I might be tempted to believe she is related to ye. I've nae ever seen blue eyes such as yers outside of Gylmyne, just now possessed by that woman and the younger lass."

Swallowing thickly, Sorcha replied without looking at Augustus.

"I don't know that woman," she lied.

Chapter Seventeen

They remained amid the busy market street for nearly an hour, in which time Augustus dictated a message to one of his soldiers and bade him seek out Robert Bruce, enlightening him about de Montfort's ambush and Augustus's depleted force and also about his plan to bring the fight to Ironwood near Caol. And with Geddy and Angus's input, they decided upon where best to spend the coin earned for the sale of the three de Monfort horses. There were no armorers, fletchers, or blacksmiths set up as vendors at the market, but a few discreet inquiries provided information on where to find those craftsmen locally, as they were in need of bows, arrows, and swords to replace the ones lost.

Unless there was an absolute need, Augustus refrained from dismounting, reluctant to abandon Sorcha, who clearly had suffered an upset when she'd noticed those two women, one young and one old, and had been uncommonly silent and still since then. Plenty of emotions he'd witnessed crossed her face by now, but not until today, in front of the livery, had she exhibited so much raw pain and stunning vulnerability.

The resemblance between Sorcha and both women was striking enough that he'd had no choice but to deduce that they were likely related. Yet, as he pondered this familial connection—and though he'd been quite certain for many years that he was incapable of any soft emotion or tender sentiment—his heart ached at the pain etched in Sorcha's expression when she was shunned. It was a stark reminder of the complexity of her past and the scars she feasibly carried, both of which he knew very little. In that moment and since Augustus felt a surge of protectiveness towards Sorcha, internally resolving that he would, as much as he was able, shield her from further hurt.

Sorcha was revived from her stupor after a while, while the discussion of how much they might be able to afford took place.

"I have coin to contribute," she said, withdrawing a tightly cinched purse from within her cloak. "I'd forgotten all about it, but it is yours—it belongs to you at any rate, for I meant to use it to free Grimm from the dungeon but you have seen to that."

Augustus laid his hand over hers, which was outstretched with the purse, and pushed it downward. "Keep yer coin, lass. Or, if it suits ye, since we'll be here at least for one night, mayhap you'll purchase a chamber at the inn."

During their parade along High Street, he was approached by the several of Gylmyne's burghers, the privileged citizens of some rank or title who usually held some role in the burgh and the market's administration. As Augustus knew them normally to be high-strung and fussy people, he was not disappointed by the trio that approached him.

They came barking at him, introducing themselves as burghers, but without offering names, demanding that his army disperse, they were making the market-goers nervous; they insisted that no poaching take place anywhere in Gylmyne's limits, which they claim extended for miles outside the town in every direction; and lastly, they argued vehemently against any encampments within the burgh walls, citing various past grievances and incidents of unruly behavior by soldiers.

And then they really pissed off Augustus, at least one of them, a natty bald man wearing a silk and fur cloak worth more coin than Augustus would see in a year, who could barely keep his eyes off Sorcha and asked bluntly after all other grievances had been voiced, "And what of this one? Kidnapped, is she? We do not stand for crimes of this ilk to be committed under our noses, my lord. And if she be a common jade, purchased with coin, we've hardly more tolerance for her kind."

Augustus and Sorcha stiffened at the same time.

"I am no such thing!" Sorcha insisted, insulted by the suggestion that she might be common, purchased, or a jade.

'Twas the first time she'd spoken in a quarter hour.

"Be verra careful how ye address my bride, sir," Augustus warned the man in a dangerous tone. He felt Sorcha bristled further and subtly tightened his hand around her waist. She would be far safer for being regarded as his wife. Already his name, given to the trio on their approach, was being bandied about High Street. He suspected that few would dare to incur his wrath, nor that of his army, by insulting or otherwise upsetting a wife of the Earl of Lochmere, long rumored to be the Rebel of Lochaber Forest.

Little did this appease the richly garbed and pinch-faced burghers, and not a word was spoken of remorse for their error.

Dismissing them with as much courtesy as they'd shown him, Augustus slowly wheeled his horse around and continued his conversation with Geddy and Angus while Wycliffe and a few others hovered nearby as well, a conversation that had been interrupted by the coming of the burghers.

"I'll take Sorcha to the inn and see what accommodations might be had," he said. "Send off the bulk of the army, outside of Gylmyne, have them set up camp at some distance, however they are able, as best they can." He understood that few tents and supplies were available to them since the ambush. "Keep a dozen inside the burgh, sleep where ye might when the time comes. Station several around the inn. I'm sure there are stables there."

With that, they took their leave of the MacKenzie officers and while the market was yet crowded, he walked the horse slowly down High Street, dismounting when they reached the first of two inns within the burgh's wall.

He wasted only a moment or so considering Wycliffe's obvious dissatisfaction with Augustus's directives. The man had to understand that he was no longer required to keep charge of Sorcha or see to her welfare. Augustus had taken on that role and did not foresee any time in the near future when he would need to give it up, certainly not before they returned to Caol and assaulted Ironwood. He far preferred that she remain in his custody, in his care. He'd not exaggerated his vow to her, that so long as he lived, so too would she. 'Twas not merely obligation that had compelled the vow from him, but rather a realization that he had, very quickly, begun to cherish and revere her in ways he had yet to fully comprehend.

The inn here in Gylmyne was well-appointed. In truth it made the Bonnie Barrel Inn and several others Augustus had visited in his travels seem as derelict hovels. While there hung about an odor of woodsmoke and garlic, it was not as stale or greasy as one might expect. The bar, tables, and benches were made of finely milled wood and gleamed with beeswax. The floor was not earthen but constructed of timber, the planks mostly clean or the cleanest Augustus had ever noticed. Augustus approached the bar, with Sorcha in his wake, inquiring of the tall and lanky barkeep about a chamber for the night.

"Aye," the man said, and turned toward the kitchen, hollering, "Jennet!"

A diminutive and yet robust women, wearing a tidy léine beneath her somewhat soiled apron, appeared, pushing through the door and bringing a bit of steam with her.

"Needs a chamber," the barkeep advised with brevity, pointing a long finger at Augustus.

The woman, with her pale gray hair neatly tucked under a mob cap, smiled profusely and waved Augustus and Sorcha down to the end of the bar. From behind the counter, she pulled out a ledger and perused the last used page.

"Only two chambers remain, milord—och, and ye're dead on yer feet, are ye nae, milady?" She paused to address Sorcha and then consulted the ledger once more. "The northeast chamber'll suit ye best, furthest away from the taproom."

"Aye, give us that," Augustus said, glancing around the taproom now, which was relatively crowded, but not as he would have expected on market day.

"They'll come in when the stalls close up," said the woman, "and right cheery it'll be all night long. Two pence, milord," she quoted. "And those are fresh linens, mind ye, on the mattress."

"Verra guid. And add supper as well."

Sorcha objected, laying her hand on Augustus's arm. "I only want to sleep," she said softly, "and...put everything behind me."

Augustus laid several coins on the counter, overlooking his suggestion to Sorcha that she might use her own. "Have a bath and maid sent up posthaste as well."

Sorcha's eyes widened, but her weariness was such that it took her following weak smile to advise that she was pleased about the prospect of a bath.

"Correction," she said, "I want only a bath and then to sleep."

Augustus grinned. "Ye'll be hungry. I'll fetch ye after a few hours to sup in the taproom."

"Oh, please don't wake me merely to dine." She faced the kindly woman behind the counter. "Mayhap a tray of bread and cheese?"

"As ye wish, milady."

While Augustus debated escorting her personally to the chamber, the proprietress guaranteed him she was in good hands and would be well cared for.

Sorcha's assurance was added to this. "Thank you, Augustus. I will be fine. I know you've plenty on your mind yet."

Nodding, he was about to take his leave when it occurred to him that as the woman thought he and Sorcha were wed, and because he'd expressed concern for Sorcha, it might seem strange if he did not kiss her ere he departed. He viewed it neither as an excuse nor an opportunity, but knew he'd be remiss if he did not act upon the notion.

Leaning down to her height, Augustus advised, "I will check in on ye this evening." And then he did kiss her, not grandly, as he'd have liked, but as a husband might kiss his wife. Ah, and how pleased he was that Sorcha did not stiffen or push him away, but softened her lips in a return kiss.

When he parted from her, he lifted and squeezed her hand, not oblivious to the small pink stains on her cheeks.

His mood improved, as much as it could be under their present circumstances—regarding what had come to pass and what yet lay beyond today—Augustus exited the inn and went in search of his men, hoping that sometime this afternoon or evening he, too, would be afforded an opportunity for a bath.

He browsed the market briefly though made no purchases and then stationed Finlay and three others inside the inn's taproom, to keep an eye on Sorcha. Next, he and Geddy and half a dozen lads rode out to the home of the fletcher, at the directions given earlier in the day. At the same time, Angus, Wycliffe, and another unit went to see the blacksmith about purchasing swords or having some quickly fashioned. Though he and Geddy did come away with several sheaves of arrows and seven bows, he was disappointed not to have amassed several grosses of arrows. Less than a hundred, all that the fletcher had on hand, was far from what would be required to lay siege to Ironwood.

Augustus and several others availed themselves of the clear water of a loch just outside Gylmyne, disrobing and plunging into the icy depths, scouring away the stench of the march and the battle. Augustus could do nothing about his garments, having lost his belongings when he lost his destrier, the latter of which still burned disturbingly.

By the time the sun had dropped low behind the tallest western mountains, both parties convened back inside the burgh of Gylmyne and found themselves occupying several tables inside the taproom of the inn where Sorcha was ensconced abovestairs.

The ale was refreshing, smooth and evidently fresh with a pleasant aroma and clear, golden color. Despite the fine quality, Augustus did not overindulge, knowing they had another long and arduous day ahead of them. One by one, Geddy and the others slipped off into the night, seeking beds as they could find them until only Augustus and Wycliffe remained.

"Ye've kept yer voice low and for guid reason," Augustus commented. "But one might presume ye are making up for all the words nae said in the past year with the way ye chattered all evening long with Angus and Finlay."

The Englishmen did not acknowledge his remark and did not mince words in his own observation.

"One might presume," he repeated, "by the way you purloined Sorcha, that you have designs on her. And I wonder if they are sincere or illicit."

He wasn't about to discuss his intentions regarding Sorcha—certainly not his desires—with this man, a suspect Englishmen hiding out with a beekeeper for the last year.

"Wonder all ye want, English," he drawled, taking a sip of his ale. "That'll be between the lass and I."

"I've told you that she won't give up her dead lover, not that sainted man," Grimm said with a shake of his head, as if he were sorry that Augustus had not heeded his caution.

Though Wycliffe did not say it, Augustus heard, *Not for you*.

Augustus chewed on the inside of his cheek and nodded, but only to acknowledge that he heard and understood. He did not rile Sorcha's former protector by hinting that maybe he did not want or need her to give up the ghost. Not more than a heartbeat passed before he realized that was only a lie he told himself.

Wycliffe stood from the long bench he'd occupied for the last few hours and said testily, "I assume you will insist on seeing to her safety overnight."

Nodding slowly, Augustus held Wycliffe's gaze.

Wycliffe nodded, and though he seemed to wrestle with some internal debate for a moment, at length he tapped the table distractedly and thought he needed to remind Augustus, "I would not hesitate to kill you if you harmed her."

"We've had this discussion. Guilty of an inordinate amount of sins I am, but mistreating women is nae one of them."

"Make sure that remains true so long as your association with Sorcha continues."

With that, the giant of a man turned and exited the taproom.

Augustus sat quietly with his thoughts, hardly any of them related to Wycliffe's warnings, and finished the last of his ale. It was yet several hours before midnight and indeed the taproom had filled considerably. The raucous din began to grate on his nerves, prompting him to take his leave.

The proprietress, Jennet, stopped him before he quit the room completely.

"Milord, here ye go," she said, holding a single key on a metal ring. "Your lady advised that ye should have this as she was expecting to lock the door from within and take to her bed. Turn right at the top of the stairs, milord, and she'll be inside the last door on the left."

He hoped he hid his shock well, murmuring his appreciation to the woman, who seemed as if she had more to say or wouldn't have minded some conversation from him. He left her disappointed, turning and making for the narrow stairwell.

Sorcha had left the key for him?

He'd planned naught but that he might make his bed outside her chamber, as retainers sometimes did when their mistress traveled alone.

Was this an invitation? Or had Sorcha simply recalled that he'd said he would look in on her tonight?

Augustus did not long ponder the reason behind the oddity, but climbed the stairs and quietly slipped the key into the lock, turning the handle slowly and pushing open the door quietly.

Flickering firelight greeted him as he stepped inside, casting a warm glow in the area closest to the hearth, where an arrangement of a pair of comfortable chairs flanking a low table invited relaxation. Immediately, his gaze sought out Sorcha in the bed, who lay peacefully upon her back, with her face turned toward the fire. Her features were softened by both her slumber and the gentle light. The cares of the day, and there had been a few, seemed to have melted away, so that her slumber was restful and her expression devoid of any consternation.

He stood over her and stared for quite a while, watching her chest rise and fall with her rhythmic breathing. He studied her face, realizing that until this moment, he'd never witnessed so serene an expression on her face. She'd slept in his lap last night, but the darkness of the forest had hindered his ability to make out her features clearly. She wasn't any more or less beautiful for the utter tranquility of her face now, but he thought himself fortunate to see this, a profoundly tranquil expression gracing her features in slumber. Still, he rather liked the animation of her wakeful face, including her stormy mien, which he encountered most often, and when her bright eyes stared with such keen perception at him.

It required all the restraint he possessed to resist the urge to wake her with a kiss, or with his hands.

He continued to study her, unwilling to move, visited by some fanciful notion that even in the grips of so deep a sleep she might or should *sense* his presence, and that she would wake. When she did not, he removed himself from the bedside and added peat to the fire so that it might last through the night before he sat in one of the chairs before the hearth, having angled it a bit so that he faced Sorcha in the bed. Leaning his head against the cushion, he closed his eyes, courting sleep.

Sleep did not come before Sorcha shifted and woke, sometime later.

Augustus watched as Sorcha sat up swiftly, possibly sensing a presence. She pushed her hair out of her eyes and peered into the shadows toward the hearth.

At the same time, Augustus announced himself. "'Tis only I, lass."

"Augustus," she said, but not with any alarm. In fact she sounded quite at ease, and even lifted her bare arms out from under the bedclothes and stretched, slowly and gracefully as would a cat. She was garbed in naught but her chemise, the fabric scant and light against her skin. "What hour is it?"

"Nae yet midnight but getting close."

She was no blushing virgin, he realized, had lived with the man, Finn, for nigh on a year, which might explain how she could so casually flip back the blankets and rise from the bed, garbed only in her shift and now receiving a man's company in her chamber. She strode across the decent-sized chamber and found the MacKenzie plaid she'd been given, folding that in half and wrapping it around her shoulders. Her feet were bare as were her legs, devoid of any hose. While he watched she paused at a small table that sat under the dormer window, picking up the small tray that had been left untouched there. With no awkwardness that he could detect, she plopped into the cushioned chair opposite him and set the tray in her lap.

Before she began to nibble on the cheese and bread, she caught herself and offered it first to Augustus.

"Nae. I supped belowstairs," he declined softly, fascinated by the way firelight danced as golden shadows across the delicate features of her face.

She ate in silence for several minutes, chewing slowly, seeming sleep-shrouded still, unblinking as she stared at the wee orange flames in the hearth.

At length he asked what had simmered in the back of his mind for half the day. "Who was that woman in town? And the lass with her?"

Still she did not blink but responded in a wooden tone. "My mother. And my sister, Gelis."

"Yer màthair dinna speak to ye?"

She smiled sorrowfully. "My mother does not even deign to acknowledge me apparently."

"Is that merited?"

Pondering this, Sorcha tipped back her head, exposing in full the graceful column of her neck. Lowering her face after a moment, she said, "Is there anything a child might do that would make her mother shun her? Anything so grievous or mournful or shameful?"

"There should nae be, I imagine. Shuns ye, because ye ran off with the beekeeper?"

Nodding, she took another bite of the crusty bread. "I will have children one day," she said around the food in her mouth and with a soft vehemence, "and I vow to you they will never—not *ever*—have cause to wonder, not at any point in their life, that they are loved. And there will be nothing they can do to earn my derision or lose my love."

He didn't doubt it. As passionate as she was about so many things—singing, her beehives, Grimm, and injustice—he expected she would be fierce when loving.

"And still, I ken, ye dinna possess a black heart," he reminded her.

Her shoulders slumped a bit. Her hand, holding a piece of bread, sat motionless in her lap. "I do know that. But aye, I do also sometimes need reminding." She turned sharply to Augustus. "I am not a bad person."

Though fervent, her tone was so flat that he could not determine if this were a question or statement.

"Ye are nae a bad person," he swore firmly.

"And yet I gave the key to Jennet to give to you," she surprised him by saying.

His body drummed suddenly with awareness, coming to life now.

"And why did ye do that?"

She smiled softly, as if she held a secret. "I believe I understand you to some degree. I predicted you would want to see for yourself that I was safe and tucked in my bed."

He sensed a bit of mockery in there somewhere and imagined at least two reasons for it: she sensed that he was protective and would not rest without such knowledge, that she was indeed safe; or she guessed, correctly, that he trusted only himself and his own instinct about things and was generally reluctant to take the word of stranger, Jennet in this instance, that all was well.

And yet....

"That's nae the only reason ye left the key for me," he said.

"No, it is not."

Sorcha stood and returned the tray to the table, pausing to take a sip from a pewter cup there. Facing the chamber again, she pulled the plaid from around her shoulders and tossed it onto the foot of the bed as she passed, and then glided toward Augustus in only her shift, causing his body to react strongly, swelling with desire. When she reached him, she bent and took the hand that rested on the chair's arm and straightened, urging him to his feet.

On his feet, Sorcha held his hand and stared at him. Possibly that was as far as her daring went. When he lifted his hand and cupped her cheek, Sorcha closed her eyes and leaned into his hand.

Recalling her supposed black heart and his actual one, Augustus hesitated to take what was so gorgeously being offered.

All the hope he'd ever known or entertained had been related to war and the battles within it, to crops and matters concerning Strontian and the people under that umbrella. Sometimes, much less frequently, he wished for peace inside his mind and for a day to come when he could lay down his sword and retire to the quiet expected at Strontian, free from the burdens of command and duty. But just now, as he looked at Sorcha, as she tempted him so beguilingly, he acknowledged long-denied hopes for other things of a lasting nature.

"Dinna come at me like this," he clipped, "out to prove something, because ye're upset by your mam's coldness, or with some misguided notion to thumb yer nose at yer mam's principles."

She sighed and melted against him, her head at his chest, her arms folding between them. "No, it's not—I just want to be loved, just for tonight." Her voice was small, laced with yearning.

"One night is nae what I'm after," he informed her; this truth had teased at the back of his mind for a while.

"But it is," she argued, tipping her face up to him. "You offered to pay for one night when first we met."

"Naught is now as it was then," he said, his voice low, less stern. Indeed, everything had changed. How short-sighted and arrogant he'd been, to have offered her coin for one night with her. "I dinna want ye like this, only trying to run further from the limitations yer own family put on ye or whatever drivel they drilled into yer head."

"But kiss me, Augustus," she pleaded, lifting her hands to his face, "no matter the reason or what you want or do not."

In truth, he was strong enough to resist—even Sorcha and her desperate plea and her warm and enticing body—but he had no desire to deny either himself or her. And frankly, there was little reason to do so. She could call it whatever she liked, could justify it however she wanted, but he knew her kiss and her passion, and sensed that it blazed for him just as fiercely as his did for her.

"Kiss me. Please."

He fixed his eyes on her soft, curved lips and lowered his head, seeking the sweet seduction of her kiss. Sorcha's long lashes fluttered closed just before he touched his mouth to hers.

Chapter Eighteen

She closed her eyes while heat spread up from her chest, into her neck and face.

His kiss was bold, and beautifully warm and now familiar. Sorcha opened eagerly to him, and he slipped his tongue inside at the same time he drew her closer with an arm around her waist. The swift jerk of that action triggered a greater hunger in her. At the same time there was great satisfaction at such a display of urgency. The warmth of his kiss turned to fire, which pulsed in her veins, same as it had every time their mouths met. Sorcha slid her hands around his neck and pulled him down to her at the same time she stood on her toes, wanting to climb up on him, to be as close as was possible. She threaded her fingers through his hair, surprised to find it damp, but then was mindless to such a small matter when his kiss was so bone melting.

His kiss was so much like him, fierce and possessive, inspired by an arrogant grace, and yet somehow as unfathomable as the man for how it consumed her.

She swirled her tongue with his, deepening the kiss, drinking in the lush fullness of her own response. With just a kiss her body quivered and ached for more.

Augustus's hands moved to her bottom, yanking her against his hard body. Her reaction was unbridled, swaying her hips and belly against him, well aware of what was obvious, his growing desire for her.

Everything was different now, as if some deeper longing had been waiting for only this, to find them alone, behind a closed door so that they could tease and taste and explore freely.

"As sorry as I am that likely you've not slept," she said against his lips, a wee breathless, "I am glad that I did find a bit of slumber. Keep me awake all night, Augustus."

To her chagrin, he straightened away from her at these words, his eyes glittering as he stared down at her. For one horrifying, nearly inconceivable moment, she feared he would say now he really did need his sleep.

"Aye, we've all night and thus nae need to rush," he said thickly, offering instant relief from her wayward concern. He placed his hands on her cheeks again, drawing her up to his kiss, which was heated but brief. "I want to love ye all night long, lass, many times."

His hands were huge and rough, and she loved absolutely everything about that, how they felt against her soft cheeks, the strength realized, the possessive way he handled her.

"Have you wanted that for a long time?" As ridiculous as it was, she felt as if her desire for him was years old and mammoth for having not been fulfilled.

"Nae," he answered, causing a womanly distress to rise until he finished. "only since first I saw ye."

Indeed, desire flashed in the blue depths of his eyes.

Her smile was instant and appreciative, selfishly gratified to know she'd not been alone in her fascination.

"I want to undress you," she said, having arrived at this decision just now and having spoken it before she'd thought it through, immediately worrying that she didn't know how or that the tantalizing act itself would make her shaky and giddy at the same time.

The look he gave in response to this, a softening of his intense features and a gaze filled with awe, as if he'd waited forever to hear her say just that, emboldened her beyond her own insecurity. In more than a year together, she'd never undressed Finn.

Augustus separated himself from her and outstretched his arms. A shadowy, lazy grin lifted his lips. "I'm all yours."

Longing drew her toward him, one step at a time, while she considered all the garments covering him, wondering where to begin.

"Start with the belt," he suggested helpfully.

Her fingers shook with anticipation as she unbuckled the leather belt, pulling the prong free from the buckle. She pulled it off him, around to the front, and because of the sword and scabbard attached to it, she laid it carefully on the floor beside them. The plaid was hence freed, and she raised her arms, gathering the weight of it from his shoulders, and drawing it away from his body. Men were particular about their plaids, maybe earls and lairds even more so, she imagined. She lifted a hesitant gaze to him, not sure how to proceed, how to fold it properly.

Augustus plucked the heavy breacan from her hands and carelessly tossed it aside. "I'm nae interested in that so much as I am in how ye will proceed."

Frankly, her own interest was piqued wildly as well. She'd already been gifted a glimpse of his chest and her hands ached to acquaint themselves with his body. And at his waistline, inescapable, the evidence of his erection inside his breeches had managed to gather heat between her legs.

Sorcha reached for his tunic, her nervous fingers lifting it upward. His stomach rippled with muscle as she moved the linen fabric up over it, his arms flexed as he raised them obligingly over his head. His dark nipples and sculpted chest were revealed as the tunic was dropped to the floor.

Slowly, her gaze wandered over him, wanting to know every inch of flesh. He was large and broad and muscled in ways previously unimaginable to her. Scars and wounds, old and new, decorated his warrior's body. She had thought him impressive atop his huge destrier the very first day she had met him, had thought him intimidating and fearsome, and yet undeniably handsome. Here, now, stripped of his tartan and sword, standing before her as an undressed man, wearing his scars as badges of honor, while his chest rose and fell with his increased breathing as he patiently allowed her to look her fill, he was beyond magnificent.

But a frown came, when she spied the slice across his skin that she herself had bandaged but that was not wrapped now. Gingerly, she reached out toward the fresh tear in his skin, one of many, and opened her mouth to question his neglect of it.

"I discarded the linen strip when I bathed," he said. "And truth be known, lass, it dinna need wrapping. I gave in to yer concern last night so that ye would nae fash about it."

She was unperturbed by this, having begun to believe he might be invincible.

After a fleeting glance into his eyes, which found his regard trained fiercely upon her, Sorcha extended her hand and touched the tips of her fingers to the slight matting of hair covering his chest. Blood pounded throughout her veins. His body pulsed with vitality, and she was briefly smitten by how small, white, and soft her hand appeared against his broad, hard body, his skin being several shades darker than her own.

In truth she was overwhelmed, but in the sense of a hungry child set before a feast, delighted and eager.

Again she met his dark gaze. "You are beautiful, Augustus," she said, a sweet reverence creeping into her tone. She thought to add a practical point. "And we haven't even gotten to the good part."

A burst of laughter erupted from him, surprising her. And then he tossed back his head and his laughter continued, nothing but joy in the sound. His laughter was rich and velvety, and twice as lovely for how genuine and pure it sounded.

Sorcha was breathless, in awe of his merriment.

In the midst of his laughter he closed the distance between them and took her up in his arms, kissing her softly, quickly. "Nae, lass," he said, still smiling against her lips. "We've nae uncovered the guid part yet." His fingers teased the flesh at the outside of her shoulder, sliding along her skin under the narrow sleeve of her shift. He lowered his head and kissed her bare shoulder. "Like silk," he murmured, "as I ken it would be. Beneath yer shift, love, or in yer blue eyes when sunlight hits them, and in yer smile—aye, there's the guid parts."

Truth be told, her heart melted right then and there. Such beautiful words. And mayhap they were only words uttered by a practiced seducer—her sphere of reference was decidedly limited—but she loved them all the same, and she blissfully judged them sincere.

He ravished her once more with his kiss, licking and tasting, and moved his hands up her back, weaving his strong fingers into the thick length of her hair, far more damp than his. A shiver engulfed her, but she was restored, nearly to cleverness, when he drew forward her hand and laid it over the waistband of his breeches.

"Get to this guid part, lass, so I can get to mine," he whispered against her cheek.

She fumbled a bit over the three buttons of his breeches but had little trouble with the drawstring of his braies beneath and tugged the cord loose as well. At the same time he began cinching up the fabric of her shift in her hands, Sorcha pushed down his breeches and braies past his lean hips. She gave them a final shove downward, all that she had time for, before Augustus had her shift gathered and she was compelled to lift her arms over her head. Her long, loose hair was the last thing tangled in the linen before that was sent away and she stood naked before him. A half foot of space separated them now but she didn't want that, and reached for him, wanting to feel the length of him pressed against her.

"Wait, love," he said, toeing off his boots and the garments that had dropped to his ankles.

And then they were both utterly and wonderfully bare.

Unable to resist, Sorcha's gaze fell onto his erection jutting out from a tangle of curly black hair. She whimpered at the sight of his manhood, tall and swaying, and desire exploded inside her.

Augustus's indrawn breath, at the sight of her nakedness, wrenched her gaze from the confirmation of his longing. She watched him study her, his mouth slowly opening as his gaze traveled slowly across her body. Her nipples tightened under the intensity of his blue eyes. She imagined that never before had she felt so worshipped and adored—and *seen*. Cool air kissed her skin, but then Augustus's heated gaze quickly scorched her flesh, everywhere his eyes touched.

Sorcha drew in her own deep breath.

Being naked with him, her body craving his touch and feverishly anticipating what was to come did not bring the expected guilt she'd long suspected. For quite some time, she'd wondered how she feel and behave in this moment, if a sense of betrayal would assail her, but it did not. She only tucked Finn's memory deeper inside, safe from intrusion. She wavered but briefly, a wee fearful of her own desire for Augustus. Since learning of Finn's death, there were nights when she lay awake, grappling with an emptiness that should have been filled by Finn. This desire now, for Augustus, was different. It resonated within her, overpowering all rationality. It screamed inside her, burning away all sensible thought. Her body pulsed with need. She could not douse it, she knew, it simply was not possible. Only Augustus could bring to life and quench the flame of her desire.

When she could no more bear the distance between them, she made it go away, stepping into his arms, searching for his kiss. Their naked chests collided, hard against soft, and they moaned their pleasure in harmony, into their kiss.

Longing to touch him she moved her hand, wanting to tangle her fingers in the dark hair at his chest. Sliding her hand upward from his waist, she felt Augustus tense. He paused his kiss to groan his pleasure as she boldly slid her hand across the flat hard flesh at his stomach. She kept going, her fingertips inching upwards until her hand settled with titillating satisfaction over his magnificent chest. Boldly, she allowed herself to explore once more, caressing the sculpted muscles and short, wiry hair. Beneath her fingers, his heart pounded almost as rapidly as her own.

Augustus held her in his steely grip, suddenly possessed of six hands it seemed, on her back and her bare buttocks, in her hair, and most satisfyingly, coming round her front and cupping her breast. The roughness of his hand made her skin tingle. Callouses grazed the underside of her breast as he stroked his thumb down the pebble of her nipple. Lowering his head, he kissed her breast and she trembled. Shafts of pleasure darted from her breast to her belly. Her breasts were small and firm and he took almost all of it in his mouth and moved his tongue around her nipple in deliciously slow circles. She slid her hands around his back as he stroked her with his tongue until the peak was rigid. Sorcha groaned her pleasure, all of which moved from the touch of his tongue, down through her belly, and lower to the very core of her. A fleeting thought of *it's been too long*, was squashed by the reality that *it had never felt like this*.

He lavished attention on one breast and then the other before he molded her breast with one hand and pulled her against him with the other, returning to her lips, his tongue slick inside her mouth.

He kissed her deeply, their bodies pressed together, his hand and tongue bedeviling her, and Sorcha struggled to focus on each sensation individually. She wanted it all, every tingling bit of pleasure, and squirmed, needing to feel his rigid hardness pressing against her.

"I'm trying to keep it slow," he whispered, the slightest quiver in his deep voice. "Ye want it now, or do ye want to savor it?"

"I want you. Everything. Yes,"

A soft chuckle answered this. "Aye, love." And he kissed her again.

Moving her hand down, she slipped it between them, encountering first the soft tip of him and a dewy drop of his pleasure. She closed her fingers around the thick length of his erection. She squeezed gently.

A low groan came from his throat and his kiss stalled briefly.

Gliding her hand up and down the length of him sent her pulse racing faster. When she did it again, his hips lurched forward. She sighed with delighted anticipation, wanting so badly to have him inside her.

The next moments were crowded with pleasure. While she stroked him and luxuriated in the feel of him, how hard and hot he was, Augustus rolled her nipple with his thumb and moved a hand between her thigh, delving into the pale curly hair. He slid one long finger over her, stroking back and forth, finding that place that was filled with so much sensitivity, teasing her, torturing her, before pressing deep inside her, stroking until her hand stopped moving against him and her breath stopped coming.

"*Jesu*, lass, but ye're wet for me," he seethed tightly against her.

She purred a low, keening sound when he withdrew his finger and she stared, befuddled when he pulled away from her. He paused and looked down at her, his gaze alight with some scalding need, and took her hand, leading her toward the narrow bed, where he sat down at the side. His erection strained mightily between his powerful thighs. He pulled his arm toward himself, bringing Sorcha to him.

Sorcha went willingly, needfully, meaning to sit beside him.

"Nae," he said, steering her between his legs.

He laid his hands at her hips and brought her breast to his mouth and there began another tender assault. Setting her hands on his shoulders, she gave herself up to the thrill of each nip of his teeth and every lick of his tongue. A shiver of liquid heat shot through her, and she arched into his touch, threading her fingers into his soft, thick hair.

His scorching caress soon had Sorcha agitated with need, an overwhelming need to be everything to him, all at once and forever.

Just as she imagined she would explode with yearning, the hands at her hips shifted and he wrenched his face from her breasts. Deliberatley, he met and held her gaze, and she wondered if her eyes and countenance looked as his, tortured by need, rigid with furious desire, eyes burning with urgency.

Moving a hand to the back of her thigh, he guided her to straddle him before both hands returned to her hips and he positioned her above his swollen manhood.

He lowered her downward and Sorcha gasped silently as the tip slid inside her slick entrance. A shudder embraced her and her entire body clenched with joy when Augustus brought her down at the same time he thrust upward, filling her completely.

As her body took him in, he leaned back and watched her. Face to face, Sorcha returned his molten stare. Her mouth opened in awe, but she could imagine no words to describe the glorious feel of him seated fully inside her.

"*This* is a guid part as well," he ground through his teeth, as if restraining himself.

"The best part," she agreed on a breathless sigh.

Again, his hands flexed, and Sorcha obediently lifted herself up and lowered herself back down onto his throbbing shaft. Repeatedly, she rose and fell, groaning deeper and louder every time she came down on him. Augustus claimed her breasts with his hands and mouth and bucked up against her until he growled, "Ye mean to kill me," and deftly swung them around, tossing her back on the bed.

There, he drove deeper inside her and she whimpered with a new thrill at the force of his thrusts, clutching his shoulders. Every nerve in her body sang with sensuous delight. She wrapped her thighs around his hips and lifted herself to meet each perfect plunge. A coiling sensation knotted deep inside her. A kaleidoscope of color swam before her eyes.

His tongue swept across her lips and into her mouth, and she took as much as she gave, pulling him closer and deeper inside her.

She sent her fingers into his hair again and clasped tightly as the magic inside her blossomed, growing, threatening to burst into flames. She arched up at him, wanting him to put out this fire. Her body clenched and ached. She stood on a precipice and had never wanted so badly to fall.

And then it came, the sweet oblivion, and she shook with a moan, locked within his embrace, whimpering as her heart soared and her body thrummed with exquisite ripples of pleasure. Sorcha clung to him and whispered his name.

As she rode the wave of her release, Augustus reared back and plunged softly now, his face twisted in gorgeous agony.

Clenching herself around him, Sorcha watched with languid eyes as he writhed and then stiffened and a hoarse cry was torn from his lips, pleasure that she had wrought in him. A moment later, he collapsed on top of her, and they remained locked together, spent, his face buried in her neck, and their bodies slick.

She didn't want to move, couldn't move.

Long moments later, she decided right then and there that the saddest sensation in all the world was the feeling of him sliding out from within her as he shifted onto his side against her.

"Dinna do that again," he said against her hair, his breathing labored still. His hand sat softly on the middle of her stomach.

"Do what?" she asked, feeling as if she were only half conscious.

"Try to kill me."

Even her smile was drained, and her lips quivered as they tried to move.

"'Twould be a beautiful death," she supposed.

"Aye, it would."

Sorcha turned her face toward him and exalted in the way he immediately kissed her, tender and soft.

"Ye smell of roses, by the way," he said.

"Mm. I wanted to give every coin in my possession to the proprietress, for how singularly glorious she'd made my bath."

Curving himself against her, compelling her to shift onto her side, and cradling her breast in his hand, Augustus's breath and words came at her hair and cheek.

"Sleep now, lass, for I fear I'll nae be able to resist waking ye soon."

Smiling sublimely, Sorcha snuggled against him and wondered how sleep would be possible with his glorious naked body tucked against her and his loving now known and already cherished.

She curled her ankle and foot around his calf, wanting to keep him near, as close as possible.

***

Sweet dreams were snuffed out by a knock that sounded firm and yet intentionally soft.

Sorcha opened her eyes but did not move.

The voice of Augustus's captain, Geddy, came through the door. "Aye, lass, and we're needing to get going as fast as ye can. We canna find the laird and will want to get a search on anon."

Sorcha's eyes widened and she lifted her face off Augustus's chest to find that he was awake, comfortably so, his arm bent under his head. The arm around her flexed and his hand stroked up and down her back.

"Lass, are ye awake?" Geddy called.

Augustus looked at Sorcha, his expression asking an obvious question. She shrugged sleepily and whispered, "It's fine."

"I'm here, Geddy," Augustus then called out, "but there's nae need to bandy that about. We'll be down shortly."

Geddy's response, though awkward, came swiftly and with a hint of scolding, "Aye, but ye just bandied it yerself to the lads with me."

Augustus used the heel of his palm to rub at his brow with some frustration. "Await us below," he instructed.

Soft footfalls carried the men away from the door. Unperturbed, Sorcha dropped her head back down, too pleasantly imbued with memories of last night to concern herself with so small a thing as who knew what.

Augustus's hand again caressed her naked back.

A moment later, he offered, "I can exit via the back door and—."

"Do not play games on my account, Augustus. I feel no shame for what we've done. And quite frankly, I don't think it will come as a surprise to many."

"For the way I look at ye?"

She let out a small laugh against the heat of his hard chest, her heart thrilled. "I was suggesting that the way I sometimes stare at you must be quite telling."

Beneath her, his muscles flexed and tightened as he moved. Pulling himself up, Sorcha was forced away and then easily onto her back. Augustus hovered over her, his elbows on either side of her shoulders. He kissed her tenderly, lingering over her lips.

"Might be, lass, this is the last bed we see for a while," he said.

Her eyes remained closed, and she wore a serene smile. "A fine thing, then, that we put it to such good use."

He had indeed woken her during the night and had loved her again, tenderly, slowly, until as before passion made them wild and she'd not whispered but had cried out his name.

"Had we time, I would use it again," he said now, laying a kiss on each of her closed eyes.

"You'll have to be sustained by memory of the two occasions it was used," she teased.

"I feel a failure," he said, which promptly opened her eyes and knit her brow. "I hinted at *many times* and fell far short."

Her lips curved again, and her eyes softened. "I imagine that even the Rebel of Lochaber Forest needs to sleep. Mayhap your efforts should be judged on quality and not quantity."

A grin teased his gorgeous mouth. "A guid plan," he said. "We'll abide by that."

Augustus kissed her smiling lips once more and retreated.

They rose at the same time, retrieving garments from the floor, smiling often and languorously at each other while they dressed. The water that remained in the ewer was cold, but she scrubbed her face and teeth and shoved her feet into her boots before gathering the MacKenzie plaid around her shoulders over her battered cloak.

When all their scarce possessions were returned to their persons, Augustus took her hand and led her from the chamber.

His languid kisses and playful good morning filled her with a warm and lovely feeling. If he'd simply risen to Geddy's alarm and had donned his clothes and taken his leave with barely a glance at the bed or a word for her, she'd likely have assumed his desire had been met, her purpose had been served, and he had no further need of her.

Chapter Nineteen

In truth, riding with Sorcha in his embrace over the last few days, with her body soft and tempting against him while desire hadn't yet been met had at times been a challenge, but sharing a saddle with her now, when the taste of her was fresh, after he'd explored nearly every inch of her delectable body, and when he knew what delights could be found in her arms, proved almost dangerous. Concentration was hard to come by, and Augustus had to force himself to resist images and a return of sensations of the night spent with her. Of course, there were moments when the trail was easy and no threat was imminent when he recounted as many moments as he was able, and to great satisfaction.

She hadn't proved so much a revelation in his arms for the passion she exhibited, and that without a shred of shame, as she had simply confirmed what he'd suspected about her: she was bold and fierce in her loving as she was in life, and completely without fear, without reservation. 'Twas as satisfying to Augustus as was her response to his touch—she desired him as he did her and wasn't afraid to show it.

What remained of the MacKenzies, their numbers mournfully depleted by thirty-two after de Montfort's attack marched north from Gylmyne under a watery gray sky that threatened at any moment to open up on them. And while the MacKenzies were generally pleased to have been reunited to this number, a pervasive somberness hung over the force, for all those lost so tragically and wastefully to one man's greed and deception. Still, Augustus understood they were profoundly fortunate to not have suffered greater losses, attributing that to the mighty prowess of his army and the unwavering fervor that regularly coursed through them in the heat of battle.

Augustus knew that when the time came, he would be called to rally them from their gloom, to raise their dispirited mindsets to defiance and robust fury, to elevate them once more to their proud fighting spirits as would be required of them to lay siege to Ironwood.

Before that, however, they needed to return to the scene of the ambush and respect their fallen. He didn't relish the tableau that awaited them. Bodies left unburied even for a few days and at the mercy of the elements, tended to decay grotesquely, and quite often became food for scavengers—birds, wild animals, and even thieves.

Sorcha, huddled in front of him with the MacKenzie plaid covering her head and all her upper body against the creeping, icy fog and the damp chill, turned her face toward him. "What will you do when this is done?" she asked. "When the siege at Ironwood is finished, to satisfaction or not, what will you do then?"

Though he suspected there was a deeper question behind the straightforward one, he answered the one she'd voiced.

"Back to war I'll go. Find the king's army and join in their battles."

Though she kept her head turned and her gaze on the dreary scenery passing at her right, she did not reply to his response, prompting Augustus to query, "And what of ye? I'll nae abandon Caol nor Ironwood until de Montfort is conquered—in what fashion I dinna ken yet—but what will ye do when he is gone?"

"I...I'm not sure. I suppose I might keep on in Caol, rebuilding my hives. Mayhap peace will come for the threat of de Montfort having been removed. But I'm not sure. I hadn't given it much thought."

Speaking from the heart, about the emotion and an idea that came to life within him, Augustus said without hesitation, "I want ye with me," he said. "Or at Strontian, waiting for me, until the fight is done."

There was no immediate response; she did not move or speak for so long a moment that Augustus held his breath, dread rising with each second that she remained silent.

"Really?" she finally replied, her voice soft and filled with wonder. "You would want that?"

Augustus blew out the breath he'd been holding, relief tempering a sudden fierceness and rigidity that had overwhelmed him. "Aye. A fine apiary has Strontian, by the way. Auld Cuilén has been keeping bees for longer than I've been alive."

She straightened against him, her interest piqued. "Is it very large? Is it just one apiary or are there many? How many bees does he have?"

Augustus chuckled. "Calm yerself, lass, lest I believe ye more interested in the bees at Strontian than its laird."

Another long stretch of silence ensued before Sorcha leaned languidly against him, her face turned toward his chest. "I am, though, very interested in Strontian's laird."

His breath caught at her words and instinctively he tightened his arm possessively around her middle. At the same time, he grappled with thoughts that seldom dared to surface before. Sorcha's presence in his life had stirred something within him, something unfamiliar and yet undeniably potent. It wasn't love, but then he couldn't be sure, having not experienced feelings so profound as what he did for Sorcha. Mayhap it wasn't love in the conventional sense that poets and minstrels sang of, but rather a newfound sense of hope, a bright flickering ember to reach for amidst the darkness of war and death and destruction.

For as long as he could remember, Augustus had been consumed by the relentless pursuit of freedom, of victory on the battlefield, and the stewardship and welfare of his people. Love and companionship had been distant concepts, relegated to the realm of fantasy as he immersed himself in the harsh realities of war and politics. The notion of a woman waiting for him at Strontian seemed surreal, a departure from the solitary, military existence he had grown accustomed to. Never before had he allowed himself to be swayed by matters of the heart, never permitted himself to become entangled in the complexities of romantic entanglements—or, in reality, had never met anyone who gave him reason to. But Sorcha with her fiery spirit and her hypnotizing beauty, was different. The prospect of her waiting for him, of finding solace in her embrace after the turmoil of battle, stirred something primal and desirous within him, for something he hadn't known he wanted or needed, but that was now within his grasp.

Yet, as he pondered the implications of his blissful obsession with Sorcha and these nebulous plans just made, a nagging uncertainty gnawed at the newfound edges of hope. Would her presence weaken his resolve, dull the edge of his sword, as his thoughts wandered to her instead of the battlefield? Could he afford the luxury of affection when the kingdom's fate hung in the balance? Would he be expected or forced to leave behind the persona he had meticulously honed over the years, the Rebel of Lochaber Forest. It was a moniker steeped in legend and fear, a symbol of defiance against tyranny and oppression. To relinquish it would be to forsake a part of himself. Augustus found himself torn as he weighed the cost of holding onto that identity against the promise of a future with Sorcha. Could he reconcile the two facets of his being, the hardened warrior and the potential lover, or would they forever remain at odds?

The answer eluded him. Whether he could truly give up his legend, his legacy, remained to be seen. But for Sorcha, he was willing to entertain the notion, and for now he could only dwell on the possibility of a life beyond the battlefield, as he'd never had cause to do before now.

When they were but half a mile out from Ashgill's Pass, a more palpable somberness settled over the ranks. The air was heavy with grief and solemnity, and then came the rain, light and cold, so that each step closer seemed even further weighed down by the burden of loss.

Augustus took the steed upon which they rode out of the marching line and waited for Wycliffe to come. Inclining his head at the Englishman, he bade him approach and when he did, announced, "Take the lass with ye. I dinna want her near the site. Keep her atop the crag, and safe."

Wycliffe nodded, understanding the assignment, that Augustus didn't want her anywhere near what would surely be a brutal scene. Sorcha said not a word as Wycliffe brought his horse directly beside the one Augustus rode, and she was transferred to the saddle with Wycliffe. Imagining that she appeared tiny when sharing the saddle with him, Augustus fleetingly noted with a raised brow that she all but disappeared inside the massive embrace of the Englishman as they trotted off.

Ere they dispersed, Augustus heard Wycliffe say to Sorcha, "No choice now but to speak to me."

Sorcha's quiet retort and the light tone in which it was delivered hinted strongly at a softening toward Wycliffe.

"I don't believe either of us expected I'd have been able to maintain the silence for as long as I did."

Wycliffe's responding chuckle grew softer the further away Augustus went.

Coming upon the site shortly thereafter, Augustus was pleased for his decision to distance Sorcha from himself and the cruel scene. Though a seasoned warrior himself, it was hard for him to see.

Though more than a hundred MacKenzies descended upon the scene, they had few implements, naught but a few short-handled spades carried in saddle bags, and two shovels they'd purchased in Gylmyne. And because of Augustus's insistence that the slain MacKenzies be buried properly—outside the pass and singularly, not in a mass grave—it took them the rest of the morning, the entire afternoon, and most of the evening to complete the heart-sickening task. All the while, the rain continued to soak them, the grim weather a fine companion to their sour and sore moods.

There was a time, shortly after noon, when the rain did briefly lessen to a fine and constant mist, and a song came down from the top of the crag. At first, it was but a faint echo, carried on the same spray of mist that fell over the narrow glen, but soon it grew in strength and clarity, piercing through the somber silence that enveloped the MacKenzie soldiers as they toiled to bury their fallen kin.

Somewhere above them, her face and figure unseen, Sorcha's voice rose like a mournful lament. The haunting melody floated downward, filling the air with a sense of sorrow and reverence.

One by one, as they realized the sound, the soldiers paused in their work to listen, sorrow and awe washing over them. Sorcha's voice, though somber, carried a note of solace, and Augustus was pleased and proud of the song she sang.

"*While shadows claim their mortal frame,*" she sang in part, "*their deeds of valor light a flame. Blessed life they were denied, but in your hearts they will abide.*"

As ever, her voice was an epiphany, conveying peace and serenity that, for several moments, seemed to soothe the weary souls of all who heard it.

Misty-eyed, Geddy commented when the final notes of the song had drifted away on the wind, "That'll stay with me, the bonniest send-off I've ever heard."

Later, they made camp atop the crag, upwind, not far from where Sorcha had sung the mournful ballad, the day having drained them too much so that moving onto Caol was put off until the morrow.

Sitting under a gracious fir, whose boughs offered minimal protection against the rain and cold, Augustus passed the night sleeping with Sorcha in his arms, inside his plaid, opened and tented over them as cover. Scarcely had they spoken, words nearly meaningless and attempts at conversation seeming an irreverence after their sorrowful labors of the day. Sorcha had kissed him tenderly when he'd come up from the glen, not as a lover but rather as a gesture to soothe his weary soul.

And though he did grieve, come the morn Augustus was ready and willing to put Ashgill's Pass behind him.

They reached the demesne of Lord Aldric de Montfort and went first to that area where Wycliffe had said the tunnels should exit. The exit point of the tunnels, Wycliffe had overheard, lay concealed amidst a copse of ancient oak trees on a hill on the southeast side of Ironwood.

While Sorcha waited, well-hidden with the majority of the army, Augustus, Wycliffe, and half a dozen more searched the location in question. Thick undergrowth and tangled brambles shrouded the area, helping to conceal the searchers as they approached the only thicket of towering oaks perceived as far as the eye could see.

Indeed, the oaks were ancient, their gnarled branches reaching for the sky like skeletal fingers. Keeping one eye on the curtain wall, somewhat visible to them, they spread out and began to examine the ground all around the trees.

Aye, access to Ironwood via tunnels would be a welcome advantage, but Augustus held out little hope that they actually existed or that those guards hadn't been purposefully, maliciously deceiving Wycliffe.

A full ten minutes passed while they searched and hope faded, until Kael called out in a whispered hiss, "Here!"

The small party gathered round the lad.

Just beyond the furthest roots of those trees, moss-covered rocks flanked the entrance, masking its presence from casual observers. Kael was lifting away a two-inch layer of earth and sweeping dirt and mud away from an unusually level section of ground.

"There's a marker," he said, pointing with his elbow as he labored, toward a subtle arrangement of stones with nails hammered through them, arranged to form a star on the ground, cunningly buried under some vines and grass until Kael discovered it.

When portions of a flat plank of timber were unveiled, Augustus, Wycliffe and the others dropped to their knees and began tearing away at the turf laid on top of it. In no time, a three foot by two foot hatch was revealed, covered with a wooden door. A metal latch was embedded into one end of the door.

They stood, one by one, and considered the door.

Augustus wiped his muddy right hand as best he could on his breeches and tunic and then drew his sword.

"Before we bring out the rest of them, let us first discover where it goes," he cautioned.

Geddy scowled and challenged this. "And why else would a hatch be laid in the earth?"

"Found the tunnels, did ye?" Said a craggy voice outside their circle.

They whirled at once, expecting to confront a threat, but found only an auld shepherd, his head and hair wrapped in a linen coif, his faced wizened with many decades.

"Might well use the front door," he said mildly. "Keep is deserted."

"De Montfort did nae return?" Augustus frowned.

"Returned, aye," said the shepherd, who was bent drastically, sporting a large hump on his back. "Came and went. Packed up his wayns—wife, bairns, silver, bedding, his silks and furs—and away they went."

"Where?"

The shepherd shrugged, the action more visible in his face than his narrow, drooped shoulders. "Canna say. South, fer sure, but nae east whence ye come, but west."

"He kent we'd come for him," Geddy presumed. "Son of a bitch, but I wanted that bastard to eat my blade."

"The keep is vacant?" Augustus wanted clarification.

Another shrug, of sorts, preceded his answer. "Nae soul in that one, Blackwood, so aye it's essentially vacant."

"Blackwood remains?" Geddy queried.

Augustus suspected that like himself, Geddy didn't much care for or have patience with the shepherd's want to speak in riddles.

"He and a handful of his minions, playing Lord soon as de Montfort quit the keep."

Griffyn, among the men listening to the shepherd's news, chuckled at this, which did not bode well for the bailiff-cum-lord of Ironwood.

Augustus and Geddy faced each other, their minds churning with plans of how to proceed.

"Save ourselves the trouble, I reckon," Geddy proposed, "and nae crawl through a quarter mile of muck or through whatever foulness this here would take us."

"March right in through the gate?" Augustus only needed a second to consider this. "Aye, that sounds guid."

True, it was rather anti-climactic, and Augustus felt cheated to have been denied—for now—his aim to deprive de Montfort of life, but practically speaking, 'twas far better than he might have hoped, and he was pleased that not one more life would be lost to de Montfort's treason.

Retreating from the shadows of the ancient oaks, they went next to spy upon Ironwood, to discern the veracity of the shepherd's news. Not more than a few minutes were needed to see that no guard stood atop the battlements and that, indeed, the gate was wide open. A home guardsman leaned negligently against the open gate, making time with a lass of flaming red hair, one Augustus recognized as a barmaid at the Bonnie Barrel Inn, a telling circumstance. Had there been any sign of heightened security, they might have assumed the shepherd had it wrong.

As it was, Augustus planted two men in his company to remain and await the full MacKenzie army, watching the wall and yard for any sign that it was not as it seemed.

Next, he sought out the army waiting for them some distance away, close to where Sorcha had kept her woodland apiary.

After a quick explanation of what they'd found, and what they'd learned from the shepherd and had since confirmed, that de Montfort had vacated the keep and likely Caol itself, Augustus ordered the men to mount and ride with him, through the gates of Ironwood. While men dashed about to collect their steeds, Sorcha lifted her hand to Augustus when he maneuvered the gray charger next to her.

When she was ensconced in the saddle with him again and while he waited just a moment until the lads were ready, Sorcha asked, "De Montfort has fled?"

"Aye, he, his wife, and kin."

"But where did he go?"

"Far away," he said tersely, reminded that he was sorry that he'd not be allowed to kill him, "far from any chance of his neck being stretched or sliced."

"He has property in England," she said, "about which he was always pleased to crow, his vast wealth."

"Little guid it will do him when his treason against Scotland catches up to him," Augustus predicted grimly, "and it will."

A quarter hour later, what remained of the MacKenzie army rode unopposed through the gates of Ironwood. Aye, their numbers were not as they'd been, but an admirable threat they presented to the few men who were left behind, apparently under the direction of the former bailiff, Blackwood.

With hardly a need to delay, Augustus strode purposefully into the hall, Sorcha's hand in his, and a quarter of his army on his heels. The rest of the MacKenzies, under Angus and Griffyn's command, were busy securing the gate and manning the wall, lest the unprotected, inviting keep was merely set as a trap. Additional men had been directed to investigate and secure the tunnels against either any possible threat or anyone's desire to escape.

Augustus sensed straightaway, from the scene that greeted him, that this was not a trap. The bailiff had made himself laird and lord, had assumed the finely carved chair at the high table and surrounded himself with platters of food and drink. He was surrounded by his loyal and equally depraved henchmen and several woman of dubious standards, garbed scantily and all wearing dim-witted expressions—all save for one figure, a woman who seemed to have no interest in their coming. She sat meekly at Blackwood's side, her head bowed toward the floor.

"Taking up right where de Montfort left off, I see," Augustus called out before he'd reached the table.

Blackwood's jaw, which had dropped with incredulity at their entrance, slackened further.

Upon hearing his commanding tone, the woman whose head was bowed raised her face. Augustus's jaw clenched at the sight she presented, her eye and lip swollen, her peasant's gown torn, and wearing a collar of heavy metal around her neck. Augustus judged she couldn't have seen more than a score of springs in her young life.

Sorcha gasped, realizing the woman's existence and condition as well. "Effie," she whispered in horror.

'Twas difficult then to maintain control of his rage. But he did manage to subdue Sorcha, whose instinct it was to rush forward to the pitiable, abused lass. He caught her wrist, forcing her to wait.

"Is that how ye coerced her to make those claims against Grimm?" Augustus asked the bailiff in a dangerous growl.

Despite the very obvious apprehension that arrested his features, Blackwood sneered. "'Tis about all she's guid fer."

Augustus smirked ruthlessly at the reckless toad, who was not worthy of the designation of *man*.

Releasing Sorcha's wrist, he stepped closer to the table, and knew a wicked delight for the way Blackwood shrank down and back in the overlarge chair.

"Y-ye have nae jurisdiction here," Blackwood stammered. "Ye canna kill me. I am an agent of an earl."

Augustus's smile increased. "I can kill ye and I will. Ye are a verra strong man, are ye nae? How easily ye take yer hand to a lass—many lasses, I ken. Take yer hand to a man instead," he sneered. "Aye, I'm feeling generous and will allow ye to fight. I'll even put a sword in yer hand. If ye win, ye may go free, and skulk back into whatever hole ye crawled out of at the beginning of yer existence."

Rising hope lifted Blackwood's bushy brows. He glanced beyond Augustus, to where stood dozens of his army. Swallowing, he asked, "Who will I fight?" No longer the bully, he sounded uncertain, whiny, his voice high-pitched with fright.

"'Twill be me, and 'twill be my honor," Augustus was pleased to answer, and then more delighted when all the blood drained from the bailiff's face.

"Get him outside," Augustus ordered the men around him. "Free the lass and put her in Sorcha's care. They're nae to be unattended. Bring me—"

"Augustus," Sorcha whispered with heavy concern. "Surely, you don't mean to—"

"I do."

"But you don't need to," she argued, wearing a strange expression as she stared at him. "Put Blackwood in chains or convene a court—"

Augustus closed the distance between them and lowered his head as his instructed her firmly, "Dinna ever question either my decisions or my commands."

Sorcha recoiled slightly, her eyes widening in disbelief at the sharp tone he'd employed, or the message delivered. Her lips parted, as if she wanted to challenge him yet, but the words seemed to catch in her throat.

"Attend the weaver," he instructed and brushed past her.

Blackwood's whimpering and the image of Sorcha's stunned gaze followed him as he walked outside into the bailey, expecting that the bailiff would be made to follow.

No sooner had he stepped outside, squinting against the mid-afternoon sun than a shout sounded from the battlements.

"Riders, ho! Riders coming!"

Expecting de Montfort's army, Augustus hurried up the stone steps to the battlements, his heart pounding with anticipation. The distant rumble of approaching hooves grew louder, drowning out the speculative murmurs of the MacKenzie men, those high on the wall and those in the yard. When he reached the top, Augustus scanned the horizon, a wee bit hampered by that bright sun. He raised his hand to his brow.

Just as he recognized first the massive size of the army thundering toward Ironwood, he noticed the particular formation of the vanguard, and the vast sea of banners that fluttered as they rode. His breath caught in his throat at the sight, a surge of adrenaline coursing through his veins.

"Look!" one of his men exclaimed, pointing toward the advancing force. "The king's banner!"

Turning toward the inside of the wall, Augustus's voice rang out across the bailey, "Open the gate! Prepare yourselves! The king has come to Caol!"

Cheers erupted from the assembled soldiers. Augustus bounded back down the stairs and helped draw out the bolt to unlock the tall wooden gate, putting his weight and strength behind the men moving the beam.

They did not wait for the king's army to approach but rather the MacKenzies spilled outside the yard and gate, throwing up their fists and raising their swords, calling out good will to the king.

Charging at them was a force five hundred strong and riding abreast of his bannerman was the imposing figure of Robert Bruce, King of Scots. Though his current circumstance must surely be daunting— named a fugitive king and on the run for more than a year—there was an undeniable aura of regality about him as he rode forth at the head of his piecemeal army.

Clad in simple but well-worn armor, sans a helm, Bruce's face was weathered, aged ten years in the last twelve months by Augustus's estimation, hardship and struggle aging him prematurely. But for his eyes, dark and piercing still, and presently surveying the scene before him with steely resolve.

Coming in hard, he drew up sharply, and all before him went to their knees and bowed their heads.

"Rise! Rise," he called, with seeming impatience.

He dismounted confidently and with ease in spite of the weight of the armor plates and plucked at the fingers of his riding gloves, removing one and then the other as he strode toward Augustus.

His broad face creased with a smile, and he opened his arms, into which Augustus stepped. Their relationship had not been long known, but it had been forged on a solid foundation.

"'Tis good to see you, my friend," said the king quietly, sincerely.

"And ye, sire," Augustus returned.

Separating, Robert Bruce glanced around at those closest to Augustus, which mostly were his officers, inclining his head at several known MacKenzie men as he said, "Your message found us naught but half a day away and on the backside of the battle with Pembroke, made a day early at my convenience," the king said with a rare show of dark humor. "Even had you not been waylaid and reduced, 'tis unlikely you would have arrived in time, so pray do not disparage your inability to come to Loudon Hill."

His reference to surprising Pembroke a day earlier than intended struck Augustus as amusing. No doubt the king did this to visit retribution upon Pembroke for a brutal deception he'd played upon the king's army last year. 'Twas near Methven when Robert Bruce found Pembroke embedded in Perth and, in chivalrous fashion, had challenged him to come out from behind the town's walls and fight. Lord Pembroke, Aylmer Valence, had responded that the day was too far gone then, and they should meet on the battlefield the next morning. And so the king's army, with whom Augustus had been joined at the time, had made camp for the night, preparing meals and making their beds. Lo and behold, Pembroke's army, which vastly outnumbered all of Robert Bruce's combined forces at the time, had come charging into their camp overnight. The Scots' army was swiftly overcome, and it required all the valor of Bruce and his defenders to merely secure a retreat.

"Pembroke has retreated to Ayr," Robert Bruce said now, "and with no enemy either on the horizon or nipping at my heels, I found myself anxious to take up the enemy you battled, as your enemies, my loyal friend, are mine as well."

"Ye do me a great honor, my king," Augustus said reverently.

"'Tis you, my lord, who regularly honors me, with your fighting spirit and unwavering faithfulness." He glanced around. "So, where is he? The scoundrel, de Montfort?" savagely, he said. "Frankly, MacKenzie, I grow daily more sickened by the infidelity of Scotland's own nobles. I mean to make an example of de Montfort."

Augustus chuckled. "You'll have to find another unfaithful noble, sire, for this one took the path of Pembroke. Gone on the wind."

Robert Bruce slapped the gloves in his hand against his thigh with some frustration. He then stared beyond Augustus, beyond the gates, his features gentling.

"Praise God for the beautiful creatures he crafts," said the king, his voice chock full of wonder, "but who is that startling woman?"

Augustus did not have to turn around to know that the king referred to Sorcha, but he did turn, finding her biting her lip as she stared with her own sense of awe at her king.

Augustus held out his hand for Sorcha to join him in the company of the king. Eyes wide now, mayhap with some womanly concern that she was unfit to meet the king in her present bedraggled state, Sorcha came forward haltingly.

"Sire, may I present Sorcha Reid, daughter of Gospatric Reid of Balquhidder and currently the beekeeper of Caol."

Sorcha gracefully lowered into a deep and reverent curtsy. "Sire, it is an honor." When she rose she stared at the king, her face tipped upwards as Robert Bruce was nearly as tall as Augustus, her expression imbued with as much wonder as the king's return study of her.

"Madam, your loveliness is a balm to this weary heart and many tired souls, I'm sure," said the king elegantly, suddenly the courtier and not the warrior. "I trow the chaos of war in my memory is turned to dust in your presence."

Barely had Sorcha's pink blush arrived at the king's evaluation than a voice, loud and insistent, called out from the depths of the king's army.

"Sorcha!"

Confusion registered on Sorcha's face. She, along with the king and Augustus and many other faces turned toward the massive crowd of soldiers of the king's retinue.

"Sorcha!" Came the call again, the voice young and eager.

Augustus surveyed the throng of mounted men and foot soldiers, most recently still but now shifting subtly as if a divide were created. A foot soldier came forward, his pale crowned head bouncing along between the mounted cavalry as he made his way to the front.

"Sorcha!" he called again, and it sounded now as a plaintive cry.

Augustus's lips parted, a sinking black dread overwhelming him. He turned to look at Sorcha.

Disbelief washed over her, her eyes widening in astonishment as she gazed upon the approaching figure. Her hand flew to her heart and her breath seemed to catch in her throat.

Slow was the progression in her from befuddlement to comprehension. Icy fingers gripped Augustus's heart as he watched her. As the lad burst from the front line of horses and into full view, tears shimmered in Sorcha's clear blue eyes and wobbly smile blossomed slowly into radiant joy.

"Finn?"

Chapter Twenty

Though confusion still reigned, Sorcha's smile was instinctive.

And yet she had cause to wonder if she were dreaming.

How was it possible that a man stood before her, wearing all the features of Finn's beloved face? How did this man possess Finn's honey-colored hair and his soft brown eyes?

"Finn?"

Once burst from the line of horses, his steps faltered as his eyes sat heavy and warm upon her. Which each step forward, Sorcha's eyes widened further, her entire being weakened by disbelief and wonder. At the same time, her smile grew and tears fell, while a piece of her heart thought lost forever was now returned to her.

"Is it true?" She asked, her voice quaking.

"What's this?" Asked the king. "A reunion, I daresay, and how fitting."

Sorcha scarcely recognized the king's words, her mind aflutter with disbelief yet.

And then, as if given leave to approach by the king's words, Finn rushed at her, his arms extended. Sorcha went willingly, if yet a wee muddled, into his embrace. His arms closed around her just as her legs threatened to give way.

Enveloped in Finn's arms, a surge of joy flooded her senses. The weight of grief and longing lifted, replaced by sheer elation at his return—at the very fact that he was alive!

Fairly quickly, though, it became apparent that there was no familiarity in this embrace. Resting her chin on his shoulder as

Finn stood not much taller than she, and with his lean arms around her, the fit and sensations seemed foreign to her.

Her eyes widened and a sudden pang of guilt washed over her, realizing that in her confusion and joy, she'd forgotten all about Augustus standing beside her. She froze in place, in Finn's arms, while the stark juxtaposition between past and present, between the love she once mourned and the prospect of love she'd found anew left her reeling.

And while sometimes of late she thought she never wanted to leave Augustus's arms, she dreaded now abandoning this embrace with Finn, but only for fear of having to face Augustus.

In a final burst of excitement, Finn picked her up and spun her around, crying out jubilantly, "I can't believe it! I imagined ye might have returned to yer father's house. But to find ye here!"

When he set her down, she now stood across from Augustus, facing him.

The expression on his face would be burned into her memory, into her heart, for as long as she lived, she knew at that moment. His jaw was clenched tight, veins rippling along his neck as if resisting a primal urge to lash out. His nostrils flared, a sure sign of his raging emotions, and his brows were gathered darkly over his piercing stare. While he held himself rigidly, intense emotion flashed as he stared at her, a turbulent storm in the deep blue sea of his eyes.

It could not be helped but that she sensed a challenge in his gaze, as he glared with such brutality at her. His eyes glittered with hardness, and Sorcha was overcome by the idea that he either expected her to announce their relationship now, or that he was about to speak in a dangerous tone, determined to protect what he considered as belonging to him.

And yet, beneath the mask of defiance, Sorcha imagined she saw something else in Augustus's eyes: pain, raw and immeasurable.

Her throat clogged with emotion and her lips parted while her heart twisted with conflict.

She waited for Augustus to unclamp his teeth and open his mouth, to claim her as his.

But it was Finn who spoke next, and Sorcha blinked, removing her gaze from Augustus while her heart constricted further.

"My liege," Finn addressed the king formally, bowing his head, "Might I have leave to reacquaint myself with my love? We've a cottage nearby"—he halted and turned to Sorcha—"Do we still?"

At her shaky nod, Finn faced the king again, his brows raised with hope.

The king inadvertently aided and abetted Finn's cause and managed to twist Augustus's mouth into an even more ugly sneer when he so generously acquiesced.

"By all means, lad, take your leave. I envy you your reunion and all the joy that comes with it."

Filled with glee, Finn smiled broadly and grabbed Sorcha's hand, pulling her away from the king and Augustus, away from the gates of Ironwood, causing her to run to keep up with his enthusiastic sprint. A short burst of lackluster cheering and ribald laughter shadowed their departure.

She went, less so willing or urged by delight than she was simply following, a wee removed from reality at the moment.

For all that she'd longed to know one more hour with Finn, one more day, she had yet to make sense of what was happening, or how it was possible. She hadn't yet grasped the concept of how

Finn could be here, tugging at her hand, running across the fallow fields of Ironwood toward her home—their home. But how could she process such a fantastic turn when she couldn't shake the vision of Augustus's handsome face twisted and tortured!

A hundred yards away from the gates of Ironwood, Finn halted abruptly, causing Sorcha to nearly crash into him. She winced and Finn laughed, catching her, taking her face in his hands.

"I can't believe I haven't kissed you."

Frantically, Sorcha covered his hands with her own, meaning to pull his hands away, to thwart his coming kiss. But he was eager and unstoppable, filled with boundless energy, and his mouth crashed onto hers before she could muster a protest.

Finn ground his lips against hers.

Sorcha squeezed her eyes closed. She waited for...for anything—a thrill, a change in her breathing, a racing heart, a tingling deep inside, that glorious reward of pleasure—but if any of those sensations arrived, they were drowned out by the memory of another kiss that stirred all of those things and more.

"Och, but how I've missed ye and how sweet ye are," Finn said with a broad smile when he pulled his lips from hers.

She tried to smile in return but feared she failed miserably. At best, it was a shaky and uneven attempt to which Finn was completely oblivious.

They walked then, hand in hand, and for this Sorcha was grateful. The idea of running all the way to the cottage was a bit extreme, and her legs were yet pudding from her shock.

"I don't understand, Finn," she said to him, "what you're—how you can be here."

He turned a stilted smile on her, confusion evident. "What do ye mean? Ye saw me come in the king's army."

"But how are you...alive?" She asked. When he stared with his own bewilderment at her, she informed him, "I was informed you had perished in a fight. Your name was called out in the notices."

He was aghast, his eyebrows shooting up into his forehead. "What?"

Nodding, Sorcha explained that his name had been recorded in the death notices, and that his, and others, had been called out by Lord Aldric.

"I canna conceive how—well, actually, 'tis nae uncommon, that names are recorded in the wrong columns after a battle."

Not discounting the possibility of such carelessness, Sorcha also wondered if de Montfort, in his lust for her, had simply added Finn's name to the roster of the dead, hoping to make her vulnerable, desperate.

"Ah, my love, how you must 'ave suffered," he commented, his warm brown eyes darting around her face. "Doubly joyous, is it nae? Is that what ye feel that has ye so reticent and stiff?"

Sorcha latched onto to that excuse, which wasn't wholly untrue. "I feel as if I've seen a ghost."

"Nae doubt, nae doubt," he concurred promptly and then his voice and mien sobered. "And that was the MacKenzie, was it nae? There at Lord Aldric's gate?"

"Yes, it was," she said, her voice small.

"Ye'd be best keeping yer distance from that one," he said. "Dinna let it get out, Sorcha, but that's the Rebel of Lochaber Forest and 'ave ye ever heard of him?"

Dumbly, she murmured, "I have."

"Then ye ken, do ye nae, how brutal that man is? And what are ye doing in his company anyway? Did ye meet him at Ironwood? Did he rout Lord Aldric and was settling accounts? Were ye summoned by him? *Jesu*, but dinna tangle with that one, Sorcha. Just dinna do it."

Rather than explain even the smallest part of her knowing Augustus, or her relationship with him, Sorcha asked, "*You* know him?"

"Nae personally. Of course nae. I'm a grunt, Sorcha, a bluidy foot soldier. The lords and lairds and generals dinna take time with us. But I've fought in his company, Sorcha, and ye would nae want to see him with his sword in hand. Bless yerself, ye'll nae ever 'ave to. Ye'd withered and die in fright, sure as I'm standing 'ere, mark my words on that."

She'd forgotten, quite frankly, how animated and exaggerated were all of Finn's mannerisms and expressions. She'd forgotten as well, how riled he would become when relating news or events, even mundane ones.

"It's true what they say, Sorcha," he went on, shaking his head to corroborate his telling. "Whatever ye've heard about the Rebel of Lochaber Forest, all the ugliness, cruelty, showing nae mercy—'tis all true. The Rebel has nae soul, Sorcha."

That is a lie, her heart screamed. She would never believe that every kindness Augustus had shown her, every attempt to keep her safe was made by a man without a soul. He was separate from his legend, she understood that now. The legend was that man on the battlefield, and rightly so, as he needed to be, not only to survive but to triumph in the war. The man was neither merciless nor unjust.

"You never wrote me," she mused quietly when Finn was quiet for a moment.

He did that sometimes, grew quiet even as he remained animated. Sorcha had always imagined that he was only scrounging around in his brain for topics or matters to discuss. Often he would chew nervously at the inside of his cheek, as if the quiet disturbed him and he was determined to fill it. And then his eyes would widen, as if pleased by the discovery, when he imagined some fresh bit of conversation to share.

Presently, a look of mild awkwardness washed across his face. He glanced at the ground as they walked. "Aye, and to that, ye understand 'tis nae so easy to do. Parchment and ink are hard to come by, and aye, ye taught me the letters but I canna say it stuck."

"Were you not in Eamon Gregory's company?" She asked, referring to a local crofter's son who was smitten with the cobbler's daughter.

"Och, sure. Best mates we are, he and I."

"He wrote to Maribel...regularly, often. She had letters once a month at least."

Finn frowned and waved his hand. "Nothing to write about," he said airily. "'Twas naught but marching and fighting and fighting and marching."

Before she'd been notified of Finn's 'death', she'd been quite put out that she'd received not one piece of correspondence from Finn—not even a postscript in Eamon's letter to pass onto her. She'd made excuses for the absence of communication at the time, but now, with his weak excuse given, she chewed her lip while a wee uncertainty crept into her consciousness.

"But it would have been nice to know that you were, indeed, alive," she argued gently. "A letter would have gone a long way invalidating the notice that you had been killed."

"But ye do ken now, Sorcha," he said blithely and then changed the subject. "Ye canna imagine my excitement when the king's lieutenant announced we were marching up to Caol—to bluidy Ironwood, he said, and nae one was more surprised than me. Two years I've been gone and aching to get back. Though, to that, I dinna expect to find ye here."

It was nearly impossible not to compare Finn's character and behavior to that of Augustus, and yet she understood it would be a precarious endeavor. Though she assumed it was natural for her to draw parallels between Finn and Augustus, she recognized that each man—every man—was unique, with his own strengths, weaknesses, and complexities. To judge one against another would require that she generalize their individuality and possibly overlook the nuances of their personalities.

At length they arrived at the cottage, which gladdened Finn until he spied the missing sections of thatch.

"God's teeth, Sorcha," he started, "but what happened to the roof? Why did ye nae repair the gaps?"

"It just happened, less than a week ago," she said sensitively, "and I've been...there's been a lot going on in the last few days."

Sweet heavens, but there was so much to tell him about all that had transpired and befallen her since he departed with the army—most of which had occurred just in the last few weeks since the arrival of the Mackenzie army and Augustus. And she'd have to tell him about Grimm eventually. But not now, when her brain was still processing his return and her anxious and increasing inner discord.

Finn pushed open the door and pulled her inside, spinning abruptly to take her in his arms. "Nae worries, lass. I'll nae be concerned with the roof while I'm here."

While her arms were trapped inside his, Finn nuzzled at her neck with his mouth.

"'Tis my Sorcha that I want," he said between kisses. "It's been too long."

Sorcha stood stiff in his embrace, unable to escape the memory of Augustus's recent expression or the lingering delight of his affection. Squirming with discomfort, Sorcha pushed away from Finn's arms.

"I can't," she said. Unable to comprehend how to explain this to Finn without telling him what she had done, how she had betrayed him, she murmured, "I'm sorry, it's still so...I feel I don't know you. This is—I'm so sorry—this is awkward." She swallowed all the guilt that surfaced with her half-truths and was caused to wonder if she would have rejected Finn just now if she'd not so recently encountered Augustus and the joyous expertise of his kiss and his touch.

For the space of a second, a veil of anger cloaked his amorous animation. He shuttered it quickly enough and said, "I kent ye'd be happy to see me."

"Of course I am," she insisted. "Simply to know you're alive, Finn, fills my heart with joy."

"But nae more than that," he guessed.

"Much more, but this....this is—just give me some time to come to terms with—"

"I'll nae have leave for long, Sorcha, mayhap more than today and tonight."

Firm in her resolve, she could only repeat, "I'm sorry, Finn."

A pang of guilt assaulted her. She could clearly see in his eyes the hope, the longing, the expectation that she would have welcomed him back with open affection. But instead she felt only turmoil, being unable to reciprocate his advances or excitement. She knew she hurt him, perhaps irreparably, with her hesitation and reluctance.

With contrived lightness, she said, "But let us spend together as much time as we are allowed, Finn. Let's tramp through the forest as we used to do—oh, I must tell you the same storm that took away portions of the thatch also destroyed the forest apiary. Come with me, Finn, and let's plan how I shall rebuild it before you return again."

Distracted, and a little curtly, he informed her, "I dinna care about the hives, Sorcha. I want to spend time with ye."

"But we will," she argued, briefly nonplussed. "We don't have to go the apiary. I can show you how well I've kept the hives here. Finn, I made new hackles completely on my own," she announced with no small amount of pride.

With much less animation, he refused this as well. "Nae. In fact, I should get back to my commander and verify what leave I might be given, if any."

"But the king said—"

"The king is my liege lord, Sorcha," Finn cut in, "but the commander of my company may nae approve of even a short departure."

"Oh."

Possibly he read her crestfallen expression; he smiled again and stepped forward to squeeze her hand and press a fleeting, harmless kiss on her cheek. "I'll return as soon as I am able."

"Of course," she allowed, fairly stunned by the quick about-face.

As quickly and unexpectedly as he had re-entered her life today, he departed it, sailing through the open door with nearly as much speed as he'd come through it a moment ago.

She stood for a moment, unmoving until she frowned in consternation and placed her hands on her hips. Her gaze drifted beyond the open door, staring rather blindly at the tall swaying grass beyond, wondering if the pain of her rejection had sent him running or if his inability to get her into bed had taken him off with such haste.

However, overriding her curiosity over this, was an undeniable relief to have sidestepped his advances.

The truth, though genuine, made her nearly sick to her stomach. *My God,* she thought, *but Augustus has ruined me for any other—including my own true love!*

Drained as she was, Sorcha flopped onto her back on her narrow cot, realizing just now that she'd been gone from this bed for several days, as she hadn't since first it had become her own. She threw her forearm over her forehead and stared at the sky through a nearly perfectly round hole in the thatch. For quite a few minutes, she tried to focus on one pertinent fact: Finn was alive. However, it was virtually hopeless to concentrate only on this and not question what it meant to her and Augustus.

Naught but a quarter hour had passed since Finn had left when she realized she was only tormenting herself mentally and she needed something else to occupy her. Though she had no idea how long Finn might be gone, she decided she likely had enough time to check in on Effie and see how she fared, even as more guilt assailed her at the thought; with the arrival of the king and his army, and Finn's resurrection, Sorcha had all but forgotten about poor Effie, whose trauma was obviously far greater than Sorcha's internal anguish.

She exited the cottage then, knowing it would take only twenty minutes or so to reach Effie's croft, which she'd once shared with a husband who had actually died in war, unless that notice had been falsely delivered as well. The announcement of Fergus's death had been recent, not more than two months ago, but this might have been the catalyst that made Effie a recent target of Blackwell's wickedness.

The route to Effie's croft on the outskirts of the village took her past the Bonnie Barrel Inn. The lane was damp, muddy in some spots, and she kept to the fringes, walking along the grass.

As she neared the Bonnie Barrel Inn, a small group of people were collected in the yard there. She recognized immediately the plaids and faces of some MacKenzie soldiers and several locals.

In their midst, at the center of the small crowd, was a man whose image shocked Sorcha. He spun about continually, as it seemed he was being harassed by those gathered round him and wanted to keep an eye on any threat. But that was the least remarkable thing about him. He wasn't very tall, was stocky and unkempt, his breeches ragged and torn in several places. His face, which might have once been handsome, was haggard and twisted with contempt as he glared at his audience. But most prominent about this man was the fact that though he had two hands, one of them had been removed at the wrist and was strung about his neck, being counterweighted with a small rock.

Sorcha covered her mouth with the back of her hand, the sight of the severed hand disturbing, for it had not only been recently removed, but appeared shriveled and nearly black, decay long ago having set in.

"Aye, poacher," one of the MacKenzie men was saying, his tone unkind, "and wot brings ye down from Strontian?"

Another Mackenzie soldier asked gruffly, "Did the laird nae tell ye, when he chopped off yer hand, to keep to yer croft and yer own affairs?"

Outside the circle of people, Sorcha gasped at what was revealed? Augustus had removed the man's hand?

The man stuttered some incomprehensible response, his words slurred beyond recognition. He listed a bit as well, advising that he might be drunk.

"Yer kind is nae welcome here, poacher," said another soldier. "Get back to where ye belong." He gave the drunk man a shove, not hardly light, that sent the man to the ground.

This was followed by snickers and sneering from all those around.

"Och, pick up that hand, mate," called another MacKenzie man. "Recall what the laird said he'd do to ye if he found ye without it."

Appalled, Sorcha stared gape-jawed at the MacKenzie soldiers, none of them at this moment the well-disciplined lads she'd met in Augustus's army. Further, her stomach-turning astonishment was heightened by the revelation that Augustus had so wickedly commanded that the man *wear* his severed hand. This then was her first true encounter with any supporting evidence about the rumors of the Rebel's callousness. True, she'd seen a bit of that in the ugly ambush, had been a wee alarmed at his dealing with Blackwood, his want of a fight that would have been clearly unfair, and now this man, with his severed hand....

Clearly, she did know Augustus. What he showed to her was only half of his character. Obviously, he'd gone out of his way to conceal the other half, that part of him that was in truth the merciless Rebel. Her head swam in light of this new information, for how easily she'd been deceived, for how easily she'd allowed herself to see what she wanted to see.

While the few townsfolk present goaded the one-hand man to leave their village and as the gathered soldiers did the same, Sorcha, still coming to grips with the ugliness of the scene, saw Grimm exiting the inn.

He noticed her directly as she was paused on the periphery of the group, and he marched directly at her.

"You don't need to see that," he said, putting his hand at the small of her back, compelling her to turn, and then leading her back the way she came. "A scrap of rubbish the MacKenzies will have removed in short order."

Sorcha went along with Grimm, less willingly than distractedly, until it dawned on her that she intended to go in the opposite direction. "No," she said, turning around again. "I was on my way to Effie's, to see what I could do for her."

"She's fine. I brought her myself to the Widow Agnes, who took her in hand," Grimm informed her. "I hadn't yet departed when three more matrons arrived, ready to lend support and aid."

"Oh," Sorcha said and allowed herself to be steered further along the lane and back home, knowing those matrons would not receive Sorcha kindly in their midst, even as her desire to see Ellie had been grounded in compassion.

Grimm dropped his hand after a few more steps. "Why are you not at home with your man?"

She panicked a bit, unprepared for the question, and what an honest answer would embarrassingly reveal; that she'd rejected Finn's advances and that he might have abandoned her because of it.

"He ah, he felt he needed to report to his immediate superior and um, confirm the length of his leave."

"Quite a shock you had," Grimm remarked mildly.

She snorted lightly. "Quite so. They just keep coming, so much upheaval."

"Hm. And yet, you're delighted with Finn's return, are you not?"

Sensing another question hidden under the one he voiced, Sorcha replied swiftly. "Of course."

Teasingly, Grimm posited, "Plenty of protectors you have now."

She cast a disapproving frown in his direction for what seemed a sardonic comment.

Grimm only grinned but sobered fairly quickly. "That makes my leavetaking less difficult, knowing you'll be safe—no matter whom you choose."

With the evidence of Augustus's cruelty only moments ago thrown in her face and because of her long-standing love for Finn, as compared to her emotions regarding Augustus—unexamined and so recent—Sorcha asserted starchily, "There is no choice. I love Finn. I had only ever dreamed that such a day might come. And yet here he is. My heart is full—but wait, what do you mean your *leavetaking*?"

Grimm stopped and faced her. "It's time for me to move on," he said.

"But why? Where?"

Another upheaval.

She'd been so grateful for the time spent together yesterday, when they'd waited above the crag while the MacKenzies had been about the unkind task of burying their dead. Her short-lived annoyance with Grimm had been superficial and she'd been so looking forward to enjoying his company even more than she already did, now returned to Caol and hopefully with all upheavals having been settled, for now being able to have conversation with him.

"But why?" Was all she could imagine to ask.

Grimm answered indirectly. "Sorcha, you are beautiful, brave, and clever, and whether you believe it or not, I always found your constant need to fill our silence with speech quite charming. I think, even without conversation, we got on very well together. I would have, and you know this, killed anyone who had harmed you. Your friendship is warm and comfortable, and what you provided me as far as relief and escape from my demons—for that I can never repay you. But there is another who holds my heart, whom I left...in an inexcusable fashion."

"And to her you will go?"

He nodded.

Sorcha smiled despite this fresh cause for grief. "That pleases me greatly." And it did, that he had someone to love, hopefully who loved him in return. "But Grimm, what kept you from her? Pray do not tell me you stayed away from her all this time merely to safeguard me? I will clobber you over the head with—"

His deep chuckle interrupted her growing exasperation.

"No, Sorcha, it was not you, but me that kept me away. And fear."

"Fear?"

"A man cannot fight as we do in this war, not with competence and success, without gathering some scars internally. I thought I shouldn't burden her with my demons, but..." he shrugged, a wee sheepish suddenly, "perhaps I'm hoping that she'll see me as you see the MacKenzie, beyond the façade of warrior and all he must possess and exude to survive, down to the heart."

Sorcha blanched a bit but advised, "You cannot be compared to Augustus Grimm. I *know* your heart is good." She glanced back toward the inn, a hundred yards away, seeing that the crowd there had dispersed. "I think in his case, what has been said about the Rebel might actually be true."

"Do not judge him by that one piece of evidence, certainly when you have not the full story."

His quick and firm defense of Augustus surprised her.

"Sorcha, you understand why the legend needs to be fed, needs to be exaggerated, to strike fear in his enemies. Likewise you know—you *know* this—that the man and his legend are not the same person."

She said nothing, not sure that she did still believe that.

"Are you planning to leave soon?" She asked, pleased to change the subject.

"I am." His lips curved upward. "I meant to give you and Finn some time before I came to give my farewell."

Her eyes were suddenly awash in tears. "Will I ever see you again?"

"I have every confidence that you will," he said.

From where came this confidence she did not know.

"The MacKenzie has invited me into his army and to imagine a life at Strontian when we're not at war," he announced, revealing the justification behind his certainty.

Of course, his sureness was predicated on an apparent belief that she, too, would one day reside at Strontian.

"But you would fight against your own?" She thought to ask.

"I will for right," he answered simply, which did sound quite like something Augustus would say.

"So this is it," she concluded.

"It is for now."

Fearing that, despite his prediction, she would never see him again, Sorcha hugged him long and tightly. "Farewell, my friend. May God ever watch over you."

When they parted, and before Grimm turned and left her, he said gently, "Listen to your intuition, Sorcha. Think for yourself and of yourself, honestly, about which man is better suited to you and holds the true affection at the core of your heart."

And with that, he bowed courteously, pivoted on his heel and walked away.

Sorcha stared after him for a long moment, somehow not surprised about his insight into her turmoil.

Chapter Twenty-One

"I remember all those weeks it took for us to thatch this roof originally," Sorcha called up from the bottom of the ladder.

"I dinna recall," Finn sent downward.

Glancing upward, she saw only his boots and legs and a compacted view of his torso, arms, and head as he stood at the top of the ladder.

"You don't remember?" Sorcha challenged. "Finn, it took us nearly a week to gather all the straw, and another for it to dry, and you an entire fortnight, working nonstop to complete the roof."

"I mean, aye, I recall that I thatched the roof," he said, a wee breathless for his labors up there. "But nae more than that."

"Don't you remember," she pressed, "we prayed the rain would hold off until it was complete, but of course it did not. We woke one night when only half the roof was done, and rain was patting us on the face. We had to move the cot to the other side of the cottage, under the finished section."

The speed of his response suggested little thought given to the memory evoked. "I dinna remember that."

"Oh."

This was either sad or curious, or mayhap both. It was odd as well, in her estimation, considering that she'd tucked away and cherished every minute detail of their time together. Chewing her lip, she wondered if the harrowing nature of war meant that Finn had been induced to bury his sweet memories even deeper and thus they were lost to consciousness.

He'd been back for two days now. Frankly, she was still reeling from his return, both joyously and guiltily.

Two days ago, after he'd fled the cottage only moments after they'd entered, he'd not returned until the evening, saying he'd had a hard time tracking down his immediate commander. He'd been told he had leave so long as the king's army remained garrisoned at Ironwood, which Robert Bruce had since assumed for his own use.

"Willna be long, though," Finn had said then. "The king has plans to lay siege to the castle at Ayr, where the English commander, Pembroke, has made his camp."

Though he seemed to be—*was*, Sorcha was certain—genuinely happy to see her, that happiness appeared to be attached to his hope to renew their intimacy. When he'd returned that evening, he'd tried again to kiss her. And though it pained her enormously to deny him—Finn, to whom she'd freely and happily given so many kisses—she had again pushed him away, having yet to come to terms with the sense of betrayal she felt at the very idea, in regard to Augustus.

She simply could not bring herself to return Finn's affection, having met and adored the expertise of Augustus's loving, and hardly able to bear the knowledge that Finn's very rudimentary and sometimes fumbling attention could not compare. However, she hadn't resisted Finn's advances merely because memories of his lovemaking did not stir in her that same breathless excitement as did the memory of being loved by Augustus. She simply—and selfishly—didn't want the perfection of her night with Augustus to fade by taking Finn to her bed. She wanted to hold onto that memory for as long as she could, until she could no more.

Finn had received this blow poorly—childishly, in her mind.

"Might well 'ave stayed with my mates, if that be the case," he'd said.

Shortly thereafter, he'd announced he would leave.

"You won't stay with me?" She'd challenged. "Because I won't lie with you yet?"

Finn had shaken this off. "Nae, Sorcha, but I was instructed I must return to my unit each night." And so he did, departing her company after spending naught but an hour with her.

Petulance of that sort was rare but not wholly unknown to her. In truth, however, she'd carefully cleaved that and other small, disconcerting traits of his from the trove of her memories over the last twelve months.

And yet the tears she'd shed that first night were not for Finn, either in gladness for is return or for how awkward they were and what a stranger he seemed to her. Tears she'd shed that first night were for having to abandon what had blossomed so wondrously between her and Augustus, for the knowledge that never again would his strong arms enfold her, never again would his kiss ravish her.

She'd woken, not well-rested and her mood scarcely improved.

Despite this, yesterday had been quite nice. Finn had come in the early afternoon and had stayed with her most of the day. For a while it was as if he had never left. They'd visited the woodland apiary, and she showed him the damage from the storm. Though Finn expressed neither great sadness nor any desire to discuss how they might rebuild and even expand, as they'd always dreamed of doing, Sorcha was sure he was pleased to revisit the hives and to spend time with her. And yet, he had changed, she decided, not unexpected for what he might have seen and done in the last year. He frowned more and spoke less, and sometimes stared at her blankly, as if he saw through her or was seeing something else rather than her.

He'd spoken of some of his experiences in war, from the very beginning, his first battle, and how terror had filled him. She might have said, *Yes, I know all about it*, but did not. She could not quite fathom what reason compelled her to withhold her own recent initiation to war, but shook herself free of this concern and concentrated on Finn's accounts.

"We met a gruesome battle at Methven," Finn had said, plucking a long blade of grass from where they'd sat in the sunny glade of the ruined apiary. "The king invited Pembroke then to meet him in battle. From beyond the walls, Pembroke declined, sayin' it was too late in the day and dawn would serve them better." He frowned down at the grass in his hand, attempting to tear the long strip in two from top to bottom. "'Twas naught but a few hours later when we were yet erecting the camp and some were out foraging and others, they were already knee-deep into preparing their meals when Pembroke and his force broke through the trees. Christ, outnumbered us three to one, we guessed." He harrumphed, recollection making him silent for a moment. He threw aside two pieces of grass, split perfectly down the middle. "I was taking a leak at that moment. I dinna ken what to do, just dropped to the ground behind the brush, and rolled off to one side until I was hidden deeper. Och, but Sorcha, the screams all around, the sound of metal striking flesh and bone, the way a horse squeals like a hog when it's been struck." He shrugged helplessly at the same time he shook his head. "I covered my ears, couldnae stand it, the madness, watching as my own mates were slain, some nae more than a dozen feet away, those that ran from camp."

Sorcha said not a word. She was torn between heartfelt compassion for how terrifying that must have been, literally caught with his breeches down and overrun by an army thrice the size of his, and a certain disappointment that Finn had hid himself, watching men die that he might have saved.

But surely, she justified, he would have perished himself if he'd announced his presence in any way to the enemy.

However, there was no way she could resist comparing this behavior to that of Augustus, who had fought valiantly at Ashgill's pass and had only fled the immediate scene—after killing as many as he did who'd attacked him—because she'd been with him. *My God, how he'd battled*, she thought.

Unless I am slain, Sorcha, Augustus proclaimed shortly before the ambush, *I vow that ye will live.*

When the roof repairs were complete, Finn went off for a while, in search of some small game out of which to make a meal. Sorcha remained inside the cottage, using what remained of her barley and oats, which she procured from Ironwood's priest's glebe, the strip within the open fields maintained by the church, and for which she bartered using beeswax and honey, the latter which Father John proclaimed he could not eat his morning bannock without. She made a small loaf of bread and foraged within sight of her cottage for mushrooms and nuts to add to the pottage she'd started fresh upon her return.

Together, Sorcha and Finn enjoyed a fine stew, including the long-legged hare that Finn had brought and the addition of an onion, gotten from where Finn would not say. Mayhap the army had stores to which the soldiers could help themselves, she guessed, hoping that in reality, Finn had not pilfered the stores of another peasant as he'd sometimes been known to do, a habit Sorcha had been trying to break him of.

He talked more of places he'd been and people he'd met and for a little while seemed more the Finn she'd known and loved and less the stranger that had first returned to her. And yet, when evening came, she almost dreaded that he might attempt once more to share their bed and knew a profound relief, though it was tangled with guilt, when he announced his intention to return to camp without making any advances.

That night she sat on the side of the narrow cot, her hands on either side of her while she soaked her feet in a basin. Dressed in only her shift, having moments ago bathed the rest of herself, she pulled the torn hem of her shift into her lap. Absently, her finger traced over the uneven edges, hardly able to credit that it had been but days ago since she'd made the tear herself and bandaged Augustus's injury.

Try as she might, she couldn't stop thinking about Augustus.

And yet as she yearned for him, she was riddled with guilt. She was being fickle, she told herself harshly, arguing within that it was Finn she loved, and had loved for years since he'd been the beekeeper at Ballechen and she the daughter of its lord. The truth was, as difficult as it was to consider, that Finn was so much better as a memory than he was in reality.

Shaking her head, Sorcha knew that was not precisely true. More precisely, she began to wonder after having spent a few days intermittently with him, if her love for Finn had been greater in her lonely recollection than when it lived between them. Possibly, his supposed death had elevated her love to mythic proportions. Had her love for him and the effect on her heart been perfected in the embrace of memory?

The issue was, as she saw it, that he stirred in her no great and tumultuous emotion. Her heart did not beat with the thrill of anticipation at his touch, her eyes did not follow every move he made, she did not stop and stare in wonder at a smile from him, there was no spark of longing deep within her soul when she looked in his eyes.

Had there ever been?

Frowning abruptly, she pushed the hem of her shift down over her legs.

"No," she told herself. "No. I love Finn. I do."

She reminded herself of the differences between Finn and Augustus where the former clearly rose above the other in terms of suitability. Augustus, the Rebel, was cruel and merciless, killed with an ease that was alarming, and was often brooding and formidable. She remembered how thoroughly intimidated she'd been when she'd first laid eyes on him.

Finn was exactly the opposite. He was steady and true, a gentle soul who apparently did not relish the killing. They shared a beautiful history together. He was neither cruel nor merciless.

The inner struggle raged on within Sorcha, tearing at her heart and pounding in her head. Pitted against the familiar, comforting love she held for Finn—as she convinced herself it was, it *must* be—was the newfound allure of Augustus, a man whose enigmatic presence intrigued, entranced, and titillated her. She was caused to wonder if her fascination bordered on obsession, or if such devotion to a man as stoic and unyielding—and possibly as cruel as the rumors portrayed—was not, indeed, simply foolish or in fact, crazy.

She might have cried all night, her head and heart at war, but it occurred to her that possibly it was all for naught, her wrestling with indecision about her feelings for Finn versus Augustus.

In all likelihood, she had overestimated her own worth in Augustus's eyes. Mayhap he didn't want her. He hadn't challenged her leaving with Finn, hadn't said one word.

And he hadn't come for her since, as she'd fully expected that he would, demanding that she belonged to him.

***

Three days later, after the arrival of the king—and the return of Sorcha's true love—Augustus rode with Robert Bruce and a small retinue about the demesne of Ironwood, wanting to examine the entire holding and all it entailed. The king had confiscated Ironwood for the Scottish monarchy, and would, as was customary, entrust it to one of the nobles who had remained or had proven faithful to him and his wearing of the crown.

"I would gladly put it in your hands," said the king to Augustus as they rode, "and will do so, if you would consider coming down from your mountains up there at Strontian. I would appreciate a good warden for Caol, one loyal and true as you have proven with such distinction."

"I am honored that you would consider it, sire," Augustus acknowledged proudly. "But I happen to like those mountains—"

"And the distance between them and other society?"

"Aye, and that, too. Strontian is home, sire, and there I will abide when comes the end of war."

"God willing, sooner rather than later," Robert Bruce said with steadfastness.

In truth, the prospect of becoming lord of Ironwood filled Augustus with a deep-seated unease, one he struggled to articulate. On the surface, and as he'd said, his refusal to accept so generous an offering was a matter of an allegiance to his Highland fortress. Beneath his refusal, however, lurked a more poignant truth: the thought of residing in Caol, with Sorcha so near but out of his reach, belonging to another, was a torment he dared not consider. The mere thought of seeing her with another man and possibly having to witness her affection for Finn, a love he suspected surpassed anything she could ever feel for him, was a wound he was not brave enough to risk.

They rode on, through the village and over fields recently planted, along the river that emptied into the loch, and through the forest. The king commented on the fine quality of the soil, the sorry state of the mill, and the density of the forest, remarking that there was suitable timber available for cutting.

What more he might have added to that last statement was forestalled by one of the king's guard giving a curt and abbreviated whistle to alert all that something was either suspicious or unknown, warranting investigation.

As the small party came to a halt inside the forest, all noise of their making ceased until only the whisper of softly rustling leaves and occasional birdsong were heard.

With a furrowed brow, Augustus scrutinized the area all around and attuned his ears. It took only a few seconds to realize what had given the guardsman pause.

It wasn't just birdsong nearby; there was another voice singing. The sound, melodious and clear, carried through the forest with a gentle cadence. It echoed softly among the trees and yet carried a warmth that was evident and raised the king's brow.

Had it not been for the king's presence, Augustus might have closed his eyes and listened to her sweet song.

Sorcha apparently was at her apiary, the storm-damaged one, which was fairly close to where they stood.

"Stand down," he said to the watchful guards. And to the king, Augustus said, "'Tis the beekeeper, sire. Sorcha Reid. Ye met her the other day when she was reunited with her man, long-believed dead."

"Ah, yes, the beauty with the luminous blue eyes," the king recalled. He studied Augustus thoughtfully while he listened to Sorcha's singing, and they had yet to move. "Hm. If her presumed-dead lover had not returned, would you then have considered my offer of Ironwood and this earldom?"

Though affairs of the heart had no place in any conversation with the king, not now when his reign was so precarious, Augustus shook his head and said honestly, "I would have taken her to Strontian with me."

Robert Bruce studied Augustus a moment more before pulling on the reins and turning his horse around, though he remained close to Augustus's side.

"I've seen all I need to see of the estate and have matters to attend inside Ironwood's keep, messages to send," said the king. "We will return, the guards and I, but you, Augustus, should visit with the beekeeper—who clearly owns the voice of one of God's angel, I trow." The king drew closer and lowered his voice ever-so-slightly. "More remarkable than her reunion with her lover was the pain etched on your face at the same time," he said. "Advise her of your imminent departure, Augustus, and make a proper farewell, my friend. Pray do not leave and regret that you hadn't done so."

He nodded and within seconds, the king and his men had melded into the trees.

Augustus sat a moment more, debating if he would truly approach Sorcha in her apiary. Like as not, the man Finn would be with her. With so limited a time and with so much to celebrate and renew, Augustus imagined that the man had barely left her side.

His nostrils flared at the very thought.

Of course he teemed with tortured emotions, none of which he wanted to either name or investigate. But aye, the king wasn't far off the mark. Though Augustus was fairly certain he'd never had a broken heart, and that he hadn't ever suffered pain at the loss of affection from any woman, he supposed that the king's description of what he'd seen on his face three days ago was apt. He'd felt as if all the air had been sucked out of his lungs, and all promises of joy had been cleaved from the realm of possibility in those moments.

Geddy had goaded him later, unintentionally Augustus was sure, but had riled him all the same, wondering almost verbatim what Augustus initially had. "That's what she'd been mooning and mourning? All those bluidy songs twisting my heart and what? They'd been sung for that one and he looks to have nae more than a score of years under his belt, naught but a downy chin of hair? Ye mean to tell me he's man enough for her? That one, and he's nae wide enough to bless himself, and I dinna ken how he might keep her safe." The captain had snorted, the sound harsh and unflattering for the opinion attached to it.

Augustus sighed with distaste. And yet, it was what it was—and it was, he'd since decided, likely for the best.

He knew what he was: brooding, proud, fierce, often unyielding, and unable to distinguish love and all its softness from weakness. He had long maintained that love was a vulnerability he could not afford, one that might compromise his strength and effectiveness.

Sorcha, he determined, needed qualities that likely Finn could and had provided, emotional support or tenderness, things he struggled to express or show. She was better off with Finn, he told himself for the hundredth time, having fully convinced himself that he was acting in her best interest. His greatest desire was Sorcha's happiness and well-being, and it was only gut-wrenchingly unfortunate that to have those things meant it would be with someone else, and that his own desires would be squashed.

For one fleeting moment, he wished he was not the man he was, nor the legend he'd allowed to grow. But nae, 'twas dangerous, such thoughts. As it was, a small part of him already had wondered if the force behind his feelings for Sorcha had the potential to destabilize his carefully constructed identity or disrupt the control he fiercely maintained over his emotions and actions—as was already proven by how ungovernable to himself he'd become since first he'd set eyes on Sorcha.

Moreover, he reminded himself of his duty, to be at the king's side, in an uphill battle where the peak was not yet in sight. Or, in this case, as the king had made his wishes known yesterday, Augustus would not immediately be at the king's side but working on his behalf.

Make a proper farewell, the king had advised.

Straightening himself in the saddle, Augustus moved forward, toward the clearing and the apiary, realizing that she'd stopped singing. He hadn't far to go, he knew, but sped up a bit, hoping he hadn't missed his opportunity.

He found her standing in the middle of the glade, garbed in the familiar worn blue cloak, curiously faced in his direction and wearing an expression of arrested wariness.

The lad, Finn, was not in attendance of Sorcha, or not seen at the moment.

Though his heart quickened at the sight of her, a wave of concern washed over Augustus, fueled by her apparent unease.

"Sorcha?" He questioned, dismounting swiftly and covering the short distance between them easily with his long strides. "What causes your distress?"

Her façade softened as he approached, the visible apprehension evaporating.

She was quick to ease his mind. "No, nothing. Nothing. I heard your horse, but I didn't know who came. It's fine. It's you."

"Oh," he said, with a great lack of cleverness. And words continued to evade him as he stared at her, realizing he was unlikely to ever see her again. His heart clenched in anguish at the idea and time seemed to slow to a crawl as he desperately tried to commit to memory every detail of her exquisite features.

Her fair golden locks, kissed by the sun, cascaded in waves over her narrow shoulders, framing a face so achingly perfect that he hoped forever its image was burned in his brain. But in truth, 'twas her eyes he would remember most, for they had captivated him from the start. Presently, they were mesmerizing pools of azure as she returned his silent regard.

Her gaze sparkled with a depth of emotion that stirred his very core, as if she too were aware that this would be the last time they would meet.

Clearing his throat, by no means anxious to become mawkish, he scowled at her and announced the reason for his presence.

"A farewell is due between us," he said. "The king and his army—your man included—will abide at Ironwood for a few more days before they head south. I and a dozen of my men will be returning briefly to Strontian at the king's behest. He is hoping that with his most recent triumph over Pembroke, and with Longshanks' health rumored to be perilous, that I might be able to gather a large force from some of the previously foot-dragging Highland clans."

"Oh," she said, every bit as unclever as he.

He assumed that this new distress was centered around having to bid farewell to Finn again. Likely she would be worried that another notice of death might come and that it would be real.

"The larger the army is, Sorcha," he advised, meaning to put her mind at ease, "the safer he will be."

"You are leaving," she said, ignoring his assurance and sounding a wee breathless. "First north and then south, to join the king and fight more battles."

He nodded, a bit confused by what seemed a fresh worry in her.

He knew not what else to say, though so much was left unsaid between them. And so it would remain.

Pride, of course, would not allow him to ask her to choose him, to come with him, or to wait for him. Still, as mighty as was his pride, he had to fight furiously to refrain from voicing the request.

Sorcha, too, seemed equally tongue-tied. After their initial long and melancholy stare, she'd spent the next little while darting glances at him, sharing her gaze with the hands she fidgeted with at her waist, as if she, too, were loath to take her leave, likely understanding as he did they would never see each other again.

Until Sorcha's gaze settled at length on him, and she whispered brokenly, "I'm so sorry, Augustus. I don't know what...if any hope you might have"—she stopped and shook herself rigidly. And then she started again. "I'm sorry this happened. Not Finn's return, of course, but that it happened...when it did and how it did, when we had barely...."

She did not finish but bit her lip and glanced again at her hands.

"Are you sorry for me or for you?"

He believed this an appropriate and justified question.

Even as her gaze lifted swiftly and her brow knit at the question, she wilted before him, her shoulders sagging. "I'm sorry for us."

He stared at her with a diligent gaze, trying to see what was unveiled in her face, and leave off reading her through his emotions, all of which were negative. The genuine distress glimpsed could not then be overlooked.

And aye, there'd been hope, and it rose again to the surface now.

If she were torn, could he convince her? He couldn't with words, having not the foggiest notion what might need to be said, having never once in his life begged for anything.

But a kiss perhaps. A kiss would remind her of their passion, might very well persuade her to choose him.

Abruptly, he moved, closing the gap between them. He was sure he appeared pitifully in need of her but did not care. He hauled her up against his chest, caged her within his arms, and captured her mouth and her startled gasp with a kiss of possessive greed. His hands swept over her tantalizing curves as he pressed his tongue inside her mouth, wanting to taste her.

Her resistance was tiny and lackluster and swiftly abandoned. Sorcha clutched at him, pressing against him with a whimper of delight, opening herself to him.

He kissed her as if he were starving and she responded ardently, as if she meant to nourish him.

For one glorious moment, his heart soared. In that time she melted against him as she had so beautifully before, she slid her tongue hungrily between his teeth and tasted him, and she molded her soft body to his. For that moment, she was his. For a moment her arms were wrapped around his shoulders but too soon, they lowered and wriggled between him and her. She pushed at his chest until he was forced to break the kiss.

Tears clouded her eyes as she pushed against him. His face twisted with raw fury for her conflicting actions.

"No," she pleaded. "No, please. Finn is back. I'm with Finn now...again."

All sense of restraint dissolved, gone in a flash. With the feel of her kiss and her equally desperate response so fresh, and the mention of her lover's name, jealousy and rage were unleashed.

"If he put his hands on you, I'll—"

"He is my husband," Sorcha contended hotly through her tears, her voice raised.

"He is nae yer husband," Augustus shot back hoarsely, "nae any more than I am. Did ye lay with him?"

Ah, Christ, why did he utter those words!

While he still held her arms, not allowing her to escape completely, Sorcha dropped the top of her head against his chest. Her hands remained there as well, her fingers splayed out above his stomach. Her shoulders shook with sobs, though she made no noise.

Mechanically, he moved his hand from her arm and slid it around her back, holding her close, drawing in a deep and tortured breath as he stared above her, into the trees, waiting for her tears to subside.

"I did not," she said after a full minute had passed. Another cry came. "I could not," she wept. "I didn't want it to weaken the memory of being in your arms."

Augustus closed his eyes and fought against all emotions while in the depths of his being, a storm raged.

He gathered Sorcha closer and held her tenderly.

"But ye will remain his?"

Another sob shuddered through her. Now fully in his embrace, with her cheek pressed against him, she nodded.

"I have to be with Finn."

"And what we shared?"

"Was...very special but—"

His noxious curse quieted her.

"Dinna pawn me off with such rubbish," he demanded severely even as he did not let her go.

And Sorcha did not immediately push to be freed. Her hands grasped at the fabric near his waist.

"My heart is broken, Augustus," she whispered in a small voice.

For the life of him, he could not bring himself to admit the truth, that his was as well.

It took another few moments for Sorcha to calm herself. He felt her draw in long, measured breaths, felt the rapid beat of her heart begin to slow.

She tipped her face up to him, her eyes shimmering with moisture, while her cheeks were wet with tears. The tip of her nose was red.

Gently now she pushed away.

And he let her go.

When she stood a few feet removed from him, she met his gaze and gave him a bittersweet smile, the last he would have from her.

"Be a good man, Augustus," she said.

While he stared, lifeless, she turned and walked away.

Chapter Twenty-Two

Finn did not visit her until late in the day. They supped together, once more on the rabbit stew, sitting at the small table in the dreary light inside the cottage. She'd been thankful that he'd not come sooner, that she didn't have to explain her tears and desolation to him. She didn't ask what kept him away until so late an hour and it wasn't until much later that she frowned over what seemed only a half-hearted want to be in her company.

She painted on a bright smile and stared absently at him while he spoke, at her request for something to occupy them, of the daily routine of the army.

"Marching is all we do, Sorcha," Finn answered between spoonfuls. "Aye, and when we're nae doing that, we have drills, and patrol, and mundane chores and uninspiring meals."

He then went on, in long-winded fashion, about an occasion when he became lost while on routine patrol, only to stumble after more than an hour upon a familiar landmark, which allowed him to eventually find his way back to camp. Sorcha listened attentively, expecting the drawn out tale to contain some bit of excitement or misadventure, but it never did.

"Ye're nae yerself tonight," he commented soon after his tedious tale. "Ye've hardly said two words. I'll be leaving shortly, Sorcha, and I dinna ken that ye'll mind so much. Ye've given nae the welcome nor the homecoming I'd expected."

Guilt ripped through her.

"I'm sorry, Finn. I really am. I want to...but...." She swallowed thickly. "Finn, do you believe we are the same people we were when first we left Ballechen?"

He frowned, possibly at her unrelated question.

"The same person?" He repeated, a hint of incredulity in his tone. "Nae, I'm nae the same person. *Jesu*, Sorcha, ye have nae idea what I've been through, what I've seen. I'm nae more a lad, stumbling through life without purpose or direction."

She was taken aback by his last words but had no time to dwell upon them as Finn continued.

"Ye're nae the same either, I can see that."

No, she was not. Though her response was not the whole truth, it was a large part of it as well. "Just as you needed to become a different person to be a confident and capable soldier, Finn, so I had to adjust to being by myself. It was daunting," she admitted, and gave a short laugh. "And quite often, certainly in the beginning, I cried as much for your loss as I did out of fear."

"Aye, but it's different, Sorcha," Finn argued. "Ye face nae life and death battles, dinna have to worry when ye would eat next—or if ye would. Ye had the townsfolk to support ye and I told Murdo to keep an eye on ye."

Nodding, Sorcha acquiesced, even as none of that was true. "You're right. Of course, the two circumstances cannot be compared."

Finn took his leave shortly after, his good night stilted after he made no attempt to hold her or kiss her, for which she was thankful and then infused with shame for feeling that way.

She was mentally exhausted, completely drained, and yet sleep eluded her. She was riddled with fear—an odd certainty—that she'd made the wrong decision.

Yesterday, she'd decided that Finn was the better man, and thus the better choice, but it just didn't feel that way.

Once more, she was driven to compare her love for Finn to her feelings for Augustus.

She shared an undeniable history with Finn, a past filled with love, companionship, and shared dreams—or so she'd thought. His statement about stumbling through life without purpose or direction had struck her as dishonest, or at the very least misremembered. Plans and dreams, of which they'd had plenty, could not be likened to aimlessness.

Finn had been her escape from a stifling and unhappy home life, and their time together had held the promise of joy and freedom. Had it always been perfect? No. But what was?

Her heart ached at the memory of joy they once shared, and she did genuinely mourn his loss deeply when she believed him to be dead. But now, in his presence again, Sorcha found herself questioning both the depth and the authenticity of her feelings for Finn. Was her love authentic? Or had it merely been a product of duty and guilt? He rescued her from a life she despised, and the weight of that debt had often hung heavy on her conscience. Many times since she'd had word that Finn had fallen in battle, Sorcha had tortured herself with guilt that if they had not ever left Ballechen, Finn might still be alive. All of this created doubt, wondering if she'd been clinging to the idea of loving him out of obligation rather than true affection.

Her brain and heart wrangled with questions about guilt, obligation, and the true nature of love.

One thing she knew for certain. Finn had changed, as had she. Had they simply outgrown one another? Apart from his attempts to be intimate with her, he'd seemed almost disinterested in the prospect of spending time with her. True, her conflicted and lukewarm welcome—a shameful thing—likely served as a strong detriment.

In contrast, while her love for Finn was known and comfortable, even if it had risen from a place of guilt and a sense of obligation—her feelings for Augustus were unbridled, colored with the joy of hope.

But that had been before she'd encountered that scene in front of the inn, and the man with the severed hand. That man and his pitiful circumstance had reminded Sorcha of Augustus's reputation, how fierce and unkind he could be. She was sorry now that she'd not taken the opportunity of meeting Augustus in the forest to question him about that man and the loss of his hand.

And yet, a part of her knew, in the depths of her soul, that there had to be more to the story. Despite his reputation, her personal knowledge of Augustus didn't align with the idea of him callously and cruelly taking off a man's hand simply for the crime of poaching.

She frowned into the darkness.

Augustus *was* a good man. She knew that he was. She felt this truth deep in her bones.

He had the power to take her, unwilling, in the beginning, but he did not.

He brought her thatch for her roof and gloves for her hands.

He freed Grimm, a man unjustly imprisoned, and on her word alone.

He'd fought as a demon during that ambush in his efforts to keep her free from harm.

He wore that gruesome expression when he climbed up from the pass where they buried the dead, his sorrow monumental all that night.

He'd loved her tenderly, rousing passion as she'd never imagined.

Closing her eyes, she allowed herself to feel his presence, his strength, and the cherished memory of his kiss.

Listen to your intuition, Grimm had suggested. *About which man is better suited to you and holds the true affection at the core of your heart.*

Sorcha bit her lip.

Oh, but I've made a terrible mistake.

***

Sorcha rose with purpose the next morning and not without a great fear that she might be too late. Pray God that Augustus hadn't yet departed for Strontian. She would make the journey herself if she had to but would much rather do so in his arms. She was visited by and quickly squashed a niggling doubt that he might not want her. No, she'd witnessed up close the depth of his pain, glinting in his steely blue eyes when she'd told him she'd chosen Finn and not him; she'd felt the power of his kiss yesterday, and all the furious emotions attached to it.

Quickly, she threw on her léine and ran her bone comb through her hair before twirling her cloak around her shoulders and pulling open the door.

She started and came to an abrupt halt at discovering Finn there, walking up from the lane.

Her first instinct was to excuse herself and ask to speak with him later. She needed to tell him of her decision as well. But Finn smiled at the sight of her even as a fleeting look of surprise brightened his face and began speaking before she might have.

"I came to advise that we're leaving a day earlier now," he said. "King Robert wants to march come tomorrow's sun."

"Oh, I see." Drawing a deep breath, she stepped backwards and invited Finn inside. "Finn, I'm glad you're—"

"Och, Sorcha," he said as he entered the cottage, "ye have to hear this. It's all over Ironwood, all through the camp. Some ne'er-do-well from the MacKenzie stronghold found his way to Caol."

Sorcha held her breath at the mention of Strontian.

"The Rebel sliced off his hand and, get this, Sorcha, made him wear it round his neck. *Jesu*, but he's a monster, aye?"

Bristling at the falsehood, Sorcha opened her mouth to refute this.

Finn kept on going though. "The man is pathetic, I guess, naught but a miserable drunk these days." He snickered haughtily. "And what did he ken would happen? I understand the poaching, 'ave done it myself, but he attacked some lass, nae but ten and three they say, and the Rebel—"

"He assaulted a young girl? The poacher with one hand?"

"Aye, that's what was told. 'Tis said the Rebel did nae kill him outright because he had a wife and bairns to support. Apparently MacKenzie kent that losing a hand would render him incapable of assaulting another, but that he could still shepherd the herd as he did. That's what was told anyway. Soft, by my reckoning," Finn said. "The Rebel, that is, for nae killing him as he needed. Should've chopped off his bits as that's what brought him to Caol, or rather from Strontian. 'Tis said he attacked another lass—or tried to—and Strontian's bailiff banished him fer guid."

Sorcha's heart soared with relief. She'd known there had to be some explanation.

She would have chopped off something as well, if the choice had been hers, for the man's attack on one so innocent.

She did not challenge Finn about his conflicting assessment of Augustus, having called him a monster and soft in the space of a few seconds.

"But I told ye, did I nae, that the Rebel was too be avoided, Sorcha? Bad news, that one. Aye, I dinna mind fighting in his company, dinna get me wrong, for he's the devil inside a fight—save that I heard de Montfort trounced him easily, naught but a week ago, I hear. And what's so mighty about him now, beaten by de Montfort's militia? They are nae but—"

"It was an ambush," Sorcha interjected tersely. "The MacKenzies were caught inside a narrow pass and de Montforts men—more than twice in number—turned on them without provocation."

Finn scowled at her, possibly wondering from where she'd gotten her information.

"Anyhow," he said, shrugging, "I dinna think he's quite what his reputation describes."

"He's not," Sorcha stated. "He's gallant and honorable and brave beyond reason. And he—"

"How the hell would ye ken that?" He laughed.

"Because I know him," she confessed. While Finn's frown returned, she added with confidence, "And I love him."

Mother of God, but that felt good, to get that out, to acknowledge that truth.

Finn's mouth opened but no words came forth.

Swallowing, and reminded of her guilt and shame regarding Finn, Sorcha winced a bit. "I'm sorry, Finn. I know that because I had believed you dead I don't need to feel guilty about loving Augustus, but I want you to know if I *hadn't* believed you dead, I absolutely would not have betrayed our...commitment." Having recently questioned the validity of her affection for Finn, she couldn't bring herself to use the word *love*.

"What...? Sorcha, what are you saying? Do ye jest?"

Softening her voice, she confirmed, "No, Finn. I love Augustus. And I want to be with him."

"He raped ye? Is that what happened? And now ye believe ye—"

"No!" She was quick to clarify. "No, he most certainly did not. Nothing I did was against my will." While he stared at her, seemingly aghast, Sorcha reiterated, "I am very sorry, Finn."

Eventually, Finn shook himself from the stupor of his shock. "But ye canna go with him or be with him," he said, as much a statement as it was a question. "Ye'll wait here for me to return again."

"Oh, Finn," she breathed, awash in guilt once more. "I cannot—"

"Ye've lain with him?" Finn interjected.

Sorcha bit her lip and nodded, her heart breaking for the shock she'd visited upon him.

Finn puffed up his cheeks with air before blowing it out, his frown still in evidence.

"'Tis nae easy a transgression to forgive, Sorcha."

I don't need your forgiveness, Finn, she thought but did not say. She watched as Finn tried to comprehend the gravity of what he'd just learned. And grimaced a bit while there was a moment of quiet contemplation, during which lines etched across his forehead and his eyes darted back and forth, searching for clarity amidst what surely was the chaos of her startling news. This was followed by a subtle shift in his expression, what seemed a blending of acceptance and determination.

Sorcha lifted her brows, hope overcoming her that he understood what this meant.

"Ye canna be with him, though. Ye ken that. Ye're nae made to be the Rebel's leman, Sorcha. Ye'll stay with me. And aye, I can forgive ye as I assume ye will my own transgressions, though mine are likely easier to justify."

"Your transgressions?" Sorcha asked.

"'Tis a long time marching, Sorcha," Finn explained matter-of-factly, addressing the ground beneath them, "and aye, sometimes I found relief in the bed of another." His ensuing chuckle was both misplaced and offensive, as it preceded the confession, "Sometimes nae in a bed, but upon grass or hay." He glanced up at Sorcha and mayhap deciphered her quiet disbelief and outrage. "'Tis nae anything to fash about. They dinna mean anything to me. And here ye are, confessing the same thing, so...."

Her jaw dropped and she stared at him, with fresh eyes and not the lens she owned years ago.

Starchily, she inquired, "Did you believe *me* dead at the time, Finn?"

He frowned, not in anger but in confusion, possibly wondering why she would have thought that.

She had been firm and confident and happy in her decision to part with Finn, had been sure that not only was Augustus the better man, but the one who owned her heart. But this was quite agreeable, she decided, to have this additional justification behind her decision.

The very fact that shock was the foremost emotion at this moment—not pain or sorrow—confirmed what she'd already guessed: that her love for Finn was not what memory had proclaimed it to be.

"The house is yours, Finn," she said indifferently, his unfaithfulness allowing her more easily to put the matter to rest. Guilt would no longer be a part of her life in this regard. "Do with it as you like. I won't be here when you return." She didn't know yet what might become of the bees, though she knew that bees had the capability to survive for years, even centuries, without attendance. Ideally, she would be able to relocate the hives to Strontian.

And unless Augustus rejected her outright and harshly, she *was* going to Strontian, either with him or to wait for him.

"Ye're serious, are ye?"

"I am. I love you, Finn, as much as I am able, and I will forever cherish what we had together."

She was, frankly, a tiny bit surprised that he seemed to accept it as well as he did.

Shrugging, glancing out the open door as if he wished to be walking through it, Finn said, "I guess there's nae reason for me to return ever to Caol." Turning back to Sorcha, he theorized, "I found a sweet spot down near Glasgow, south of there, fine burgh it is, Renfrew. I might eventually find myself there."

Some intuition prompted her to ask, "A woman lives there? One who caught yer fancy?"

Finn hesitated but then nodded.

Sorcha smiled. "Mayhap we were both living in the past, tied to it by what we felt was obligation. You should have told me, Finn," she said gently, lightened by the removal of so much anxiety.

"Aye, I might have," he said. "Truth be told, Sorcha, if ye'd received me better, with more passion, I'd have been happy to keep ye."

Of course it was worded all wrong, nearly offensively, but Sorcha did not take issue with it. She did, however, remind him of something she'd not have borne. "But I wouldn't have endured your infidelity, Finn."

For a moment they stared at each other.

"I wish you well, Finn, in wherever you go."

"And ye, Sorcha. I dinna ken about a life for ye with the Rebel, but I ken yer mind and that ye're impossible to stop once ye set it to something."

They embraced warmly. Sorcha closed her eyes, a bit teary-eyed after all for this, what would be their final parting, though it was nothing compared to the raw pain what ripped through her yesterday when she'd embraced Augustus, fearing that was the last time she would ever touch him.

"Assuming he dinna yet ken of yer decision," Finn said when they broke apart, "I might suggest ye get a move on. The MacKenzies were gathering near the gates when I went by."

Sorcha's heart skipped a beat. She pecked a quick kiss on Finn's cheek and fled through the open door.

"Goodbye, Finn!" She called over her shoulder. "Stay safe!" She said, but her mind had already put him behind her.

She forced herself into a sprint, her mind racing with fright that she might already be too late, and ran as if her life depended on it, knowing that every second counted. Her heart pounded in her chest as she ran along the lane and then dashed up the heather-strewn knoll and pushed through the trees in the wooded vale until finally she burst upon the fields of Ironwood, the castle and wall visible now in the distance. She breathed raggedly and paused, trying to decipher what she saw, still so far away. There, just in front of the towering gates stood the MacKenzie unit, unsurprisingly small since Augustus had told her he would travel with only a dozen men. There they were, clad in their blue plaids and brandishing their targes. They were already in formation, was all she could make out from several hundred yards away.

With the surge of determination, Sorcha burst into another sprint, the fear of losing Augustus propelling her forward. Her shoes were sucked into the recently turned-over earth of the field, and she struggled to gain traction, losing time and momentum, until finally she simply discarded her shoes and ran barefoot.

To her dismay, a great distance remained between her and Augustus when the small force began to move, not to the south, which would have brought them much closer to her, but around the wall and toward the north.

"Augustus!" she cried out, her voice ringing with desperation as she fought to make herself heard across the distance. "Wait."

No one heard and she kept running, stumbling twice and having to put her hands into the moist dirt to prevent herself from landing on her face. The fact that the MacKenzie men were only walking along, that they hadn't broken into a canter or gallop did not seem to matter as she seemed never closer to them.

She screamed again, crying out only a loud noise, and raised her arms as she ran, scissoring them above her head.

Please see me.

Her chest heaved with exertion, but she kept moving, cutting the distance from the edge of the trees in half at the same time the last of the mounted soldiers turned the corner around the wall.

Sorcha stopped and fisted her muddy hands. With her feet planted wide, she tipped her face to the heavens and screeched his name. "Augustus!"

Breathless and hopeless, she sagged a bit and returned her gaze to Ironwood's wall. For one brief moment, it appeared that the last pair of soldiers, at the end of the wall and just near the corner, had noticed her or heard her. She squinted, trying to decide if they had paused and were looking in her direction. But she could not be sure and then they, too, disappeared from view, rounding the corner of the curtain wall.

Dismayed and dejected, Sorcha stared in anguish for another moment. And then she glanced down at her feet and toes, buried in four inches of mud. She considered her hands, caked with the same brown wet dirt.

Her heart sank and so did she, plopping gracelessly down onto her butt, with this brief defeat.

She would catch her breath, she decided, and begin immediately working on her plans to journey alone to Strontian.

While her lungs continued to protest her mad dash, Sorcha's heart broke, knowing Augustus had actually left her.

He had left her, hadn't fought for her heart.

Mayhap there was no reason to go to Strontian after all.

Oh, but there was. 'Twas not much that she owned, but she'd wager it all against Augustus's pride being the culprit, preventing him from fighting for her, for them.

The jangle of a harness, followed by her realizing the clopping sounds of a horse close by jerked her from her reverie. She closed her eyes in despair, imagining she was about to be confronted by one of the crofters and given a scolding for clomping through their runrig. Or possibly one of the king's guard, about patrol, wondered what she was doing, nearly encased in mud.

She lifted one dirty hand and held it above her head and gave a single wave. "I'm fine. Everything is fine."

"Ye dinna look it."

Sorcha startled and turned. But the horse was so close that all she saw was it's head and not the rider in the saddle.

Augustus?

She tried to stand, to hop to her feet, but was prevented from doing so by the grasping mud.

"Sweet Mother of God," she blasphemed gruffly, forced to turn onto all fours.

A hand appeared under her arm and hauled her to her feet.

On her feet, she pushed the wayward hair out of her face, unknowingly leaving a swath of mud along her brow, and glanced into a pair of perfect blue eyes.

"What are you—" she stopped and turned back toward Ironwood. There was no sign of his army, none at all. She faced Augustus again, too witless with hope and jolted by confusion to suffer any anxiety at the moment over her appearance. "But I just saw you leave," she accused, pointing her finger over her shoulder toward the keep.

"Ye saw the lads of the unit leave," he informed her.

His fierce gaze searched every inch of her face, piercing and probing in its intensity.

Sorcha's heart skipped a delicious beat as she returned his thorough scrutiny. She would never not be captivated by his face, all those broad angles and sharp lines coming together to form so handsome a visage.

Blinking, she was returned to awareness.

"What are you—why are you not with your men, going to Strontian?" Frankly, she was just befuddled enough that it was implausible that hope stood a chance of developing.

"Ye first, lass. Why do ye go barefoot through the muck and screech my name across the fields?"

"I was trying to reach you...before you left," she finished weakly.

"For what purpose?" He asked, his scowl heavy.

'Twas not the conditions she'd imagined—or rather she hadn't actually plotted out what might happen if she'd reached him in time and was able to have her say—so that she spoke from the heart, even as a huge awkwardness struck her.

"I meant to beg you to take me with you to Strontian."

"Did ye?" He asked, giving nothing away as far as his reaction; his scowl did not ease.

Sorcha nodded jerkily.

"Yesterday ye said you had to be with Finn," he reminded her shortly.

"I know," she said and bowed her head, shame filling her for how she'd doubted the truth, what she felt for Augustus.

He said nothing until she lifted her gaze again to him.

"How did ye plan to convince me?"

"What?"

"What did ye plan to say?"

Finally, his scowl departed, as his brow rose in expectation.

Ah, he wanted an allocution.

Clearing her throat, Sorcha lifted her chin and boldly stated what she knew to be true.

"I planned to tell you I was wrong and that I love you. I love *you*, Augustus."

He listened and watched her but said nothing.

"You're angry—hurt, more likely," she rushed out. "I would be, too. It seemed...well, you didn't stop me when I went with Finn."

"Ye dinna want to be stopped."

"Oh, but I did." Deep down, beyond the shock of Finn's return, she'd wanted Augustus to speak up. "I love you," she repeated, forcing out more words to convince him of her heart. "For me at least," she said and tapped her muddy fist against her chest, "for me can you set aside your intractable pride for one moment? For this moment? You do love me. I saw it in your eyes when Finn came, it was there beside the heartbreak. I know you love me. And you will probably holler at me not to tell you what you think or feel. And I will say that I have to; if you won't acknowledge it, then I must."

"And what of your man?" He asked through clenched teeth.

"Finn is not my man. I told him so only this morning. He's not...you. I seem to understand finally what life ought to be—what love ought to be! I'm no longer afraid, or making decisions based on fear or guilt or—I love you. I'm going with you," she announced with grit, unwilling to be cast aside. She let no silence sit between her words, too fearful that his continued fierce expression meant that she might have, unbelievably, misread every blessed look and touch and kiss. "You invited me to Strontian. You wanted me there, and so I'm going, either with you or—wait, but why are you not with the men going to Strontian now?"

Completely devoid of any softening, his response came in a level and mild tone, utterly at odds with the heart-melting content of his answer.

"I'll be catching up with them," he answered. "I went by yer place, intending to compel or cajole or simply abduct ye."

Sorcha opened her mouth and stared at him, the meaning behind his words washing over her, flooding her heart with lightness and joy, and an overwhelming sense of relief.

Though she was layered in dirt and standing barefoot in a field, her toes cold now under the mud, and though the sky was overcast, the world around her seemed to shimmer with newfound brightness.

Keeping a smile at bay, as he had done, she boldly inquired, "And you? What had you intended to say to me?"

His slowly evolving grin was uncharacteristically mischievous, a beautiful sight to behold.

"Naturally, my plea would have been stated succinctly: Ye belong with me, Sorcha."

Reawakened to vitality, Sorcha grimaced a bit in mock dissatisfaction. "Um, I think you would have said that you love me."

"I might have," he teased. "We'll never ken."

"Why did you make me suffer just now? Dragging out of me all that begging and giving me not one hint in your expression that you felt the same way?"

"I dinna do it intentionally, love, but aye, I was weighing your statements against what ye said yesterday, which was the exact opposite. I needed to ken it's what is true inside ye."

"Do you doubt me now? Still?"

"I dinna doubt ye love me, Sorcha. I questioned whether your guilt would allow ye to express it or embrace it."

They hadn't touched yet, save for when Augustus brought her to her feet. They stood nearly two feet apart.

"It feels good, doesn't it?" Sorcha asked.

"What's that? The mud between yer toes?"

"All questions answered," she corrected. "All doubt erased."

"There was nae doubt in my mind, lass. I told ye I wanted ye at Strontian. That has nae changed."

"Will you take me in your arms now?"

"Are ye stuck, that ye canna launch yerself at me? I rather had that in mind, as to what yer reaction would be."

"Oh, I want to," she assured him, smiling broadly, charmed that he'd envisioned such a thing. "Alas, I am actually stuck."

Grinning widely, Augustus stepped forward and wrapped her in his strong arms, plucking her out of the mud as he lifted her off her feet.

Nose to nose, he said somberly, "I love ye, Sorcha. I dinna see it coming, and I'm not sure exactly—I've nae ever felt like this. It will take some getting used to."

"I look forward to discovering love—and everything—with you, Augustus."

"Aye, we've a lifetime to indulge in it."

Warm in his embrace and the promise of his love, Sorcha asked, "Would you really have abducted me?"

He kissed her long and luxuriously before he answered. She was breathless and yearning when he pulled his lips from hers.

"I am the Rebel, lass," he said, a devilish gleam in his blue eyes. "Aye, I would have."

The End

Thank you for reading *The Rebel of Lochaber Forest.*
Gaining exposure as an independent author
relies mostly on word-of-mouth,
so if you have the time
and inclination, please consider
leaving a short review wherever you can.
Thanks!

Other Books by Rebecca Ruger

Highlander: The Legends
The Beast of Lismore Abbey
The Lion of Blacklaw Tower
The Scoundrel of Beauly Glen
The Wolf of Carnoch Cross
The Blackguard of Windless Woods
The Devil of Helburn by the Sea
(and coming soon...)
The Rebel of Lochaber Forest
The Avenger of Castle Wick
The Dragon of Lochlan Hall

Heart of a Highlander Series
Heart of Shadows
Heart of Stone
Heart of Fire

Heart of Iron
Heart of Winter
Heart of Ice

Far From Home: A Scottish Time-Travel Romance
And Be My Love
Eternal Summer
Crazy In Love
Beyond Dreams
Only The Brave
When & Where
Get the Free Novella (Nicol and Eloise's story) by signing up to my Newsletter
A Year of Days
(and coming soon...)
Beloved Enemy
Winter Longing
Here in Your Arms

The Highlander Heroes Series
The Touch of Her Hand
The Memory of Her Kiss
The Shadow of Her Smile
The Depths of Her Soul
The Truth of Her Heart
The Love of Her Life

Sign-Up for My Newsletter
and hear about all the upcoming books.
Stay Up To Date!
www.rebeccaruger.com

Printed in Great Britain
by Amazon